SOUL MAGIC

A Wing Slayer Hunter Novel

JENNIFER LYON

SOUL MAGIC: A WING SLAYER HUNTER NOVEL

Copyright © 2009, 2015 Jennifer Apodaca
All rights reserved.

Published by JenniferLyonBooks
www.jenniferlyonbooks.com

ISBN: 978-0-9887923-8-8

Cover Design: Jaycee DeLorenzo of Sweet 'N Spicy Designs
Copy Editor: http://www.kimberlycannoneditor.com/
Formatted by: Author E.M.S.
Wing Slayer Hunter Logo Design: Jaycee DeLorenzo of Sweet 'N Spicy Designs

Originally published by Ballantine Books 2009

Published in the United States of America

THE WING SLAYER HUNTER SERIES

≫ 1 ≪

SEX WASN'T WORKING FOR HIM anymore.

Sutton West leaned against a black acrylic bar etched in fiery red lights. The nightclub, "Axel of Evil," had a whole hellish theme going on. The music pounded, the colored strobe lights flashed, and the smell of sweat and alcohol permeated the room.

It was last call.

A few mortal women lingered on the dance floor, and some witch hunters lounged by the two fire pits watching them with pointed interest.

Sutton returned his attention to the dancers, looking for one to take to bed to ease the pain of his cravings. He spotted a woman with long, shimmering black hair, chocolate eyes and long legs. His interest barely stirred.

He shifted his gaze to the two blondes, one in a yellow dress, the other in tight jeans and a black top. Both were hot, but when another man walked up and started dancing with them, he moved on without a stitch of regret.

Sutton had an absolute rule about women: They were helping him beat back the curse, and he would treat them with the respect they deserved. The redhead deserved more than he had to give tonight, and he looked around the club again. This lack of interest in sex worried him. Sex was how the hunters controlled their compulsion for witch blood. If they gave in to the compulsion and killed a witch, they lost their souls and went rogue—living only for the next "fix" of witch blood. For Sutton, losing interest in sex meant the curse was getting a foothold in him. He'd touched the blood of a witch, and now he was on the edge of losing control. He tightened his jaw in determination. *Never.* He'd never give in to the curse. His father had set the standard, and Sutton would live up to it.

Which meant he'd die before he let the curse win and take his soul.

Pushing his dark thoughts aside, he focused on the three men returning from hunting rogues. Key and Phoenix went to report to Axel, while Linc headed toward him.

Linc was one of their two candidates set to be inducted into the Wing Slayer Hunters. They both had the outline of their wings tattooed on their bodies: Linc Dillinger had chosen a falcon and Brigg Cusack had chosen a crow.

Now they all waited. Each of the two men was preparing to face a test that would prove him loyal to the Wing Slayer. The test was an unknown, but Axel Locke, their leader, would recognize it when it happened.

Linc came to a stop next to Sutton with barely a whisper from the perfectly cut slacks and coat over an open-collared shirt. His brown hair was expertly tousled. His gold eyes were dark and troubled under the pulsing strobe lights. "You heard anything from Brigg?"

Sutton shook his head. Brigg had left the club two nights ago and evidently no one had seen him since.

"I looked for him tonight. I couldn't find anything, not a goddamned trace of him. It's not like him to just vanish like this."

The tension of waiting for their mysterious test was taking a toll on both men. "Maybe he found a party and hasn't come up for air." They all had their times when the curse drove them to extremes. Sutton took himself off to the most isolated spots he could reach. He climbed, hiked, ran and swam trying like hell to sweat out the curse. Then he'd return to civilization and find a willing woman. As many as it took.

"He should have checked in," Linc said.

Sutton silently agreed. It was giving him a bad feeling, too. "Could be getting cold feet about becoming a Wing Slayer Hunter. It'll make him a target for the rogues." Wing Slayer had created the witch hunters to hunt and kill demon witches while protecting innocent earth witches. Because Wing Slayer was half demon and half god, invoking his god powers required complete and total acknowledgment from his witch hunters that he was their god. The demon Asmodeus had his demon witches cast the curse to break the bond between the Wing Slayer and his hunters so he could gain power on earth. It had been working until the five of them recommitted to Wing Slayer, reinstating his god powers.

Linc shook his head. "No. Brigg is hard-core about passing the test and getting fully winged at the Ceremony of Induction. We both are. We want to vow our allegiance to the Wing Slayer, take our oath to protect the innocent, and never give in to the curse."

"Might be that Brigg is facing his test now," he pointed out. "There are some things a man has to do alone." The man was really worried about Brigg, but under that was the resentment that Brigg might be facing his test and would be ready to take his wings first.

Linc let the silence stretch out, then he shrugged, looked around and said, "Any claims on that redhead?" He tilted his head to the woman Sutton had noticed earlier.

"Nope. She's yours if she'll have you."

He looked at Sutton with a gleam in his gold eyes. "Thousand bucks says she does."

"Sucker bet and I'm not a sucker." The hunter was throwing off pheromones so heavy that women across the club were glancing his way.

Linc chuckled and strode off to the dance floor.

Sutton turned back to the job at hand, closing down the club for the night. He glanced at Key, Ram, Axel and Phoenix. They were spread out around the club, checking things out, closing down the bar, saying good night to patrons, and making damn sure a rogue hadn't gotten in. The rogues had been quiet for the last couple of months. Witches still disappeared, but the rogues weren't challenging the Wing Slayer Hunters openly. They were scurrying in the shadows.

He knew from his constant efforts to hack into their new databases that they were rebuilding the Rogue Cadre. They had created new and better firewalls, showing a sophistication that did not bode well. They were also trying to recruit witch hunters to go rogue and fill their ranks. Quinn Young, the rogue leader, had to find a way to kill all the witches. He had a very demanding master—a demon—who wanted all the earth witches dead. Young and his rogues were out there, strategizing and planning to make it happen.

Sutton got the all-clear signal from the others. He dropped his crossed arms and raised one hand.

The music cut off, the colored strobes died and the house lights went on.

Witch hunters and the women started making their way out.

One woman hung back, a mortal with wavy brown

4

hair and bright brown eyes, wearing an emerald-green dress that swirled around her thighs. She was rooting around in her purse with a frown. He walked over to her. "Lose something?"

She lifted her face, and he saw the sheen of sweat from dancing. Flashing him a smile, she said, "I don't think I should drive home."

They were prepared for that. "We have several cabs out front."

She moved up closer to him. "Or you could drive me home."

She smelled of peppermint blended with her natural scent. Maybe he should take her up on it. Take her home, give them both a little pleasure and leave.

Too much effort.

He'd rather go to the warehouse to work on cracking the firewalls into the Rogue Cadre databases. "Maybe another night. But I'll help you to a cab."

She shook her head, looking embarrassed. "No thanks. I'm fine. I just got a little overheated from dancing." She started walking away, putting her hand back into her purse, probably looking for her car keys.

He regretted embarrassing her, and turned away to make a last circuit of the club.

He heard a click and whirled around, spotting the gun in the woman's hand just as she fired at him.

The sound exploded in the club.

He caught sight of Ram pulling out his knife. Sutton bellowed "No!" and spun to protect his heart. The bullet tore into his right shoulder.

The searing pain lit his nerve endings on fire. He snapped his teeth together and forced himself to breathe. Damn, that was one woman who didn't take rejection well. But it didn't make any sense; why had she shot him? He looked up. Key had wrenched the gun from the woman's hand and held her by the arm.

Axel strode up, his green eyes furious. He held a

5

white bar towel in his hand. "Sit down, let me look."

"Later." He took the towel from Axel, pressed it against his shoulder, and walked over to where the woman was standing.

Her eyes were wide, sweat coated her face and her hands trembled. "I shot you. My God, I shot you!"

"Why?" Sutton asked. The pain in his shoulder was burrowing into the nerves and firing his compulsion for witch blood. But this woman wasn't a witch, she was a mortal. A harmless little thing, she barely reached his shoulder.

"I don't know! I don't remember! I...I don't even have a gun!"

Sutton watched as Axel faced the woman and looked into her eyes. Witch hunters had the ability to travel the optic nerve mentally and shift memories. Axel was seeing what he could get by touching her memories.

He turned to meet Sutton's gaze, his face grim. "Rogues."

The scream jerked Dr. Carla Fisk from a light doze.

She jumped up off the couch, her head spinning at the sudden movement. Her small office was dim, lit only by her desk lamp.

Another scream.

She kicked aside the shoes she'd taken off before lying down and raced out the door, lifting her long skirt out of the way as she took the stairs two at a time. By the second floor, she could hear the broken sobbing.

Then Max Bayer's soothing tones. "Josie, honey, wake up. You're safe."

Carla slowed her steps, composing herself. She loved to listen to Max gentle their residents. The transitional clinic was Max's baby. His specialty was tracking and extracting people who had been indoctrinated into cults. Whether they were lured, seduced, or forced, if he could find them, he got them out.

Carla had worked closely with Max to design the program to reverse the brainwashing. She admired him, respected him, liked him...

But she didn't feel anything romantic toward him, only admiration for his work and friendship.

As her heart calmed down, she turned and walked into the room.

In the light from the nightstand lamp, she saw that Josie was sitting up in the bed closest to the door. She had her knees drawn up tightly to her chest, her arms wrapped around them. Her face was tight and splotchy from crying.

Max was on his knees, his back to Carla. He wore a pair of gray sweatpants and nothing else. His back was lean, his arms wiry and strong. "Josie, you're hyperventilating. Try breathing with me, like Carla taught you."

Josie kept her eyes fixed on the wall across the room. "They'll find me."

She saw the muscles ripple across Max's back. She could feel his need to pull Josie into his arms and swear to her that he would never let that happen.

But Max resisted the impulse. Josie had only been out of the cult two days. Men frightened her. In the place she'd been, men had total, brutal and humiliating control over the women. Max was the gentlest man alive, and yet Josie couldn't relax around him.

It always killed Max that these young women were afraid of him. Eventually, they came to trust him. And then he let them go back into the world.

Carla put her hand on Max's shoulder.

He looked up at her, his dark eyes full of impotent fury. Max had once had a purely scientific curiosity about cults, and had worked closely with a young research assistant trying to infiltrate a cult. Then the research assistant had gotten in too deep and the cult had killed her. The curious sociologist in Max died, and this man, full of passion, grief, anger and guilt, was born.

She squeezed his shoulder. "How about getting Josie some water?"

He rose. "I'll be back in a few minutes."

His bare feet made little sound on the wood floors.

"Is he mad at me?"

Carla sat down on the side of Josie's bed. It was a child's question. "No. Max isn't going to get mad at you for being scared or having nightmares." She reached out, putting her hand over Josie's cold fingers. Opening her first four chakras with a swift popping sensation that started at her pelvis and rose to her heart, Carla sent calming energy to the frightened girl.

Her eyes widened. "How do you do that?"

"In our hypnosis sessions, I've been giving you calming suggestions. When I touch you, your brain remembers the suggestions." And, of course, she was a witch. But Josie didn't need to know that. She believed Carla worked her healing with hypnosis alone.

The girl's breathing settled down to an even, healthy rhythm. "Do you think they can find me here?"

"No. You were kept in Arizona, out in the desert. This is Los Angeles, they wouldn't even know where to look. But more important, do you think Max or any of his men wandering around here would let them take you?" Max's team doubled as protection for the clinic when they weren't out on a mission to extract someone from a cult.

"Yesterday, that big guy, umm, Rich?"

Carla nodded.

"He watched me walk in and out the front door. Never said a word."

Testing to see if they'd stop her from walking out. To see if she was a prisoner. "Did you think he'd stop you?"

She shrugged, then picked at the blanket. "You tell me that I'm free now, that I'm safe, but I can't seem to accept that."

Carla fought down her anger at the bastards who had done this to a nineteen-year-old girl. "Honey, they brainwashed you. They tried to destroy your individual self. But you are an amazing, strong and smart young woman—and they failed. Your brain is fighting back and the nightmares are the result."

She took a deep breath. "Really?"

"Really. Ready to go back to sleep?"

"I don't know if I can."

Carla glanced at the bedside clock, it was just after two A.M. Softly, she said, "I can help you sleep."

"Okay."

Carla concentrated to funnel the elemental power of the earth up through her four opened chakras. That was the easy part.

The hard part was trying to open the top three chakras. Actually it was nearly impossible ever since the curse had destroyed the witches' bonds with their familiars. The special bond with an animal helped focus and control a witch's power to open the chakras, as well as provide some protection from demons if they were using ley lines. Without their familiars, the witches just didn't have enough control over their power to access the higher magic. Carla could open her fifth chakra, which was her communication with other realms, but she couldn't open her sixth chakra, which was her third eye, or her seventh, which was knowledge.

She needed her fifth chakra to guide Josie's spirit

to the astral plane. She concentrated and pictured the blue chakra at her throat, then she began funneling her powers up faster and faster, focusing on that one spot.

The vibrations grew stronger, and she felt a choking sensation. She pushed harder, her body trembling as she struggled to control her magic. She felt a burst of sudden relief as the chakra flew open. Her body dropped away and she floated on a plane of blue.

The astral plane.

"Doctor?"

"I'm right here," Carla said, and her doppelganger body took shape. For reasons known only to the universe, a mirror-image body usually appeared with the subconscious on the spiritual plane. Perhaps because it was the only way the human mind could grasp the reality of this level of existence. But, in Carla's experience, one body didn't know what happened to the other in real time. For instance, if Josie's body on the physical plane was hurt, her body on the spiritual plane wouldn't know it. At least not until her subconscious returned to the body to "experience" it.

Josie appeared standing next to her. "I love this place." As soon as Josie said it, a large green pasture opened up before them, dotted with grazing horses. They'd practiced creating these places that Josie loved.

A dot in the sky surprised Carla. She watched it soar closer until she could make out a huge eagle with wings spread majestically. Then it vanished. "Did you see the bird?" she asked Josie, wondering if the girl was adding to her dreams. Maybe the eagle signified freedom?

"No. Can I go ride the horses?"

"Of course. Your body on the physical plane is asleep already. This is your dream. You're safe here, you control what happens."

Josie smiled at her. "How do you make me feel so safe?"

"Magic," she answered with a laugh. She took a quick glance around, but there was no sign of the eagle. Brushing it off, she said encouragingly, "Now go ride your horses."

While the girl moved off, Carla kept a tight hold on her spirit, and began guiding all but the dreaming fraction of her spirit back to Josie's sleeping body.

Dreams were actually a part of the spirit leaving the body and exploring other realms. The small portion of Josie's spirit on the astral plane would return without a hitch once the girl woke up.

Returning to the physical plane, Carla settled back into her own body, feeling heavy and tired. It took a tremendous amount of energy to control the magic of her fifth chakra.

Josie was asleep where she sat, her face relaxed. Carla laid Josie down and covered her, while allowing herself to feel a moment of contentment. Carla hadn't ever fit in anywhere, not with witches and not with scientists. But these young women needed her special combination of skills both as a witch and a psychologist. It validated her, gave her a place in the world where she belonged. She glanced at the bedside light and it went out. Then she turned and walked into the hallway.

Max leaned against the wall, holding a cold bottle of water. He handed it to Carla. "You might as well drink it. She's not going to wake for hours now."

Carla took the bottle.

"Have I told you lately how amazing you are?"

Many times. "Josie wouldn't have the chance to recover and live a full life if you hadn't found her and gotten her out."

He studied her, raising an eyebrow. "Same shirt and skirt you wore yesterday. You haven't gone home. Let me get dressed and I'll take you home now."

"I'm fine. I have a change of clothes in my office."

"You slept on the couch again."

She drank down a gulp of the cool water, avoiding his gaze. "I worked late, and—" And she had nothing to go home to. The loneliness was a constant ache. Insomnia was bad enough, but when she slept, the nightmares caught up with her. The memory of the knives, the pain, the helpless terror...

And then the witch hunter who'd saved her.

Her dream always shifted then, the horror giving way to being touched and stroked and filled until she felt whole. When she woke, she was left aching for something that wasn't real. Carla had spent her life trying to find a way to meld together the two parts of her psyche; the logical scientist and the emotional witch. Always pulled in two directions.

Max reached out, laying his palm on her bare arm.

The warm touch hurt her all the more because she didn't feel the connection he wanted. She cared about him, but he didn't stir her passion.

And if he ever found out she was a witch, he'd want to use her like her father had. She tried to smile. "Go back to bed, Max."

He dropped his arm. "Try to get some sleep," he said and walked away.

Carla took her bottle of water downstairs, ignored her office, turned left, passed through a dining room and went to the small, walled courtyard. She keyed off the alarm system for the slider, then opened it and slipped out into the cool night.

She sat in the chair, propped her feet on the edge of the stone fountain. There were large pots of geraniums dotting the patio. Soft colored lights in the center illuminated the bubbling stone waterfall cascading down. The tiny sliver of moonlight barely touched her skin, but it was enough.

It fed her chakras, eased her exhaustion.

The faint scent of incense bloomed, then faded. It wasn't real, she knew that. Every now and again, her grief manifested an image of eagles or the smell of incense—things that reminded her of Keri. It had been two years since her sister's murder, and the grief, guilt and regret still took up too much space inside her. She had to let Keri go, had to accept that her sister's soul had gone on to her next life. The scar across her lower back, the one she'd gotten trying to save Keri, ached slightly. It was time to let it all go. She breathed deeply, drawing the cool damp night air into her lungs.

She was just releasing the air when her cell phone vibrated. Reaching into her skirt pocket, she pulled the phone out and opened it.

The image of her best friend, Darcy, stared back at her. "Carla, where are you?"

Darcy was using magic to project her image through the phone. Carla spoke to the picture. "The clinic. What's wrong?" It was after two in the morning; Darcy wasn't calling for a chat. "Is a witch missing?"

Darcy shook her head. "Not that I know of."

Darcy and Axel had broken the thirty-year-old curse on the witches and witch hunters, making Darcy the most powerful witch they knew of. She was struggling to find her place among the witches, while her mate, Axel, led the Wing Slayer Hunters in their fight against rogues. Like the rogues who had killed Keri. So if Darcy wasn't calling about a missing witch... "Then what is it?" Worry pulled tighter in her stomach.

Her face was troubled. "A woman shot Sutton tonight."

Carla dropped her feet from the edge of the fountain, sitting up. Her skin tingled from her neck to her thighs—all the places that Sutton West's T-shirt had touched her when he had rescued her from rogues. The dreams of him were making her restless, making her need something she couldn't have. "Is he alive?"

Darcy's brown eyes glinted with silver lights. "Yes. He's fine, she missed his heart."

Her own heart skipped a beat and caused her to struggle for her breath. Finally, she said, "Why did the woman shoot him?" Witch hunters gave off pheromones that attracted women. They used sex to help them fight down the bloodlust from the curse...did some woman want more from him? Get angry or jealous? "Was it, uh, personal?" And why did that thought make her chest burn?

Darcy shook her head. "A rogue has been in her head, Axel is sure of that much. But he's never seen this kind of thing before. He can't tell if it's brain damage from some witch hunter repeatedly shifting her memories or..."

"You think the rogues are trying to kill Wing Slayer Hunters using a mortal woman?" Carla processed that. "Like some kind of mind control? Do the rogues have that kind of power?"

"We've never seen it, but I'm worried. We have the woman but she's in shock. I can't get much out of her. The rogues have been fairly quiet since Axel and the men took a stand against them. But this..."

She remembered the night Axel and his men destroyed the Rogue Cadre's base of operations. She'd been there, strapped down on a table, her skin cut to disable her powers. Then Sutton had arrived, killing rogues until he got to her. He could have killed her, could have given in to the curse that made him sweat and shake with the craving for her blood. Instead he'd ripped the restraints off her and covered her with his shirt. Ever since that night...

Darcy's voice interrupted her thoughts. "What if

the rogues are reorganizing and using some kind of brainwashing on mortals? What if this woman isn't the only one?"

"Bring her to me."

"Too dangerous. The rogue would be able to track her and we don't want them to find the clinic or the house you're staying in."

Carla couldn't endanger their residents, Max, or the staff. She made a quick decision. "Where are you? I'll come there."

"I was hoping you'd say that."

Prickles of unease skittered up her spine. "What do you mean?"

A large shadow passed overhead. Carla jerked her head up in time to see a huge creature with wings fill up the night sky. He swooped in, his gold and brown wings catching the moonlight as he shifted on the air current so that he landed on his feet a yard away from Carla. His wings spread across most of the courtyard, lifted up and folded to disappear into the tattoo on his back.

Carla turned to Darcy. "No way, I am not flying!" She still couldn't get used to the idea of a man with wings who could fly.

"You'll be safer with Axel. Please, Carla. Let him bring you here."

Carla turned to look at the man in question. He stood well over six feet, his muscles gleaming in the moonlight. His wings ripped holes in his shirts, so he usually flew bare-chested. She looked into his green eyes. "We could drive my car."

He smiled. "We could try, but Darcy will magically disable it."

Her curiosity outweighed her fear. She looked at Darcy. "You so owe me for this."

2

THEY LANDED IN THE DIRT in front of a rustic cabin built into the hills overlooking the ocean in Glassbreakers, California. It was a rugged piece of land that required four-wheel drive or wings to access. Carla didn't need to ask which hunter this house belonged to. The rough finished logs, beamed ceilings and simple furniture reflected Sutton's rugged side.

The man was complex and highly skilled—a self-taught computer expert. She'd learned that while disguising herself behind a crone avatar to help Darcy learn to control her powers. Sutton had found a way to track her down and learn her identity in spite of her magical cover. He was formidably smart, and followed no one's rules. She knew he'd have a high-tech computer set up somewhere in this cabin.

Just walking into his house caused her skin to tingle with hyperawareness. Her self-diagnosis? She craved the man who could kill her. That was not a sign of a healthy mind. She had to stop thinking about Sutton and concentrate on the woman she came to see.

She followed Axel to the bedroom. It was large for a cabin. There was a big stone fireplace in the far wall, and next to that was the oversize chair Darcy sat in. Directly across from the bed was a sliding glass door that would let in the cool ocean breeze. On Carla's right, a doorway led to a bathroom. Shifting her gaze, she looked down at the sleeping woman on the huge wood-framed bed. There were dark half-moons beneath her eyes and her cheeks had sunken into her bone structure.

Darcy said, "I'm surprised she fell asleep, she was so agitated. Kept saying she couldn't believe she shot him."

"Sleep could be an escape." Carla'd seen the reaction to severe stress before.

"When I touched her, I got a sense of massive confusion. As if she couldn't understand what she'd done."

That could be a form of brainwashing but Carla needed more information. She shifted her attention to Axel standing by Darcy. "What did you find?"

"Definite memory-shifting by a rogue, but something more, too. The way we shift memories is to go through the optic nerve to the short-term memory. But I felt a web of pathways opening up so I pulled out. I didn't want to do more damage."

After watching her sister and friends murdered by rogues, Carla had been terrified by all witch hunters. She hadn't realized how many of them were fighting against this curse that tortured them. Her respect went up another notch. Even though this woman had shot Sutton, Axel had been careful not to hurt her. They all had. Which made her finally ask the question that had been burning on her mind. "Where is Sutton? Did you heal him?"

Rolling her eyes, Darcy said, "Eventually. A mortal getting the drop on him made him a little testy." Her tone indicated that was an understatement. "He's out there somewhere." She lifted her hand to the darkness beyond the sliding glass door. "Looking for any rogues that might be trying to track our guest here. He's standing guard, but he can't be too close."

To her. With Axel and Darcy soul-bonded now, they were both free of the curse. Although still a witch, Darcy's magic no longer incited the bloodlust in hunters. But even if Sutton was a danger to her, it made Carla feel better, safer, to know he was out there. He wouldn't let a rogue sneak up on them. She shuddered at the thought, then said, "Let's get started then. Do you know her name?"

Darcy said, "There was no identification on her, but she said her name was Pam when I asked."

Carla dropped her gaze to Pam. She looked tiny on the massive bed, her green dress too bright against the simple chocolate-colored comforter. Carla took a deep breath and opened her first four chakras with a series of small pops. Her elemental powers releasing created a swirling sensation inside her stomach. Then she focused on the fifth one and realized how very tired she was as she tried to force a stream of magical pressure against her communication chakra. Her throat tightened and vibrated until finally, the chakra released. As her powers mixed, a hum rose inside her.

"Is she all right?" Axel asked.

"Yes," Darcy's voice responded. "It's hard to control the fifth chakra power without a familiar and it's taking a tremendous amount of will to do it."

Carla ignored them and concentrated on keeping the communication chakra open, and her powers mixing correctly to put Pam in a hypnotic state and lead her to the astral plane. Finally, she touched her hand to the woman's shoulder. She felt the immediate suction against her fingertips, which created the link with the woman's spirit so that Carla wouldn't lose her on the astral plane.

The physical world dropped away and they

appeared on the endless, formless blue of the spiritual world. "Pam, you're going to wake up now and be calm. You're safe. Everything you remember will feel far away from you, as if you are watching it in a movie. Open your eyes."

Pam's eyelids lifted slowly. "Where am I? Who are you?"

Her voice was calm and untroubled in her hypnotic state. "I'm Dr. Carla Fisk, and you're safe in the astral plane. Nothing can hurt you here. Right now, I'm talking to your subconscious, the part of your brain that you are often unaware of, but it's always there."

"Am I dead?"

"Absolutely not. You are very much alive and I'll take you back to full consciousness on the physical plane any time you like." Carla never lied to her patients, and always made sure they felt like they had control in the session. It was the only way to gain their full trust.

"It's nice here. I don't feel guilty and ashamed." She looked around at all the endless blue, then turned back to Carla. "No one is trying to kill me here, right?"

Hmm, Carla thought, paranoia. "You're safe here. What's your name?"

"Pam Miller."

Carla smiled. "Tell me a little bit about yourself, Pam."

"Uh..." she trailed off. "I am, uh, I work at a hair salon."

Carla felt a backwash of anxiety tightening her stomach and throat. If Pam had been awake, this question would upset her. "Oh, do you like cutting hair?"

"I...don't know."

Carla kept leading her. "What about your family?"

"I'm not allowed to see them. Or I don't want to see them?" She frowned. "Why don't I remember?"

19

"What's the last thing you do remember?"

"I shot that man at the club. I can't believe I did that. He didn't seem like he was going to kill me. He was nice. But I had to shoot him...didn't I?"

Pam's physical body was backwashing more agitation and confusion. Her subconscious knew something was wrong. "Tell me about the guilt and shame you mentioned."

"I thought I'd feel relief if I shot him. But I felt horrible. I couldn't believe I did it."

"We're going to figure this out together," Carla said gently, but she was dead sure the woman had been brainwashed. Her uncertainty about who she was indicated that someone had tampered with her individual sense of self, which was why Pam didn't know if she liked her job or what she cared about. Separating her from her family and support system created a desperate dependence on the brainwasher. Who was it? "You're doing wonderfully, Pam. Can you tell me who you spend a lot of time with?"

"Styx."

"Is that a man? Or a woman? A child?"

"A man."

"Good." Carla had to focus to keep her fifth chakra funneling through her voice and into Pam. She knew she was getting closer to answers. "Is Styx a first name or last name?"

"Just a name. It's all I know."

He was being careful not to give Pam too much information. "What happened yesterday? Did you wake up at Styx's house?"

"Yes."

"What happened then?"

"He told me that I had to prove myself to him or he wasn't going to let me be his girlfriend anymore. I would have to leave and go back to the people who hate me and want to kill me."

And there was the typical pattern. The rogue had isolated her, damaged some of her sense of self in her brain, then overlaid false memories of abuse and attempted murder. Then he showed her kindness and gave her a new identity as his girlfriend. With the damage and confusion in her brain, that identity was all she had to hold on to.

Pam went on in her monotone voice. "He showed me a picture of one of the men who was trying to kill me and told me his name was Sutton. Then he said I had to kill Sutton. He said I had to be clever and use the only talent I had—sex."

Carla felt the waves of shame and terror Styx had forced her to experience. The weight of it pressed on her chest, making it hard to breathe. Flashes of light burst on the edges of her vision.

But the lights weren't emanating from Pam; they were coming from somewhere else. Carla fought to keep control, something she'd never had to do before. Maybe she was too tired, or they'd been out of their bodies too long. Tightening her hand on Pam's spirit, she struggled to keep her chakras open and maintain their connection.

Losing Pam now would cause her spirit to break from her body. In mortal terms, Pam would be in a coma. Carla had never, ever lost a patient. Forcing herself to sound calm, she said, "Pam, stay with me. Keep looking at me."

Her eyes shifted away. "What is that? It's bright and warm. It's calling me..."

"No! Don't look at it." Another entity was on the astral plane, and struggling to get their attention. A soul? A demon? "We're going to travel back, and you're going to settle into your body."

"I like it here. I felt awful there..."

Carla hadn't considered this. She'd been so quick to want to see what had happened to cause the mortal to shoot Sutton, she hadn't thought out Pam's mental state. Since Pam had been asleep, Carla hadn't talked to her to assess the danger. She struggled to block out everything but Pam and guiding her back to the physical plane. The snaps of light were drawing together into a single mass. *Don't look,* she warned herself. "I'm going to help you with those feelings, I promise. Right now, I just want you to—"

The light burst over Carla, severing her connection to Pam and dragging her to some other place. A place filled with blood and screams.

No matter how far he went, it wasn't far enough. Sutton had made a mile-wide sweep around his cabin.

No rogues.

But he knew the witch was in his cabin. He would always know when she was nearby—he'd touched her blood.

For two months now, he'd been trying to purge her from his body and mind. He'd touched her blood when he'd rescued her from the rogues, and now she was seductive poison to him. His body tightened with a blast of white-hot lust at just the thought of her. His skin burned to feel the cool power of her witch's blood.

Her blood had killed his desire for other women, and saddled him with the dual cravings for sex and blood. The man in him wanted to make love to her, the curse wanted to cut her and bleed her to death. If that didn't make a man insane, he didn't know what would.

He stood on the rocks with his arms crossed and watched the powerful waves crash below him. The dawn hadn't yet broken, but he could see perfectly well.

He could feel her in his cabin. His home. The place

where he had always felt at peace. Alone in the middle of nature.

He'd been alone since he was seventeen.

He watched as another wave swelled and lifted higher and higher, then broke. Like the curse inside him that was swelling and unfurling more each day.

When would he break?

His uncle had been thirty-one when he broke. His dad had been thirty-seven when he knew he was on the verge of breaking and ended his own life in a fiery plane crash.

Sutton was thirty-two.

He closed his eyes, trying to draw in the tang of the ocean and wash out his memories.

Instead she filled his mind. Carla. Long white-blond hair, searing eyes with the colors of green, yellow and brown, her incredible body...it was an unendurable torture to want her so badly and know he couldn't have her.

He dreamed of making love to her, of bringing her to his bed, stripping off her clothes, looking, touching and tasting his fill. Then filling her with his cock, joining with her as deep as she could take him. Her sweet moans making his balls ache...

Then her screams ripped the dream into a nightmare. He saw the silver knife stabbing her, butchering her.

It was his knife, Sutton was sure of it. He was going rogue, inch by inch, day by day. The nightmare of killing her was becoming more frequent, more violent, until he'd awoken, covered in sweat and the gut-cramping fear that he'd killed her.

His dad had known when he'd broken, when the curse had him, and he'd done the right thing.

Sutton knew Carla was the witch who could break him.

How much longer before he broke completely? Not

yet, not today, he decided. Not as long as he still cared that she was putting herself in danger from the rogues by hypnotizing the woman who'd shot him.

Not today, but tomorrow? He didn't know.

Carla's spirit slammed into her body, leaving her dizzy and nauseous. She looked at Pam's slack face and the full impact hit her. "Oh God, I've lost her! I have to go back."

"Wait, slow down. What happened?"

Carla turned to see that Darcy was next to her. She'd obviously moved to her side when Carla was on the astral plane with Pam. "I don't know, exactly. Something else showed up on the astral plane. Then it dragged me into a vision and I lost my hold on Pam's spirit." Turning back to the figure on the bed, she added, "Now she's in a coma while her spirit is wandering on the astral plane."

"Was it a demon?" Axel asked sharply from Darcy's other side.

Carla took a minute to breathe and pull herself together. "I don't know. It didn't feel like a demon. Whatever it was showed me a witch being murdered with a silver knife. I assumed it was a rogue killing her." She turned to Darcy. "Maybe it was the soul of the witch trying to show me how she was killed. But the dead have never talked to me before." It didn't make sense.

Darcy's cool fingers touched her arm. "What exactly did you see?"

She tried to get it right. "It was like I was *inside* the knife, stabbing her over and over. She kept screaming, the blood was splashing all over me..."

"Have you ever seen a soul on the astral plane before?"

Carla shook her head. "That's not how the astral plane works, though. We were there to find out about Pam and why she shot Sutton. I was able to catch a few images that were manifested from Pam's subconscious. But it's rare to see something not of your choosing. It's a spiritual plane, not physical."

"Is it possible that the poor witch's soul was so traumatized by her murder that she got stuck on the astral plane on her way to Summerland? And somehow she found you?"

She didn't have an answer. "I have no idea, but I have to go back and find Pam. I can't just leave her like this..." She waved her hand toward the bed.

Darcy said softly, "Do you think I could do it? Axel can help me."

Carla shook her head. "She won't recognize you, may not be able to hear you because you don't have the connection to her spirit. I can't believe I lost her."

"It wasn't your fault; something got in your way. We'll find a way to fix this. But you can't go back right now. You're too upset and we don't know what you encountered."

Axel looked over Darcy's head and said, "Did you find out anything about the rogue who messed with Pam? Is it brainwashing?"

She lifted her gaze to him, glad to have an answer to at least one question. "Yes." She recounted Pam's story about Styx brainwashing Pam into trying to kill Sutton.

"It's the rogues, they've reorganized. Now they are using mortals in this war." Axel's voice was grim.

Carla knew the rogues' goal was to kill all the witches. The demon, Asmodeus, had promised them he'd grant them immortality once they'd done that. With their souls gone, the rogues were desperate to live forever so they wouldn't spend eternity as formless, pain-racked shades walking the between-worlds. But now that the Wing Slayer Hunters were actively hunting and killing rogues to protect witches, the rogues had to get rid of them, too. "Whoever did it used his memory-shifting to destroy her memories of herself, then he forced new memories of people she'd thought she trusted beating her and trying to kill her. Once Pam's self-identity was lost, the rogue began to reconstruct her into what he wanted. Normally, brainwashing takes significant time, but this was compressed into a week or two."

Darcy and Axel looked troubled. Darcy asked, "Do you think they could do this with any mortal?"

Sadly, she answered, "No, but a young, still-impressionable woman, particularly if she wants to please the people in her life, is usually a good candidate." The psyche was delicate, shaped by so many things, and more easily damaged than most people wanted to believe. She could help Pam, help her find her real memories, rediscover herself and then have enough confidence in herself to be less susceptible to outside influences. But first she had to reunite her spirit with her physical body.

Axel said, "The rogue must be tracking her."

She shook her head. "The tracking works by marking the brain, and right now, Pam's brain is off-line. He can't track her."

Axel slid his hand under Darcy's hair, absently kneading her neck. "The rogue could have been tracking her before she went into the coma. We have to move her."

There was no question about this. "She has to stay with me so I can work to get her back."

"All right. We'll move her to the safe house where you're staying."

Sutton was in his zone. He scanned in a picture of Pam, entered the pertinent facts like height, weight, hair and eye color, then wrote a program to crawl through police missing person reports. After that, he hacked into the Department of Motor Vehicles, and used another program to find licenses that matched a woman with the first name of Pam or Pamela, last name Miller, and her approximate age and physical description.

He could hear the other hunters moving around the warehouse, the huge cavernous building Axel owned next to his club. Inside was a gym, a small sitting area with a refrigerator, a tattoo station and a large pool table in the center of the room. The music was blaring and the men were talking, but his world was narrowed to his corner, the state-of-the-art computer station he'd designed. He glanced up at the wall of monitors above his workstation, which displayed feeds from the video cameras set up within the club.

He shifted his gaze to a screen that showed several angles of the outside Dr. Carla Fisk's house. He'd wired the security there himself, trusting her safety to no one else. The outside of the house was quiet. She was safe.

As long as she stayed away from him.

Another screen flashed a warning that the warehouse security was paused, and Sutton shifted his gaze to that monitor to see Axel coming in the back door. He rearmed the security system and cut the music in the warehouse.

Axel stopped by the pool table and said, "Given what's happened, we have to take more seriously the fact that Brigg is missing." He zeroed his gaze in on Linc. "That's why I wanted you here. You might be a target, too. It's not a secret that you and Brigg have the outline of your wings."

Linc straddled a roller chair, his arms folded over

the back of the seat. It looked casual, but his jaw was clenched tight. "If he was killed by some mortal chick controlled by rogues, wouldn't they dump his body to show us that they killed him?"

Axel met the man's gaze. "Not if he was the test to see if their brainwashing worked, and they have something bigger planned." He added, "Starting now, we're actively looking for Brigg. Fully winged or not, he's one of ours. We're going to hunt down rogues and find out what they know. But we have to prepare for the other outcome."

"He's not rogue," Linc said. "He'd die before he let that happen."

Key, known to the world as Kieran DeMicca, author of a dark comic book series, lifted his head from the drawing he was working on. At just over six feet, with spiky blond hair, a ladykiller smile and a dragon tattooed on his muscular chest, he looked the least threatening of the men. More than one dead man had made the mistake of believing that. "What went down with Carla and Pam?"

Sutton watched Axel walk over to the fridge and grab a beer while explaining why Carla thought Pam was brainwashed by a man named Styx. Axel looked at him. "Got anything on a Styx?"

Sutton turned and opened his files on known rogues. He was building the most comprehensive database outside the Rogue Cadre. He ran a few searches, then said, "It doesn't pop. Nothing on a Styx."

Linc said, "Can't the doctor get more from Pam?"

Axel told them about the interference on the astral plane, and that Pam was in a coma.

Sutton's blood began to pound in his head, and he involuntarily turned to study the monitor that showed the outside of Carla's house. Forcing himself to swivel back around in his chair, he felt the burn start under his skin.

A voice in his head whispered, *Carla's yours. Go get her, before someone else does.* His skin itched.

"Any leads on who Pam is?" Axel asked. "The rogues had to get her from someplace."

"I'm running searches, but she'd have to be in the system somewhere to pop. The DMV search will only narrow it down to women her general size and description with a first name of Pam. It'll take days to go through that. The missing persons police reports are our best bet. But if she's from out of state, then I'll have to widen the parameters."

Key said, "Back to Styx. He probably gave Pam a fake name. Let's look at this from another angle. Where did he take her? Where did he keep her while he screwed with her head repeatedly?"

"We've searched every place we can think of." Phoenix Torq's boots echoed on the cement of the warehouse as he paced by the pool table in the center of the cavernous room. Frustration flexed the wings of the phoenix tattooed on his massive biceps. Defeat was not in his vocabulary. In his hobby of hunting down human scum that preyed on women, he never gave up until he got his man. "Where is the Rogue Cadre's new headquarters? Where's Quinn Young?"

Ramsey Virtos stood with his legs spread, his hands folded behind his back, and his thunderbird tattoo hidden beneath his shirt. He studied the computer monitor with the grid he'd designed. The methodical search worked from the outsides of the city and moved inward. His military background had honed his precision. "Quinn Young has changed the battle plan. He found out that drawing us to them didn't work."

Sutton had to fight down the vivid memory of that night. The rogues had kidnapped Carla, along with Darcy's cousin Joe and the woman he loved, Morgan.

They took them to the rogue compound and sent a video to the Wing Slayer Hunters.

A taunt.

He could see Carla again, strapped down like a sacrifice on that steel table, naked and bleeding...

All to get to Darcy. Quinn Young had to kill off his witch-daughter and her soul-mirror mate. Ironically it had been Darcy who had arrived and saved the day with her magic. Which brought him back to Ram—the witch hunter was right. Young was smart and adaptable. "He's trying another method of attack."

"Using mortal women." Phoenix's disgust was clear in his tone.

Axel shoved away from the pool table he was leaning on. "He's using the women to try to kill off the unbonded Wing Slayer Hunters before you find your soul mirrors. These women can't kill Darcy or me, we're immortal." He ran his hand through his dark hair.

Ram's blue eyes were icy with controlled rage. "But Young does have the Immortal Death Dagger, the one thing that can kill the two of you. He's out there somewhere, just waiting for his chance to do it."

Phoenix said, "They are killing witches, feeding their sick craving for the blood, right under our noses. Witches are still disappearing. Right now, they could be killing a witch who is one of our soul mirrors!" His fury pulsed in his voice.

Sutton knew they all feared they wouldn't find their soul mirrors in time. But it was already too late for him. Every hour brought him closer to his breaking point. He stood up. "I'm going to my house. Maybe I'll get lucky and a rogue will show up." Killing would release some of his stress.

Axel met him at the door. "You have women friends. You need to go see one of them. You're on the edge."

He and Axel had been friends for years, ever since they'd met working for an elite security team for the club circuit. They'd both had the same goal: Never give in to the curse and kill a witch. Axel knew him better than anyone else, so he told him the truth. "Sex isn't helping anymore, A."

Axel put his hand on Sutton's shoulder. "Give it another try. You just have to hang in there until you find your soul mirror."

It was time they all started facing the truth. "Not all of us are going to find our soul mirror in time. I won't turn, at least not if I can help it." The rogues were trying to compel witch hunters to turn by blooding them, bringing them into contact with witch blood. "I'll end it before I turn. But if the worst does happen, you made a vow." All the Wing Slayer Hunters had made the vow when they tattooed the wings. They would fight the curse, but if one of them went rogue, the others would kill him.

Axel clenched his jaw, his fingers tightening on Sutton's shoulder. "It won't happen."

"But if it does?" He needed to know that they would stop him if he reached the point of no return, stop him before he killed a witch and lost his soul. Dying wasn't a big deal, but living as a soulless creature killing the very witches they had been created to protect...that was an abomination.

Spending an eternity as a pain-racked shade didn't appeal to him much either.

Axel narrowed his eyes. "I will honor the vow. We all will."

3

CARLA WAS STAYING IN A Mediterranean-style house in
Glassbreakers. The family room, large kitchen and
breakfast nook all overlooked the patio at the back of
the house. The floors were done in terra-cotta tile, and
curved archways gave the rooms character.

Pam rested in one of the bedrooms while Carla
and Darcy worked with the Circle Witches on
the computers. It was too dangerous for witches to
gather in person, so they used the Internet to work
together.

Ten minutes after the two of them sent a query
about the situation with Pam, and the soul that
interfered on the astral plane, responses started
pouring in.

Darcy narrowed her eyes and read aloud: "Carla
has overstepped the boundaries and endangered a
mortal. I recommend that she be banished from the
Circle Witches."

Carla sighed. "Silver. She formed the Circle
Witches. She's losing control of the group and doesn't
like it. Just ignore her." She read the next email out
loud. "We've never heard of a soul trapped on the
astral plane and unable to get to Summerland. It

seems like this soul is trying to reach you. Try talking to the soul and find out."

Darcy read the next email. "Are you sure it's a soul? Why would the soul of an earth witch harm a mortal and trap her on the astral plane?"

Carla had considered that, but the soul might not understand the danger to Pam. Or...her attention snapped back to the screen when she saw the pixels break apart, then re-form into a picture of a woman with long, dark-blond hair pulled back into a low ponytail, her green eyes bracketed by lines of worry.

"Mom."

"Sweetheart, I just read your query. Are you all right?"

"I'm fine. Just worried that I lost Pam. I've never lost anyone on the astral plane."

Chandra drew her eyebrows together. "You've always had a singular ability with the spiritual plane. What do you think happened?"

Her frustration and fatigue bubbled up. "I don't know."

"I think you'd better find out who that soul is, but be careful. You're doing high magic without a familiar. A demon could find you, or you could lose control..." Her mom trailed off, then swallowed. "But find out. Then you'll be able to figure out what to do next."

That was the most logical step. "Thanks, Mom."

Chandra looked over her shoulder, then back at the laptop. "Got a batch of cookies in the oven. I have to run. Let me know." The picture dissolved and re-formed into an eagle.

Startled, Carla blinked and looked again, but the eagle was gone. Obviously, losing Pam had really rattled her.

"You know," Darcy said dryly, "most moms would tell their daughters to stay out of danger."

That eased her shoulders and she grinned. "Mom's worried about me or she wouldn't have popped in. Her bakery is probably packed with the morning pre-work crowd."

Darcy broke into a full grin. "The Cookie Witch! I've seen your mom on talk shows with cooking segments. She's really awesome. Does she use magic in her cookies?"

Carla shook her head. "She bakes most of her cookies like any mortal. She came up with the idea to call herself the Cookie Witch, opened the bakery so people can watch her 'casting spells' as she bakes, and it just took off. Her natural quirkiness just adds to the charm."

Darcy picked up her mug of tea. "Your mom is hiding in plain sight."

"Mom was a fairly powerful witch until the curse. She'd been with her familiar for ten years, and then he disappeared. She was grief-stricken by the loss, which was bad enough, but her top three chakras closed off, too. She was reduced to elemental magic, and she didn't know how to function. Then the witch kills started and she was terrified. All the witches were. Witch karma prevented them from using their powers to protect themselves from the rogues. The witch hunters they had always relied on to protect them were now killing them."

"It looks like your mom adjusted, found a way to cope."

Carla sipped her own tea. "Not without some missteps." Like her dad for instance. He was a huge misstep. He knew exactly what her mom was, and used her—and later, his twin daughters. "But Mom is right. The best way to figure out what I need to do is to find out who the soul is and what she wants." She stood up.

Darcy rose, too. "I'm not letting you do this alone.

What you saw last time..." She shuddered. "You're not going to be alone."

They walked out into the family room, then left into a hallway that led to three bedrooms. The master bedroom was on the other side of the house behind the family room, but Carla had chosen the first bedroom on this side. The house belonged to the Wing Slayer Hunters, and when Carla had first come here, Darcy and Axel had stayed with her a few nights to make sure she was safe, and they'd slept in the master bedroom.

In the doorway of the room, she stopped and looked at Darcy. "Rogues using mortals like Pam to kill the Wing Slayer Hunters...that's just evil." Anger heated her blood and flushed her skin.

"We won't let them win. We're going to save Pam and help her be whole again."

The burden on her chest eased. "Let's see what I can find out." She headed into the bedroom. Pam hadn't moved from where Axel had placed her on the bed. Working quickly, she opened her chakras and touched Pam's shoulder to establish a connection to her. Then she let her spirit rise and stretch past the earth's physical plane.

The astral plane appeared in the vast blue. To move around the plane, she needed to just focus on what she wanted. She focused on Pam, calling to the woman's spirit.

Instantly the atmosphere changed into Axel's nightclub. Carla had never been there, but she recognized it from Pam's memories. She saw the throbbing colored lights on the dark dance floor. Pam was dancing among a group of women. Then she spotted Sutton by one of the bars.

Through Pam's eyes, he looked hot in a scary, overwhelming way. He was well over six feet and wore black pants over black hiking boots paired with a

JENNIFER LYON

muscle shirt that revealed muscular arms. His bald head, vigilant blue eyes, and the gold eagle earring in his left ear elevated him from sexy to almost untouchable.

Yet Carla wanted to touch him. Even though she was viewing Pam's creation on the astral plane, she longed to touch Sutton. Even amid a hundred throbbing bodies, he looked alone. It bothered her deeply, made her want to ease him.

She forced herself to stop focusing on him and look at the whole picture. After a few seconds, she realized that Pam was reliving her experience in the club. The astral plane was tricky, giving the spirit what it longed for, letting the subconscious work out problems, issues, or feelings by reenacting things. Carla watched carefully to see that the club was closing down, and the pack of women who had been dancing were leaving. But Pam hung back, looking in her purse.

Sutton approached her and Carla witnessed the exchange between them up to the point when Sutton walked away and Pam put her hand in her purse.

She pulled out the gun and her hand began to tremble.

Carla's chest tightened in sympathy for the woman. "Pam," she called softly. "It's time to go back now."

Pam looked up at her and the gun vanished from her hand. "I can't change what happened, can I?"

"No."

"Are you sure I'm not dead?"

"Very sure. I'm going to take care of you, bring you back to your physical self. Then we're going to help you get your life back together."

"Okay, how do I go back?"

"Take my hand." Carla held out her hand to Pam.

Pam began moving toward Carla.

It was working. Carla would return Pam to the physical plane, then come back and talk to the soul.

36

Happiness and relief made everything around her seem brighter and more...

A small starburst of lights ruptured between them.

"That light is back," Pam said, then her voice tightened with tension. "Dr. Fisk? I can't see you. Where are you?"

The light was cutting Pam off from her. Carla felt her body on the physical plane react, her heart seizing, then starting to hammer. Her chakras wanted to close off. She struggled to keep her communication chakra open. "Pam, think harder, imagine getting on the other side of the light to me."

The light suddenly brightened into a flare shaped like a blade, and pulled Carla's spirit in like a vacuum. Everything went cold and her doppelganger body vanished. Her spirit was trapped in something! She tried to force her spirit out of the object, but the press of cool metal surrounded her, along with remnants of magic. *Think!* The object had to be silver to conduct magic, but a silver what? She let her spirit fill the space until she could feel the outline. It was familiar...long, with a sharp end...oh crap, she was inside a silver knife.

"No!" She struggled to focus her energy into moving outside the knife and back to her doppelganger body. But she was trapped.

How could that be? On the astral plane she should be in control.

A woman appeared. She had dark eyes that had the witch tilt to them, and smooth, flawless olive skin. The witch was outside the knife, while Carla was inside.

And then the knife was moving. Oh God, she was in the knife that was going to kill the witch! Carla could feel the knife moving, slashing downward.

Blood welled up along the cut on the woman's thigh as her scream echoed shrilly in the knife.

A man's hand smearing the blood. "Mine," a voice

behind the knife said. "More!" The knife slashed again, slicing the witch's stomach.

More screams. More pain. More blood. More...

Carla couldn't bear it anymore. She couldn't watch the torture of a woman born to bring comfort and aid to earth's people. To avoid looking, she squeezed her eyes closed and told herself: *I'm on the astral plane. The knife isn't real.* But the light that was holding her in the knife was real.

It had to be the soul of one of the witches the knife had killed. That made sense. The soul was manifesting the knife, reenacting something just as Pam had been reenacting the scene where she had shot Sutton. Pam had been trying, futilely, to change the outcome; what was the soul doing? Trying to tell Carla something? What? Dear Ancestors, if ever she wished she could open her sixth chakra—the one that held her third eye—it was now. Her third eye could see what her regular eyes could not. But she couldn't, so instead she used the vibration of her communication chakra to ask, "Who are you? What do you want? Are you trapped?"

Trapped.

That voice! It vibrated in her head, and recognition stunned her so badly she felt her physical body on the earth's plane slip to the ground.

"Carla! Get your spirit ass back here, or I'm coming after you."

Darcy's strident voice gave her the boost she needed to slide out of the knife. But her spirit hesitated, and in that second, she felt the echo of power that could only belong to one person. She stood on the astral plane, looking at the shifting light that shimmered between her and Pam. "Keri?" Dear Ancestors, it was her sister! They'd shared power often enough that Carla knew her sister's magic as well her own. She was trapped in a rogue's knife!

Find the eagle. Free me.

She reached out her hand, desperate to touch her sister, but the astral plane pulled back, shrinking away from her like water swirling down the drain.

Then it was gone. She was on the cold tile floor, her right elbow and the side of her head aching badly enough that she knew she was back in her body.

Darcy was bent over her, her face pale, her brown eyes intense. "What the hell happened?"

Carla shoved herself up to a sitting position as the full impact hit her. *No, no!* her brain screamed, but she knew it was true. She had to grit her teeth to stop her body from shivering. Finally, she said, "The soul isn't trapped on the astral plane, it's trapped in the knife that killed her."

Darcy dropped onto her butt and crossed her legs so that she faced her. "How is that possible?"

"I don't know, but she's in there. She was forced to watch as the rogue who has it killed witch after witch." The room was standing still now, but her head pounded and her heart beat frantically.

"Who?"

"Keri. My twin sister."

"Find the eagle. Free me." Carla walked around the wrought-iron table and chairs on the patio that led to a swatch of green grass surrounded by flowers. Bees buzzed around doing their work, while birds chattered in nearby trees, and each breath she took added another crack to her breaking heart.

Her eyes burned. She put her hand over her chest, trying to ease the knot within.

"Carla, why didn't you tell me that one of the people who was murdered at your clinic two years ago was your twin sister?"

She forced a deep breath, walked back to the table and sat down. "At first, I didn't tell you because you didn't know you were a witch. Frankly, if I had even started talking about Keri to you, I'd have told you everything. I didn't think you were ready, and maybe I wasn't ready to talk about her."

"And since then?" Darcy asked gently.

Carla looked into her eyes. "I would have told you, at some point when it was just the two of us talking. I knew you'd listen and be there. Maybe I was saving it for the day I really needed you." She dropped into the chair and rubbed at the pain in the center of her chest.

Darcy said softly, "God, Carla. For you to have been there, to see your sister murdered by a rogue, I don't know how you stood it."

She dropped her hand and said, "That's the thing, Darcy. She saved me. I was late to work that day, late for an appointment with my client. I got to the Holistic Healing Clinic and I went in the front way through the waiting room. I walked in on a rogue attacking Keri." She kept her eyes wide and focused on Darcy, because if she closed them, she'd see the scene behind her eyelids. "I didn't know it at the time, but my client was already dead in my office, and the other two witches, an herbalist and a midwife, were being drained by a rogue in the office kitchen." The guilt and horror dried out her mouth. "But all I heard were Keri's screams. I attacked the rogue to get him off Keri. There was a clinical part of my mind that knew Keri was already dying, but I had to try to save her or die with her. I had to make him stop cutting her. Somehow I got between her and the rogue, and that's when he cut me."

"The scar on your lower back?" Darcy asked.

"Yes." The scar tingled as she tried to explain. "It all happened so fast. The shock of pain, then suddenly, Keri used her powers to lift me off her and throw me across the room to the door." At Darcy's skeptical look, she said, "What?"

"That doesn't sound right," she said with a frown of concentration. "The first thing the rogue would have done was cut Keri enough to close off her chakras so she couldn't do magic. That's why he started cutting you, too. Rogues usually use three cuts on different parts of our bodies to shut down our magic. Carla, your sister didn't have her powers to save you."

"Keri's powers were closed off. But we were identical twins, we could share power. She managed to connect her mind to my chakras and use that power to hurl me across the room."

"You were very close, weren't you? Keri must have loved you very much."

"Keri loved everyone. Where I'm half scientist, half witch, Keri was all witch. Her greatest joy was helping other people. She was the one who wanted to open the Holistic Healing Clinic. I hadn't planned on joining."

"So why did you? You told me you were a witch activist, lobbying for witches to come out of hiding and do the right thing—helping humans."

Carla took a deep breath. "It all comes back to my dad. I told you my dad was a geneticist, but he's not just any scientist, he's Dr. Jerome Wagner."

Darcy's eyebrows shot up as she placed the name. "Your dad is the famous mad scientist who insists that humans can do magic?" She sucked in her lips with a groan and said, "Sorry. I wasn't thinking. And obviously he's not crazy, magic does exist."

"He prefers the term psi-geneticist," Carla said dryly. "And yeah, that's him. He's spent his life working to discover the genetic breakthrough that will validate his beliefs that humans can become superhuman. He met my mother on a talk show. She was there to make cookies, and he realized there was something special about her."

41

"Amazing. Your dad's a mortal though, right?"

Carla's feelings about her dad had mellowed enough that a little amusement slipped through. "Oh yeah. Much to his frustration. And once he met my mother, he was even more convinced he could isolate the gene that transformed mortals into witches. The fact that witches evolved from mortals just fed his certainty. He is determined to prove that he isn't a crackpot, but a legitimate scientist. He plans to change the world."

Darcy's face tightened. "You and Keri were his research subjects?"

"Pretty convenient, huh? Anyway, Keri stopped cooperating with him in her late teens. She became much more interested in yoga, holistic healing and her eagles. Her passion was to help witches stop hiding. She hated that. Keri was passionate and..." How could she explain it? "In many ways, she and my dad were alike. Both were stubborn and believed one hundred percent, no holds barred, in their causes. And Jerome made it worse."

"How?"

The old guilt surfaced. "He favored me. I tested out smarter than Keri, and in Jerome's world, being smarter must make me a more powerful witch, too. But that wasn't true. In the witch world, Keri was more powerful. But her power crested and thrived when she was helping people. In the lab? Her power was flat."

"Why?"

She searched for an explanation. "Keri was a strong telepath, a psychic witch. But she had a natural anxiety that was only calmed by contact with other people. Sometimes when she was alone, she could pull enough from me to be okay, but too much isolation drove her crazy and drained her powers." It felt really good to talk about Keri, to tell someone who could understand who her sister was. "Plus, she knew in her heart that our dad would never isolate this gene that made us witches, because, well, it's evolution that happened over time, and with cause. It's the one thing Jerome never got. All evolutionary changes happen for a reason, and over time. In Keri's mind, he fundamentally didn't understand the reason."

"Mortals needed us. We can heal, teach and banish demons. At least we could before the curse, anyway."

In so short a time, Darcy had absorbed an incredible amount about witches. "Yes. And when she tried to tell him that, he wouldn't listen. He would tell her that she couldn't grasp the scientific principles."

Darcy asked, "So she stopped cooperating, but what about you?"

"I was torn between them. I identified with my dad more than Keri did. I wondered what we could do if we did find out more about our genetics." She dropped her eyes to the table and said, "I have my mother in me, too—I wondered if there was a scientific solution to the curse." Slowly she lifted her gaze to Darcy's face.

"Ah, now I see what you meant about your mom's missteps. She thought Jerome could break the curse and return her to her full power."

Carla explained, "They fell in love for the wrong reasons. Mom wanted to believe he could fix the curse, and Jerome wanted to believe she would help him with his big breakthrough. By the time Keri and I were two years old, they didn't have anything left between them."

Darcy asked, "Do you think that it's possible science can break the curse?"

She shook her head. "No. I wanted to believe it, but no. The curse was a soul-destructive magic, not science. And I realized just how fragile souls can be when our dad found out that Keri was trying to talk me into working at the Holistic Healing Clinic. He went ballistic and screamed at her that if she wanted to waste her life jumping from one silly idea to the next, that was her choice. But I was too smart and valuable to waste on her frivolous crap."

Darcy's eyes widened, and her face flushed. "That was cruel and horrible."

Carla winced at the memory. "I felt her pain that day. She was shocked and hurt. Always, deep in her heart, Keri had hoped that one day Dad would figure out on his own how gifted she was at witchcraft, and that was without a familiar. But in that moment, his words destroyed her hopes. It just..." She shook her head, pulling herself from the past. In a more clinical voice, she said, "I realized how unfair he had been to Keri, and that I had been condoning it. His genetic link had turned him into an unfeeling monster. I walked out and started work at the clinic."

"What did your dad do?"

"He was furious and said I'd realize the mistake I'd made and come crawling back." Her smile was real. "But you know what? I found what I loved. It was the perfect mix of the science of the brain and witchcraft. I saw what we were accomplishing with both mortals and witches. I believed Keri had been right, witches had to stop hiding and help people."

"Did you ever talk to your dad?"

She grimaced. "It was strained. He couldn't see past his own obsession. He swore Keri was going to destroy me."

"Oh, Carla. How awful."

She closed her eyes. The pain in her chest felt like her heart had frozen solid, then been cracked open with a hammer. "After Keri was murdered, I ran to my mother. We were both inconsolable. Mom called Dad. He arrived, hugged us, then said to me, 'Now you can come back to your real job.' I was furious. Keri was dead! Murdered! And he was worried about his research?" The old wound tore open and the rage pounded in her head and chest. Opening her eyes, she said, "Dad told me that I was the one who let Keri get murdered by abandoning our research, and if I walked out on him..."

"What?"

She could still hear his words ringing in her ears. "I shouldn't come back."

"Carla, I'm so sorry."

She looked up. "They were both wrong. Keri was wrong about witches coming out of hiding, and my dad was wrong about me. I wasn't the smarter or more powerful witch. And he'll never find the link to prove his theories. He threw Keri away for nothing."

"And you," Darcy said softly.

The pain cut off her breath. "Even when she was dying, Keri tried to save me. And now she's trapped in a rogue's knife. How did she get in there? A witch's soul doesn't accidentally get trapped, it has to be bound magically."

Darcy said, "My mother bound her soul to the tapestry and stayed there for twenty-six years. She did it for me."

A light went on in Carla's head. "Keri wasn't just getting into my chakras, she was trying to bind her soul to me! To my silver armband! Silver conducts power. It's why all our witch books are made of silver. She was trying to give me the extra strength to live..." It was so horrible. But she had to say it, she had to face it so she could fix it. "She missed the armband, and instead, bound herself to the very knife that was killing her."

"It was an accident." Darcy reached out and took her hand.

She looked up at her friend's pale face. "But how could I have not known? I've always felt Keri's emotions, and she felt mine. We were connected!

She's been suffering for two years, trapped in a knife and forced to witness witch kill after witch kill while I did nothing."

Darcy's face hardened. "Stop it, Carla. What we have to do now is figure out how to free her. Not fall apart and leave her to suffer. She said, 'Find the eagle. Free me.' What could that mean?"

Carla closed her eyes for a second to think and caught a whiff of a familiar scent. Snapping her eyes open, she said, "Do you smell incense?"

Darcy inhaled, then shook her head.

Her heart fluttered. "It's Keri! She's been doing that, trying to reach me. For a couple months, I've been getting a whiff of incense—she always smelled like incense—or I see eagles. Either eagles in flight or... Oh, Ancestors!" She reached into her pants pocket and yanked out her cell phone.

Darcy leaned forward, her shoulders tense. "What?"

Using her magic, Carla re-created the image she had seen on the computer after talking to her mom on her cell phone screen. Then she held it out to Darcy. "Look familiar?"

She sucked in her breath. "That's Sutton's eagle tattoo."

The scent of incense grew stronger. "I know. I saw it the night he saved me when he gave me his shirt. And if I saw it, then Keri saw it." She tried to put it together, to understand what Keri was trying to tell her.

"How long did you say you've been smelling Keri's scent and seeing the eagle pictures?"

"Two months..." The answer clicked. "Since that night Sutton rescued me. Keri loves eagles. She would identify with that tattoo. Sutton's the eagle Keri meant. But what can he do? How can he help her?" Carla would do anything to get Keri free of that knife.

Darcy's eyes were thoughtful. "Sutton has the most complete list of rogues, he can help you find the knife Keri's in."

Carla's stomach turned over. To see him again, touch him...no. She couldn't risk it. Sutton was cursed, he'd touched her blood once. Next time, he could kill her. Did she have a death wish?

Maybe. As a psychologist, she knew about survivor guilt. Keri had died, and she'd lived. She should have died that day with her sister.

No, Carla would do this the safe way. She summoned her powers and used her phone to connect to Sutton, either his phone or computer, whichever he was closest to.

The screen on her phone went black. Both her magic and the phone were dead. "Keri, damn it!" She and Keri had done this to each other a million times while growing up. She could feel her sister cutting off the mind-chakra connection she needed to access her magic.

Darcy jumped in her seat. "What?"

Carla looked up at her friend. "She's blocking my magic. Seeing her on the astral plane must have triggered something. I had my fifth chakra opened. That's our communication with other realms, and Keri could have used it to strengthen our connection."

"Why would she stop you from calling Sutton?"

"She wants me to go to him in person."

4

SUTTON RAISED THE AX HIGH over his head, and brought it down with a satisfying crack.

Anything to keep from thinking about the nightmare. He'd slept less than an hour before he'd been pulled into the dream. He saw his large fist closed around the wickedly gleaming silver knife before plunging the knife into Carla's chest.

Sutton had jerked awake with sweat running down his back and legs, his heart pounding viciously, and his mind shouting a denial. It took long seconds for him to realize it had been a nightmare.

Not real.

Not yet. He hadn't killed Carla...yet.

Then he'd smelled her scent, still lingering from when she'd been in his cabin earlier. His morning hard-on had throbbed for the feel of her, while his craving for her blood loomed darkly in his head. He'd leaped off the bed, yanked on his hiking boots and headed outside, trying to escape his nightmares and her scent.

The sun was shining brightly, helping to shove his nightmares back into the shadows. He set the ax down, stripped off his shirt and tossed it on the porch railing. With the sun on his shoulders and back, he bent to pick up the ax when his phone began beeping an alarm.

The skin on the back of his neck tightened at the signal that his security had been breached. The cabin was remote, set up on the rugged cliffs overlooking the ocean. He owned the surrounding land, and had it wired with infrared cameras and various security devices. He pulled his phone out to see what had tripped his security.

The screen showed three bodies about forty yards away. They had to be witch hunters in stealth mode, invisible to a normal camera, but his infrareds picked up their body heat as they moved between knotty, twisted trees, the chaparral, sagebrush and cacti.

Sutton regularly cleared the brush close to his cabin. He dropped the ax and shielded himself so he appeared invisible even in the bright sunlight. The bodies on his small cell phone screen were moving fast, much faster than humans.

His blood surged at the prospect of a down-and-dirty fight. They were close enough for him to inhale and catch the scent of copper over the earthiness of the land.

Rogues. Were they looking for Pam? Or him? Did they think Pam had succeeded in killing him? Failed? He'd find out soon enough. The scent was getting stronger. He set his phone down, able to track them by noise and smell now. Judging by the faint rustling, he'd say they were about twenty yards away. He moved like he'd been taught since he could walk: silently and blending in with the land around him.

Sweeping his gaze back and forth, he spotted a movement in the brush about a half-dozen yards away. He had his large knife tucked in the holster at his back, but he left it there for hand-to-hand fighting.

First he'd flush them out. Dropping his left arm, he snapped his wrist and a smaller knife with a thin, wicked-sharp blade sprang into his fingers. He checked once more.

He could see the dirt ahead of him depress with the footstep of an invisible rogue. He measured the distance carefully, determining that the lead rogue's heart was about five and a half feet straight up from that imprint. In a rapid movement, he drew his arm back and threw the knife.

A bellow of surprise cut through the unnatural quiet. Then a man appeared, the thin silver knife buried in his chest, and he tumbled to the ground.

Two other rogues appeared behind him.

Witch hunters couldn't hold the shield of invisibility while fighting, which meant Sutton was now visible, too, and standing out in the open. He moved in a blur, slamming himself up against the shady side of his house. He assessed the situation quickly. The rogue in the green shirt seemed faster, while the one in the white T-shirt was bigger and had both a gun and a knife. Moving swiftly, he dropped his right arm to release the second knife.

He picked up another sound over the roar of the ocean—uneven footsteps and labored breathing. Not a rogue, too clumsy. Damn it, now he had to worry about keeping a human alive while dealing with the rogues.

The rogue in the white T-shirt fired.

Sutton jumped to the right and let his small knife fly at the exact instant that the bullet grooved into the side of his cabin. His knife hit the mark, causing the man to tumble backward as blood spread on his shirt. He was dead when he hit the ground.

The last rogue pivoted on his heel to the right and broke into a run, disappearing from view as he shielded himself.

Furious, Sutton took off after him. Who were these bastards? Was one of them Styx, the rogue that brainwashed Pam? Did they know anything about Brigg? He pushed his body up to at least twenty miles an hour as he covered the rocky, uneven terrain, darting around trees and bushes.

The bastard turned and headed for the cliffs overlooking the ocean. On the right was the access road, on the left was a sheer drop. He seemed to be speeding up.

Going to jump? It was his best chance to escape. The drop was at least thirty feet. If he didn't crush his heart on a rock, he'd survive and heal.

And Sutton would probably lose him. He couldn't let that happen; he needed to question the man before he sent him to his eternity as a shade. Who the hell was Styx and where was Brigg?

He increased his speed, pushing himself and inhaling to stay on the copper scent.

The back of his neck went tight at a new smell—lavender laced with the spicy scent of a witch. He instantly recognized that scent.

Oh, hell no! The words exploded in his head. Not Carla. If he could smell her, then...

The path the rogue was churning in the ground abruptly turned right toward the access road.

Shit! A double shot of adrenaline hit his blood. He pulled his knife from his back holster. Just then, Carla's white-blond head appeared as she crested the top of the road.

She was on foot!

What the hell was she doing here?

Her hair was piled on top of her head, and falling down around her sweaty face. The shimmer of her skin—the one that mortal eyes couldn't see but witch hunters could—glittered like a neon sign.

His blood roared, exploding into fiery pain. A

sinister voice in his mind screamed for him to get her, get the witch blood!

A rogue materialize just a couple yards from Carla. She froze, her eyes going wide, her mouth dropping open.

Mine! His mind bellowed and he leaped, every muscle and tendon straining to get to her.

The rogue got within a few feet of Carla, one hand reaching out to grab her, the other arcing his knife toward her side.

Sutton flew between them, bringing one arm up to deflect the knife and using the other to shove Carla to the ground.

The knife slashed to the bone of his arm. The hot pain incited his rage. Sutton landed on the ground, rolled up to his feet, and in one continuous movement slammed his body into the rogue.

"The witch is mine!" The crazed rogue fought, thrashing his body and screaming curses.

With a possessive roar, Sutton pinned the knife-wielding hand to the ground and levered up to get his knee in the man's stomach. He looked down into the rogue's light-blue eyes staring at Carla, his whole body twitching with the blood-craving. Sutton moved in a blur, stabbing his knife into the rogue's heart.

The man jerked, his mouth opened in a soundless scream. Then death stilled his movements.

Jacked up, his heart pounding and his muscles stretched, Sutton shoved up to his feet.

Carla stood just a few feet away.

The impact of seeing her knocked the air from his lungs. It hurt to look at her, but he couldn't tear his gaze away. She was as stunningly beautiful as she was a mess. Her hair had been torn loose from the clip and hung in clumps. Her face was shiny with sweat. Her cat-tilted eyes were wide, revealing layered colors of green, yellow and brown. She wore jeans, a tank top and tennis shoes that to his trained eye looked like they were spotless under a fresh layer of trail dirt. All her exposed skin had a silvery shimmer.

Her lavender scent made him think of soft skin, sultry nights and hardcore sex. But the wickedly enticing Arabian coffee aroma invoked a dark memory of touching her blood two months ago. The dual hungers for sex and blood cramped his gut and burned his veins.

"Sutton, you're hurt." She lifted her hands as if to summon her magic, then must have remembered the danger of her power inflaming the curse and dropped her arms. She pulled her mouth tight in concern.

"Carla..." Oh God, to touch her, just to make sure she was okay. No! He didn't dare. She was the one who would drive him rogue. He tore his gaze away, seeing the dead rogue who had gotten too close to her. A shudder ran through him. She wasn't safe out here; more rogues might come looking for their friends. He had no choice. "We'll go to my cabin."

She looked around, then her gaze shot back to him and his shirtless chest. Her silvery witch-shimmer took on a dusky gold tone, warm and sensual. When she returned her stare to his injured arm, she reached down, grabbed the edge of her tank and pulled it off.

He couldn't believe it. "What the hell are you doing?"

Wearing only her jeans and a black bra, she closed the distance between them. "I'm not moving until we take care of that arm."

Her scent almost drowned his lungs. She was so close, too damned close, her full breasts spilling over the delicate black cups. "Get back! And put your shirt on, damn it!" Was she trying to make him lose control?

She lifted her eyes, and the green heat in them damn near knocked him senseless. "You've seen me naked. You took care of me." She grabbed his hand and started to wrap her shirt around his arm.

Naked. Sex. Carla. Holy fucking hell, the feel of her small hand on his...he took hold of her shirt, tugged it loose from her fingers and finished wrapping up his arm before the last thinning thread of his control snapped. "You're playing with fire, little witch."

"And you're always saving me." She looked around, her expression grave as she saw the dead men. "Thank you for that."

He blinked and his gaze locked on her breasts. Her nipples hardened beneath that thin layer of material. She was reacting to him. Had to be the pheromones he gave off. The curse was burning so hot in him, he was probably spurting the damn things. He had to get himself under control! Jerking his gaze up to her face, he said, "My cabin." He started walking, hoping like hell he wasn't leading her to her own murder. By his hand.

She walked beside him.

He had to shorten his stride so she could keep up. He kept his eyes and ears opened to any threat as they walked, while wondering why she would risk her life to see him. By the time they reached the steps of his cabin, his neck and shoulder muscles felt like rocks, and sweat slid down the center of his back. The effort of not touching her...

Half of him wanted to pull her to him, run his hands and mouth over all that warm, bare skin. Make her sigh and writhe to feel his touch. Then bury his cock inside her, *make her his.*

The other half, that cursed animal, saw all that bare skin as invitation to palm his knife and cut her over and over. The idea of her power-laced blood welling up set his veins on fire with murderous craving.

Sutton strode up the steps, snatched his shirt off the railing where he'd tossed it while cutting the wood, and threw it at Carla. "Put this on." He didn't look at her and tried not to breathe in her scent as they went inside the cabin. He could bear it more easily if she covered up.

Shutting the door, he ignored the living room and turned right. He used his palm print to open his environmentally controlled computer room. He had to contact Axel to report in about the rogue attack and to have him come get Carla.

Now.

Before he lost control.

"What is this?" Carla walked into the room the size of a master bedroom and looked around.

She had put his shirt on, a big black garment that hung down to her knees. Knowing it was his shirt on her, the shirt that had touched his skin just an hour ago was now touching hers, sent his blood rushing to his dick. He focused on answering her with, "Server, hard drives, monitors, printer, big-screen TV. I keep the Wing Slayer Hunters' computer network backed up here." Yeah, he was showing off a little. Carla had a PhD; she was elegant, smart and beautiful. He was self-taught, but hell, he wasn't without skills. He went to the keyboard of his main computer and accessed the warehouse to connect to Axel.

With every strike of the keys, he felt Carla's presence behind him. Felt her breathing. Smelled her scent.

Her blood.

A low roar started in his head. He looked up to the monitor, expecting to see Axel or one of the other hunters.

Instead he saw... "What the hell?" His eagle tattoo filled all the monitors in the room. It was even on the big-screen TV. No fucking way! Someone hacked—

Carla inhaled sharply behind him. "It's Keri. She's using my magic to block your computer."

Her words hit him square in the back at the same time that he felt magic sizzle through him. He turned to look at Carla. "Why are you here trying to make me kill you?" It was all he could do to stand down, hold his position.

Her hazel eyes bloomed a pain-filled yellow, her witch-shimmer dimmed to a gray dust color. She brought her hand up to knead the spot between her breasts. "Keri's my twin sister. She was murdered two years ago..."

Sutton reached behind him, curling his fingers around the computer table, and anchored himself to the spot while Carla told her story. He didn't dare let himself feel anything, no pity, sympathy, or rage that Carla had seen her twin sister murdered. Or that the rogue had sliced Carla with his knife. He had to stay in control, cold and logical. Keep the curse locked down tight. When she finished, he said, "Keri's using your magic to hijack my computers. Why? What does she want from me?"

Carla had bunched the front of the oversize shirt in her hands and twisted the material. Now she dropped the shirt and smoothed it down as she explained. "Find the eagle. Free me. That's what Keri said." She took another breath, lifted her shoulders, and added, "Keri always loved eagles from the time she was two years old. She'd hike to all kinds of places to see them. To Keri, you're the eagle that can save her. She needs you."

"Just because I have an eagle tattoo?" That was a hell of a stretch. "Lots of men have eagle tattoos."

Carla stared him down. "You saw what she did, putting your tattoo on the monitors. It's you. Keri believes you can free her. You can find her. You have all these resources." She looked around at all his equipment. "You can find the rogue who killed her and has the knife she's trapped in. And once you locate the knife, I'll find a spell or a way to free her soul so she can go on to Summerland." She took a breath. "Keri hates being trapped."

Her pain and desperate determination stirred the dark craving in him until he couldn't think. Carla's scent was filling the room, and his mind was saturating with her. The memory of his dream, of seeing his hand hold the knife that cut Carla shoved him into motion, and he walked toward the door. He needed a little space...

The door closed. By magic. He was trapped in the computer room with the one witch he'd seen himself cut in his dreams.

It was his nightmare come to life.

"I didn't fight hard enough for Keri when she was alive, I'm going to fight for her to my last breath now." Carla stared at Sutton's naked back, his huge muscles bunching and twitching beneath the eagle tattoo. The brown and black wings spread from the edge of his pants on his left side to the top of his right shoulder. The white hood and tail stood out in stark contrast. The bird's dark, intense eyes seemed to be watching her. The creature looked so real, it even had the yellow beak and feet. She wanted to touch the bird, and touch Sutton. Craved it. Needed it. She wanted to rip off the shirt Sutton gave her and press her body up against him. What the hell was wrong with her? Keri had been the impulsive thrill-seeker, not her, Carla the coward.

Sutton slowly turned from the door. He dominated the room, towering over the electronics and her. His dark pants sat loosely away from his narrowed hips, then bulged at his thighs and again at his calves. His hiking boots were huge, nearly twice the size of her own feet. His eyes bore into her. "I can smell the magic in your blood." He took a step toward her, then stopped as if he'd put the brakes on. He crossed his arms over his massive chest and glared at her. "Open the door. Give me some space."

"You'll do it? Look for the knife Keri's in?" It felt like she needed more than that from him, but what? Her skin heated, and her powers twirled restlessly deep inside her stomach, seeking some elusive thing she didn't understand. This was crazy, yet her hands itched with a need to touch him, to run her fingers and palms over the bare skin of his chest, shoulders, and all the way down his arms to his thick wristbands. Her gaze snapped back to her blood-soaked shirt wrapped around Sutton's left arm. Her chakras bubbled and her scar heated.

Almost without thought, she used her magic to get rid of the shirt, leaving his arm bare and the wound gaping open, oozing blood. Carla's stomach clenched...the pain he must be feeling! The scar on her lower back was burning now, fueling the need to touch him. Heal the wound.

"Carla..." Sutton growled out the warning.

She looked up to see his bald head gleaming in the overhead lights. His jaw was clenched, his throat worked.

But she couldn't stop. The scar pushed her, made her *need* to touch him. Part of her brain yelled the warning that this was the collision they had both been trying to avoid. Something irreversible. Another step, and her skin pebbled. Then she lifted her hand, the pain in her lower back a branding agony now. She looked up into his fierce blue eyes. "Have to." She laid her hand over the wound.

Sutton hissed, then froze as if by sheer will he'd turned himself to a statue.

Carla's first four chakras burst open, and her powers poured out in breath-stealing waves, rushing around her body and humming. Then they poured down to her hand, and light flared from her palm, growing brighter as her powers began healing him. Every pulse of her magic opened up a yawning need inside her, desperate to pull Sutton into her. Her nipples ached to be stroked by him. Her womb throbbed to be filled by him. The hot, sexual desire burned inside her.

"Can't...oh shit." Sutton wrapped his free arm around her and yanked her off her feet. With his arm locked around her waist, his head an inch from hers, they both turned to see that his blood coated her palm. Then it began to vanish.

The burning in her scar faded as her body absorbed his blood. The heat of Sutton's body surrounded her, caressed her until the yearning inside her ramped up to bright, fierce, painful need.

"Can't let you go," Sutton said tightly as he slipped a hand under her leg and hooked her thigh over his hip.

His erection pressed against her core. Her breath rushed out as pleasure raced along her nerve endings. Sutton pulled her tighter and lowered his face and brushed his full lips against hers. "Need you." Then he sank into her mouth.

A voice exploded from the computer. "Sutton, what the hell is going on?"

Sutton's arm tightened around her as he jerked his head up. "Mine," he snarled.

Carla tried to clear the haze from her mind and looked around the room.

Axel's green eyes stared out at them from all the monitors. "I just got your message that you killed three rogues, and Carla is in danger."

What the hell was she doing? "Put me down."

Sutton seemed to struggle with himself for an endless second before he slid her down to her feet.

"Get here, Axel. Now," he said in a dark voice as he backed away from her.

Carla looked down at her hand. The blood was gone. That was what Keri had wanted—Sutton's blood. But why? The answer stunned her, taking her breath away. Soul mirrors were the two halves of one soul ripped apart when the curse was thrown. When those two halves of the souls found each other, they used a blood exchange and sex to re-form the bond and make the two souls whole again.

Oh, Ancestors, had she just kissed her dead sister's soul mirror?

⇒ 5 ⇐

CARLA WAS WALKING ON THE astral plane, on a graceful path of colored stones with beautiful vines on either side of her. Huge white and purple flowers bloomed as she passed by. The path gave way to soft grass surrounding a rock waterfall that splashed into a pool. Mist from the waterfall kept her cool. She wasn't even walking, but gliding.

Sutton walked beside her. He was shirtless, the eagle on his back fluttering and stretching its wings inside the tattoo. She couldn't stop looking at him.

She wanted to touch him, to feel all of his skin.

That was when she realized she was naked, her body soft and warm, feeling fluid and desperate for his touch.

He turned to look at her, his blue eyes lighting up with interest.

Then Keri appeared in the pathway in front of them. "Carla, you found him! You found the eagle!" She held out her hands and Sutton forgot about Carla, his gaze latching onto Keri. He moved to her, sweeping her up into his arms. Now they were both naked, and Carla had to look away.

She woke up, feeling the wash of vivid humiliation and stabbing loss. The grief for her sister was always with her but this was tinged with feelings that made her uncomfortable. Jealousy, and shame for feeling that way.

Pushing up, she swung her legs over the side of the bed and glanced at the clock. Just after one in the morning. Her room was velvety dark and cool. She sat there, letting her emotions calm down.

She wouldn't sleep any longer. Getting to her feet, she decided that now was an excellent time to go to the astral plane and retrieve Pam. She'd assure Keri that she would find the knife and free her. She didn't need to hold Pam hostage.

Although, as she walked out into the hallway, she had to admit that didn't sound like Keri. Was there another reason she was keeping Pam's spirit on the astral plane?

Carla opened the door to Pam's room and stopped. The room was filled with flickering candles, gentle sounds of the rain forest floated in the air, and on the ceiling over the bed were pictures of animals and babies playing.

Most telling of all was the scent of fresh-baked sugar cookies.

"Mom, what are you doing here?"

Chandra Fisk sat in a chair by the bed, her long, dark blond hair in a braid, wearing flowing green silk pajamas and working on her laptop. She lifted her green eyes. "I drove straight through. Keri needs us." She glanced toward the bed. "And so does Pam. You don't have to do this on your own, Carla."

Was she still dreaming? "You know about Keri?"

Her eyes darkened. "She's not at rest. I've known that ever since that horrible day she was murdered."

Carla went into the room and softly closed the door. "Why didn't you tell me?"

Her mom's smile was sad. "You would have told me that it was grief."

Carla opened her mouth to protest, then realized that that's exactly what she would have done. She'd have pulled out her training and explained how grief can twist reality. "I'm sorry."

Chandra set her laptop down on the bed, stood up and crossed the room to hug Carla. She took her hand and the two of them sat on the end of the double bed. "Don't be sorry. I wasn't sure. How could I be? We were both devastated by Keri's murder. My mind could have been playing tricks. These days, without our familiars, we can't be certain of anything. And I was scared for you. The rogue had marked you with his knife. Nothing we did healed that wound. I was terrified he'd be able to find you."

"I know." They had both worried about that possibility. Carla had left San Francisco to hide, and also to draw any rogues away from her mother. Chandra had only agreed because she thought it would be safer for Carla.

Chandra looked into her eyes. "It's Keri's soul that was on the astral plane."

"Yes." Squeezing her mom's hand, Carla said, "She tried to bind herself to my armband and got trapped in the rogue's knife. How could she have been trapped and didn't know?"

Chandra's mouth pulled tight and her eyes filled with pain.

Carla said softly, "Mom, I'll find her and free her. I promise, I'll do it."

"Oh, Carla, this isn't your fault. You couldn't have known. Binding a soul like that takes tremendous power and is always dangerous."

"Keri was powerful, Mom. And danger never stopped her. I should have known she wouldn't leave me." Her throat tightened with memories of Keri.

"Remember when we used to fight? I'd go away to cool off, but Keri couldn't stand it, she'd follow me. Like the time she used magic to get Mark Tanner to like me enough to ask me out?"

Chandra smiled at the memory. "Keri's version of helping."

"Of course, I felt Keri's magic and was furious. Embarrassed. I told him no, yelled at her and went to Dad's lab to work off my anger. Keri followed me. She brought me brownies and ice cream and wouldn't leave me alone until I forgave her." God, she missed Keri so much. She was infuriating, wild and loving. Keri had a quick temper that evaporated as quickly as it came. Carla was the one who could hold a grudge, and then Keri would tease her out of it. Tears welled up in her eyes. "Mom, I should have known Keri wouldn't leave me, not when I was in danger!"

Her mom hugged her again. "Carla, honey, we didn't know. But now we do. I'm not leaving. Not you, or Keri. We'll figure this out together."

Carla swallowed and pulled herself together. Her mom was right. She looked over her shoulder at Pam. Chandra had dressed the woman in lemon-yellow pajamas and combed out her hair. Her chest rose and fell softly as she slept.

"She looks peaceful."

Chandra smiled. "Pam suffered a terrible shock from shooting that witch hunter. We want to make her body feel pleasant and relaxed, and maybe her spirit will want to return."

"Thank you, Mom. I should have done more of this." She waved her hand around.

"I'm happy to help." Chandra shook her head. "You need to focus on Pam's spirit and Keri's soul. There's much more going on here than we understand."

"Thanks. I came in here to go back to the astral plane." She explained about Keri wanting her to find the eagle, who turned out to be Sutton, and that Carla was going to send him as much as she remembered about the rogue who killed Keri. Maybe he could track the knife. But Carla didn't tell her mom about the blood, or kissing him. She wasn't ready to talk about that yet. Instead she finished with, "I'm going to tell Keri we're doing everything we can and to let Pam's spirit go. I'll bring Pam back if I can get her to do that."

"And if not?"

"I don't know yet. But I'll think of something." She stood up and walked to the edge of the bed where Pam lay so still. Laying her hand on the woman, she began opening her chakras. "Let's see what happens."

"You look like shit."

Sutton didn't bother looking at Linc. "Got anything?"

"Checked three places tonight. No one can connect the names you gave me to the name Styx."

They had identified the three rogues Sutton had killed at his cabin, but so far, it didn't look like their brainwashing rogue was one of them. Who was Styx? What was his next move? Was he working for Quinn Young or on his own? Sutton focused on Linc. The other man topped six feet, and wore perfectly draped custom-made suits; his shoes alone probably cost more than Sutton's cabin. No doubt he paid for those shoes with his winnings from high-stakes gambling. "Thought you had connections."

He lifted one corner of his mouth. "I'm not the Ghost Whisperer. Give me a real name and concrete details. Your Styx is a phantom."

"He's real and he's alive. I'm going to find him." Furious, he added, "I might have gotten something out of the last rogue I killed if Carla hadn't shown up." Once he realized that rogue wanted Carla, he'd killed the man. The witch was making him lose control.

Linc turned to the bar, ordered a vodka neat, then downed it in one swallow. He set his empty glass down and eyed Sutton. "There a reason you look like something I ran over three days ago?"

Sutton snagged a beer and refused to let himself think about Carla. Draining the bottle, he shifted his gaze to the witch hunter. "It'd take more than your pretty-boy car to run over me." Actually, Linc had a powerful Viper, but the concept still held—his body would smash the front end of that beauty. All he'd get for the trouble was maybe a bruise that would heal in a day.

Linc winced. "Point taken. But you still look like hell."

Sutton plunked down his beer bottle. "Makes me all warm that you worry."

Linc narrowed his gold eyes. "You're supposed to be the computer genius but I don't see you doing anything genius-like. Brigg is missing and you haven't found a damn thing."

"Nothing on Brigg's accounts, I told you that. The man hasn't charged anything, used his debit card, or done any kind of electronic transaction. I have it flagged to beep me if anything pops. Until then, crawl back out of my ass and leave me the hell alone."

"You think he's dead."

Sutton gave it to him straight. "Or gone rogue. They could have turned him—you'd better get used to the idea."

"I'll believe it when I see it." Linc stalked away, snagged the hand of a classy-looking blonde and pulled her onto the fire-etched acrylic dance floor.

"He have anything?" Axel spoke as he and Ram settled next to Sutton.

"Besides an attitude? No." Suddenly, the club started to spin. Flashing lights burst in his head, and his entire body was covered in prickly sensations like a thousand needles had been shoved into his skin. He went weightless. The thick scent of the club's sweat and alcohol was replaced by lavender and blood.

What the fuck? Had he been shot again?

This wasn't right. The astral plane didn't appear as the formless, endless blue Carla normally saw when she began her journey. Nor was it something from Pam's mind. No, this was straight from her dream. "Pam?" she called, trying to force the dream back and bring the mortal woman's doppelganger forward.

Unsuccessful, she found herself still walking down the colored pathway, surrounded on both sides by leafy vegetation dotted with large white and purple flowers. Just ahead was the grassy area and the waterfall. She could feel her hair blowing out behind her. She looked down.

Naked.

Oh, God. Why was she reenacting her dream? She had to get control of her thoughts. Concentrate on Pam, and talk to Keri when she appeared. She closed her eyes and called up the image of Pam lying in the bed, looking peaceful.

She felt a warm touch on her skin, just above her arm-band. Good, she'd found Pam. She opened her eyes, turned and forgot to breathe.

"Where am I?"

"Sutton!" He was here, on the astral plane. With her. The heat of his gaze scorched right through the cool, wet mist of the waterfall. First her face flamed hot, then the skin on her neck heated and the feeling poured down her chest as his eyes followed.

His stare lingered on her breasts, making her nipples ache. They lowered to her belly, and sparks lit up her insides. She blurted out, "Astral plane!"

His gaze rose. "What?"

"You're on the astral plane. This isn't real. You shouldn't be here. Maybe you're not really here." She was babbling, but she couldn't think fast enough, not with his incredible blue eyes looking at her. Seeing her stripped bare. For him. Oh God, the humiliation alone. She'd wished him here with her. She wanted to look and confirm her suspicions that he was naked, too.

"Carla, what the hell is going on?"

"I don't know." She had never done anything like this before. She sure as hell hadn't ever pulled a witch hunter onto the astral plane. She'd only done it with the people she hypnotized, and that was so they'd be in a place they felt safe. This wasn't making sense.

"You're naked."

She was desperately trying to conjure clothes to cover up. "I can't seem to make my clothes appear." Was this Keri? It was harder to tell on the astral plane. She wasn't used to feeling Keri's power in her doppelganger body.

He dropped his stare. "I like you this way."

She took a breath. "You have to go back. Leave."

"I don't know how the hell I got here." He finally looked up. "Or where my clothes went."

That was it. She lost her willpower and took a peek. Tiny droplets of mist beaded on his massive shoulders and ran in thin rivulets over the swells and valleys of his arms and chest, catching in the crisp light-brown hair. Since he kept his head bald, she'd never really thought about his hair color.

She couldn't stop herself now.

His wide chest narrowed into a flat stomach. The thin streams of water ran over the ridges and down in a V pattern.

Yep, his hair was brown.

Her breath caught, her nipples grew taut at the sight of him. His penis was engorged, standing up long and thick, deepening in color as she watched. Her mouth dried, and she curled her fingers into her palms to keep from touching him. Would it feel hot? Would the skin stretched over the hard length feel soft? She lowered her eyes, taking in his muscular thighs all the way down to his very large feet on the red, brown and gray pavers. She really didn't know what to say. "Nothing like this has ever happened before."

"I don't feel the curse. I can smell your blood, but...oh, hell, I was shot again, wasn't I? Am I dead?"

She snapped up her head, fear blasting through her like a cork had popped. Was he dead? No! She didn't see dead people! "What's the last thing you remember?"

"Talking to Axel. The club was getting ready to close. Then suddenly"—he shrugged and all his muscles rippled—"I got dizzy and here I am."

"No pain?"

"The lights started to flash, there was a needles sensation, then I could smell you."

"I don't think you're dead. Plus...I don't think you'd, uh, have your body if you were dead."

He looked down. "Yep, all there." He lifted his head with a grin. His white teeth flashed, then he said, "But we should make sure." He reached out both hands, capturing her shoulders.

"Uh..."

He crowded into her; his chest touched her breasts, his thighs cradled her hips, his erection pressed up against her belly. "Problem, doctor? Either I'm dead or I'm not really here, isn't that what you said?"

He sure felt real. "Yes, but at your cabin—"

His eyes gleamed. "I was trying not to kill you.

Here, I don't want to kill you. I want to finish what we started."

She could feel what he wanted pressed up against her. His hands were warm on her shoulders. His breath felt like a caress. His voice dropped to pure seduction. "Do you know what it feels like to be free of the fear that I'll hurt you? How I longed to touch you without worrying about losing control and slaughtering you?" He ran his hands down her arms.

Shivers raced through her, her chakra flung open and poured out to swirl and writhe. She shouldn't be feeling physical sensations like this on the astral plane, but she was. More than ever. "I thought I just incited bloodlust in you. Then today, maybe it was Keri—"

He shook his head. "It's you." He kept up the sensual glide of his hands over her arms until he stopped at the band on her left biceps. He traced the silver, his fingers dipping in and out of the loops. "Ever since the first night I caught your scent at your house I wanted you, craved you."

"You were outside." He had been there to guard her, Joe and Morgan, but he'd stayed outside.

"I smelled you. The scent was on your car, around the flowers, your lawn furniture...anywhere you had been. Lavender is the scent of your skin. That scent made me desperate to touch you and make love to you. But the darker scent of your blood, it brought out the curse, and I didn't dare get too close to you." He closed his eyes, his face going tight. "The night the rogues took you, nothing could stop me from tracking you and rescuing you...but I was sure that once I found you the blood-curse was going to win. Axel swore he'd kill me before I could harm you."

"You touched my blood when you tore open the metal clamps. But you never hurt me." He'd given her his shirt, just like he'd done earlier today. Her powers reached, searching for him, trying to connect with him. "You made me feel safe."

He inhaled sharply and his dick twitched hard against her belly. He lowered his head. Slowly. His eyes on her.

She could stop this madness. But she was held in his gaze. Still, she tried to make sense of it. "This can't be real."

He paused. "A dream? If it's a dream, what's the harm? I can smell your desire."

"But—"

He raised his eyebrows. "Are you going to say you aren't wet for me?"

She wouldn't babble like a teenager. She had nothing to be embarrassed about. "That proves this isn't real."

He blinked, then slid one hand from her shoulders into her hair to cradle the back of her head. "Your desire is real. It was real at my cabin and it's real now."

"No. It's not mine. Can't be. I've been numb since Keri died." She was trying to make sense of what was happening. But the truth was that she loved the idea that he wanted her.

Something swept across the blue in his eyes, something black and brown, with a feathered edge. "It's been hard on you, hasn't it? Losing your sister?"

Oh, no. She wasn't doing this. She could take anything but his sympathy. She had held it together ever since her complete breakdown the first day of Keri's murder. She said the first thing that popped into her mind. "Shut up and kiss me."

He wrapped his arm around her back, pulling her more tightly into his body, and his mouth. He brushed his lips across hers, igniting a pool of warm liquid in her belly. He smelled of forest and earth along with a trace of beer. She wanted more of him, she wanted to taste him.

He made a noise in the back of his throat, his fingers sliding from her hair to stroke the skin along her nape. Shivers broke out, racing along her nerves. The warm sensation turned to white-hot lava. Her powers jumped and shot through her in a wild pattern. She was losing control with just a kiss.

The slide of his tongue against hers filled a vast and barren loneliness inside her. She dug her fingers into the warmth of his biceps muscles, aching for more of him.

His hand slid over her shoulder blade, down the curve of her waist to the flare of her hip. The heat of his rough hand made her shiver, then all she felt was a soft caress. From the breeze? The waterfall? It felt like feathers. She arched into the sensation.

His fingers spread over the scar at the base of her spine. Sutton lifted his head, his blue eyes boring into hers. "This is the scar from the rogue's knife?"

He was getting too close, touching her in her most vulnerable place. Keri's murder had left her feeling like she'd been torn in half, and the scar was a symbol of that tear. She wanted to tell him not to touch the scar, not to invade her like that. But she couldn't. His touch had shifted from purely sexy to warm and gentle. Like her scar was something to be treated with care. She nodded wordlessly.

"Does it hurt?"

"No. Normally it's numb."

He arched an eyebrow. "Not now?"

His fingers kept brushing the healed marks, firing a deep sense of relaxation into her. "I can feel your touch. And today, at your cabin, it was hot."

He slid his hands to rest on her hips, then turned her around so that her back was to him.

Carla stared at the beautiful flowers, inhaling the

rich fragrance, and knew she was acting out of character. Letting Sutton in too deep.

The silence behind her tightened her shoulders. What did he see?

His hands wrapped around her hips. Then she felt...oh, sweet Ancestors, his mouth against her scar. His lips full and firm, then his warm tongue tracing the path that had been burned into her with the knife.

He was on his knees behind her, kissing her scar, kissing her pain.

Emotions and sensations erupted in her. Every touch of his mouth and tongue ignited a fire that swelled her nipples and between her legs. That he somehow seemed to understand her pain and loneliness forced her to feel more than she wanted to. The intimacy of it stripped her emotionally bare.

How could Sutton touch so much of her? Like he knew her right down to her soul?

He kept up laving at her lower back, his hands tightening slightly on her hips. Then he kissed his way up her spine as he rose to his feet. Pulling her back to his chest, he said, "Let me make love to you."

Overwhelmed by the feel of him surrounding her from behind, she said, "This can't be real."

"Feels real."

No!

The scream shattered through the velvety atmosphere of waterfall mist and foliage. The falls vanished, and the flowers and vines wilted brown.

"Keri? Keri!" It was her sister's voice. Where was she?

Sutton spun her around and shoved her back up against a trellis holding the dead vines. "My knife, where is it?" He demanded.

"Move! It's Keri!" She shoved him, but he wouldn't budge.

The smell of sulfur burned her nose and throat.

Dear Ancestors, that smell wasn't Keri. The air grew heavy and cold sweat froze the sensuality into ice. She shivered behind Sutton. The elemental knowledge closed her chakras up tight. "Demon."

"Where?" He barked the demand at her.

"I don't know!" The trellis behind her disappeared. She fell backward, windmilling her arms in sheer panic.

Sutton blurred into movement, spinning around to catch hold of her arms before she hit the ground. He pulled her up, shifted her around and stood her next to him with his heavy arm anchoring her to his side. "Can you bring my knife to me?"

She shook her head, realizing that she couldn't control anything! Her chakras were closed.

Where the trellis had been now looked like some kind of horrific explosion had taken place. Fires burned and blackened unidentifiable lumps. A hot wind blew the stench of sulfur and ashes. Pools of what looked like blood bubbled up from the charred ground. There was a hideous echo of screams.

Then the bloody, blackened ground exploded like a volcano. In the spew of black smoke, a form took the shape of three heads on a thick body.

"Asmodeus!" He'd found her on the astral plane.

Sutton shoved her behind him. She found herself suddenly staring at the eagle gaze of his tattoo. Then the wings seemed to lift, rising off Sutton's skin.

As if the bird was trying to shield her, too.

No! Sutton had fought for her once, risking his life and his soul. She couldn't let him do it again, he would lose against Asmodeus. She had to get him off the astral plane.

How?

Frantically, she thought of her sister's furious *No!* "Keri, help me!" She cried out, raising her arms high and forcing as many of her chakras open as she could.

"Stop, witch! You will not escape me!" the demon cried.

The pops along her spine rushed through her. She felt Keri close by and pulled all the power she could from her sister.

Then she mentally shoved Sutton and his eagle from the astral plane.

Sutton turned to look over his shoulder at her, his eyes burning with rage.

Then he was gone, vanished. She was left facing Asmodeus. Her powers rushed back into her chakras, leaving her dizzy.

"Excellent," one of the demon heads said.

"Yes. Very good," another head agreed, its bulbous eyes watching something.

The third head turned its evil gaze to her. "How badly do you want your sister's soul freed? Enough to sacrifice your own?"

Oh, shit. Too late, she realized what she'd done. Turning, she caught the trace of Keri's magical shimmer as it arched from the astral plane down into the physical plane. Carla didn't have enough power to follow its trail once it disappeared from the astral plane.

But the demon had more power than she did, and he knew it.

He knew where her sister was! Asmodeus's thick, horrible, blood-tasting laughter echoed in her head as she slammed back into herself on the physical plane.

"Carla!" Her mom was bending over her.

She opened her eyes and found herself sitting in the rocking chair her mom had been in earlier. Her head throbbed, bile burned her throat and her stomach roiled sickeningly. The buzzing in her ears made it hard to think.

Then she remembered.

Leaning forward, she grabbed her mom's arm. "Keri! Asmodeus knows where she is!"

6

THROWN BACK ONTO THE PHYSICAL plane, Sutton was helpless to return to Carla. The club was empty, except for the four other Wing Slayer Hunters.

"Where's Darcy?" Sutton demanded. "I have to go back! Carla's alone on the astral plane with Asmodeus. I need Darcy to send me back."

Axel said, "Easy, man. I'll have Darcy check on Carla." He pulled out his phone.

Sutton realized he was holding his knife. He'd whipped out his knife before he'd fully regained his senses in the physical plane. The damned tattoo on his back was clawing and ripping.

Axel hung up. "Darcy said she can't send you back to the astral plane, but she's going to open her third eye and check on Carla."

Sutton's heart was pounding with fear and fury. He couldn't make himself sheath his knife. Here he was fully clothed, and his erection had diminished to semi-hard. But he could still taste Carla's mouth and skin. Still smell her fragrance. Still feel the softness of her. Holy shit, he had never felt anything like her.

Incredibly, he hadn't felt a trace of the curse.

"What happened to you?" Phoenix asked. "It's like

you checked out of your body. The lights were on but no one was home."

He shifted to look at the leathered man knocking back a Coke. "Somehow Carla pulled me onto the astral plane with her."

Key asked, "What happened with Asmodeus?"

He grip tightened on his knife. "There was a scream; it had to be her sister, Keri. She screamed the word *no*. Then Asmodeus exploded out of the ground. Carla begged her sister to help her. The next thing I know, I'm standing here with you." Leaving Carla alone with a demon, damn it.

Ram stood quiet, a bit apart from the rest of them, his blue eyes taking it all in. Then he walked a circle around Sutton and stopped to face him. "Your back is bleeding."

Key's gray eyes lit up with interest and he prowled to Sutton's back. "Take off your shirt."

"I don't give a shit about my back." He glared at Axel. "What is taking Darcy so long?"

Axel narrowed his eyes in warning. "She's working on it."

He sucked in a gulp of air and self-control. As Darcy's soul mirror, Axel could feel Darcy using her powers, just like a familiar would. She was just above them in Axel's condo, and even from that distance, he funneled and focused her witchcraft. Sutton knew it, but he was too restless and agitated to wait. "I can't believe Carla tossed me out just when she was in danger."

"Curious," Phoenix agreed mildly. "But dude, you're starting to drip blood on the floor. That's not cool."

It did feel like his back was sliced up. Sighing, he sheathed his knife. Then he reached over his shoulder to grab a handful of his bloody shirt and yanked it off. Key's sharp whistle echoed in the empty club.

Phoenix said, "You got one pissed-off tat."

Sutton looked over his shoulder. All four hunters were staring at his back.

Ram lifted his gaze to Sutton's. "The eagle's talons are ripping open your back. I'd suggest you think of something to calm it down."

"I can see the claws slicing through from the inside, like it's trying to get out," Axel said. "That's got to hurt."

Sutton focused on the important thing. "Can you call Darcy?" He wasn't trying to insult Axel's witch, but he couldn't just stand there waiting.

"She'll call—" Axel's phone rang and he answered with, "What do you have, Darce?"

Someone pressed a damp towel to Sutton's back. But he didn't care what the tattoo was doing to his skin. Instead he watched Axel's face for some sign of Carla's safety, but the man showed nothing, as usual.

Axel hung up and said, "Carla's okay. She only stayed a minute or two after you left. She's back at the house. Darcy hasn't talked to her yet, but she saw her leave the astral plane with her third eye."

His knees damn near buckled in relief.

"Move the towel, Ram," Key said.

Sutton felt the towel lift off of his back.

"Hmm," Key said.

He was starting to get curious now that he knew Carla was back. He glanced at Key. "What?"

"As soon as you found out Carla was safe, the bird stopped ripping the shit out of your back."

The implication took the air out of the club. All the men were silent. Was it possible?

"Your tattoo's coming to life," Ram added.

Key said what they were all thinking. "Carla's your soul mirror."

Axel jerked off his T-shirt. "Put this on and go." Sutton grabbed the shirt with a nod of thanks. They didn't leave the other halves of their souls unprotected.

On the fifteen-minute drive, he was in a state, worried about Carla, and worried about her reaction to being his soul mirror. Once he arrived at the safe house, he bypassed the alarm and stormed inside, desperate to see her. He had wired the house himself and could bypass it anytime he chose.

He chose now. He'd better damn well find Carla alive and healthy on the physical plane, or he was going to do some serious ass-kicking.

What the hell had she been thinking? That demon bastard Asmodeus had found her, and the little witch had thrown his ass out of the astral plane to face the demon alone. It defied logic and proved to him that the witch needed a keeper.

Him.

He couldn't breathe until he saw her. His chest was a tight band of strangling fear. He'd seen her sliced up once before...and it had nearly destroyed him then.

The thought of her dead left him...barren. The very idea of it made the skin of his tattoo feel numb and dead.

He hadn't been this out of control, this wild, since he was seventeen years old. Since then, he'd perfected cold logic.

Until now. Until the witch doctor.

His excitement and worry rolled up and out of his chest in a bellow. "Carla!" He strode soundlessly across the tiled floor and was almost to the kitchen before his sense of smell halted him.

Cookies?

He heard a clatter in the kitchen, then, "Get out! Stay away from her!"

A large glass bowl came flying at him. Followed, by a cookie sheet, a mixing spoon, a carton of eggs and a large mixer.

JENNIFER LYON

He dodged the missiles, unable to believe this shit. It wasn't Carla, but it was a pissed-off witch. He could smell the spicy power in her blood as she hurled things at him.

"Hey! Stop it!" Carla's voice thundered as she ran past him into the path of a large brown bottle.

Sutton grabbed her around the waist, turned and shielded her with his body.

"Let go of me!" She swung her elbow into his ribs.

Sutton frowned. "That woman is a lunatic!" But a tiny lunatic, and if he tackled her, he'd probably hurt her. Then there was the whole witch problem.

"She's my mother!"

"Mother?" Sutton slackened his grip around her waist. Mothers were something he had very little experience with.

Carla shoved out of his hold and turned to glare at him. "You scared her!" Then she pivoted on a bare foot and ran to the woman.

Sutton straightened up and noticed that Carla was wearing a short little robe the color of hot chocolate. It floated down to end at midthigh, leaving the rest of her legs bare. Her long hair was wet and tangled, soaking the satin robe. *This woman is mine, mine to care for and protect and love.* The idea of it took his breath away. Was it possible? Would she accept him? He'd been alone for so many years, and now his salvation, his partner, stood just feet away from him. If she would have him, he'd take her somewhere private, strip her to her skin, and—

"He's a witch hunter!"

"I know, Mom." Carla put her arm around the smaller woman's shoulders. Then she lifted her free hand, and the broken pieces of the bowl rose, reassembled, and floated back to the kitchen. Followed by the spoon, the cookie sheet and the mixer. Lastly, the broken, scattered eggs repaired themselves and went back to the egg carton. Then the carton floated into Carla's hand.

Sutton had opened his mouth to assure Carla's mom that he wouldn't hurt them, but a sudden vibration rolled through him. Carla's magic trembled through his body, much like a bass playing in his intestines. Then it was gone, leaving the scent of two witches assaulting him. His veins started to burn, his temples throbbed. He concentrated on breathing and keeping the curse locked down tight.

Carla set the eggs down on the counter, then she looked at her mom. "Why don't you go sit with Pam? Use the back hallway." She tilted her head to the doorway that opened off the breakfast nook.

Chandra shook her head. "It's too risky."

Carla looked over at him, then back to her mom. "He'll leave. Go wait with Pam."

Her mom glared at Sutton, then turned, walked across the kitchen and disappeared down the hallway.

He heard a door open and close. Her scent grew fainter.

Then Carla shifted to look at him. "What are you doing here?"

He opened his mouth, but what should he say? Being attacked by her mother threw him off his stride. Not that he'd actually had a plan...he'd just rushed right over here. Damn. Holding himself in place, fighting the growing urge to touch her, he blurted out, "You threw me out of the astral plane. You were in danger."

Her face tightened. Leaning a hip against the bar, she said, "It was too dangerous. The astral plane is spiritual. You can't fight physically like you do here. If you'd gone with your instincts, then Asmodeus could have gotten between me and you, and in doing that, he'd break the link between your spirit and your body. Then you'd be in a coma like Pam."

He crossed his arms, trying to contain his roiling emotions. The bird tattoo seemed to react to his anxiety, shifting in his skin. "You could have told me that." Did she think he wouldn't understand? Sure, he didn't have all her fancy degrees but he could grasp simple words. The impotent fury of not having been able to protect her beat at him. "Instead you threw me out."

She straightened up, her elegant chin thrusting out. "I didn't bring you there in the first place."

"Of course you did. I'm not a witch. How else would I have gotten there?"

"Keri." Her witch-glow dimmed, and her eyes filled with yellow pain. "I went to the astral plane to retrieve Pam, but when I got there, I wasn't in control. I think Keri was."

"How? How could a dead witch have that much power?"

She flinched.

Instantly, he remembered her thick grief buried in that scar. He was an ass, hurting the woman he was supposed to protect and care for. Dropping his arms, he said, "I'm sorry, that came out cruel. I meant—"

She cut him off, her expression bleak. "I can only guess. I'm still putting it all together, and I've asked Darcy to talk to the Ancestors to see what they know. But Keri and I shared power all our lives, and since her soul is still earthbound, under the right circumstances, she's able to access my power. The astral plane has different rules, but Keri was in control. She wanted you there, and you were there."

"*You* wanted me there." He had to clench his fists at his sides to keep himself from taking her in his arms and proving it. *Touch her. Make her yours. Claim her.* The longing played through his head. But it was bittersweet. He wanted to touch her so badly, it made his fingers ache. But his blood was heating to a boil that made his skin hot and his head throb. A darker voice chanted, *Cut her, get her blood. Look what she's doing to you—taunting you! Cut her, cut her...* He remembered his nightmares of killing her and held himself in check.

He could destroy the very witch who was his salvation.

Or she could destroy you, the voice of the curse reminded him.

He told himself to focus. "What happened after I was gone?" He had to know if that demon did anything to her. Hurt her.

She shivered, drawing her robe tighter, and stacking one bare foot on top of the other. "Asmodeus found Keri."

"How?"

Her eyes were haunted as she explained. "Asmodeus saw Keri's magical trail from me to the knife. He knows who has the knife she's trapped in." Her face bleached of color, her witch-shimmer muddied, and she shifted from foot to foot. "I couldn't see the trail. I have to find her! Asmodeus can't pull her into the Underworld, but he can hide her, or make the rogue who has her kill over and over, torturing her. If I don't find her..."

Every fiber of his body needed to protect her from danger and from pain. He longed to be able to touch her now, but he couldn't risk it. Forcing his voice to stay calm, he said, "If you don't find her; then what?"

She took a breath, visibly calming herself. "Asmodeus asked me if I was willing to go far enough to bargain with my soul."

A screech ripped through his head. His tattooed wings burned and clawed his back, trying to break free. Every molecule of air he dragged in burned like he was breathing fire. "You won't."

"I... Her voice trailed off into a gasp. "Sutton, you're bleeding!"

He didn't care. "Carla, listen to me, I'll help you find the knife with your sister in it."

She walked toward him. "That's blood on your T-shirt! I can see it on your side."

He backed up a step. "It's the tattoo. Forget it. Just swear you won't deal with Asmodeus." He couldn't imagine Carla turning to demon magic, but he'd felt her grief for Keri. He knew how much she loved her sister, how desperate she was to free her soul. But at the cost of her own?

"Sutton, you're hurt. What happened?"

Her lavender scent was swirling around him, filling him. Marking him as hers, and opening up a pit of yearning in his gut that only she could fill if he could just touch her. At the same time, the bloodlust began to shred his veins, desperate for the cool pleasure her blood would give him. It was insane, the conflicting needs rising in him.

"Take your shirt off. Let me see your back."

"No." Not a chance. If she touched him, would he yank her up to him and kiss her? Or pull out his knife and cut her? He couldn't trust himself, and that made him an animal. He saw her take another half step and told her, "It's the eagle tattoo. It's coming to life."

She halted, her mouth parting, then she sucked in her lips. "You're getting wings like Axel?"

He snorted. "Mostly I'm getting my back shredded every time the tat thinks you're in danger."

She shook her head and fingered the edges of her robe. "He's not coming to life for me."

His eagle wilted heavily against his skin. Sutton knew how the stupid bird felt. What had they expected? Carla was elegant, refined and educated, while he'd grown up with little formal education as a survivalist and a tracker.

84

She lifted her eyes. "Keri wanted me to touch your blood yesterday. Your blood is giving her strength. She's bringing your eagle to life. Keri's the one who loved eagles. She's the one who insisted I find her eagle."

It's not me, it's my dead sister? Was she serious? "I wasn't kissing your sister. I kissed you. Both in my cabin and in the astral plane. You're the one, Carla."

She shook her head. "But I'm not like you, I don't even like eagles."

Getting pissed, he snapped, "I get it, Doctor. But I touched your blood two months ago, and you touched my blood yesterday. Remember? Blood and sex seal the bond. We've covered the blood part."

Her face thinned with tension. "Well yes, but—"

He took the step toward her, his control slipping with every word she uttered. "You liked kissing me on the astral plane. Five more minutes, and I'd have been buried so deep inside of you, you'd forget other men existed. You'd be bonded to me. Or are you going to deny you wanted me?" He was being a jerk. The physical attraction was part of the complex blood and sex curse that halved their souls three decades ago. Carla had responded physically to him because he was the other half of her soul. But intellectually she didn't want him.

Her face flushed. "It's Keri! She's projecting through me!"

He laughed. "Tell yourself whatever you want. It's you. You're my soul mirror."

Her chest, those perfect breasts he'd felt flush against his skin on the astral plane, rose and fell in a pant. "You don't understand."

"Enlighten me."

She composed herself in seconds. "It's the twin bond you're reacting to. Keri claimed you," she said softly.

He didn't buy it. "I claim you." He belonged to her. His eagle came to life for her.

She dropped her shoulders. "Even if that was true, I can't risk it. If we had sex, if my soul bonded to yours and became whole...Keri might not be able to reach me anymore. She'd be alone."

"Carla..." It was torn from him. He had to touch her. Ease her. Do something.

"Leave, Sutton. Please."

He saw her strained face, felt her powers bubbling in agitation, and did as she asked.

For now.

It was late when Carla went into Pam's room and sent her mom to bed. Chandra was tired and afraid. Sutton had her agitated enough that she'd burned her cookies.

For that alone, Chandra'd never forgive him.

That made Carla smile. She had been working for hours. She'd gone by the Transitional Clinic to check on the residents, then she'd come home to do research to help Keri and Pam.

The Circle Witches were meditating and searching their witch books for any information on trapped souls and lost spirits on the astral plane.

She opened her laptop and was surprised to see Darcy on the screen. "Hey. Don't you need to sleep?"

"I have something from the Ancestors."

Her stomach tightened. "What?"

"They said it's possible Keri is projecting through you and Sutton might be reacting to her. Being identical twins makes a lot of things possible."

Her stomach emptied out, leaving her hollow. Desolation weighed down on her. The night he'd rescued her, when he'd touched her, she'd felt a bone-deep connection. She'd tried to tell herself it was some kind of hero-worship because he'd saved her. But it had been more, deeper. And then in his cabin and on the astral plane, she'd wanted to believe it was her that Sutton desired. Her he cared about.

It wasn't.

She made herself answer. "I figured that."

Darcy's gaze was filled with soft sympathy. "They said Sutton may be able to help increase your power, whether he's your soul mirror or hers. But you have to be careful to, uh, *not* finish the bond. If he's your soul mirror and you do that, your souls will meld and Keri will lose her connection to you."

The scar across her back throbbed like an old toothache. "Why don't they know who he belongs to?"

"They are not gods, Carla," Darcy said, her own frustration sharpening her voice. "They are old souls who have reincarnated until they are extremely knowledgeable. But they aren't gods."

Feeling a bit ashamed, she answered, "Thanks, Darcy."

"They did say that you and Sutton could work together on the astral plane. Try to draw Keri in and use your communication chakra to talk to her. If you can open your third eye, then you can find her."

A new hope touched her. "I'd be able to see her magical trail. With the help of Sutton and Keri, I might be able to do it."

"But be careful of Asmodeus."

A dark cold fear slithered inside of her. "I have no intention of becoming a demon witch. But I will find a way to free Keri."

7

SUTTON COULD SMELL THE RANK copper scent of the rogue bastard. And he could smell the witch blood. The craving hit him so hard he could barely stand up. He tightened his grip on his knife.

His enhanced hearing caught the gurgled shriek of pain that faded into a moan. It ignited his rage, enabling him to push back the sick desire for witch blood and track the bastard.

The night was dark, the moon shadowed by clouds. He tracked the scent to a trailer parked in an abandoned lot.

Disgust rolled through him. *Witch kills on wheels.* How convenient.

Carla's face filled his mind and his fury exploded. He grabbed one of the double doors, yanking so hard he ripped it off the hinges and it flew across the yard. Sutton leaped up into the trailer, his boots landing with a thud that rocked the entire vehicle.

A man the size of a grizzly bear slammed into him, throwing both of them back onto the hard-packed dirt. A searing pain sliced his side. That enraged him, and he flipped the bastard off him and leaped to his feet.

With a roar of rage, the rogue flew at him again, his

knife ready. Witch blood had given him more strength and speed.

Sutton released his knives into his dropped hands, kicked the knife from the rogue's hand, and jammed his blades into the man's stomach. Then he jerked upward.

Blood spurted and the rogue howled, throwing wild punches.

An elbow caught Sutton in his cheekbone, splitting his skin. But he held the knives grimly. Finally the blood loss and pain weakened the rogue.

Sutton twisted the knives to get his attention. "Where is Quinn Young?"

Fear widened his eyes. "No."

Young had that effect on everyone. A demon's death dagger burned into his forearm was enough to scare anyone. He twisted the knives again.

The man screamed. "We don't know!" He started struggling again, then went limp.

"Shit." He must have nicked the heart. He wanted answers before the rogue died and turned shade. "Where is your headquarters? Who is running the rogues?"

Blood trickled from his mouth, his eyes rolled back and he was dead.

Sutton yanked out his knives. Shit. They had nothing. He turned and jumped up into the trailer to see if the witch was still alive.

She was young, maybe twenty-five. A tiny thing with black hair. Her clothes were sliced from her body, and wounds were everywhere. He noticed the delicate silver rings on her fingers.

Her blood scent was dying.

The witch was already dead. Although she'd been badly cut, he didn't think she'd bled out, but her heart had given out from the stress, pain and shock. Too much horror. Heavy disgust settled over him. If he'd gotten there sooner, Carla and Darcy could have saved her.

He turned, leapt out of the trailer to the ground, pulled out his phone and called Axel. "It's me. I have a dead rogue and a dead witch." He walked over and picked up the rogue's knife.

His thumb felt the insignia, rubbing over the grove of letters at the base of the blade. Glancing down, he felt his throat tighten. BC for Brigg Cusack. *Shit.* "I have bad news, A. The rogue had Cusack's knife."

"Be there in five."

Sutton shut the phone and shoved it into his pants, then he leaned back against the side of the trailer. Cusack was dead or possibly rogue. The helpless fury beat at him. Brigg had worked hard over the last couple months, proving his loyalty, showing that he wanted to make a real commitment to the Wing Slayer. Like all of them, he struggled with the curse. Jesus, he hoped the man was dead, that he'd died with his soul intact.

Sutton hadn't felt like this since he, his father and his uncle had gone out to track a missing girl. They'd followed the girl to a remote shit-hole shack and discovered that she was a witch taken by a rogue. All hell broke loose. Sutton had seen his father make the hardest decision of his life.

They'd saved the young witch but the cost...

He rested his head back against the cool side of the trailer. Inside was a dead witch he'd failed to save.

A breeze told him Axel had arrived. He opened his eyes and silently held out the silver knife with the monogram.

Axel's hard green gaze tracked over him. "You're cut. Face and side."

A thick regret made his voice harsh. "I look better than the witch inside."

Axel took the knife and studied it. His massive

wings lifted then disappeared into the tattoo of hawk wings on his back. The cords on his neck stood out, and his mouth flattened. Then he lifted his stare. "Cusack is either dead or rogue."

"It wasn't a rogue that took him unaware in the street, he had to have been tricked by a woman. A test, just like you said." He sucked in a breath, reaching for his cold logic. "They struck at our weakness, our need for sex."

Axel's hand closed around the knife until his knuckles were bleached white. "If they've turned Cusack he's going to come back at us."

Sutton felt that. "Linc."

Axel's eyes filled with the weight of his position as the hawk. "If that happens, it'll be Linc's test. If he kills Cusack, he'll prove himself loyal to the Wing Slayer. He'll earn the right to be a Wing Slayer Hunter."

"He has to make the choice to kill his friend in the Wing Slayer's name."

Axel's face was pitiless. "We've all had to prove ourselves. If Cusack is rogue, his soul is gone and he must be killed."

Sutton agreed, although it didn't make it any easier. His phone vibrating cut off his thoughts. He pulled out his cell, looked at the screen. "It's Phoenix," he told Axel, then answered the cell with, "What's up?"

"Not my dick. Chick shot me. Then she tried to turn the gun on herself. I wrestled her, got the gun away, then she sprayed me with pepper spray and ran. I'm still seeing double."

Damn, they couldn't get a break tonight. "Where are you?" Sutton watched as Ram and Key pulled up in a truck. Axel waved them over.

"My house. Goddamnit, I can't even see to dig this damn bullet out."

Sutton's gut tightened. "Hang tight, we'll be there." He hung up and filled in the three witch hunters.

Axel ordered, "Sutton, Key, go. Let me know if Phoenix needs Darcy to heal him. Ram and I will deal with this."

Knowing it was easier for Axel to handle the still somewhat fresh witch blood since he was bonded to Darcy, Sutton and Key raced over to Phoenix's house.

Carla jammed her keys into the door of the clinic, feeling a creeping sensation run down her spine. It was still dark on the streets, just after four A.M.

She looked over her shoulder as she turned the lock, but no one was there. Just the parking lot and adjacent park. On the other side of the clinic was a physical therapy clinic that didn't open until nine A.M. There was no sign of movement.

Of course, rogues had the ability to make themselves invisible.

She shoved open the door, rushed in and shut it. Then she hit the code into the keypad to set the alarm. Once inside, she felt a little better, but still uneasy. The clinic was an old two-story house with lots of wood paneling, pocket doors and charm.

Max walked into the living room that had an overstuffed sofa, big comfortable chairs and a fireplace. "Carla, thanks for coming."

"What's the situation?" She fell into step with Max as they walked through the living spaces to an examination room.

"She was in the park. John found her when he did a sweep outside the clinic. She was sitting on a bench like she was waiting for a bus. I tried to talk to her, but got no response. She has blood spattered all over her. I didn't see any injury on her to account for it. She had no purse and no ID."

"Just sitting out there in the middle of the night?"

"All alone. She's not reacting or talking. You can see for yourself." He opened the door to the exam room.

Carla smiled a greeting to John, who was standing by the table, hovering in case the woman tried to leave or hurt herself.

"Morning, Doc. Now that you're here, I'm going to take a look around outside." He tilted his head toward the shade-covered window that faced the park side of the house. "See if someone is looking for this woman."

Carla looked at the fabric-covered shade, thinking that normally, the park was a relaxing view for residents who needed medical attention. Max had two medical doctors who donated several hours a week to the clinic. But he'd called her first, thinking this woman's mind was in the most desperate need of care. She turned her attention to the young woman lying on the exam table. Her brown eyes were open, staring at the lights. Her arms were stretched at her sides with her fingers curled into claws. She had dark gore covering the front of her black-and-white spandex top and low-cut jeans. Carla set down her purse and turned back to the woman. "Hi there. I'm Dr. Fisk. What's your name?"

Her jaw moved, her teeth grinding, but her eyes stayed opened and fixed.

Carla touched her bare arm, and felt a backwash of cold fear, like brackish, bitter water. "She's suffered a severe shock to her mind."

"She's catatonic," Max said.

She realized he was standing right behind her, looking over her shoulder.

"Yes." Carla needed to move fast. The girl was mentally slipping further and further away. "I'm going to see if I can hypnotize her, maybe calm her mind enough to talk to us."

Max stepped back, silently watching her.

Her hand on the girl's arm, she formed a link with her physical body. Carla started popping open her chakras then struggled to force open the fifth one. Then she reached her spirit into the woman to lead her to the astral plane.

A loud crash shattered the stillness.

Alarms screamed around them.

"Shit!" Max grabbed her, shoving her away from the window. Her shoulder slammed into the wall, and she had to fight to get her balance. She looked up and saw two men leap through the broken window, ripping the blind off and shattering glass.

Carla smelled the copper. *Rogues!* The first one looked at her and his pupils dilated, his entire body jerking with excitement. Terror and memories held her frozen. Not again!

The second rogue grabbed the girl on the table and tossed her over his shoulder in a fireman's hold.

"Get away from her!" Max bellowed.

The attacker spun, one hand anchoring the girl, his free hand brandishing a knife as Max leaped at him.

Carla sent a wave of energy to the knife, knocking it from his hand.

"Cut the witch!" The rogue threw the girl to the ground, grabbed Max by the throat, jerked him over the table, slammed his fist into the side of Max's head and dropped him to the ground.

The first rogue grabbed Carla, his knife flashing in front of her eyes. It was all happening in fast-forward...so quick she could barely see it. She would not be cut again. She sent her powers into the blade arcing toward her thigh.

The knife flew from the rogue's grip, the handle slamming into his stomach. "Bitch!"

One second later, the witch karma backlash blasted into her belly. She doubled over as the breath was knocked out of her. She fell to her knees, gasping as her locked lungs struggled for air.

From the floor, she saw the other rogue snatch up his knife and kick aside the broken body of the girl.

The alarms kept shrieking.

Her rogue snatched up his knife and latched on to her arm when Carla heard the screech of an eagle in her head. She knew right down to her cellular level that Sutton was there. Two men burst into the room, one going to the rogue who was closer to the window.

The second body slammed the rogue who had hold of her. They tumbled past her, and swear to the Ancestors, she thought she felt a brush of feathers.

The alarm kept screaming a pulsing shriek. Carla looked at the girl on the floor and could see by the unnatural angle of her head and the pool of blood that she was dead, but what about Max? The pain in her stomach prevented her from standing so she crawled toward him. Broken glass crunched and her hands slipped in warm blood. *Don't think about it. Oh, God, this isn't happening.* She focused on Max's feet, then his legs, his black shirt and finally, his face. He was lying on his left side, legs splayed, eyes closed, but his chest was moving. He was breathing. They were both alive. She reached his side, sat down and pulled his head into her lap.

The left side of his face was dark red and swelling but not cut. Concussion? She put her hand over his temple and cheekbone. "Max, open your eyes."

Nothing. She couldn't lose him. Tears filled her throat. "Please, Max!" She lifted her hand and saw blood. Her head spun until she realized it was her blood. She'd cut her hands crawling over the glass.

Focus. She could help him. She pulled in deeper to

herself, blocking out the horror of the night, and reconnected with her chakras. It was like trying to pry a stubborn top off a bottle of soda, but finally, the first four opened.

That was all she needed. Laying her hand over the injured part of his face, she sent cooling energy to stop any swelling. She followed that with healing light.

"She's using her powers."

The voice was from the witch hunter with Sutton. She ignored them, concentrating on Max.

"Key, get rid of these bodies," Sutton said.

She heard him but didn't care. Max wasn't a body, he was her friend and she loved him, not like he wanted her to, but she did love him.

She refused to think about that poor dead woman on the floor.

Max's eyes began to flutter, then open. His incredibly soulful dark eyes brimmed with confusion. "What happened?"

Her first relief, first bit of respite, flowed through her. She brushed his hair back, looking through the blood smears from her hands to see that the swelling was gone. "We were attacked."

He reached up and held her wrist. "Are you okay?"

"Fine." *Liar.* She could feel cold tremors trying to set in. More people were pouring into the small room. Carla looked up and saw Josie and the two other women huddled together outside the door. *I should help them, calm their fears.* The thought passed through her head, but her gaze skimmed over the blood and glass she'd crawled over. She shuddered.

Where was that poor young woman?

The piercing pulse of the alarm stopped.

A shadow fell over them. Then Sutton kneeled beside her. "I'm going to take you out of here, Carla." Max's wiry body tensed and he sat up. His gaze searched the room and his face leached of more color when he saw all the blood. "Oh, Christ. Where's John?"

Sutton said, "That your guard? I'm sorry, but he's dead outside the window. The woman is dead, too. I had my men take her and the two who attacked you both out."

"They must have tracked her here. One of them picked her up like he was going to take her away, then when Max attacked, he just threw her down. She hit her head. There was so much blood," Carla whispered. Bile rushed up the back of her throat, but she fought it down. "The girls, I have to take care of the girls."

"Who are you?" Max demanded.

"Sutton West."

"Carla, do you know him?"

"Yes." She wiped her hands on her jeans but they kept bleeding. "He's okay, Max."

"You're hurt." Max reached out and took hold of her wrist, turning her palm up. Blood welled from at least a dozen cuts.

"Just let me up." She took her hand back and tried to get her feet under her.

Sutton put his massive hands under her arms and lifted her to her feet.

Her left shoulder hurt, and her stomach cramped sickly. "I'm fine." She walked out of his hold, over the crunchy, blood-slippery glass and out of the room. She went to the girls. "It's okay, it's all over."

Josie said, "Were they here for me?"

Carla reached out and put her hand on Josie's arm, fighting to funnel calming energy into her. It made her dizzy. "No. This wasn't about any of you. It was a woman Max brought in early this morning. It's over now."

Joe MacAlister and Morgan Reed walked in. "Axel called, said he wants me to cover security for this place." He visually searched the exam room, then put his arm around her. "Bad night?"

She ignored the pain in her shoulder for the comfort of Joe. He was Darcy's cousin, an unusual mortal who, once he found out Darcy was a witch, had barely missed a beat. He and Darcy had a close relationship.

Then Joe had fallen in love with the wife of a rogue witch hunter. Morgan had suffered significant brain damage at the hands of the rogue from his particularly brutal memory-shifting, and she was pregnant by him. Carla had worked with her for the last two months, and now she was blooming with the pregnancy and had recovered most of her memories. Joe now headed the mortal end of security for the Wing Slayer Hunters.

Morgan walked up to the girls and introduced herself, then she led them up the stairs back to the rooms.

"She has a knack," Carla said.

Joe looked down into her face. "She does. She'll take care of the girls. Sutton said the upstairs has been cleared. I have four very good men coming over. We're going to keep this place safe."

She believed him. "How did Sutton find me?"

"Been a lot going down tonight, Doc. Phoenix was shot. Darcy's with him now."

There was a buzzing in her head. "How is he?"

"Pissed. We think your woman was the one who shot him. The rogues tracked her here."

"Guess they were trying to get her back." But they'd killed her instead.

Max and Sutton walked up. Max reached for her hands. "You might need stitches."

She pulled her hands back. "No, it's not all my blood." Her stomach rolled over at the memory of crawling through the blood. Quickly, she said, "I just need to wash them. I'll make some tea..." She turned and hurried across the dining room into the kitchen. It was a wide rectangle kitchen with industrial-grade appliances. She went to the deep stainless-steel sink and just stood there wondering if she had enough power to heal herself.

Every movement hurt her shoulder and stomach.

Finally, she forced herself to turn the water on, but her bloody hand slipped off the handle. "I have to get the blood off," she whispered, staring to tremble, and hot tears burning her eyes. She struggled to blink them back to stay in control.

Two large hands reached around her. One hand turned on the faucet. The other hand squeezed soap into her palm, then pushed her hands under the warm water.

Sutton. His musky scent surrounded and comforted her.

His body pressed against her back; his breath touched her face as he leaned over her. He didn't say a word. He used his fingers to gently lather her palms and rinsed them.

The soap burned but his touch soothed her.

He poured more soap into one of his hands, lathered it, and washed the skin of her wrists and forearms with soft, easy strokes. He rinsed her, then he grabbed a towel, keeping his body pressed to hers, and gently dried her.

The torn skin on her palms and fingers barely bled. As she watched, her powers started to close the wounds, almost without her making any effort.

"Good girl." He ran his fingers over the closed skin. "Now tell me where else it hurts."

"My shoulder. But it's not that bad." She raised her left shoulder to loosen it.

Sutton lifted his hand and put it on her shoulder, then used his fingers to caress the muscles and tendons from her neck to her upper arm. "Here?"

The sweep of his fingers warmed her, made her lean back into his body. "Yes, but—"

He leaned his head down, replacing his fingers with his mouth, his lips dragging across her skin, then a touch of his tongue.

Her powers blew up from her center and raced to each cell he touched. Against her skin, he whispered, "I can taste the exotic spice of your powers."

She had to be inciting bloodlust in him. Not that she could ever imagine Sutton turning into a rogue. "My shoulder is healed."

He lifted his head, dragged in a breath. "Where else are you hurt?"

"My stomach, but it's from witch karma."

He stepped back and turned her around. Clenching his fists at his side, he said, "You used witchcraft to fight the rogues?"

She lifted her chin. "He was going to stab me—damn right I did! The knife flew, handle first, into his stomach."

Sutton winced. "Thank God it wasn't the blade side. As it is you probably took a hell of hit from witch karma." He dropped to one knee.

As he lowered himself down, she got her first real look at him. "Sutton! Your face!" There was a line where the skin had closed over a bad cut, and bruising.

He put his hands on her hips. "Healing, barely feel it. We're going to take care of you." With one hand, he lifted her T-shirt.

The cool air caressed her skin, followed by his warm breath. Then the soft touch of his fingers sliding over her vividly bruising stomach. "Focus your powers here." He kept gently brushing the area between her belly button and left hip bone.

She didn't have to focus her powers. They took on a life of their own and rushed for his fingers. "It's witch karma, I can't heal it." The punishment for using her powers for harm was that she wasn't allowed to heal herself. Another witch might be able to do it, but right now, she barely felt the pain at all.

Instead she felt the brush of his fingers stroking her in soft caressing circles. Her powers kept following his fingers, doing nothing to heal the injury, instead opening a pit of longing deep in her belly. It was a desire, the bone-deep ache, to be touched and filled.

Her eyes filled again and she blinked away the tears. *Shock.* It had to be shock making her crave a connection. Sex was a healing gift, but in the two years since Keri died, she hadn't been able to connect with anyone that way. Until now. Sutton's touch was more than skin-deep, more intimate than anything she'd ever experienced. But he might not belong to her.

And he was a witch hunter. "You have to stop. The bloodlust..."

He looked up at her, his eyes filled with a fierce heat that burned like the center of a gas flame. He rose to tower over her, and lifted her face to see his blazing eyes. "When I walked in and smelled your blood...yeah. But then I touched you and it's not the kind of lust I'm feeling."

What were they doing? She had to bring them both back to reality. A mortal woman had been murdered. Phoenix was shot. And her sister was still trapped somewhere in a rogue's knife. She caught sight of the gold eagle earring in his left ear and blurted out, "I can't do this."

He dropped his hand and rose to his full height. Picking up a teakettle off the stove, he reached around her to fill it with water. "Who is Max?"

He had both arms around her to reach the sink, while looking down at her. "My friend."

"More."

She blinked at his soft command. "He's a doctor of sociology but found his calling in helping people who have been indoctrinated into cults. He extracts them, and then works with them here in this Transitional Clinic to undo the brainwashing."

"Doctor of sociology. So he's book-smart." He shut off the faucet and went to the stove. Setting the kettle down, he turned on the flame.

She had no idea what he meant by that. "He's street-smart, too."

Sutton turned. "Know how I found you, Carla? We were tracking the woman who shot Phoenix. She has to be another brainwashing vic of the rogues. We tracked her to the park when my eagle starting keening and scratching my skin raw. I knew you were in danger. I could feel your fear. That's how I found you." His eyes practically lit up the kitchen. "I would have found you anywhere."

She busied herself getting cups and tea bags out. "Keri loved eagles." She didn't have the energy to argue with him.

"And you love Max," he said softly.

A mug slid from her hand.

Sutton moved swiftly, catching the cup. He set it down and took her face in his hands. "Tell me. Do you care for him? Love him? Is he that important to you that you'd crawl through blood and glass to get to him and save his life?"

She was trapped in his stare. His words were gentle. "He's my friend."

He let her go. "Doctor, your friend is in love with you. You'd better figure out if you feel the same." He walked out of the kitchen.

SUTTON DIDN'T STOP WALKING WHEN Joe called his name as he passed through the dining room. He couldn't. The dual drives in him were ripping him apart, bone by bone, muscle by muscle, tendon by tendon.

When he touched her, he craved her heart and body.

When he took his hands off her, he craved her blood. The cuts on her hands made him hurt to feel her blood.

He stormed out of the house and across the street into the park. Far enough away to get control of himself, but close enough to watch out for Carla. It was still dark, but he could see perfectly well. Standing in the grass, he lifted his hands and looked at them. They tingled from the feel of her blood. Even mixed with the mortal's blood, soap and water, he could feel the dark pleasure of it sinking into him and feeding the curse, making him want more. But that need had been muted by touching her. He recognized Axel's tread as he walked up behind him.

"You touched her blood?"

"She was bleeding. She crawled over glass to get to

another man." His eagle shifted and itched at the memory of Carla crawling toward that man to save him.

"Easy, Sutton."

"He's a doctor. Like Carla. Smart like her." Not like him. How many times had she told him that she was nothing like him?

"You think she cares for this man?"

He shrugged. "I killed that rogue right in front of her and she crawled away." Trying to get away from him? From his brutal violence? Everything inside him roared for her to come to him. Run to his arms, his protection, his comfort.

Axel put his hand on his shoulder. "Witches are emotional creatures, they will crawl to the one who needs them."

He needed her. "She keeps insisting Keri's my soul mirror, not her."

"What do you think?"

He turned to Axel. "It's Carla. She's the other half of my soul."

Axel nodded.

They had been friends for a decade. Axel was giving him the space he needed to box up his emotions and shove them back under control. "Let's go back inside."

"I've got this covered. Go home. Sleep."

He shook his head, meeting his friend's green eyes. "Can't leave her." He took a breath. "I'm solid, let's go."

Sutton bypassed the table where Darcy, Joe, Max and Carla were sitting and moved as far across the room from Carla as he could get. He planted himself by the sliding glass door that led to the small courtyard with a fountain.

Darcy poured out a steaming mug of coffee and brought it to him.

He smiled at Axel's witch. At Phoenix's house,

she'd insisted on healing his face and side. He barely remembered his mother, and he didn't have sisters. It was a surprise to discover that the female caretaking trait was kind of cool. And she made Axel happy, made him whole. As Darcy returned to sit next to Axel, his gaze searched out Carla. She sat next to Max.

The man had dark hair, dark eyes, a lean body and a book brain. He saved girls and women from cults. Do-gooder doctor, just like Carla.

Sutton hated him. He could crush him like a bug, spilling his guts all over the shiny dining room table.

Except Carla had crawled over broken glass to save the man.

He ignored the coffee in his hand and tried to focus on the conversation.

Max turned to Carla as if he'd just remembered something. He reached out and took hold of one of her hands. "How? Your hands were cut, I saw them."

Sutton had to fight the instinct to grab him and toss him across the room. He didn't want Max touching Carla.

Carla looked up into his eyes. "It was mostly that poor girl's blood, not mine."

Sutton felt a vibration pass through him and knew it was Carla using a bit of magic to convince Max.

He frowned, wondering why she didn't just tell the mortal she was a witch if they were so close.

Carla pulled her hand free. "Max, it doesn't matter. What's important is that we keep the clinic safe. Joe MacAlister and his team are the best at security. Let them help us protect the clinic."

He turned from Carla, looking around the table. "How did you just happen to be here?"

Sutton answered that with, "The woman who was killed here tonight shot one of our men. We tracked her to the park. Then I heard the alarm go off and we came over to see what the trouble was. We found your man, John, with his throat cut outside the window." Not exactly true. He did hear the alarm, but what yanked him there was Carla. He and his eagle felt her sudden, intense fear.

Max seemed to be putting the pieces together. "That would explain the blood on her clothes."

Carla said, "We think it's brainwashing. Someone extremely skilled is brainwashing young women into becoming killers."

Max turned to look at her. "That's hard to do. It would take months at least, possibly years, unless the person was already predisposed to killing, maybe a sociopath."

"Normally yes, but in this case, we think he's doing it quicker."

Max kept her stare. "Someone with your...skills?" Sutton felt Carla's sudden unease prickled against his spine. What was this?

She said, "Maybe. Hypnosis might have been used to enhance the brainwashing."

Max looked away from Carla. "Why was the woman in the park?"

"We tracked her straight there," Sutton said. "My guess is she was told to go there and wait for someone to pick her up. She had no identification and no ride that we could find." He would put her into the tracking program he was using to find information on Pam. But so far, it was a dead end. Where were these girls coming from?

His brow furrowed, his dark eyes searching each face. "She was unresponsive when I found her."

Carla said, "Her mind couldn't accept what she'd done. She was being forced to act against her own morals. Her brain couldn't take the stress and shut down."

Max took a deep breath, looked at the wall over Darcy's shoulder, and said, "John was murdered tonight Carla. John, one of ours. You and I could have both been killed. I think I deserve the truth."

Sutton was astonished to see that Max was purposely avoiding looking at Carla. He knew, if not consciously, then subconsciously; he recognized her power.

Her shoulders dropped. "It's a cult worse than anything you've ever seen. Axel, Sutton and their team have been fighting this cult for a while. It's not your fight, Max. Let them do it."

Max turned to look at her, as if he couldn't help it. "What kind of cult? Let me help you. Trust me."

Sutton was getting tired of the kid-glove bullshit. If the man wanted the truth, he'd give it to him. "They aren't mortal. They are witch hunters, created to protect earth witches and kill demon witches. But thirty years ago, we were all cursed. Now we crave witch blood. If we kill a witch, we lose our souls and become the monsters you saw tonight. That's the cult we're dealing with, and it's way out of your league."

Max's dark gaze slammed into him, then cut back to Carla. "True?"

She closed her eyes, her chest heaving with some terrible weight, then she opened her eyes and said, "Yes."

"You're a witch."

"Does it matter?" she asked softly. "We've worked together for well over a year, does it matter?"

"Hell yes, it matters. That's how you do it, how you reverse the brainwashing in these victims. What else can you do? Find the cults? Stop them before they start? Save girls before they get sucked in? The research we could do! How does being a witch affect—"

"No." The word was sliced painfully from Carla. Her witch-shimmer had taken on a dirty brown. She stood up. "Let Joe and his team protect the clinic. I'm going home."

Sutton didn't understand it. What was she angry about? Axel, Joe, and Darcy all started to move, but Sutton got to her side first. "I'll take you home."

She looked up at him.

"Give me your keys, Carla. It's not safe and you know it." He knew she was roiling with emotions, but she wasn't stupid.

"Carla—" Max's voice was confused and beseeching.

She turned to look at him. "I'm not an experiment." She handed Sutton her keys and walked out.

The cool, predawn stillness stretched out in a comforting, heavy silence. Carla walked to her white Explorer, desperate to keep her composure. She knew her worth, understood her gifts of witchcraft mixed with her knowledge of science.

She helped people.

But she would not be dissected and reduced to her genetic structure, her power and intellect carefully measured, but her heart and soul ignored, as if they had no value.

Sutton moved silently next to her.

She said, "How do you move so quietly when you're so huge? That much mass should create more noise."

"The same way we can bend light to make ourselves appear invisible, we also mute sound waves. Plus, I grew up tracking through deep wildernesses. It's always wise to keep silent and not alert any predators to my presence."

She cut right to go to the passenger side of her car. He followed her and she asked, "You grew up tracking? Where?"

He clicked open the lock and looked down at her.

"That's your question? Not surprised that I know about bending light or muting sound waves?"

She saw his earring again, that fierce-looking eagle, and wanted desperately to touch the gold nestled in the lobe of his ear. What was wrong with her? "You'd have to know in order to do it. I suspect witch hunters knew before the scientists who made the breakthroughs in the mortal world." Sutton was intelligent and precise. He didn't just use a computer, but understood how the computer worked. Like tonight when he'd killed the rogue; he'd used a very calculated leap to get the momentum to push the rogue from her while grabbing the hand that held the knife. Everything had been measured. She turned and climbed up to the seat.

Sutton shut the door and in less than a second, was opening the other door and sliding in. He had to push the seat as far back as it would go, then he started the car.

She wanted to know more about him. "Where'd you grow up?"

"Our base house was out by Palm Desert. We had an airstrip so we could go anywhere we were called. We tracked idiots who got lost, or in some cases, criminals who tried to get lost in forests, mountains, deserts, anywhere."

"We? Your family?"

"My dad and uncle."

Carla was fascinated. "What about your mom?"

He shrugged, his hands tightening on the steering wheel. "She wasn't there."

No mother? "Ever?" The psychologist and the witch inside her were horrified. A mother's love and nurturing the first years of life gave a child a strong foundation.

He looked over at her, the starkness in his eyes filling her with a need to ease him. "She left when I was three."

"Why? How could she leave her own child?" It wasn't right. Many fathers have raised their babies with all the love they needed, but Carla factored in a dad and uncle probably trying not to go rogue, and she didn't like the odds of them lavishing love on Sutton. More like, they lavished structure and discipline.

He rolled his head and stretched his neck like the memory was cramping up his muscles. "The curse. Someone they knew went rogue and killed his family. She couldn't deal, so she left."

Instinctively, she put her hand on his forearm. Her chakras opened and her power bubbled up like a geyser, pouring out to him. "I'm sorry."

"Pull back your powers."

She saw the sweat bead on his forehead, felt the tightly coiled energy under his skin begin to simmer. Yanking her hand from his arm, she clasped her fingers in her lap. "Sorry. I didn't think." She'd just reacted, wanting to comfort him. And maybe wanting a little comfort for herself. Every time he touched her, she felt real and whole and more than a sum of her magic and intellect. Max's reaction to discovering she was a witch felt like a painful betrayal. Turning away, she looked out her window. "You should have let Joe take me home. I can't keep doing this to you." She watched the gray horizon begin to lighten.

"I want to take you home. I'd rather take you to my house, fill up my bathtub and take you in there, washing away everything you had to see and feel tonight. But I can't do that...I can't trust myself to touch you like that and control myself."

She turned to see his hard profile. "The bloodlust?"

"This second, yes. It's eating me up. But the instant I touch you, it'll be a kind of lust that has no words. I won't stop touching you until I've sealed the bond."

With sex. But it wouldn't be just sex, but a joining of two souls, or not. If she wasn't his soul mirror, if she

110

touched him as her own then found out he belonged to Keri, it would shatter her. "Sutton, I'm not..."

His blue eyes blazed in the cab of her car. "You wouldn't stop me. I can feel how badly you need me to touch you. How your skin prickles with the ache, how your heart is hurting. How much you need comfort because a man you cared about in some way, either love or friendship, hurt you tonight. Deeply, in a place where no simple magic can fix it." He ripped his gaze from her, his forearms bulging as he gripped the steering wheel.

"How can you know that?" It felt like her shell had been ripped back to reveal her insides. Every time she was with him, she was exposed. "The men I dated, I always had to be careful. I could only show them my scientist side, not the witch. I couldn't ever tell them I was a witch."

"Like you couldn't tell Max?"

She looked at Sutton's hard profile and found herself telling him why. "I told Doctor Lorenzo Zellweger. He was a well-known psychiatrist and author. I was working on my PhD in psychology at the time, and I thought I loved him. We were making dinner together one night when he knocked over a wineglass and cut his hand badly. I figured that was as good a time as any, so I healed the cut. He..." The memory seared her with shame. Why had she started this?

Sutton's fingers tightened on the steering wheel. "What did he do, Carla?"

She remembered the disgust in his eyes, and the clamminess of his skin as he backed away from her. He looked at her like she was something growing in a lab dish. "He was freaked out. Sickened." She wrapped her arms around her waist, trying to hold it together. "He wouldn't answer my phone calls for a week, and then he called. Said he was sorry, that I just surprised him." She stared out the windshield, remembering how quickly her hope had bloomed. Maybe she'd just shocked him. He'd needed time to process it. But he'd called her and everything would be fine. She'd looked up to Lorenzo so much, and she'd wanted his approval.

"What happened? Did you see him again?" Sutton's voice was neutral.

"Yes. He asked me to meet him at his office." Why was she telling him this? "I went, thinking we were going to talk."

Sutton turned his gaze to her.

"He wanted to examine me. Blood work, EKG..." She turned away, looking out the side window. "He already had on latex gloves when I got there. Didn't want to touch me."

The car swerved to the side of the road and Sutton put it in park. He reached over and took hold of her wrist, pulling her arm from her waist. Then he wrapped his big fingers around her hand. "That son of a bitch. I'll find him and kill him."

His touch warmed her right to her soul. "Keri said the same thing. Then she filled his Porsche with sea water. He opened the door and the water poured out." She grinned at the memory. Keri had always been on her side.

His mouth twitched. "Almost as good as killing him." His thumb rubbed circles on her skin. "I like touching you, love touching you." He sucked in a breath. "My problem is that it is almost impossible for me to *stop* touching you once I start."

She looked down at his hand around hers. She could feel the pain building in him, the compulsion. "Thank you," she said softly. She lifted her gaze. "I've learned to face the truth. And this...thing...between us, we have to face the truth about that, too." She took a deep breath, gently pulled her hand away, and said,

"The Ancestors told Darcy that Keri could be projecting through me and you might be reacting to her, not me."

"Bullshit," he growled, turning back around. He put the car into gear and pulled back out onto the road. "My eagle knows you. I know you."

Oh, Ancestors, she wanted to believe that. Like she'd wanted to believe that Lorenzo would love her, both as the scientist and the witch. But Carla had worked with her dad in genetics, and she was a witch. Both sides of her knew that it was all too possible that he was reacting to Keri, not her. To get some distance and bring her wild thoughts under control, she parroted what Darcy had told her. "If we are soul mirrors, sealing the bond will break my connection to Keri. I won't be able to find her. How am I supposed to choose? You or my twin sister?"

Sutton would never make her choose. He pounded through the woods surrounding his cabin, doing his damnedest to outrun the monster in him.

He had slept a couple hours on the ground behind her house to make sure she was safe. He'd been careful taking her home last night and knew they hadn't been followed, but still...he had to be sure. Then he'd called Joe, got a couple guys to watch her house, and gone home to his cabin. But the minute he walked inside, he'd smelled her. Felt her. Needed her. He'd spun around and left the cabin to go for a run.

He'd gone five miles when he slowed and walked back. He'd grab a shower and go to the warehouse, start working. He wasn't getting any hits on missing person reports for Pam or the girl that the rogues killed in Carla's clinic. The program was still working, though the Department of Motor Vehicles might be a dead end if Pam was from out of state. He was hoping that finding out where Pam came from would give them some idea of how she'd crossed paths with Styx. They were getting these girls from somewhere.

Finding the rogue that killed Carla's sister two years ago was going to be even harder. He'd start by going through his rogue files and narrowing down all the names that had been in San Francisco at the time, but it was a needle in a haystack. There had to be a way, he just needed to...

Sudden dizziness stopped him in his tracks. The trees and thick brush began to spin around him, moving away as a blue fog swirled in, like he was in the middle of a vortex. All the weight of gravity dropped off and he smelled lavender.

Oh, hell, she was pulling him into the astral plane again. Briefly, he worried about leaving his body unprotected outside his cabin; then he caught sight of Carla and nothing else mattered.

He could see her perfectly in profile, her long white-blond hair falling straight, eyes full of confusion and underlined by dark fatigue as she stared at something. But everything beyond her was fuzzy. "Carla?"

She turned to look at him. "I don't know where I am. I was asleep." She squeezed her eyes shut. "Can you hear the screams?"

His eagle started that clawing shit until Sutton moved to her. Once he put his arm around her shoulder, the eagle settled down, except for the sensation of feathers trying to slide across his skin to reach her.

Then the feathers froze when the first scream sounded in the distance. "What is it?" He tightened his arm, bringing her in closer to his body.

"Witches. They are cutting witches. Where are we? How did we get here?"

If she didn't know, then they were in trouble. Something else was controlling them. How did he fight what he couldn't see and didn't understand? Sutton turned and saw some kind of small room, maybe twelve by twelve, and a huge naked man pacing back and forth as if the walls couldn't contain him. He and Carla were looking down on the scene, as though they were hovering eight feet off the floor. "He doesn't see us, does he?"

"No."

Sutton watched the man turn to walk away from them and was slapped with shock. "It's Brigg." He recognized the outline of an unfinished crow on his back.

"Your missing witch hunter?"

"Yes," he said, then called out, "Brigg? Can you hear me?"

The man kept pacing, showing no sign that he'd heard.

Another scream made Sutton grit his teeth, and he felt the goose bumps on Carla's skin beneath his hand.

Brigg's head snapped up.

Sutton saw it then, the faint trace of fading blood on his chest and abdomen. "Jesus. They've blooded him." The man's blue eyes were nearly black, his pupils dilated fully. Sweat ran rivers down his body. In a sudden spasm he dropped to his knees, rubbing his hands across the fading blood on his stomach.

"What's that?"

He knew what was coming. Everything in him screamed to stop it. "They put witch blood on him, then left it to sink in and take hold. Carla, can we reach him? They are turning him rogue! We have to stop them!"

"I can't! I'm not controlling this."

Helpless fury whipped through his words. "Who the fuck is?"

She closed her eyes, and his stomach went tight, then began to vibrate. He could feel her powers, and so could his eagle. The creature thrummed with new life, clearly wanting to help her. Carla's words jerked his attention to her.

"He has a lock on me. My power. Oh!" She shuddered and opened her eyes.

The power streaming through him shut off. "What?"

Her eyes filled with yellow and she shuddered. "He's fighting me for control of my mind. I can feel his excitement to destroy me. Like a game."

The terrified, pain-filled shrieks jerked both their attention back to the scene before them.

"No!" Brigg bellowed but his head snapped up, his nostrils flared, and Jesus, his dick went hard. Not for sex, but blood. Two witches were dragged in, naked and bleeding from too many cuts to count. They were dropped in front of Brigg like an offering.

Then a rogue put a silver knife in Brigg's trembling hand.

"Please, no," Carla whispered.

Her plea wrenched his heart. The scene before him inflamed his rage. He snatched his arm from Carla and took a long stride forward, determined to put a stop to this nightmare.

"Sutton, no!" Carla grabbed his arm. "I don't think this is real time, but something that's already done. That's why Brigg can't see us. We can't stop it." Her voice broke. "We're seeing what's already happened."

He looked down at her, saw her desperate eyes, and brought himself under control. She was being torn apart and tortured by some animal, and he was adding to that by making her feel guilty for not being able to stop it.

Neither of them could stop it but it didn't mean they would stand here and be forced to watch it.

He reached out to her. "Carla, concentrate. Come here." He pulled her into his chest. He had to get her out of here. Putting his hand to the back of her head, he held her tight against him. "Feel my arms around you?"

"Yes."

"Put your arms around me." Her neck and back muscles were viciously knotted.

She lifted her slender arms and wrapped them around his waist, turning to him the way he'd desperately wanted her to after the rogue attack in her clinic. He and the bird stroked her. "All right. Good. Now you're going to take us out of here. Can you take us someplace where we can talk? Someplace safe?"

Screams bounced around them, horrible sounds of flesh being cut, innocent witches being tortured. And he knew then, Brigg had made his choice. This was what it sounded like for a man to lose his soul. Brigg could have turned that knife on himself—could have died with his soul intact. Sutton had seen some bad shit in his life, but even he didn't want to look. He talked to her, drowning out as much as he could. "Come on, baby. Fight. Break that bastard's hold on you. On us. I mean us. I'm not leaving you alone here, not a chance, so don't even..."

A quiver took root inside him and built with the beat of her rising magic. "That's it, baby." *She is doing it* was his last thought as the world began to spin into a white and blue fog and they were pulled, pushed and hurled, and then they were feeling the wet spray from the waterfall.

Sutton held on tight to Carla and lifted his head to see that they stood on the same stone path they'd been on before. They were surrounded by the leafy foliage with the blooming flowers that mixed with her lavender scent. They were damp with mist from the waterfall just ahead of them.

Asmodeus had found them here before, but for a few minutes, it would do. He ran his hand down her long hair. Beneath her hair, he could feel her skin.

They were both naked again. It meant something that they were both naked in her safe place. She trusted him that deeply. He pulled her head back, looking down into her haunted, tight face. "This isn't your fault. We couldn't save those witches or Brigg."

Some of the rich brown and green began to darken in her eyes as she relaxed into his hold. "I know that intellectually. But I still wanted to."

"I know." As awful as realizing exactly what had happened to Brigg was, as terrible as seeing witches slaughtered, holding Carla in his arms was a gift. He knew they only dared stay here a few minutes. "Are you all right? Tell me what he's doing to you. *Who* is doing it to you?"

"Asmodeus must have zeroed in on more than just Keri; he found the wavelength of my bond to her. Someone is slipping in and pulling me into visions they want me to see. It's a psychological game to break me down so he can get control of my mind."

Sutton didn't know how to fight this. Armed rogues, yeah, he could fight them. But this? "How? Why?"

"I don't know. I couldn't...I was scared. Maybe a demon witch but I don't know. I've never had it happen before."

The feel of her in his arms, the absolute bliss of touching her with no curse threatening to erupt, eased his pulsing rage. His dick had gone hard seconds after they landed here, but this wasn't the time. "How did you pull me in?"

She leaned back and said, "The only other person I could pull into the astral plane from a distance was Keri."

"Did you ever try anyone else?"

She hesitated, and finally said, "My father. He had me try it on him after..."

The scent of incense floated on the mist of the waterfall, threaded with the sound of laughter.

Carla went stiff, then pushed out of his arms. "Keri? Where are you?" She turned around, her hair swinging out to brush his chest. "Keri?"

From the corner of his eye, Sutton thought he saw a starburst of lights that formed into two young teenage girls dancing amid swirling fog next to the waterfall. They were both in fancy dresses that made them look like girls playing dress up. When he turned his head to get a better look, the image disappeared. Chills danced over Sutton's skin.

The scent and laughter faded.

"Did you see that? What was that?" He turned to find Carla staring at the spot where the image had been, her hands lifted and reaching.

She dropped her hands. "That was me and Keri. The first time I pulled her into the astral plane from a distance. Our dad had been doing one of his endless tests on us, and Keri was bored, restless and miserable."

He reached for her hand. She was more beautiful than ever, the glow of the memory warming her skin, lifting her breasts. Tugging her closer to him, he forced himself to focus on her words. "What test?"

"Dad was testing our powers. He'd have us perform various magic, then test our blood in an attempt to isolate the genetic markers in witches. On that day, he was doing it with us separated. Keri hated the testing, but forcing her to be alone in a room like that was worse. Keri was a strong telepath, and I could feel how miserable she was. So I reached out in the next room, grabbed her spirit, and took us both out of our bodies to the astral plane. We summoned music and danced and laughed at thwarting Dad."

Sutton could feel her joy in the memory. "Why were you in those dresses? Yours was delicate gold, and Keri's was white."

Surprise widened her eyes. "You can tell us apart."

He frowned at her and squeezed her hand in his. "I can always tell and so can the eagle. So why the dresses? They almost looked like wedding dresses."

A real smile warmed up her face, making her eyes sparkle and her witch-shimmer dance over her skin. "They kind of were. Keri and I had this fascination with the Ancestors. What they look like, who they are. We thought they must be like princesses or goddesses. We imagined that they wore these long flowing dresses, sort of like a bride. We'd pore over magazines, and when we had enough power, we'd create our Ancestor Dresses. Kind of like little girls dreaming of their wedding."

He could see it so clearly, the two little witches playing their own kind of dress up. "It was a game you only played with Keri, right?" And Keri had shown him, somehow she'd given him the gift of seeing Carla as a girl, and shown him how close the two sisters had been.

"Right."

Touching her face, he shifted to the subject that seemed to trouble her. "Your dad—"

Her joy dimmed. "Is the psi-geneticist Jerome Wagner. Keri and I were his test subjects. I haven't talked to him since Keri's murder."

Sutton pulled her against him. Time was ticking by and he needed to get her to some form of safety. He wished he could keep her here forever where he could touch her and make love to her, but the risk was too great. "If Keri was the only other person you could pull from a distance, how did you pull me into that vision?" She lifted her head, taking a deep breath.

Sutton drifted his gaze down her face, her long

neck, to her breasts. His dick twitched hard against her stomach, seeing her nipples peak as he stared. His tongue stuck to the roof of his mouth. His hands tightened on her back, wishing he could stroke and tease her breasts.

His eagle quivered, feeling the same desperate excitement, lust and sheer joy of just being able to look. The eagle recognized Carla as his and didn't understand that they couldn't complete the bond that would truly free him and make them all whole.

She finally said, "I think I'm going to have to ask my father for help." Dryly, she added, "Maybe all those years of study will actually mean something."

9

WHEN CARLA AWOKE FROM THE vision, she found her mom in the kitchen talking to the computer while rolling out cookie dough. "Tawny, I have to stay here. What's the problem exactly?"

"We have two parties that want us to provide magical cookies!" The young witch's blue eyes were wide, and panic had paled her face so that her freckles stood out.

Chandra set the rolling pin down, picked up her glass of ice water, and leaned her hip against the counter. "When?"

"Two weeks. One's a bridal shower and the other is a charity event for an animal rescue center."

"Relax, it's a piece of cake. I can whip those up in two days. All I need is for you to get them to fill out the spell sheets."

Carla made herself a cup of tea while listening to the conversation. Spell sheets were actually questionnaires to find out how many guests, the theme, and all the details her mom would need to create the right cookies, each with its own rolled-up spell and wrapped with a pretty ribbon. Carla and Keri had spent a good number of their growing-up years in

Chandra's cookie shop. Carla had created quite a few disasters with her scientific/witch experiments she'd attempted while her mom worked. Carla took each and every disaster as a personal insult for about three seconds, but Keri would be laughing so hard, Carla would end up laughing, too.

Just like they'd laughed when they had escaped their dad to the astral plane. She missed Keri.

Her mom said goodbye to her assistant, picked up star and moon cookie cutters, and got to work on the dough. "Stalling won't make it any easier to tell me.

Carla set down her tea. "How do you know I'm stalling?"

Her mom moved with a sweeping grace, cutting the cookies, arranging them on the sheet, taking one batch out of the oven to cool, and sliding the next batch in. "Honey, Keri was the one who would rip the Band-Aid off in one pull. You'd design a scientific protocol for removing a Band-Aid painlessly as a delaying tactic."

Grinning in memory, she said, "Keri would get so annoyed, she'd rip my Band-Aid off."

Her mom laughed. "She was our brave, take-on-the-world girl, wasn't she?"

The ache in her chest matched the pain in the scar on her lower back. "You know she saved me. The day she died, she connected to my chakras, and threw me across the room. It's not fair that she's dead and I'm alive."

Her mom stood up and turned, her eyes filling with tears. "Carla, don't. You would have done the same for her if you could have. You know that."

"But I wouldn't have been so reckless! Trying to bind herself to my armband was too dangerous. She should have gone on to Summerland, not risked her soul to save me. Now she's trapped in that knife. I can feel her, Mom, but I can't reach her."

"Honey." Her mom rushed over, putting her arms around her. "You're trying!"

Miserable, she said, "Something else is getting in. I don't know how. I can't track him or her. They are trying to destroy both Keri and me. I'm not going to let them hurt her anymore."

Her mom leaned back to look in her face. "Carla, you listen to me. If it comes down to a choice, you will let Keri go. Do you hear me? I won't lose you! I won't! Somewhere in that oversize brain of yours, you think I would have picked Keri over you. But I love you both. You're my girls. I could never choose."

She was acting like a child. It was Keri who was emotional and reached out like this when she needed comfort. Not Carla. It was Keri who'd curled up on her bed and hugged her stuffed eagles when she was sad. Carla would work on something in the lab until she got her dad's approval, that was how she got her comfort. Carla hugged her mother tightly. "I know that, Mom. I mean it. I never thought you loved Keri more. You always made us both feel special." It was true. She'd accepted each of them for who they were. Maybe in some ways, she understood Keri better, but she had loved Carla as much as Keri.

"I can feel the witch hunter on you."

Carla took a deep breath to get control of herself and let her mom go. "While I was sleeping, I got pulled into some kind of vision, and Sutton was there, too. He's in the bond with Keri and me."

Her mom's green eyes deepened in color. She reached down and took Carla's hand. "Then he must be your soul mirror."

"Or Keri's." How did she explain it to her mom? "Sutton would rip the Band-Aid off."

"Like Keri," her mom said softly.

Very much like her. But every time she heard his voice, or saw him, or felt his touch, she wanted to crawl into his arms and curl up against him. *She wanted to claim him as hers!* She wanted him to fill her up and make her feel whole again. Sutton had understood that Max had hurt her without even understanding how. She had told him about Lorenzo, and he'd understood that, too. It was like he saw inside her. But would he be able to do that as Keri's mate because Keri could see inside her? "I need help, Mom. Twin witches are rare, and this is way out of the Circle Witches' realm of experience. Something is tracking me using Keri's bond. Something evil. I don't know how it's doing it."

Her mom firmed up her expression. "Okay, tell me what you're thinking. Spit it out, Carla."

"Dad."

Her jaw dropped and she stepped back almost as a reflex. "Jerome?" She jerked and said, "Cookies!" She turned, waved her hand to open the oven door. The hot cookie sheet floated out to sit on the counter. A new one slid into the oven and the door closed.

Carla waited, letting her mom work and have a moment.

Chandra turned to her daughter. "You haven't talked to him in two years, have you?"

Carla shook her head. "No."

"He blames himself for Keri's murder. It's taken a toll on him."

She refrained from reminding her mom that Jerome had blamed her. Chandra had tried to stay in contact with Jerome, and Carla never wanted to put her in the middle.

Chandra went on. "He sold his research lab, and basically became a hermit. He won't let me see him. He hasn't written a book, given a lecture...nothing." She paused, then asked, "How do you think he can help?"

Surprised at the twist of sympathy she felt for her

dad, she wondered if she had been too harsh. Keri used to tell her that it wasn't good for her to hold on to a grudge. "I don't understand the link, the magic, or the force that's pulling me into the vision. He's studied Keri and me exhaustively. I think he might be able to help me figure this out."

"Are you sure you're not just looking for a scientific protocol to a magical problem?"

Carla was honest. "I don't know, Mom. But I don't know where else to turn. When I took Sutton back to my spot on the astral plane, Keri seemed to be able to connect with both of us for a few seconds, then she was gone again. But she wasn't the one who showed Sutton and me the vision. That was something else." She took a breath and said, "I'm scared, Mom. I never thought I'd have to go to Dad and ask for help, but right now, I'll do whatever it takes for Keri."

Her mom's skin blanched. "You think Asmodeus has her?"

Carla put her hand on her mom's shoulder. "Not the demon specifically. Keri's not a demon witch so he can't pull her into the Underworld. But he may have sent his henchman, Quinn Young, after her."

"How will we get the knife from him? He has the Immortal Death Dagger!"

"I will. Whatever it takes." There had to be a way, whether through magic, science, or both. "I'll call Dad." She lifted her hand, and her cell phone floated out from where she'd left it in her bedroom. She made the call before she could talk herself out of it.

The first ring set her heart to pounding. The next two rings twisted her nerves tighter and tighter. What would she say? How would she ask him for help when they hadn't talked in two years?

"Huh?" A bleary voice answered.

Carla checked the clock. It was almost noon. "Dad?"

"Charra?" There was the sound of fumbling, then he was back on the line. "Carla?"

"It's me, Dad."

"Are you and your mother all right?" The words were carefully enunciated.

"Yes, but I, we, need your help." She shifted her weight from one foot to the other; then back again, trying to ease the tension in her muscles.

Silence.

"Dad?"

"Help with what?" The words came out in a slur.

Her stomach jiggled with nerves. Had she thought this would be easy? Before she lost her nerve, she blurted out, "It's Keri, Dad. Her soul is trapped in a rogue's knife and things are happening that I don't understand. You've studied magic..."

In a hopeless voice, he said, "I'm out of it. I don't study magic anymore. I'm a mortal, I can't help you. Go find a witch who has real power. Keri never wanted my help. None of you did." He hung up.

Carla dropped her hand holding the phone, staring at her mom. "He said no. Hung up. He didn't sound right."

Chandra seemed to shrink a couple inches. "I heard he was drinking."

Years of rage grabbed her by the throat. "Keri needs him this one last time and he's too busy getting drunk."

"Carla..."

"Don't defend him. Don't. I'll find Keri without him. He can drink himself to death and he'd better not come crawling to me when his abused liver poisons him! I'm not going to use witchcraft to heal him when he wouldn't lift a finger to help Keri." She would not cry. She would not fall apart. What the hell had she been thinking to believe her dad would help her and Keri? He'd only wanted them for their magic.

Her cell phone rang, and she snapped it open. Caller ID told her it was Max. She dropped the phone on the counter and stormed out.

A beep told him there was another match. Sutton was in the warehouse working at the large computer console that took up an entire corner of the huge room. He looked up at the two pictures displayed side by side on the largest monitor. The image on the left was his digital shot of Pam. The one on the right was a Pamela Lynn Miller of Glendale, California.

Not their Pam. He shifted back to the keyboard and deleted that picture. The program hummed along looking for the next match to the criteria he'd set.

Sutton turned back to working on hacking into the Rogue Cadre's computer network. He had taken a cell phone off one of the rogues he had killed at his cabin. Now he was working on tracking the computer that sent the rogue the directions to kill Sutton.

The email had been routed through anonymous proxy servers. Sutton had been raised a tracker, and computer tracking wasn't much different. It took the same concentration and patience. He would find the computer that sent this email eventually, he just had to keep picking up each thread and following it. He'd discovered that the Rogue Cadre was using a complicated pool of proxy servers and that it switched them around in a random order, routing emails through several of them.

Hitting another dead end, he shoved his roller chair back, stretched out his legs and crossed his arms over his chest, studying the monitors. He needed to get into the Rogue Cadre's network to see what the hell was going on. For one thing, it could lead him to the knife that Keri was trapped in. There might be communications in there about that knife. Sutton had a partial list of rogues known to have been in the San Francisco area two years ago, but it wasn't leading anywhere helpful. He'd known it wouldn't, there were too many variables, the biggest one being Asmodeus. The demon had done something with the knife after he'd found Carla on the astral plane. That knife had something to do with pulling Carla into that vision.

Then she, or someone, pulled him in, too.

His mind hummed in time with the computer, trying to arrange all the pieces into a pattern. Asmodeus, Keri in the rogue knife, Styx, the brainwashed woman who they could tie to Styx from what Pam had told Carla...were they all connected? How?

Who the hell was Styx and where was he?

Where was Styx getting these women he was brainwashing? Did he have more of them imprisoned? A number of women disappearing would send up an alarm. Pam wasn't a druggie or hooker that no one noticed missing.

Who or what managed to get control of Carla's mind?

How were these things connected? There was a pattern, he just had to find it.

The eagle shifted and fretted in the cage of his skin. He was as restless and agitated as the bird. They both needed Carla, were desperate for her. But he knew if he got near her, if he smelled her rich Arabian-spiced blood, the curse would rise with a vengeance. The dual drives yanked him out of his chair as he tried to pace off his pounding frustration. He stalked past the pool table in the center, ignored Key's drafting table, and turned right into the open gym area.

Since they were all in one place, Sutton told them what he'd learned with Carla. "Brigg is rogue."

Linc's gold eyes were defiant. "You saw him? Saw him actually kill a witch?"

"In a vision. Carla pulled me into it. When we left, two witches had been cut and dumped into a locked room with him."

Linc slammed down three hundred pounds of barbell and rolled up from the bench. His skin was nearly the color of his gold eyes and soaked with sweat. His chin thrust out. "You didn't see him go rogue. He could have fought..."

"We found his knife," Axel said. He had stood back by the treadmills, letting Sutton break the news. Now he walked forward and handed Linc the knife.

The witch hunter dropped his gaze. His gold eyes darkened, his hands curled into fists. "He fought, they killed him. That's the only way a rogue got his knife." He lifted his boiling stare and dared any of them to argue. Then he snatched up the knife and stormed out the alley door.

Sutton looked at Key doing curls, Ram cleaning weapons and Phoenix fiddling with his earbuds from his iPod. "He went rogue. I didn't watch him cut the two witches, but I heard it." He had practically felt the man's soul die off. It pissed him off. Brigg got a raw deal, but in the end, he'd had a choice. He could have used the knife on himself instead of the witches.

"The knife tells me he's dead or rogue, and if he shows up stinking of copper, I'll kill him," Phoenix said, yanking out his earbuds. "Second broken pair."

Ram held out one hand. "Let me see." He took the earbuds and examined the wires. "I don't doubt what you saw or heard, Sutton. But I am really worried about what you and Carla are getting pulled into. You couldn't tell who was doing it?" Ram slanted a glance to Phoenix. "Hand over your iPod."

Sutton shook his head. "All I could see clearly at first was Carla. Then when I touched her, Brigg came into focus in the cement room and I could hear witch screams from somewhere nearby. Carla was there first."

Axel said, "The soul-mirror bond pulled you in."

"Yes." He and Carla both believed that, the problem was she wanted to believe he was her twin's soul mirror.

"Powerful for being incomplete," Key mused, as he switched the free weight to the other hand.

Axel pointed out, "All we know about the soul-mirror bond is what we learned from Darcy and me. Each pairing could be different."

Ram handed the iPod and earbuds back to Phoenix. "Nothing wrong with them. They sound fine." Phoenix's dark-as-death eyes glared at the offending unit, then shifted to Key. "Then someone's been messing with my playlist. You screwing with me, Dragon Boy?"

Key dropped the dumbbell to the black mat on the cement floor. The jewel-colored dragon tattooed on his chest almost looked like it was grinning. "Nope. Maybe the mortal that shot you shorted out your hearing."

"I hear fine. It's the damned iPod. It keeps playing ballads." He shuddered in disgust and walked out of the gym area. "I'm going to delete and resync my playlist." His footsteps echoed as he crossed the large warehouse to the banks of computers Sutton ran.

Key laughed. "Hell, wish I'd thought of it. I'd have filled your playlist with boy bands."

Sutton ignored them. "Damn it, we need a break. Styx hasn't popped and we haven't heard anything from Quinn Young. That rogue I killed the other night was terrified when I just mentioned Young's name."

"Only reaction I get, too," Key said. "It's that death dagger burned into his arm. The bastard's crazy."

Phoenix called out, "You stick needles in your chest

all the time working on that big-ass dragon! Tell me that's not sick."

"Did you call her ass *big?*" Key demanded.

Sutton talked right over them, used to the bickering. "The rogues don't know where Young is. He doesn't live with any of them—too risky that someone would try to kill him to get that death dagger."

"Right," Ram said. "He puts a leader in each section; L.A., San Diego, San Francisco, one who answers to him."

"Styx might be the rogue area leader here. Young would be impressed that he can brainwash mortals." Axel turned to Sutton. "You didn't recognize the two rogues who dragged the witches in during the vision?"

He shook his head. "Haven't seen them before." The eagle shuffled uneasily in the cage of his skin, missing Carla. They both hated being away from her, but Sutton couldn't be near her for too long.

"Sutton, you got an incoming," Phoenix called out.

Straightening up, he turned, going around the partition and out into the open area of the warehouse. "Something about Styx? Or another possible match on Pam?" Did they finally have a break?

He was racing past the pool table when Phoenix said, "Nope. Carla's mom."

Her mom? Was something wrong? Practically shoving Phoenix out of his favorite rolling chair, he sat down and faced the screen. "Chandra. What's wrong? I have a security team there." He shifted his gaze to the cameras he had watching the safe house they were living in. He didn't see any signs of trouble.

"Sutton, I need you to do something for me. For Carla."

Ice formed in his veins. He didn't know much about mothers, his own having bailed when she realized she'd married a man who could turn monster and had a son who could do the same. Was this the *Leave my daughter alone or I'll hex you* videoconference?

Axel kicked his chair.

Mothers liked manners, right? Good manners meant introductions. "This is Axel, he's the leader of the Wing Slayer Hunters." He gestured over his left shoulder where Axel stood. "The others are Key, Phoenix and Ram." They each lifted a hand in greeting.

"Hello," Chandra said.

He didn't know the rules here. "They're cool, you can talk in front of them." Would she tell him to kiss off in front of the men?

"I can't get used to trusting witch hunters."

What was he supposed to say to that?

Axel cleared his throat. "Carla is the best friend to my soul mirror, Darcy, Chandra. We only want to protect her, not hurt her. If there's something she needs, we'll get it for her. I can get Darcy if you'd be more comfortable talking to her."

Well, shit, Sutton could have said something like that. If he'd thought of it. His hands were sweating. Christ. He curled his fingers into fists so the other hunters didn't notice that he was scared of Carla's mother. He had to say something to reassure her. "Uh, yeah. What Axel said."

Ah hell. He didn't have this trouble talking to Carla.

There was shuffling from the men behind him. Dumb shits, he knew they were looking at each other and smirking behind his back.

Enough, he had to take control. "Ma'am, is Carla all right?"

Phoenix snickered and muttered, "He called her ma'am."

Chandra's lips twitched. "Actually, Sutton, she's not all right. She called her dad, and he refused to help her."

Sutton snapped up in his chair. "What kind of bastard is he?"

"A drunk one. Carla and her dad's relationship is complicated. Jerome loved the girls, but he used them, too. He was so desperate to prove his theories right to the scientific community that had laughed at him for believing magic did exist, and that he could isolate the chakra gene to prove it."

He leaned forward. "Chandra, tell me where her father is. I'll bring him to her. He'll help her." Sutton would change his mind with whatever method it took. If Carla needed her dad, then she would have him.

"Okay." Her face relaxed, her eyes brightening. "Do you boys like cookies?"

"Hell, yes!" Phoenix said and slapped Sutton's shoulder. "She's the Cookie Witch, you idiot."

"Famous in San Francisco and many places outside the city, too." Key explained.

Ram chuckled. "We love cookies, Chandra."

The witch looked pleased. "I'll give the security guy outside a few dozen." She looked over the men again. "Several dozen," she amended.

Axel kicked the bottom of Sutton's chair again.

Sutton sputtered, "Uh, thanks. I need Jerome's address." He had more important things to think about than cookies.

"I'll send it in an e-mail. And Sutton, thank you."

His vocal cords froze, but he managed to croak out, "Sure."

The picture faded.

"Sure?" Phoenix hit Sutton's shoulder again then doubled over laughing.

"Ma'am?" Key shouted as he dissolved into fits of laughter.

"He's afraid of Carla's mother!" Phoenix bellowed, holding his stomach. "Ice-for-blood Sutton is afraid of a mother!"

Ram started to laugh.

Sutton surged to his feet. "Shut the fuck up! I'm not afraid." He was terrified, that's what he was. "Assholes."

Key wiped tears from his eyes. "Dude, I thought you were going to swallow your tongue."

"Enough," Axel said.

Sutton looked over at him with gratitude until he saw that Axel was fighting a grin. That was it. He stormed toward the rear door. He'd go find Carla's dad and explain to the man how much he wanted to help his daughter. He hit the door so hard, it slammed into the outside of the building and almost rebounded into Ram.

Ram agilely dodged the door and raced after him. "Sutton."

"Fuck off."

Ram paced by his side. "I printed all the information about Doctor Jerome Wagner that Chandra sent."

Sutton never lost control. Ever.

Until now.

Until the witch doctor and her mother, the Cookie Witch. He'd never heard of the Cookie Witch. How was he supposed to know this stuff? It was probably some kind of grave insult that he hadn't known. What exactly was a Cookie Witch?

Ram held out the sheet of printer paper.

"Thanks." He took the paper, but just stood there ten feet from his truck, staring at the dank exterior of the warehouse. "They're right."

"You're afraid of Chandra?"

"I don't know shit about mothers." Made him feel like the biggest loser ever.

Ram nodded without any sign of a smirk.

"My mother booked when I was three. Her mother tried to kill me with cooking utensils the first time she saw me. Woman has an arm on her."

Ram's mouth twitched, but he kept his eyes blank.

"I'm not good enough for Carla. Her mother has to know that. Carla's smart. She's a doctor."

"You're a computer wizard," Ram said.

He snorted. "Big deal. Taught myself all that shit. I went through sixth grade before I was homeschooled. That doctor she works with, he's smart like her. He loves her." Except he'd hurt her, and Sutton had an urge to knock him on his ass for that. What was happening to him? He was cold and logical, not this...crazed mass of insecurity, desperation, and this thick choking need to be the man who kept Carla safe and happy.

"I had a mom."

Sutton's wild, spinning thoughts slowed. "Yeah?" Ram rarely talked about himself.

"Military mom. When I couldn't go with her, I stayed with her retired military dad."

A military background made sense. Ram had a buzz cut and pressed, perfect clothes. Even his workout clothes tended to be precise. "So the rumors are true? You were a kid once?"

Ram allowed himself a measured half smile. "My mom expected a hell of a lot from me. I was raised on duty, discipline and denial."

His own confusion took a large step back. "Yeah?"

"My mom and her parents refused to acknowledge that I was not a regular mortal kid. I had no idea, no..." He straightened his shoulders and lifted his chin, pulling his military posture back into line. "My mom wanted the best for me. Insisted on it. I don't think Carla's mom would be so different. She wants her daughter safe and happy. She's not going to care about degrees as much as character."

The man had his reasons for keeping his past to himself. But Ram had broken rank, this one time, to reassure him. Friends like that made getting through the days possible. "Yeah, okay. Got you. Uh, what exactly is a cookie witch?"

Ram shook his head. "It's a famous bakery in San Francisco. Mortals have no idea Chandra really is a witch, but they love her cookies."

Sutton raised his brow. "A weakness, Ram? Cookies?"

The man shrugged. "First you taste her cookies, then tell me they aren't a necessity, not a weakness."

He felt better. More in control again. The fact that he had something to do, some action to take, helped. But the tat on his back started fretting, which reminded him. "While I'm gone..."

Ram cut him off. "Goes without saying that we'll watch out for your witch and her mom."

The eagle settled down. "Later."

⇒ *10* ⇐

LESS THAN FIVE HOURS LATER, Sutton drove into San Francisco, and went straight to the address that Chandra had e-mailed him. The tall, thin two-story had a faded front door, peeling cream-colored paint, and a dirty front window covered by yellowed blinds. Sutton pounded on the door.

"G'way," a voice muttered from inside.

It took an effort not to kick the door in. Instead he tried the doorknob, found it unlocked and walked in.

A man deep into his fifties sat on a couch covered in an avalanche of books and yellow tablets. There were two laptops on the scarred wood coffee table, along with a couple of booze bottles. Gin. The room stank of stale breath and old food.

"Who're you?"

Sutton sized up the man. He had bleary brown eyes, blond hair that had grown to a shaggy bowl cut, and a ragged beard. He wore a dingy white T-shirt and old sweats. "Sutton. I'm taking you to Glassbreakers to see Carla. You have ten minutes to clean up."

He frowned. "Not going. Get out." He reached for a mug filled with gin.

Sutton whipped out his knife and threw it,

knocking the cup out of Jerome's hand. The cup crashed down on the table, spilling its contents. The knife embedded itself in the couch. "Nine minutes, Doctor." Sutton was trying to hold on to his temper. Frankly, he didn't see how this drunk could be any help.

Jerome's gaze sharpened. "You're not a mortal."

Sutton hid his surprise. He stepped closer to the couch, looming over the man. "Carla needs you. She needs your help, and you're going to give it to her. Clear?"

His eyes grew wider. "I can't help her. I'm done with magic." He waved his hand around the mess of books and papers. "I'm debunking my own discoveries in a new book. Going to tell the world magic doesn't exist."

Sutton narrowed his eyes. "Why?"

"It's all I have left to give them. Keep them safe in case anyone's looking for them." His slack face tightened. "I failed, and Keri's dead. Carla said something about a rogue on the phone. No way am I going to be a part of something that might get her killed, too."

He'd never let that happen. *Unless he was the rogue,* an ugly voice in his head said. Sutton reached out and hauled Jerome to his feet by the front of his shirt. "Your plans just changed."

Jerome's shoulders sagged and he looked away. "I don't want to see her."

There was no fear in this man. All Sutton smelled was booze and regret. "She wants you, you're going." Jerome shifted his gaze back to Sutton, opening his mouth—

Sutton locked his stare onto the man's eyes, following the optic nerve, and sent the message that he had to clean up and go see Carla. He let go of the man.

Jerome's eyes turned cunning. "You're a witch hunter. Let me see your palm."

Surprised, Sutton held his hand out, palm up.

Jerome studied his lifelines. "Not rogue."

In spite of the alcohol and decay, Sutton saw two things clearly: where Carla got her intellect, and that this man cared about Carla in spite of trying very hard not to. "Six minutes, Doctor."

Carla opened her fifth chakra and went to the astral plane to try to bring Pam back, but all she saw was blue static.

Interference.

"Keri, what are you doing?" Carla begged her sister.

Keri was somehow dragging down her powers, or interrupting them. She'd latched on to Carla's chakras enough to do that, but she couldn't show herself.

"Keri, are you mad? Because of Sutton? Is he yours?" Carla reached for her sister with everything she had.

Nothing but static. Reminding herself why she was on the astral plane, Carla said, "Pam, it's Carla. How are you doing, Pam?" She focused as much of her thoughts on the mortal woman as she could summon.

The static crackled like a TV station that had gone off the air.

She was tired, emotionally charged up and bordering on desperate. Carla closed off her communication chakra and slipped back into her physical body. The room was lit by candles in the falling night. Pam's closed eyes appeared sunken into her face. Her skin was taking on an unhealthy waxiness. Setting Pam's hand on the bed, she tucked the covers around her and quietly left the room.

Crossing the family room, she rubbed her pounding

temples, and went into her small office. Dropping into her chair, she touched her mouse to wake up her computer. There were several messages on the Circle Witches' links.

She chose the one from Darcy first. *There will be no more discussion of censoring or banishing Dr. Carla Fisk. What happened was an accident, not an abuse of power. There was no witch-karma punishment, and we will not abandon a sister-witch. Anyone who disagrees may leave the Circle Witches.*

Carla smiled. She didn't have to read the other messages to know Silver was inciting rebellion. Before Darcy came along—gaining extraordinary power, a familiar in the form of a soul mirror and the ability to talk to the Ancestors—Silver had pretty much run the Circle Witches.

She didn't like change, didn't like Darcy being so powerful, didn't trust witch hunters, and hated being made irrelevant.

Carla clicked on Silver's response. *Witches have a long and valued history, Darcy. We will not be treated like the subjects of a Supreme Goddess. Our mission is to heal and care for mortals while learning as much as we can in each lifetime. We do that by working together, making decisions together, not by blindly following a witch who claims to have seen the Ancestors while screwing a witch hunter. We know your spell to heal the child failed.*

"That bitch," Carla muttered. Darcy had tried desperately to heal Axel's four-year-old sister, Hannah, from a demon witch's death curse. She had managed to push the curse back, but not break it entirely. Silver was mischaracterizing what had happened to fuel a growing fracture in the Circle Witches.

Pushing back her headache, Carla focused and used her powers to summon Darcy through her computer.

Darcy appeared on the screen, her brown eyes filled with dark fury. "They will not banish you."

Carla grinned. Leave it to Darcy to be worked up over the insults to Carla but not those to herself. "Silver is playing politics to wrest control back from you."

Darcy shoved her hair off her face. "Lovely, witch politics."

"Yeah. Well, there's a solution. You could try the Moon Witch Advisor Ceremony."

Darcy dropped her hands. "What's that?"

"You call down the moon, call up the power of the ley lines, and cut yourself. If your blood heals into a silver scar in the shape of the moon that makes you the chosen Moon Witch Advisor."

"Chosen by whom?"

Carla laughed at the disgruntled look on her friend's face. Darcy didn't play politics well. "Ancestors. Even Silver can't argue with that."

"What makes you think I'd be this Moon Witch? And what is she exactly?"

"Silver is right that we don't have a Supreme Goddess. Witches are each on their own journey, and we don't do well being told how to live. We are supposed to find the right paths for ourselves."

"Tell Silver that. She's the one—"

"Darcy," Carla admonished.

She settled back into her seat and took a breath. "Fine. I'm listening. Why do you think I'd be this Moon Witch?"

Darcy's outrage on her behalf was part of their deep friendship. It felt like a burst of stunning moonlight on a dark night. "She serves as an advisor in times of serious trouble. I'd say we're in that kind of trouble, what with the curse and the rogues. I think you might fill the role because the Moon Witch must be able to open her seventh chakra. I don't know of any other witch who can.

142

Her dark eyes took on gold lights. "Hmm."

It was a little scary to watch Darcy thinking; the results were often a surprise. She could be devious and clever when the situation called for it.

"There's a downside, though. If you attempt the ceremony and fail, Silver will marginalize you. That's why I haven't suggested it before."

"Because I failed with Hannah."

"You didn't fail!" Carla had been there, she'd felt the incredible power from Darcy. "You didn't have everything you needed."

Darcy rolled her eyes. "I know that and you know that. Silver doesn't. She's only able to cause this much dissension because the witches are scared and they feel powerless. The curse severely limited their powers. Witch karma prevented them from effectively using what powers remained for defense. And the witch hunters, the men created to protect us, are turning rogue and killing us. That fear is what gives Silver her power. So you and I, we have to be very careful not to let her feed their fears anymore. A public failure on my part would give her more cachet."

"You'll know when the time is right, Darcy. It's something to consider. Of course, you'd have to have two witch witnesses, and witches try not to gather in public like that. Too big a target." Witches always had to be careful. While the threat of rogues was probably the worst, witch hunts over the centuries had conditioned witches to a natural secrecy. Especially since the humans were killing mortals, not witches. It made them all feel guilty and responsible for the deaths of mortals they were supposed to protect.

"All right, I'll think about it. But I'm not always going to be the only witch with a soul mirror. Others may pass me in power, and they will most certainly bring skills I don't have." She leaned toward the screen, her eyes filled with the light of hope.

"Carla, for all we know, you could be the Moon Witch."

"We don't know who Sutton belongs to, me or Keri." But Carla wanted him. He made her feel alive, made her crave his touch and he made her feel safe. Had she ever felt like this? It wasn't right! Here she was, infatuated like a teenager while Keri was trapped in a rogue's knife. She thought of trying to reach Keri on the astral plane and a new thought scared her. "Keri's getting weaker. What if I'm shutting her out because I want Sutton for myself?" Could she be that horrible?

"You're not. You're doing everything you can to hold on to her."

"How do you know?"

Darcy stared at her. "Easy. You would have slept with him. Your need for his touch is so strong I can feel it. It's getting worse for you. Hurting you. And Sutton's turning into a bear. No, you're holding on to Keri. We're going to free her."

"Right, okay, just checking." She laughed, trying to close up the gulf of fear. "As long as I don't jump him, I'm good."

Chandra stuck her head in the office. "Carla, a man named Max is here to see you and he's rather determined."

"Carla." Max moved up behind her mom. "Please, talk to me."

Darcy waved from the screen and disappeared. Carla watched as Max walked into her office, around the desk to sit on the comer near her chair. He fixed his dark soulful eyes on her and said, "I know you're mad at me, but I need to understand why exactly."

She steadied herself and answered, "I was mad at myself for telling you."

He took that hit with a wince. "Why? Didn't you think I'd believe you?"

"I knew you'd believe me." He had, she noticed.

Immediately. Some of it was Max's sociology studies. He'd need an open mind for that kind of study, and then, over time, he'd studied enough different cultures to realize how big the world really was. And he'd seen her work.

"So you tell me, then get angry when I react? When I hope that your ability might allow us to do more good, save more people?"

Put like that, she wondered if she'd overreacted. Everyone had their emotional buttons.

He picked up a small silver eagle and played with it in his fingers. "I was hurt that you never told me, never confided in me. I felt like an outsider in my own clinic. Everyone else there knew. And John's murder..." He dropped his gaze to the figurine in his hands.

Her own throat constricted. "I'm so sorry about John. He was a good man—and he had no chance against rogues." Her eyes burned with tears. John had been a big man with a large heart. The girls had learned to trust his quiet ways. How many of them had he taught to shoot and basic self-defense, making them feel more powerful? She closed her eyes and leaned her head back.

Max picked up her hand. How many times had he touched her and she'd wished she felt something more? She could always feel the need in him, but in herself, she felt only friendship.

"You saved my life, didn't you? In that exam room, after that killer hit me, I felt something explode in my head, then everything went black."

"I was pretty sure you had a concussion. I did what I could to stop the swelling and heal the damage."

"You care about me. You know I care about you. We're a team. Look at the work we do. It doesn't have to change, but we can deepen it. Care for and comfort each other. I can be there for you, Carla. It doesn't matter to me that you're a witch. It matters that you're Carla."

This was the world she belonged in, a mixed world of science and magic. A controlled world. Not Sutton's wild and passionate world.

Keri's world.

"Carla," a deep voice said from her doorway.

"Sutton!" She dropped Max's hand and jumped to her feet. Her heart lurched, then pounded. "What are you doing here?" His body overflowed the doorframe as if the space couldn't contain him.

"Your father is here. Thought you'd like to know." He turned and walked away.

Max had risen to his feet and stood, watching.

Carla rushed past Max. "My father? Sutton, wait!"

In the family room, he stopped, keeping his back to her. "He's in the kitchen with your mom."

"What? How?" She barely skidded to a stop on her bare feet before running into him. Reaching out, she touched his back. "Sutton." All his muscles contracted into steel, but she thought she felt a brush of feathers so poignant and sad that it brought tears to her eyes. What was this? "Please, tell me what's going on."

He turned and looked down at her. "You needed your dad, I got him for you."

"I don't understand." Her nerves were dancing all over her skin, making her wish he'd touch her.

"Your mom said you needed him and he refused to help you. I changed his mind, now he's here. I have to go."

"No!"

He surprised her by touching her face.

All the sparking on her skin settled down and her stomach warmed. For a second, it felt like the world would be okay. Then he shattered her.

"It's okay, Carla. Don't look so guilty. If Max is who

you care about—" He bit off the words. "I just need to leave."

She grabbed on to his hand against her face. "We're just friends."

His eyes were heartbreaking. "Baby, I have enhanced hearing. I heard you and him talking even before we got inside the house. I saw you crawling across the glass and blood to get to him."

That wasn't fair. Nothing about this was fair. "And on the astral plane? Do you think I'd be naked there with every man I find?"

He ground his jaw for a second, making the eagle earring twitch and catch light. Finally, he said, "No. You're the other half of my soul, you can't help the physical reaction. We can't help it." He lifted his palm off her face, shook off her hand, turned and left.

The loss of his touch left her raw with pain. She knew Max and her mom were watching her, and she couldn't even think about her father. Instead, she ran out of the house after Sutton. "You aren't going to walk out on Keri, damn it!"

He was halfway inside his truck. He backed out of the door and whipped around. "Keri? Or you?"

It was tearing her up, breaking her into chunks. Her powers churned and roiled painfully inside of her. "I'm barely holding on to her. Keri's slipping away."

"Answer me, Carla. Are you afraid I'm walking out on Keri or you?"

She was in so deep, it didn't matter. "Me."

He reached out in a blur, lifting her off her bare feet, and pulling her into his chest. "I'm here. We'll find Keri."

She buried her face in his chest, feeling the weight of her fears ease. "I went to the astral plane and she wasn't there. What if I'm doing it? What if I'm letting her go?"

Sutton turned around and settled her on the seat of

his truck. Bracing his arms on the doorframe, he said, "Look at me."

She lifted her head and looked into his eyes. "The curse, aren't you—"

He shook his head. "I was. Until I touched you. Now tell me why you think you'd let Keri go?"

She'd already told Darcy. But still, her stomach clenched, while her chakras opened wide, trying to pull at Sutton. He'd been so honest with her. He'd even gone to San Francisco and gotten her dad to help them. As much as she wanted to look away, to hide, she kept his gaze and answered, "So I can have you."

His eyes flared and his body went absolutely still. "You're not going to have to choose. You won't ever have to choose."

She couldn't get her emotions under control, but she could clear up his misunderstanding. "I don't want Max. Not like that. I knew he had feelings for me, and I kept thinking maybe once I got past my grief for Keri, I'd feel something for him." Sutton deserved the truth from her. "But then I met you."

His eyebrows rose. "And?"

He had her caged in the truck with his massive body, yet she wasn't afraid. "You brought me my father." He didn't do it to get anything from her, he did it because she needed her dad. He wasn't trying to use her for her powers, or dissect her. She never had to pretend with Sutton.

Trying to rein in her feelings, she let her gaze slide from his. Over his massive chest covered in a dark T-shirt, down to his camouflage pants that did nothing to camouflage his huge erection. Her mouth went dry and desire swept through her. She was causing him pain, either bloodlust or sex lust. And he let her, because he wouldn't force her to choose. Instead he protected her, cared enough to hunt down and bring her father to her.

"I want to be the one who frees you from the curse. I want to but I can't let Keri stay trapped in a rogue's knife. And I can't take you from her if you belong to her."

His hand slid to her hair, gliding his palm over her scalp and down the length. "I belong to you. But we aren't going to take any chances with Keri. I won't risk your bond with her." He sifted her hair through his fingers, then closed his empty fist.

She was hurting him! She couldn't do anything about it, couldn't use her powers to ease him, nor could she touch him. She squeezed her hands together. "None of this is fair to you. I'm using you. You're doing everything and I'm giving nothing in return." She was like her father, taking and using. Pain took hold behind her eyes while her stomach boiled with frustration as her powers struggled to get to him, but they couldn't find a connection. It felt like electricity building until the pressure was nearly unbearable.

His blue eyes darkened. "You're my reason to keep breathing." His body shuddered and she saw him anchor his arms to the doorframe. "When I was seventeen, I learned that we can only hold out against the curse for so long, then we have to make the right choice. My dad, uncle and I rescued a witch. But my uncle's time was up, and he went after the girl. My father shot him through the heart, killing him while he still had his soul."

Her skin hurt with the need to touch him, and she clutched her hands together in her lap to resist. "He killed his own brother." Carla couldn't imagine making the choice. But at the same time, Sutton's dad had saved his brother's soul. "What happened after that?"

He took a breath and said, "Dad and I got the girl to safety. Then my dad told me that when our time came, we had a choice—we could die honorably with our souls, or live as monsters. Then he got into our small airplane and flew off into a mountainside."

"Leaving you alone?"

"I'm not alone, not anymore." He leaned an inch closer. "You are my soul, Carly. I can endure anything for you."

It took her breath away the way he caressed her name into an endearment. "I want to touch you."

His voice throttled down. "Bring me to the astral plane when you're finished talking to your father. I will touch you. Kiss you. Hold you."

She felt her powers tremble in her throat. Her communication chakra wanted to explode open and do exactly what he said. But caution reared up in the form of Keri. "We can't finish the bond, not even there."

His smile was wicked. "We won't. And that's as much as I promise. Now go. Before I lose control." He stepped back from the opening of the truck.

She slipped down to the ground, then glanced up at his white fingers digging into the roof of the truck. The hell of it was that she almost wanted him to lose control. She turned and forced herself to go into the house.

11

HER LEGS FELT LIKE LEAD, her head buzzed with too many thoughts, and her heart was racing. She walked inside, shut the door and listened to Sutton's truck drive away.

"You never trusted me, did you?"

Caught by surprise, she jerked her thoughts to the man confronting her. *Max.* His lean body threw off angry vibes, while his deep brown eyes were a stew of hurt and betrayal.

"Your father is the psi-geneticist Dr. Wagner, and you never thought to mention that? I've read most of his research, Carla. I've probably mentioned him to you half a dozen times and you never said a word. You're just full of secrets, aren't you?"

Tired of defending herself, she said, "Keri and I grew up keeping our father's identity something of a secret. Jerome insisted. He was in the media so much that if anyone ever made the connection that his daughters were witches, it would be easy for rogue witch hunters to find us. He didn't want us in danger." *Didn't want to lose his test subjects.* She knew that was unfair of her. Jerome did love her and Keri as much as he was capable.

"And you think I would have betrayed you?"

She hesitated.

His shoulders stiffened. "Shit, Carla, I've dedicated my life to protecting victims!"

"Exactly," she said. "And if it came down to a choice of keeping my secrets, or theirs, which would you choose?"

He jerked back and glared at her. "What kind of question is that?"

"Answering a question with a question is a defense mechanism." It told her what she hadn't wanted to know. She'd worked with him for well over a year, developed a solid friendship, but he was right that she hadn't ever trusted him.

Not like she trusted Sutton.

"I'm not one of your patients," he fumed in a low voice.

"You know what's interesting, Max?" She didn't let him answer. "You haven't asked me who Keri is." Nor had he asked her about her relationship with Sutton. He was too focused on her father.

His expression clouded as he obviously backtracked through the conversation. "She's your sister. You said 'Keri and I grew up keeping our father's identity something of a secret.'"

"She's my *twin* sister and she was murdered by a rogue witch hunter right in front of me. And my dad's reaction—that world-famous psi-geneticist you admire so much—on the day of Keri's murder was to tell me that now that she was dead, I could go back to work with him. And if I refused, then he didn't ever want to see me again."

He reached out to her. "Carla, maybe he thought work would help you cope."

She shrugged off his touch. "No, he was furious because I had chosen Keri over him. Keri and I worked in a holistic healing clinic. But with Keri dead, Jerome thought he could have me back. I was his lab rat, his 'subject' for his research. Keri and I both were until she wised up and rebelled."

"Lab rats? Subjects? Don't you think you're being a little dramatic? He's trying to help mankind, Carla. It didn't mean he didn't love you, or grieve for your sister. But can you imagine what identifying the magic gene would mean?"

She reached over and yanked the front door open. "Goodbye, Max."

He walked through the doorway, then turned and looked back at her. "Carla..."

"Don't. You used to look at me and see a woman who happened to be a psychologist with special skills. Now you look at me as a witch and a scientific curiosity. *This* is why I never told you." She shut the door.

She heard her parents' voices coming from the kitchen, but she leaned back against the entryway wall and took a moment to get her anger under control. She had to face her father calmly.

He'd hung up on her when she'd called and asked him for help. She put her fist over the hole that burned between her ribs. All his promises to her about how they were going to combine science and magic... "Enough," she said softly.

She thought of Sutton wrapping his arms around her, pulling her off her feet and into his chest. She heard his words. *"I'm here,"* he'd said. *"We're going to find Keri."* They weren't pretty or fancy words, but they were real words that she could count on. They meant everything to her.

He had brought Jerome to her.

And she would take it from there. Sutton hadn't missed how hard this was for her. He'd understood that Jerome made her choose between two people she'd loved, her sister and her father. And yet, Sutton had never once suggested that she couldn't handle dealing with him.

She followed the voices into the kitchen. Her parents sat at the breakfast nook table. Jerome was hunched over a cup of coffee, his hair hanging over his bearded face. His shoulder blades protruded beneath his long-sleeved pullover. The last two years sat on him like a full decade. Something she hadn't expected tugged behind her ribs. Love. She still loved her father. Before she could think about that too much, she walked to the table and sat in the chair across from him.

That put her mom between them.

Chandra laid her hand on Carla's forearm. "I've been telling Jerome as much as I know."

Her mom's palm was slightly clammy from worry and maybe nerves at having Jerome there. She could feel the residue of her mom's magic in the air, and assumed Chandra'd been clearing the alcohol toxins from her dad's body. Carla covered her mom's hand. "We're going to find Keri." She turned to look her dad in the eyes for the first time in two years. "And he's going to help us."

"Not like you're giving me much choice."

His brown eyes were pale and empty, as if the broken blood vessels around his nose had bled out his passion. He used to care...maybe he cared too much. Loved his science and his theories too much, but he had cared, damn it. Cold rage iced her words. "Keri's soul is trapped in a knife. She's alone, forced to watch bloody slaughters of other witches. We can't leave her like that. I won't leave her like that." She leaned forward and added, "She doesn't have a choice—so why the hell should you?"

His brown eyes sharpened. "She wouldn't listen." He slapped his hand down on the table, rattling his cup. "She never listened. She practically advertised to rogues with that damned clinic. And it got her killed!"

"Stop it now," Chandra's voice was firm. "Keri is dead. We can't change that. All we can do is free her from the knife so she can go on to her next life. Jerome. Do this for Keri. I know you loved her."

The skin on his face tightened, pulling back over his bones so that for a brief second, there was naked grief. Then he dropped his shoulders and chin. It seemed a real effort to look at Carla. "You are sure she's trapped in this knife?"

She blinked at the shift in him. "Yes."

His gaze sharpened. "How? Have you tested this theory?"

She could feel the years peeling away under his questions. Like she was a young witch again, doing the magic, measuring the results, then doing blood tests to see if he could isolate any changed markers. "I know from our twin bond. You tested that yourself, Jerome. You know Keri and I were linked psychically."

He frowned. "Death didn't break the bond?"

Her mother's hand spasmed on her arm, and her heart matched the motion. But she had to concentrate. "For almost two years, I thought it had. When I did feel her, I thought it was just a manifestation of my grief. That day when Keri died, I think she was trying to bind her soul to my witch book." Carla held up her arm with the silver band around her biceps. "But she accidentally got caught in the rogue's knife."

He turned his cup between his hands. "What's she connecting to in you?"

"Residual power. We shared power, and could access each other's chakras."

He looked up, his bloodshot eyes grim. "I have to see what happened, Carla. Show me what happened the day she was killed."

She jerked her gaze to her mom.

"Go ahead."

Carla rose, picked up Chandra's computer, then she sat down next to her dad. Angling the screen so she and her dad could both see it, she said, "I'm going to use my communication chakra and project my memory onto the screen." Carla closed her eyes and felt the first four pops along her spine. Then she pushed the powers and opened her fifth chakra. Reaching for the memory, she directed it to the screen.

In seconds the memory dragged her back to two years ago. She was running late. Wearing a black skirt and a yellow sweater, she juggled a cup of hot tea and shoved open the front door with her hip. She was thinking about her patient, a woman suffering brain damage from a rogue's brainwashing. They were making excellent progress, she thought, as she let the door shut behind her.

She froze in fear. *Copper!* She smelled rank copper and blood.

She turned to face the reception area. On the right was a bamboo desk in front of a forest-print silk screen. The rest of the walls were pale green and lined with bamboo chairs. Blood spattered everything in sight.

The cup of hot tea slid from her hand and hit the floor. She remembered that hot spatter on her legs. But what she saw ripped through her shock. A huge man smelling of old copper was on top of Keri, slicing her up and covering himself in her blood.

Carla raced across the room, jumping on him, trying to pull him off Keri.

She saw her sister beneath him, her hazel eyes almost completely yellow with pain. Her skin was pale, her witch-shimmer was limp and gray, clearly dying.

The rogue jumped up, throwing her off him. Carla remembered landing on her back on the woven mat covering the bamboo floor, rolling to her hands and knees, and reaching out her fingers to Keri.

Then the sudden slide of cold across her lower back, and a second later, searing agony. She'd been cut! But still she reached for Keri.

Keri turned and looked at her, and Carla felt her chakra suddenly fill up. She recognized her sister grabbing hold of her chakras. Then she was picked up and thrown back by Keri using Carla's power. Carla hit the wall, and slid down.

"Run!" Keri screamed.

Carla jumped to her feet, her gaze locked on her sister while her chakras shivered and trembled as Keri summoned tremendous magic...

At the same time, the rogue arced his knife down and hit her heart.

Carla's chakras deflated like a balloon, and she heard the echo of Keri's voice begging her, "Run! Go, Carla!"

Carla opened her eyes and the computer screen went blank. Thick greasy nausea roiled in her stomach. "I didn't know it then, but he stabbed her that last time just as she pulled enough power from my chakras to send her soul to my armband. But her soul hit the silver knife that killed her." She swallowed hard. "And I ran." Carla the coward. She should have let the rogue kill her with that knife. If she had, she would have sensed Keri's soul and pulled it with her to Summerland.

Shutting the computer, she looked up at her dad.

He leaned back in his chair and closed his eyes. "She didn't have to die. If you two had listened, had stayed with me in the lab and worked—"

"This isn't about you," Carla said coldly.

He opened his eyes. "Her soul is in that knife. Watching it on the computer, I saw a flash of light that burst from her body and hit the knife." He spread his hands on the table, looking at his fingers. "Tell me what she's doing to make you think she's communicating with you."

Carla outlined the two months of smelling incense and seeing eagles, then described the incident with Pam.

Jerome shook his head in amazement. "Keri never tested out with this kind of power or discipline."

"Keri hated being cooped up and forced to sit still. She needed to physically move and be with people. Her power grew when she was with people. I tried to tell you this, but you wouldn't listen. Witches need touch, and Keri especially needed contact with other people. I believe that energy fed her psychic powers, calming her so she could access her chakras. But when you tried to isolate her, make her sit in a room, her chakras closed up."

Her dad slammed his fist down on the table. "I was trying to find the answer to keep you alive!"

"Jerome." Chandra reached out and put her hand on his arm.

His mouth pulled tight, accentuating the tired lines around his eyes. He folded his hand around the coffee cup and dropped his head. "Carla, what is it that you want from me? I don't have the magic to get Keri out of the knife."

Carla looked at her mom across the table. "Did you tell him about soul mirrors?"

"As much as I know."

Looking back at her dad, she said, "Sutton, the man who brought you here is either my soul mirror, or Keri's. We're not sure which." She traced the top of the laptop on the table. "It gets more complicated. Sutton is being pulled into the bond Keri and I have. Maybe he's giving our bond more strength since soul mirrors act like familiars."

Jerome's eyebrows drew together and he turned to

Chandra. "That's why you lost your familiar. Your soul was halved. I wasn't going to be able to solve the problem with science."

Chandra kept her hand on his arm. "We didn't know. You were trying to help me when I was so desperate." Her dad didn't seem to know where to look. He studied his mug before finally returning his gaze to Carla. "So why can't you use the twin bond to find Keri?"

She had to make this as clear as she could. "Asmodeus found Sutton and me on the astral plane. When he appeared Keri screamed a warning, then she helped me get Sutton back to the mortal world."

Her father's eyes widened.

Carla went on. "And since then, something has happened. Someone was able to pull me into a vision that has nothing to do with my or Keri's magic. Sutton was there, too, but I didn't see or feel Keri."

"What was it?"

"I don't know. I couldn't get a feel for their power or track them. It's like he trapped my mind or... I don't know."

"You panicked."

"Yes." No sense in denying it. "I need you to help me find out what this is that's pulling me into visions. And I need to understand what this bond is so I can find Keri." He lifted his mug and drained the coffee in it. Then he set it down. "We need to design a way for you to resist panicking and track..."

His voice faded and she was spiritually yanked out of her body. The kitchen fell away from her and she felt her mind being shoved into a dark place. Then suddenly, a massive brick wall was rising up around her in a tight circle, going up and up until the isolated terror made her scream. But the scream echoed back on her in waves of endless agony.

A tiny hole appeared in the prison, and began to

widen. Carla was desperate to break out of the dark trap, but terrified of what she was going to see.

Sutton drove around the back of the Axel of Evil nightclub. He started to pull into the parking garage of the warehouse when he saw a shadow. He cut the engine and the lights of the car, jumped out, and got a nose full of copper.

A new rogue. The older the rogue, the more witch blood they absorbed through their skin and the ranker they smelled. Mortals couldn't smell it, but witches and hunters could.

Was it Brigg?

The pulsing beat of music and loud voices bled out of the club, but he didn't hear anything else. His eagle had gone deadly silent and still, seeing the rogue as a threat to Carla. He didn't understand this new, vivid awareness of what should just be a tattoo, but the creature was as real to him as his own heart beating in his chest. Both man and eagle began to hunt, tracking the scent of new rogue.

The club and warehouse were in one huge two-story building. Facing the back of the building, the club was on the left, the warehouse on the right. The second floor held condominiums and offices. Axel had a large condo. Joe and Morgan also had one. There were empty ones that the men used as needed. But the rogue scent slipped away from the building, heading down the alley into the part of town where entrepreneurs conducted business out of condemned buildings shadowed by broken streetlights and human desperation.

Sutton concentrated and shielded his presence, then followed the scent. The rogue was invisible, too, but the scent-trail led him over broken sidewalk, around a sleeping drunk, and into the dark halls of a building that had recently been destroyed by fire. The back part of the building was gone, and the front was a maze of smoke-blackened walls. The burned smell confused the copper scent.

It hit him that this was a trap. He'd fallen for the lure like a mouse for cheese.

Stopping, he pulled out his phone, hit 911, and sent a text to all the Wing Slayer Hunters. The GPS on his phone would lead them to him.

A woman's scream came from his left, raising the hairs on his arms and neck. He inhaled, catching a scent of rogue in the smoke damage, but no witch scent. It had to be a mortal woman screaming. Keeping his shield of invisibility, he tracked the sound, going deeper into the remaining shell. It was a maze of hallways and partitions.

A light spilled out of a doorway down a hall, and the sound of a woman crying. He followed the sound, slowly, silently.

Behind the last door in the hallway, a mortal woman was hunched down in the corner. A lantern sat on the floor next to her. Her clothes were torn, blood trickled out of her mouth, and a fresh handprint blazed across her face. The room was empty, except for her. Someone had obviously hit her and made her scream, but where was that someone? Materializing, Sutton took a step into the room just as he saw that she was holding something in her hand.

She lifted her big brown eyes to him.

The blankness there caused all the hairs on his skin rose. He stopped.

The woman brought up her hand.

Before he could react, the room exploded with a huge flash and deafening bang. He thought he felt rough hands on his shirt yanking him back just as his brain registered *bomb*.

He couldn't hold on to the thought because the whole burned-out building was spinning away from him, replaced by a vortex of white and blue fog. He must be spinning into death. Had the mortal woman killed them both? Why?

Then he smelled lavender.

The spinning stopped, and in the fog a woman began to take shape. He could only see her outline. "Carly." Was he dead and saying goodbye to her? Losing her for eternity?

She turned, stress tightening the shape of her face. "Sutton. Keri can't help them. I can't help them."

"Carla, baby, take my hand." He held out his arm, reaching for her. He had no idea what was going on, but he needed her touch to find out.

Her hand slid into his.

The fog pushed back and they were looking down into a room again. They stood there, but they weren't really there. Sutton could feel Carla's hand, but if he reached out to touch a wall, it wasn't there. His hand just moved through it.

He focused on the scene. The witch was middle-aged, with streaks of silver in her short, sleek hair, now darkened with blood and sweat. She was covered in wounds, and the two rogues were on her like animals, burying their hands in her blood, smearing it on their chests.

Then it would fade and disappear.

The witch wasn't screaming anymore.

He couldn't stand there and watch this, couldn't let Carla just watch. "Carla, get us out of here."

"No. I can't panic." Her voice was strong and furious. "The knife. Look, they are sharing a knife."

He looked down and saw that they had been passing a knife back and forth. Witch hunters were particular about their knives. It went back to the pre-curse days when they would take their wings. When the hawk-leader agreed, a witch hunter would have the wings of his choice tattooed on his body. If the Wing Slayer accepted the hunter as one of his, the ring of immortality would appear around the base of his thumbs and the same wings he chose for his tattoo would be magically impressed in the hilt of his knife. That knife was used in duty to the Wing Slayer. Witch hunters, even rogues, were fiercely possessive of their knives.

"Listen."

He unlinked their hands to put his arm around Carla, pulling her in closer to his body. Then he listened.

Free me. Dying. Can't hold on much more.

Chills chased over his skin and he looked down at her. "Your sister?"

Her eyes were dry with horror. "She's in that knife down there. The rogues can't hear us, but Keri can."

"Can she tell us anything else?"

Carla's voice was brittle when she said, "Keri, who has you?"

Styx.

The horror of Carla's twin trapped in a rogue's knife cut Sutton to his soul. He said, "Hang on, Keri. We're going to get you. Keri, you hear me?"

Eagle...

They were thrown from the vision. Sutton desperately tried to hold on to Carla but she was wrenched from him.

When he slammed into his body, there were hands holding him down. He jerked and fought.

"Sutton! It's me," Axel yelled at him.

"Where am I? I need a computer!" His head was still spinning, and his eagle was clawing him so deeply he could feel the talons in his chest.

Axel had both hands on his shoulders. "In the warehouse. Your face and chest are burned, but Linc pulled you back before the blast killed you. Darcy's trying to heal you, lie still."

He felt Darcy's warm, small hands moving on his chest. But he didn't have time for this. "Carla! She's..."

Axel snapped, "Ram, get Carla on the phone or computer. Darcy?"

"I've got the chair leg out and closed up as much of it as I can."

At his questioning look, Axel explained, "It was blown into the pectoral muscle. Too close to your heart. Linc saved your life. If he hadn't jerked you when he did, it would have gone straight through your heart."

He'd be dead. The pain in his chest was beginning to make sense. He had assumed it was the eagle clawing at him, worried about Carla, but normally he only felt that on his back.

"I've got Carla on the computer, she's okay." Ram's shadow fell over them.

"Let me sit up. A, give me your shirt. I don't want her to see my chest." He shoved to a sitting position. Pain stabbed through the right side of his chest. Fuck, that hurt.

Axel stood, reached down and lifted Sutton to his feet, got him to the black leather couch and eased him down. "No shirt. Darcy's already telling Carla." He tilted his head.

Sutton saw Darcy talking to Carla while Ram stood there obediently holding the laptop for her.

"I got it out, and the deeper wound closed, but I can't seem to heal him any more." Her dark eyes glanced at him, then back at the screen. "What am I doing wrong?"

Carla's voice floated from the computer speakers. "Nothing, it's me. I'm the one hurting him."

Sutton fisted his hands at his sides, hating the pain in her voice. "It's not your fault." He knew she'd hear him; the mike on the computer was very sensitive.

"Yes, it is," her voice came back. "Somehow I pulled Sutton's spirit out of his body and into a vision with me. My magical hold on his spirit is blocking some of your magic trying to heal his body."

He started to rise, needing to see Carla's face. Damn it, he needed to touch her.

Darcy took the computer from Ram, walked over to Sutton and sat down next to him. She set the machine on her lap and angled the screen to him.

Carla's gaze stared out, the layers of color in her gaze sharpening. "Oh, Sutton." She tracked over his face and chest, the yellow color dominating in her hazel eyes, showing her worry. "I'm coming over."

"No." He closed his eyes, fighting down the growing dual hungers for her. He ached to touch her and seal the bond that would make them both whole. His eagle fretted and pined for her, wanting to be her creature, her familiar. But the fierce burn on his chest and face stirred the ugly craving for her blood. He could almost smell the rich Arabian coffee scent that would cool the pain burning his skin and deeper into his bones. He remembered the feel of her blood, so cool and powerful...

"I can't stand to see you hurt. I can heal you." Her voice was soft, almost pleading.

He pulled himself back from the brink of darkness. "It's too dangerous for you to come here. I just got ambushed. A rogue witch hunter lured me into a building, then smacked around a mortal woman, making her scream so I'd respond. When I found her, she was alone in a room. It was a mortal woman, Carla. She had the control to the bomb in her hand, and once she saw me, she pressed the button to blow us both up. You are not coming near this place." He looked up at Ram. "Where were the explosives?"

"They were strapped to the woman. She's dead."

Linc and Key walked in from the back alley. Key added, "No identification anywhere. We've searched, but there's no sign of the rogue."

Sutton looked past Key to Linc. "It was Brigg. I saw a shadow and smelled a new rogue. It was him lurking around the back of the club when I pulled up. I followed him and—"

Linc's eyes shuttered. "Did you actually see him?"

He had to think. "No."

Linc nodded but didn't comment.

Remembering what Axel had told him, he said, "You pulled me out, why were you there?" The 911 he sent only went to Axel, Ram, Phoenix and Key. It automatically activated the GPS on the sender's cell, so each phone was getting directions to where the 911 call came from. But he hadn't added Linc to the emergency system yet.

"I was in the club," Linc answered.

Key added, "Phoenix is dealing with the police. Telling them it's a meth lab that blew, that we heard it at the club and checked it out."

"That works." Sutton returned his gaze to the computer.

Carla's face was pale, but her eyes were bright and furious. "It was another brainwashed woman. It's Styx. He has my sister, and he's brainwashing these women into killing."

The edge in her voice made his eagle tat twitch and shuffle, infuriated that he couldn't touch her. Couldn't use his feathers to cuddle and stroke her. Sutton wanted to touch her so goddamned badly, he could barely resist going to her now. His entire body went tight with vicious need, while the pain of the burns made him dizzy. Christ. They needed answers. "What does your father say?"

She looked away from him, then turned the

computer and shifted so the two of them sat together.

Jerome looked at Sutton. "From the way Carla describes him getting a lock on her mind, yanking her from her body, and dropping her into a room, then almost instantaneously building a brick prison around her, I'd say you're dealing with a very powerful psychic. Or more specifically, a psychic who has found a way to amp up his or her natural abilities. In my studies, I've found most mortals who are psychic have low-level abilities, like knowing a phone will ring seconds before it does."

Sutton shifted his gaze to Carla. "That's what it feels like? Like your mind is being captured?"

"That's the best way to describe it."

How did she endure it? He remembered her refusing to leave this time, looking around and realizing that the knife being used on the witch had her sister in it. Her mind had been held prisoner but she'd had the strength to think and observe. "You don't think it's a witch, maybe a demon witch?"

"Few witches have the kind of power to separate the mind from the body."

Pride filled him as he said, "You do."

Her eyes lit up at his tone of voice, then she sobered. "I do, but it makes even witches nervous. Witches who can open their communication chakra can meditate themselves to the astral plane, but most can't take the subconscious of another with them."

From his left, Darcy added, "Some in the Circle Witches are trying to say that Carla's misusing her power."

Sutton whipped his head around to Darcy, caught the gold fury in her brown eyes and shifted back to Carla. "You didn't tell me that."

She waved a hand. "It's not important. My point is that I know what that kind of witchcraft feels like and this isn't it."

The witches weren't supporting her and she called that unimportant?

Darcy put her hand on his tense arm. "Carla has friends, Sutton. It's just a few in the Circle causing some trouble. We'll handle it. More important is finding a way to track this psychic."

Carla had been the one witch to help Darcy when no other would risk it. She was strong, smart and resourceful. And she had a hell of a friend in Darcy. He asked Carla, "How is he locking onto you?"

Jerome said, "My hypothesis is that he's got Keri and he's locking onto the twin-witch bond. We believe you're in that bond, too. It's become a three-way bond."

Darcy inhaled next to him. Sutton saw the agony color Carla's eyes. "What does that mean?"

"Keri's soul is tapping in to Carla's blood and power. And you've partly formed your soul-mirror bond with one of them by touching her blood, then Carla touching yours."

Sutton didn't like this. "Carla's my soul mirror."

"You don't know that," Carla whispered.

She had told him her fear that she was letting Keri slip away from her to keep Sutton for herself. But he knew, his eagle knew, they belonged to her. "I know, baby." He didn't give a shit who heard him. "My eagle knows. He recognizes you."

"She called you Eagle."

Her sadness was making his eagle tat burn as badly as his chest. "My eagle belongs to you. Only you. Believe in that, Carla. In the meantime, we won't do anything to cut Keri out of the bond. We'll both hold on to her until we can find and free her." He would never make her choose. He already knew she was coming to care for him, to trust in him. He could feel it. No matter how painful it was, they would wait until Keri was freed to go on to her next life and Carla was ready.

Her gaze softened. "I need to heal you, Sutton. You won't help Keri or me like this."

His eagle danced over the back of his skin, wanting to do her bidding and practically quivering for her touch. But it was too dangerous, he was too close to losing control of himself. "I can't." He closed his eyes, struggling to restrain the raging hungers boiling inside him. The pain in his chest and face fed the dueling agonies of dark curse and unfulfilled soul-mirror bond. Her sister's soul was dying. They had to find Styx and do it now, before he managed to destroy Carla or kill off Keri. He opened his eyes and said, "I'm fine, I heal fast. Right now I'm going to get to work to find Styx so we can free Keri."

$\rightleftharpoons$ *12* $\rightleftharpoons$

CARLA CHECKED ON HER FATHER. He was working in her little office, hunched over her computer and his laptop. There were deep craters beneath his eyes, his skin was loose and he was too thin. That tug behind her ribs tightened. "Do you need anything?"

He looked up at her. "Why can't Keri get out of the knife? If she got in, why can't she get out?"

"She doesn't actually have her powers. She's tapping into mine because we're connected."

"How would she have gotten out of your armband if she had bound her soul there?"

Carla leaned against the doorframe. "Maybe I could have freed her with a spell, but that would probably take higher magic than I have. But—worst-case scenario—she'd stay there until I died, then her soul would leave with mine."

"Because of the twin bond, you could keep her soul alive."

"Yes."

"You're keeping her soul alive now?"

Her skin went icy and sweaty at the same time. She hadn't thought of it that way. "Yes. She existed for two years, maybe able to pull just enough from me. But

170

Dad, what she's seeing, what she's experiencing, it's destroying her soul..." She trailed off as the scent of incense filled the room.

"She's dying all over again," he said. "Why couldn't she reach you before now, Carla?"

Why did she smell the incense? Was Keri trying to reach their father? Softly, she asked, "Do you miss her at all, Dad?"

He jerked his gaze up to Carla, then away. "What difference does it make? It didn't make any difference to her."

Carla rubbed the ache in the scar at the base of her spine.

"What allowed Keri to reach you after two years?"

"I think Sutton touched my blood and that began to form the soul-mirror bond. It strengthened either my power or hers. And she recognized him." Sutton kept saying he recognized Carla, but Keri was the one who recognized him. "Somehow it gave her the strength to reach me. And she saw Pam on the astral plane and got between us. She's been protecting Pam." That was just like Keri.

Heal him.

She jumped at the voice. "Keri?"

Jerome shook his head impatiently. "Yes, we're talking about Keri. What about when Pam shot Sutton? If Keri thinks Sutton belongs to her..."

Had she imagined hearing Keri's voice? "Yes. I knew Sutton had been shot, so Keri would have known, too. That could have been the thing that gave her enough power to reach out to me on the astral plane." She frowned. "What does all this have to do with tracking down the psychic?"

"I need to understand how the power matrix is operating. I've never seen anything like this."

She studied her dad, remembering how much she had idolized him, how hard she'd tried to please him.

"She's your daughter. I'm your daughter. Not some power matrix..." She trailed off, mad at herself for doing this. Her dad was there to help her find Keri, that was it.

Her dad's face tightened. "I don't have magic, Carla, all I have is science. Keri turned away from me because of it. Do you know how that felt, to be seen as lacking in your own daughter's eyes?"

His words sucked the air out of her lungs. "No. She never thought that."

His eyes lost their shine, going flat and determined. "Fine, believe what you want. All I have left to help Keri is science to figure out a way for you to use your magic to track her to this Styx. And keep Styx from destroying you with the twin bond. That's all I have left to give either of you. Let me work."

Carla walked out of the office, and made her way across the family room. The scent of incense moved with her. "Is that what you thought, Keri? That Dad wasn't worthy because he didn't have magic?"

Hurry. Heal the Eagle.

She paused at the hallway. "Sutton?"

The scar warmed and tingled.

Her heart skipped a beat. "Keri." Her voice trembled with emotion. "Sutton doesn't want me to go to him." She leaned back against the wall in the hallway, afraid to move, afraid to lose her connection. There was so much she wanted to tell Keri, the words, thoughts and emotions backed up in her throat.

A soft laughter floated around her. *"Don't ask him. Heal him."*

She could feel her sister laughing at Carla's caution. At the same time, the incense scent faded, and her scar cooled. She couldn't lose contact! "Keri! I have to know: Is he your soul mirror?"

She was gone. A deep ache of loneliness settled between her breasts. Her mom and Pam were settled for the night, so she went into her own room. Her thoughts were tired and confused, and she had a lingering headache from mentally tangling with Styx.

But Keri was right; Carla was a witch, and she wasn't going to leave Sutton suffering. The image of Sutton with his burned, blistered face and chest made her stomach roll.

He had to be in agony.

She'd seen the jagged line where Darcy had removed the chair leg from his chest and closed the cut. She hadn't been able to heal Sutton any further because Carla had pulled him into the vision.

So it was up to her to heal him. She could do that in the astral plane, but she needed to make sure they were safe from Asmodeus first. She didn't have enough power to set a salt circle that would protect them, but she knew someone who did. She picked up her cell and called Darcy.

Sutton stared at the computer monitor, trying to find a comfortable position to sit in. He wore only pants and boots. His skin was a black-and-red blistered mess. Some blisters oozed a clear crap and it was annoying as hell, almost as annoying as trying to crack the Rogue Cadre computer network.

But his careful tracking had paid off. He'd managed to follow a route from the pool of anonymous proxy servers to the computer that sent a message to one of the rogue's cell phones.

He was in. Now he needed a user name and password to get into the system.

What would Quinn Young use?

Ram walked in, set a cold beer down on his workstation, and then stood behind him and watched. He said, "Key and Phoenix are asking around, seeing if any of the witch hunters have heard of a psychic rogue." Sutton grunted, his brain spinning over the problem of the name and password. "He can't hide forever. His psychic shit won't work on a witch hunter so someone's going to remember him. You know what's bugging me?"

"The third-degree burns?" Ram asked dryly.

He ignored that. "What would Young use to password protect his computer?"

"Can't you do one of your programs to crack it?"

"Tried, the network recognized a threat and shut down. I had to wait for the system to reboot. I have to do this the hard way." And he had to do it fast. Carla had been pulled into visions twice now.

"What makes you think it's Young? He has flunkies do all the work, right?"

Sutton sat up, barely concealing a wince at the flash of pain from the burns. "Shit! That's it. Styx. He's the one sending out the brainwashed mortals to kill us. He's pulling Carla into visions. He's the Rogue Leader, at least in this area."

"But we don't know who he is, just the name Styx."

Sutton felt the burned skin on his face crack when he smiled. "Styx isn't his real name. He chose it. Styx is the river that forms the boundary between earth and Hades in Greek mythology. The souls were ferried across by Charon."

Ram said, "You think he'd use something from that legend to password protect the computer network?"

Sutton reached over, picked up the beer and took a long pull, then let the cold bottle rest in his burned palm. "He's building a whole identity for himself. The powerful river taking people into hell." He set the beer down and said out loud to Styx, "What would you use for a name? Not Styx, but...ah! The whole point of the river is to get into Hades." He typed in *Hades* for the name. "Now the password that crosses us over into the

Rogue Cadre network." He typed in *Charon* for the password. He hit ENTER and waited.

"What happens if it fails?"

Noticing blood oozing from one hand, he wiped it on his pants. "The computer network will shut down." He looked at the screen and almost crowed in triumph. "We're in!"

"Excellent," Ram said while looking over his shoulder. "Now what?"

He started looking at files, beginning with the database of rogues. "Looking for who Styx is." The list of names wasn't that long. When the Wing Slayer Hunters had destroyed the Rogue Cadre compound and computers months ago, they had lost everything. Rebuilding was taking time.

"Sutton."

"Yeah?" He was on a mission now and time was crucial. The need to protect Carla drove him. He noticed that his hand trembled briefly on the mouse. He cared about her. Maybe he loved her. He didn't know.

"I don't see Brigg Cusack's name."

Sutton skipped down to the last names beginning with 'C.' "You're right." But he knew Cusack was rogue. "I'm sure it was him I saw tonight. It smelled like a new rogue, and the shape was right."

"You could be wrong," Ram said.

He wished he was. "I'm not."

"He could be dead."

"Yeah. Shit. But dead is better than rogue." He scrolled up the list, then stopped. "Branch."

"So?"

Sutton leaned back and picked up his beer. "You really do think you're clever, don't you?" The cool glass felt good against his hand. He looked up at Ram. "The name *John River Branch*. I'd bet anything that's our psychic bastard rogue."

Ram snorted. "Branch could mean stick, and spelled another way..."

"Styx. River Styx. River Branch." Sutton drank some beer, enjoying the feel of success, finally. Lowering the bottle, he said, "Got you, you mind-raping bastard. Now I just have to find you..." He frowned as his eagle tat suddenly itched. The room started spinning around him, and the beer bottle slid from his hand. The computer workstation faded into a thick fog.

He smelled lavender and knew. *Carla*. In seconds, he appeared...in a bathroom? He looked around, confused. Then he saw Carla and his brain flatlined. She stood completely naked on a black marble floor, her white-blond hair falling in silvery sheets to her waist. Her witch-shimmer was bright silver, stretching over her shoulders, down her breasts, making her dark nipples stand out enticingly. Her belly had a gentle slope that made him long to bury his face against her and let all that softness surround him. Her hips curved gently and the hair at the apex of her thighs was blond and damp. Her lavender scent was layered with desire and something else...worry? He looked up and caught sight of her armband, the one she was never without as far as he knew. Trying to get his brain off her body, off the need for her beating thickly in his cock, he asked, "Where are we? It looks like a bathroom." There was a huge black marble tub to his right.

She jerked her gaze up. "It is. From Axel and Darcy's condo. Darcy helped me."

He clenched his fists to fight the need to touch her. After he'd brought her father to her house, he'd told her to bring him to the astral plane. Here he could touch Carla, hold her, and he'd intended to show her how much she meant to him, how important she was, making love to her with his hands and mouth. But that was before he'd turned into a burned, leaky mess. She wouldn't let him touch her now, so he had to ask, "To do what?"

"Darcy set a salt circle for me. It's spell magic and I can't do it. So she set it up, then I pulled the scene into the astral plane. It should work."

"To keep Asmodeus out." Did she want to talk, try to figure out what to do next? How to find Keri? She wasn't going to let him touch her while he was such a mess. No woman would. And yet, she'd pulled him into the astral plane naked. That told him how deeply Carla trusted him, and desired him when he wasn't looking like something that had just been barbecued.

She shifted on her small feet, looking uncomfortable. "Yes, I wanted to make sure you'd be safe while I heal you."

Shock rushed him, and he was at a loss for words. It didn't make sense. He was supposed to be protecting her. She had Darcy set a salt circle to protect him?

She moved to his side, her hair brushing across his back and sliding over the tattoo. The eagle shuffled and preened, liking that. Then she put her hand on the small of his back. "Come sit on the edge of the tub and you can lean back against the tile. You're not feeling the curse, right?"

Hell, no, he was feeling confusion. The touch of her hand was branding his skin. He let her push him to the tub and he sat, bringing him eye level with her breasts. His mouth dried up as he watched her sway and bob as she moved, those dark nipples so close. Her scent filled his nostrils. He clenched his fists as the cold tile did nothing to ease the ache in his balls. "You don't have to do this."

She fixed her gaze on him. "I want to. You're going to let me."

His cock jumped at her demand. Damn she was sexy when she was bossing him around. "I am?" He sucked in a sharp breath when she placed both her hands on the sides of his face. The burns went poker-hot at the contact, making him hiss. They cooled in seconds, and he could almost feel the dead layers peeling off and new skin growing.

Amazed, he realized she really was healing him.

She pushed his head back to rest against the cool wall and said in a soft voice, "Close your eyes. I need to do this. It hurts me to see you in pain, it makes my chakras ache."

He'd never felt anything like this, the sensation of her taking care of him. He almost didn't want it to end. He wanted her hands on him, needed her touch. Her powers swirled around him, and the eagle seemed to stretch his feathers, wanting to bask in the feel of her coffee-scented witchcraft. It felt like pure energy lighting up his insides and sparkling against his skin. She slid her hands down his neck and over his shoulders. Same thing—the skin sizzled at contact, then cooled and healed, while her powers shivered through him. The sensation traveled down his arms, to his hands.

The eagle stopped spreading and preening, and froze.

He ignored the tattoo. Her hands sloped over his pectorals. He hissed again, the shock of pain fading instantly into cool relief. Caring. It was like being cared for. This was what it felt like?

The tattoo ripped a talon across his back. "Hey!" He snapped open his eyes, jerking his back off the wall.

Carla had dropped to her knees and her hands were on his abdomen. Her beautiful hair curtained her face but her scent was wrong.

He smelled sweat and the sour scent of pain. His tattoo was trying to rip a hole in his back to get out, the bird screeching in his head. He ignored it, lifted a hand, and pushed back Carla's hair.

Her face... Oh, Jesus...her skin was clammy and pale. Her witch-shimmer looked like red holes were burning through the beautiful silver. *She was taking his pain!* Her hands trembled against his stomach. "Stop! Goddamnit, stop!"

She flinched, her hands slipping off him. "What?" Her hazel eyes were swimming in yellow pain. He couldn't believe this. "What is wrong with you!"

She sank back on her heels, her hands twisting in her lap as she panted.

The eagle took another searing swipe of his back, letting him know he was an asshole. He leaned down, scooping her up and bringing her to his chest. "God, baby, I'm sorry I yelled at you." Desperation clogged his throat and he barely got the words out. "Tell me what to do, how to stop your pain."

"Not finished."

Her whole body was trembling. He had to think, but he didn't know enough about witches. How did he help her? Damn it, they were on the astral plane, he couldn't exactly call Darcy and ask her. He didn't have herbs. Hell, he wouldn't know what to do with an herb. He looked around the bathroom, frantically trying to find something...

The tub. Water. Water was the second chakra. Earth elements were essential to witches, so water might help her. He reached out to turn on the tub, but the controls didn't work. They didn't turn on. "Carla." He leaned back, put his hand on her face. "Carla, look at me."

She opened her eyes. "I can finish now. I'm fine."

No way. But he wasn't about to challenge her and make her feel like he didn't appreciate what she'd done for him. She cared enough about him to take his pain. He couldn't even think about that until he took care of her. Instead, he tried to reassure her. "You healed me. Can you fill the bath? Turn on the jets?"

The rules on the astral plane were different. He could move around, and God knows he could feel, but he needed Carla's magic to turn on the water.

Her brows knitted. "I can feel your pain."

He gave her the partial truth and hoped it would satisfy her. "Because my eagle tattoo tried to dig out of my back when he realized you were hurting. He's protecting you. Can you fill the tub? It'll make him feel better if we take care of you."

The water turned on full force. Seconds later the jets started to pulse and stir the water. He rose with her in his arms, stepped over the edge into the half-filled tub and sat down.

She tried to sit up. "I need to look and make sure you're healed."

The swirling hot water made the remaining burns at the base of his stomach feel like someone was skinning him layer by layer. To keep her from seeing, he put his hand on the back of her head and pressed her into his chest. "Let the water take the pain away from you." He watched as her hair floated on the rising water. Having her in his arms, just being able to be skin to skin with Carla, filled him with a warm, rich feeling he couldn't identify.

She had healed him. Taken his pain.

"What about your back?"

He smiled at that. "The eagle is happy now." The tattoo was trying to burrow deeper, like he could crawl through Sutton's back to his chest to touch Carla. Hell, he couldn't blame the bird; he'd crawl through anything to touch and hold her.

She pushed back against his hand cupping her head to look up at him. "He's real to you?"

The water was working, fading the red holes in her shimmer. His chest eased at the sight. "Yes."

She turned to glance at the spigot and the water turned off. Then she shifted her gaze back to him, put her hand on his shoulder, and brushed lightly down to stroke the tattoo.

"Feathers. He's soft."

The tattoo was quivering and all but dancing in his skin. Her touch sent lightning strikes of lust through his balls, and his dick twitched hard in the water.

Her witch-shimmer cleared of all the pain, and brightened to a stunning silver that began to dust with specks of rich gold. Even with the water, he smelled her desire. Her pleasure in stroking his tat was just one of the sexy things about her. He loved watching her.

Her eyes were brimming with her powers. "He feels real to me, too."

"He's yours, Carly."

She shivered in his arms. "Keri told me to bring you here and heal you."

He looked into her eyes while she explained her encounter with her sister. Brushing his fingers over the soft skin of her face, he said, "She sent you to me, baby." He leaned down and brushed his mouth over her full lips. Her taste was like nothing else, warm and slightly sweet, slightly tangy. It filled his mouth and rushed over the back of his tongue, making him want more. He sank into her mouth.

She tightened her hand on the eagle, and slid her tongue against his.

He wanted more of her. He wanted to know what made her moan, what made her sigh, and what would reach deep inside her and wrap around her heart as she had captured his. He'd never had a woman care for him like she had when she healed him. She hadn't even minded touching his burns and cuts. And now, holy God, her small hands were digging into his shoulders as she gave her mouth to him. He broke the kiss.

She opened her eyes, her head angled back over his left arm. "What?"

"I want to touch you." He drew his fingers over her jaw into the hollow of her neck.

She shivered, her witch-shimmer picking up more gold.

He watched his hand trailing over her clavicle bone, riding the slope of her breast. The gold flakes in her shimmer spun around his fingers like dust motes in the sun.

He is touching her magic.

His stomach twisted with the need to slide deep into her body and feel the very core of her. He drew his fingers over her pebbled nipple, and felt the reaction jolt through her body. He cradled the weight of her breast in his palm and drew in a breath, reminding himself of the promise he'd made that they wouldn't seal their soul-mirror connection.

But he could touch her, fill her with pleasure. He moved his hand down her belly, soft and white, then spread his hand out, covering the slope and dipping his thumb down into her pubic hair.

She lifted her gaze. "We—"

The colors of her hazel eyes were blurred with need. His heart pounded and his blood raced. He could fulfill that need. He would. "Trust me. Like I trusted you to heal me. Lift your legs, and rest them on the side of the tub." Carla hadn't yet shown any embarrassment or shame about her body. She had no reason to, she was his perfect golden witch. His heart was thudding louder than the jets pulsing around them. He could barely get his breath and his mouth was bone-dry when he added, "And spread them open for me." His balls were tightening up at the mere thought of her spread open so he could see her. Touch her.

Her belly constricted beneath his palm as she lifted her legs, draping them over the side of the big Jacuzzi tub.

He looked down her long white legs, shimmering with gold. He recognized the gold as her lust, her need, her beauty she was showing only to him. Christ, he wanted to drag his tongue over every golden inch of her until he got to her center, when he'd lap at her until she shattered, and then he'd keep licking her until he could make himself stop. Maybe for hours. Days.

Slow down. She hadn't given her body to anyone in a couple years. To him, it was more than her body, she was sharing her very essence with her trust. She believed in him, knew he wouldn't seal their bond by lifting her up, spreading her thighs, and pressing her down onto his rigid cock. Jesus, he wanted to feel her slick and tight around him, he craved the joining that would bind their souls. But it would cost her too much by breaking her bond with her sister. Instead, he laid his hand on her right thigh. He'd take his joy in stroking her until she came apart for him.

Her muscles clenched, then she let her thighs fall apart.

His dick twitched, his balls seized up. He didn't care. He shifted his gaze to the triangle of blond hair at the junction of her thighs. He trailed his hand upward, watching as his large, dark fingers slipped into her hair.

She made a mewling noise of desire in her throat.

Letting his hand rest so that his middle finger was pressing on her seam, he looked at her face. Her eyes were closed, her mouth open, and her breasts were rising and falling in a beat he recognized. "You want me to touch you, Carly." He needed a response from her, needed to know she wanted this, too.

"Please," she said, her hips rising against his hand.

He parted her hair, and then her folds, and found her slick and warm. Exploring her, he traced her tender flesh, circling the entrance to her body, and he shivered as he felt tiny pulses trying to draw him in.

She shifted against him, her body arching in a wordless plea.

Not yet.

It was like he'd waited his whole life to stroke his witch. Every time he'd seen her on the physical plane, he'd longed to touch her. Learn her. Now he would. Sliding his hand back up, he discovered her little clitoris. He had to see, and leaning over he had a perfect view of her wet, pink flesh just beneath the waterline of the tub. He stroked her clit and watched as each touch swelled and infused it with a gold color.

Lust thudded in his ears.

He wanted more. Curling his left arm tighter around her back, he brought Carla closer into his chest so he could feel the heat blooming on her skin as he slid a finger inside her. How much could she take of him? Her body was hot and wet, and sucking him in. Sweat broke out on his forehead as his finger slid in up to the first knuckle.

Then the second.

Carla was breathing hard, her hips rising to take more.

He could barely breathe as he fed her as much of his finger as she could take until he could almost touch her womb.

"Sutton!" She grabbed on to his wrist with both hands, her fingers digging into his skin. "Too much."

He froze, and started to pull his hand away from her. But when he looked at her face, he noted the intense green in her eyes. Her slick walls began to pulse around his finger and her body threw off more gold into her witch-shimmer. And most telling of all, his eagle quivered in excitement, not anger.

"No," she panted. "Not hurting. Too much. Can't control it."

Her powers squeezed harder, causing her body to buck and thrash, splashing water around them.

Her eyes filled with tears as she thrust against his hand, and he understood what was happening. Her powers were surging up and filling her, trying to reach out to him to pull him in. They were reacting to the soul-mirror connection. Another wave of raw power undulated through her. He could almost feel the brutal ache for relief inside her. An orgasm would release some of the energy pulsing in her.

Sutton leaned over her, feeling a wave of tenderness that nearly left him breathless. He brushed his mouth over her wet cheeks. Using his thumb, he stroked her clit, reveling in the wet flesh infused with her magic. In soft words, he said, "You don't need to be in control, my beautiful, golden witch." He stroked her, sliding his finger in and out of her while keeping that feathering touch on her clit. "I can feel your powers sucking me in, deeper and deeper." He shuddered, letting her feel his desire for her.

More power undulated through her and clamped around his finger. She arched up, desperate for relief.

Sutton licked his way over her jaw, and nuzzled into the hollow of her neck. He couldn't get enough of her, and damn it, he wanted to bury his face between her legs and devour her, but she needed release now. He dragged his tongue over her breast, and then told her, "I can taste your power." His voice was rough with pounding hunger for her. He latched on to her nipple, filling his mouth with her. His tenderness gave way to raw passion. He sucked her as he pistoned his finger as far as she could take him, withdrew, and did it again until he had her bucking and making deep-throated, unbearably sexy noises.

His hips were slapping against the soft flesh, his cock desperate for her. He didn't care, didn't hold back. He was demanding Carla lose control with him, so he could lose control with her.

"Oh!" she cried, and letting go of his wrist, she

reached up and cradled his head, holding him to her breast. He could feel her body tightening and racing toward completion. He pressed the heel of his hand to her clit and pumped his finger in the rhythm that made her whole body tremble. She was so close and so fucking beautiful. He growled against her nipple.

She slammed her hips into him, her body beginning to crest.

No! Mine! a voice screamed.

Not Carla. It wasn't Carla! The instinct to protect her burst inside him. Sutton reacted at hyperspeed, releasing her nipple from his mouth, easing his hand from her body. He jerked her up into his arms, shoved her to the back corner edge of the black marble tub and turned to block her with his body.

He didn't see anything in the bathroom, didn't know where the hell the threat was coming from. He looked back at Carla. "Is it Asmodeus? Did he get through the salt circle?"

$\Longrightarrow$ *13* $\Longleftarrow$

CARLA COULDN'T GATHER HER THOUGHTS. Another sharp pain sliced through her head. Sutton had shoved her onto the edge of the tub and blocked her as if he could protect her.

But the threat was inside her head. From her own sister.

"It's not Asmodeus." It's worse, she thought, as the cold weight of guilt and shame settled over her, escalating her sudden headache. Her voice sounded as tortured as she felt. "It's Keri."

He looked back over his shoulder, the eagle earring in his left ear catching the light. His pupils were still large, but instead of darkening his eyes to sexy midnight blue, now they looked menacing. "I only heard two words. What's she saying now?"

My soul mirror! Keri continued to screech inside her head, making her eyes burn. Carla summed it up for him. "She's saying that I'm letting Pam die. That I'm trying to steal her soul mirror. That I'm letting her die so I can have you."

Furious, he said, "I thought Keri loved you. Why would she...wait, something is wrong." His eyes calmed as he thought.

187

"What?"

"It's not her. Carla, think! First off, Keri told you to take me to the astral plane. And Keri doesn't call me her soul mirror, she calls me *Eagle*, like it's my name. Remember in the last vision when I told her we'd find her? She addressed me as *Eagle*, not by my name. Baby, try touching my tattoo."

Carla lowered her gaze and saw the bird watching her. She moved her hand from her temple to lay it on his back. Instantly, the headache eased and the warm feathers felt like they were folding around her hand. She had the sensation of the bird trying to push his head into her palm and nuzzle her. "He's moving. Touching me."

He kept watching her over his shoulder. "Can you still hear Keri?"

The voice was gone. "No. Just a headache now. What's happening?"

"That bastard Styx is screwing with your mind, screwing with us. I know who he is now. His name is John River Branch. I'll find him. I won't let him do this to you."

A tremor of rage moved through his entire body beneath her hand. Carla stroked her fingers over the majestic eagle soaring across Sutton's back, and she felt both man and bird calming from her touch. To have that kind of power stunned her. She wanted so much to believe that Sutton was hers. She was falling in love with the man and the bird. The man who was so shocked that she would heal him. She wanted to be the one who healed Sutton, who comforted him, who stroked his eagle as she was now, calming his fury. But Keri's voice had felt so real. "You really don't think it was her? Staking her claim?"

He turned around, facing her while on his knees in the water, and laid his hands on her cheeks. "If it was her claim to make, the eagle wouldn't keep her out."

She looked into his eyes, so dark with emotion. Her powers began the bubbling rush, popping and sparking, causing goose bumps on her skin. She tried to focus. "I don't know. I want you so badly, what if I'm blocking her out? Letting her soul die?"

He studied her face, then began to massage her temples. "Trust in my eagle, our eagle. He wouldn't block Keri out. He's helping us hold on to her, not destroy her. Keri knows that, she told you to find the eagle. And she told you to bring me here to heal me."

It made sense. She remembered Keri's soft laughter when Carla'd said Sutton told her not to heal him. She seemed to want Carla with Sutton, not apart from him. She squeezed her eyes shut, trying to sort out what was Keri and what were Styx's mind games.

He kept up the gentle circles on her temples. "Your head hurts?"

"It's better now. Too much power racing through me, then Keri—"

His face darkened. "Not Keri. It was Styx, attacking you psychically."

She was trying to get this to make sense. "You heard the first two words, but not the rest?"

He smiled. "I was touching you, and your power was touching me. I could hear very clearly. But once I let go, I didn't hear any more." He leaned forward and brushed his mouth over hers.

She shivered at the feel of his lips on hers. The power ached, the need for release surged. She tensed, the ache turning to pain. Oh, God, what if she couldn't control her powers and lost Sutton on the astral plane like she'd lost Pam? "We have to go back. I can't...we..."

Still holding her face, he said, "What is it?"

"My powers, I can't control them." She felt a wave a panic claw through her roiling emotions.

His eyes narrowed and his jaw hardened. "This is

bullshit. That bastard Styx forced us to stop before you had release and now you're suffering." His hands hardened on her face. "I felt your powers rising and swelling, but now they are backing up inside you. And I can't do a goddamned thing now to help you. Not without risking another psychic attack on you."

She understood that when he touched her, all her powers opened wide and maybe that gave Styx access. And, she reminded herself, it would be wrong to have an orgasm with the eagle that might not belong to her, or touch him as if he belonged to her. Her twin bond with Keri could be confusing the eagle, making him think she was his soul mirror when it really was Keri. She had to close her eyes to keep hot tears from leaking out. She wanted to make love to him, wanted to touch and taste all of him. The longing twisted inside her, but she tried to reassure Sutton by saying, "It's okay."

"The hell it is! You need my touch and I can't touch you."

Pain spiked through her head, making her wince. Even her skin hurt.

His hands on her face gentled. "All right, baby. Look at me."

She opened her eyes, seeing that his face was tight with worry.

"Breathe with me, now." He took a breath in.

She followed.

He breathed out slowly.

She did the same. Her respiration fell into sync with his, and then she felt the gentle whisper of feathers rubbing up and down her arms, soft and slow. Her panic eased back and her powers began to settle.

"Better?"

"Yes. I can take us back."

"I never doubted it. Before we go, you have to know one thing."

Feeling more in control, she asked, "What?"

"You're my golden witch. I will do anything for you." His eyes glittered with diamond-hard meaning. "I'm going to find and free your sister and kill Styx so he can't hurt you ever again."

Her heart trembled. "Sutton..."

He shook his head to silence her. "Listen to me. I see the love and guilt over your sister hurting you. Tearing you apart. I want you to know that if something happens to me, whatever happens to me, it's okay. I am doing this because I want to. Because you have given me a reason to fight. I want you to live and be happy." He leaned down, kissing her, then he added, "And if it ever comes down to a choice, let me go."

"No. I won't..."

He pulled her off the edge of the marble and into his arms. "Yes, you'll let me go with a free heart. You don't have to ever choose, just let me go."

With her cheek pressed up against his strong chest, she could feel the beat of his heart. Hear how her heart fell into sync with his. She couldn't face a choice like that; how did she pick between her twin sister or the man who might be the other half of her soul?

Sutton's hand caressed her back. "Now take us back. I'm going to do what I was born to do—hunt and kill the rogue who dares to threaten my witch."

"He's a leech," Jerome said. "Mortal psychics vary from low levels—really just very sensitive, perceptive people—to the higher-functioning psychic ability that goes beyond perception to actually picking up and reading brain waves. We can see that they have extra activity on their brain scans, but we've never been able to isolate what causes it."

Carla looked over her dad's shoulder at the computer where he had a brain-mapping example that he had pulled from his files. "I see that. But what do you mean by leech?" She had told her dad about Keri yelling at her, and that Sutton didn't believe it was Keri.

"Generally, a mortal psychic pulls information from people physically close to them by reading their brain waves. Think of it like the pebble in the pond and the resulting ripples. Our brain waves send out ripples into the atmosphere. The ripples are strongest near our brains, then they fade the farther they travel." Her dad's eyes got that keen, curious light he always had when researching. "Now theoretically, a very strong psychic can project his brain waves into another person's brain waves and alter their thoughts."

In spite of a few hours' sleep, she still had a low-level headache. Rubbing her forehead, she said, "Okay. They aren't using chakras like witches, right?"

He shook his head. "No, they don't have magical powers like an earth witch, like Keri, who pulled on her chakras to connect with you telepathically. It's more like they have advanced brain waves that can actually read and interpret another person's brain waves. Now, if you're right and Styx was using Keri's voice and projecting it to you on the astral plane, that would be virtually impossible for a mortal psychic. In most cases he couldn't reach across an average city, let alone to another plane of existence. His brain waves just wouldn't be that strong."

She began to understand. "That's why you called him a leech. He's leeching from Keri. She has a connection to me and that creates a magical trail between us. He's using that trail to send his psychic attack. That's how he's getting to me."

"Right. I don't know how he used her voice,

probably some kind of memory trick, shuffling Keri's words that are stored in your brain."

Unless it was *Keri.* Stop it, she told herself. She was letting him win by allowing the doubts he was seeding to take hold. She remembered the anger that had come through in the attack. "He's mad, Dad. I could feel the rage in Keri's screaming. It wasn't Keri's rage. She was quick to anger, and even quicker to get over it. Remember? Her anger always felt like a huge puff of hot air that dissipated quickly."

Jerome took a drink of his coffee, set the cup down. "What did it feel like?"

Carla moved to the side to sit on the edge of her desk. "Like being stabbed repeatedly." She rubbed her head again, trying to get rid of the residual ache.

"That's not Keri." He frowned at her. "Your sister would never hurt you, Carla. Never. She always cried when you got hurt. It's the psychic, he is trying to hurt you. We have to find a way to safeguard you."

She couldn't believe it: Her dad was defending Keri. "But we can't cut Keri off. Her connection to me is keeping her soul alive so she can go to Summerland and reincarnate. Sutton knows Styx's real name, maybe he'll be able to track him down and we can get Keri away from him."

Her dad's back straightened in the chair. "What's his name?"

Carla had to think. "It was an odd name... John River Branch."

"Branch," her dad said slowly, and shut down his brain-mapping files to do a search.

"What are you doing?"

"I've interviewed several psychics, and that last name is familiar."

She didn't see how that would help. "Styx is a rogue. If he'd been anywhere near Keri, Mom, or me, he'd have smelled us."

"Here, found it. A woman named Acacia Branch. She lived in Colorado, but she came to consult with me after seeing me on TV, let's see"—he squinted at the date on his files—"thirteen years ago."

"She was psychic?"

Jerome said, "The real deal. She could read brain waves...everyone's but her husband's and son's. I tested her and she was the highest level I'd ever seen. That's why I remember her name."

"What did she want from you?"

He looked up at her. "To know why she couldn't read her husband and son."

"Did you know why?"

He shook his head. "Some people have natural filters that dilute their brain waves as they go out into the environment, making them too weak to read. That might be it."

Carla thought about that. She'd run into various forms of mental blocks in her work, but she could always get around them with witchcraft. "Why did she want to know about her husband and son?"

"It was her son. He was fourteen, I remember her saying that, and he would just disappear. She didn't know where he was going or what he was doing. The fact that she couldn't read him made her more suspicious." He looked up at her. "What if her husband and son were witch hunters?"

"That would explain why she couldn't read them. Do you think she knew that?"

"At the time, I didn't think to ask. I was more interested in her ability. But looking back, yeah, I think she did. I know she was very worried about her son. She wanted to know if her ability was hereditary."

"Maybe, maybe not," Carla answered, as if he'd asked her the question. "We can't be sure until we isolate the gene or markers. But it probably is hereditary to some extent. Do you think we could talk to her?" Jerome switched to the Internet to look up the Branch family. "I can try. Let me see if they are still at the same address. They had a bed-and-breakfast up in the mountains."

Carla was thinking hard. "It might be better if I talk to her. I could go there..." She broke off, and reined in her excitement. "Nix that. Her husband and son might very well be witch hunters. It would be stupid of me to show up there. And it's not a good idea for me to be that far away from Pam."

"They still own the Branch Bed and Breakfast. So yeah, she's still there. I can fly up and talk to her."

Carla shook her head. "Thanks, Dad. But you're too recognizable." And she didn't want him in danger either. "I'll tell Sutton about this, or better yet, I can e-mail him all the information you have. We'll let the Wing Slayer Hunters check it out. Hunting rogues is what they do."

Pulling his mouth tight, her dad stood up. "Looks like you don't need me." He picked up his coffee and walked out.

"I fucking hate flying," Phoenix groused as he unfolded his long body from the black SUV they'd rented. "And this altitude is interfering with my iPod."

Sutton glanced over at Key. "Told you to tranq him."

Key shrugged. "I wasn't sure Carla wouldn't pull you out of your body while you were flying the plane. If I had to fly the Cessna, I wanted him to suffer along with me."

Phoenix froze midstride, turning his death-eating stare on them both. "What the fuck! Your witch could have...that's it, I'm driving back." He turned away. "Key can't fly worth shit. Men aren't supposed to fly."

195

"Axel flies. He has wings," Key pointed out with a wicked grin. "Hey, Phoenix, maybe you'll get wings."

"Shut. The. Fuck. Up." Phoenix put his earbuds in and cranked up the volume.

"Going to have to tranq him to get him back." Sutton shook his head. Key and Phoenix fought with each other all the time. But when it came time to fight rogues, they normally fought back-to-back and decimated the enemy. They were best friends.

Key looked around. "So this is Colorado?"

"Crested Butte," Sutton answered, still impressed as hell by Carla. She had contacted him with all the information. He saw the vivid curiosity about the psychic Acacia Branch in the image she magically projected on his monitor. Between her psychology degrees and her hypnosis work, Carla was professionally fascinated.

But she'd trusted him to handle this. His eagle liked that. If he could have, he'd have been strutting across Sutton's back while he and Carla talked via the computer.

Sutton had cracked into the Colorado Department of Public Health and Environment Vital Records and found the birth certificate for River Branch—his parents were Acacia and Drake Branch. Then he'd verified that they still owned the Branch Bed and Breakfast.

This was their first solid break. He had to find Keri before Styx got further into Carla's head. He didn't know how much of the mind shit Styx was doing she could take before something in her broke. It seemed to be getting worse; now he was using Keri against her.

It was tearing Carla up.

The bastard was going to die for that alone.

"Easy, dude," Key said.

The witch hunter's voice drew him back. They were at the Branch Bed and Breakfast to verify the facts and gain whatever insight they could to find out where Styx was.

The house was a sprawling, two-story home, all white and trimmed in red. There was a large redwood balcony with a matching redwood deck below it. The three of them walked up to the door and knocked.

Key elbowed Phoenix. "Turn off your iPod."

Phoenix pulled out the earbuds, shoved them into his pants, and frowned. "What is that noise?"

"What noise?" It was late afternoon, and Sutton could hear kids playing down the street. Someone was using a power tool inside, like a cordless screwdriver, and he heard the steady hum of a motor...maybe a spa? Sounded like a hot tub bubbling.

"That...singing." Phoenix twisted his mouth. "Some chick singing in the shower, I guess. Christ, you'd think she'd pick something better than that mournful tune."

Sutton looked at Key. "You hear it?"

"Nope. Dude's taken too many hits to the head." Phoenix snorted. "You two are losing your hearing. I have excellent hearing. Like right now, I can hear someone walking inside the house."

The front door opened and a young woman, about twenty-five, with chemically dark streaks in her blond hair answered. "Hello, do you have reservations?"

Sutton said, "We're looking for Acacia Branch."

"I'm Trinity. Mrs. Branch is out, but I can take care of you."

"Can you now?" Phoenix shouldered Key out of his way to look down at Trinity.

Her fair skin colored. "Uh, well sure. Do you want to book a room? We're full up right now for the wedding this weekend, but if you'd like to book for a future date, I'm sure I can help you." She flashed a set of dimples and bounced a bit on her toes.

Phoenix softened his hard face with a small grin. "How about a tour? Is that a hot tub I hear?"

Her eyes widened in surprise. "There are two of them on the back porch."

He held out his hand. "Care to show me?"

She shifted her gaze to Sutton and Key, a fleeting sense of caution slipping into her eyes.

Sutton eased back slightly so that she didn't feel like the three of them were looming over her. "When do you expect Mrs. Branch back? Is Mr. Branch around?"

Her right hand twitched like she wanted to take Phoenix's outstretched fingers. "Mrs. Branch is over helping with the bridal tea. She should be back anytime. Mr. Branch—" Her cheeks grew redder and her gaze fell to the ground. "He's around. Somewhere."

Sutton had the feeling Mr. Branch had sampled the help, then shifted her memory. She probably didn't know why she felt a sense of unease or shame when she thought of him. Disgust brewed in his gut. The witch hunters had a huge sex drive from the curse, and sex helped control the compulsion for witch blood, but it didn't excuse that kind of behavior. And why the hell had he married if he was going to screw around?

In a slow, seductive voice, Phoenix said, "Trinity, take me around back to the hot tubs. My friends will find Mr. Branch."

At the name Mr. Branch, she moved closer to Phoenix. Sutton had seen it over and over. Women trusted Phoenix. Some deep feminine instinct told them he wouldn't hurt them. True enough, but he would most definitely hurt the men who dared to abuse a woman. Mr. Branch was not going to want to meet up with Phoenix.

Key stepped through the opened door. "We'd better find the witch hunter before Phoenix does."

"He'll be busy for a while." He'd caught the scent of desire from Trinity as soon as she touched Phoenix.

The difference was that Phoenix wasn't married, he'd make sure she wanted sex with him, and leave her feeling happy about herself. Not screw with her body and mind. God, Drake Branch was beginning to piss him off.

Key looked around inside and said, "I could kick it here."

Sutton shut the door and checked it out. The front room was huge, with a big stone fireplace in the wall on the right. The floors were stained a dark walnut. A group of couches and chairs was in front of the fireplace. On the left side of the room were leather-covered benches and deep chairs around a distressed walnut table. Across the room there was an alcove under a massive stairway. The desk across the opening of the alcove appeared to be the place where guests signed in.

Sutton passed the stairway and walked into a dining room that had a long table, and went into a square kitchen. On the granite bar sat coffee, iced tea, and a plate of cookies.

Key grabbed a cookie and bit into it. "Not as good as the Cookie Witch."

Sutton frowned at him. "They are just cookies."

"Dude, you are so wrong." He took another bite. "Still good." He tilted his head. "You hear that?"

Sutton looked up at the ceiling, and caught the faint female voice saying, "What are you doing in here?"

"I thought you were at the tea. This sink was leaking. I'll be out of here...you look great."

"Thanks. I had a headache. I took some aspirin, but I thought I'd sit outside in the hot tub."

"Maybe I can help."

"What are you doing?"

"Rubbing your shoulders. Your neck is so tight—"

Sutton had heard enough. He backtracked to the stairs and took them three at a time with Key right behind him. On the left was a set of double doors. He detected no sound behind them. On the right was a hallway with two closed doors on either side.

Key pointed to the left.

They followed the voices to the second door.

Key disappeared from view, and Sutton shielded his presence, too, then he opened the door and slipped through.

The room was painted light blue, with a bed covered in a dark blue spread and some kind of fancy white overlay. The voices came from behind a half-closed door.

"You don't have to do this. I'll just go downstairs..." The female voice was uncertain, confused.

A deeper voice said, "You want me to. You came back to see me."

"I don't think, I mean I don't remember..."

Sutton walked silently to the bathroom door. He didn't like the confused voice of the woman and pushed the door open.

The man was big, probably over six and a half feet. He took up most of the space in the compact bathroom. He was crowding the woman against the counter, forcing her to look up at him. "You remember. You want me to seduce you. You've wanted me—"

Sutton dropped his shield at the same time Key did. "Leave the woman alone."

The man swiveled his head around, complete shock stiffening his entire body. "Who the hell are you?"

Key walked into the bathroom and took the woman's hand. "Come on, darlin'. I'm taking you downstairs."

"I don't...who are you?"

"Kieran DeMicca. I'm going to get you something cold to drink." Key put his arm around her and walked her out of the room.

Turning back to Drake, he answered, "Sutton West. How many of your guests do you try and pull that shit on?" God, he was furious. It wasn't that hard to find willing women, but this asshole had been trying to memory-shift the woman into believing she wanted sex with him.

Drake walked past him into the bedroom. "She came on to me. The guests were supposed to be at a tea. She came back early—"

"Save the lies for your wife."

The hunter sank down onto the bed. "I don't usually do that. I really was working in the bathroom. She caught me by surprise...and I...the curse is winning."

"Then do the world—and women especially—a favor. Kill yourself."

He snapped his head up, glaring. "I know who you are. You're one of the Wing Slayer Hunters. But you're just like me, fighting the curse."

Sutton took a step toward the man. "I am nothing like you." He'd never tried to coerce a woman.

"What the hell do you want? You've all declared war on rogues, I'm not a rogue, so what are you doing here?"

"You have a son named John River Branch. Correct?"

His eyes slid to the left. "So?"

"Where is he?"

"Not here."

Sutton took a breath, striving for patience. He needed enough information to wipe Styx from the earth and get the knife Keri was in. For Carla.

Before Styx destroyed Carla.

He clenched his fists. Beating Drake up wasn't going to do anything constructive. The man wasn't rogue, he had no smell of copper on him. He was just weak. He lowered his face and said, "You want to cooperate with me, Drake. Or I'm going to tell your wife about the woman you just tried to coerce into sex using memory-shifting."

Drake lifted his chin. "She came on to me."

"What about Trinity? I can uncover the real memory of what you did to her." Actually he couldn't, but Carla could. "Your wife is psychic, and all she'd have to do is read Trinity's mind."

He paled. "How do you know that?"

"I know what I need to. Your son inherited the psychic ability, didn't he?"

"Maybe." He sighed, apparently realizing he had little choice. "After John was born, we moved here, up in the mountains because witches usually stay closer to the ocean. I wanted to keep my soul and raise our son. Acacia and I thought this would be a good environment. We can handpick our guests, we're a little off the beaten track, but close enough for guests to enjoy the lodge and shops. Acacia is a strong woman with strong ideas."

"She knows you're a witch hunter?"

"Yes. I mean she's always been different, too. She got it. I love her, I do. But, I have needs."

"So I saw," he said dryly.

Drake narrowed his eyes. "Don't be so judgmental. I've outlasted most witch hunters. You're still young, what, in your thirties?"

Sutton crossed his arms and stared.

"Over the years, the pain wears you down. The burn gets worse. But I had to hide the women, Acacia doesn't understand." His shoulders sagged. "Maybe John got the wrong idea. He saw me screwing women that weren't his mother, and I told him to keep quiet."

Again, he said nothing. But he thought of his dad and his uncle. Women came around occasionally, and they were treated with respect and kindness. It had been years before he'd figured out that either his dad or uncle was having sex with whatever woman was around. He remembered the time he'd come home early from something or other he'd been doing. He was fifteen, and he'd already felt the curse. He heard his father talking and grunting. Curious, he'd looked through the window.

Mattie. He remembered her name. Sable-brown hair, a nice smile and a hideous scar on her face. Some ex-boyfriend had done that. She and his dad had a casual relationship. His dad had his back to Sutton, buck naked. He had Mattie balanced on the back of the couch, her long legs wrapped around him, and was thrusting into her. Sutton had been a teenage boy, and the curse rode him hard. His dick had gone from flaccid to rock hard and ready to blow. But what he remembered was the way his dad held Mattie in his arms, leaning over her, kissing her. She tried to turn her face away, tried to hide the scar. His dad turned her face back, and kissed her along the scar. Her body had convulsed then, sweet little cries of pleasure spilling from her. That seemed to set his dad off, his back bowing as he came inside her.

Sutton had learned how to treat a woman who gave her body to him. His dad never said a bad word about any woman that he could remember.

But this man taught his son that the women were a dirty secret, to be used and discarded.

With his coldest stare, he said, "I will never be you."

"You're so sure. Wait until year after year of craving witch blood eats through your soul."

He raised both eyebrows. "We're not talking about me, we're talking about your son. He's gone rogue."

Drake's defensive demeanor crumbled.

Sutton didn't let up. "He's running a group of rogues in Glassbreakers, Los Angeles."

"Killing witches. So his soul is gone."

"And using mortal women. He's brainwashing them, getting them to kill for him, even blow themselves up."

Drake's face grayed, his fingers curled. "I tried to teach him...I mean, yeah, we gotta use women to fight the curse. But he looked at me like I was weak. Then I found him...Christ."

He felt no pity for the man. "Found him what?"

"It started with little things. He'd get the female guests to do his chores. He thought it was funny to brainwash a guest into cleaning the toilets. But it escalated. He'd force women to have sex with his friends and make money off it. When I tried to put a stop to it, he got a woman to lay naked in my bed for my wife to find."

Rage choked him. "He has no conscience." This man had raised a psychic sociopathic witch hunter who had gone rogue. "And when you went along with him?"

Drake wouldn't look at him.

Sutton grabbed him by the shirt and hauled him up. "Do you know where he is?"

"No. I don't talk to him."

He smelled of fear.

"My wife does. Acacia talks to him. She might know where he is."

The coward was throwing his wife to the wolves. "Does she know what he is?" Sutton registered the sound of two women, Key and Phoenix coming up the stairs.

Drake answered, "She's in denial. She was really worried about him up until the time he took off at eighteen. Then he started calling and sweet-talking her."

"Does he ever visit?"

"Maybe twice in a decade."

"Call your wife and tell her to come home."

Drake looked at the wood floor. "She rode with one of the guests."

Key walked into the room. "Get him out of here. Trinity is going to help Jessica pack. She doesn't want to stay here any longer."

Sutton looked over at the opened doorway. Trinity and Jessica stood together behind Key and next to Phoenix.

Drake said, "No need to leave, Jessica. It was just a misunderstanding."

Phoenix stormed past Key, heading for Drake.

Sutton cut Phoenix off, body-blocking him. He put a hand on his bulging forearm. "Later. Right now, pack up, Jessica. One of you drive her in her car to the tea, or to another hotel if she'd rather. The other one follow to bring Mrs. Branch back here."

Phoenix wasn't looking at Sutton, but kept his glare on Drake. Finally, he said, "Trinity comes with me."

Sutton looked over at the girl.

She said, "I should go, that way I can let Mrs. Branch know that you guys helped Jessica out. I'll explain that there's a problem here and you drove me to find her."

"You know she's psychic?" Sutton asked her.

"She knows things, even things you don't tell her." She looked at Drake. "She knows more than he thinks. She'll want to come back."

"Good enough. We'll wait downstairs while you pack up Jessica then go get Mrs. Branch."

Drake said, "You can't just come in my house and—"

Phoenix shoved Sutton aside. "Listen up, asshole, you either shut the fuck up and do what you're told, or I'm going to dice you up into beef jerky, then feed the rotting meat to the vultures."

Drake shut up.

≈ 14 ≈

"SHE'S NOT LOOKING GOOD. HER eyes are sinking into her face, and her skin feels waxy." Carla poured out some lotion and rubbed it into Pam's arms and hands.

The candles in the room went out.

Chandra looked up from where she was smoothing lotion into the woman's legs. "We'll get her back, Carla." She lifted a hand and waved at the candles, relighting them.

"Sorry," Carla muttered, lifting the pajama shirt to pour the lotion on Pam's stomach. The skin-to-skin contact was important, essential.

"Want to tell me about it?"

She ran her hands up Pam's sides, willing her to feel the caring she was trying to pour into her. "Not really."

The candles went out again.

"Carla." Her mom relit the candles, then switched to Pam's other leg.

She had the insane urge to throw herself into her mother's arms. That had never been like her. Keri was the one who had craved touch. "I want him, Mom. I want him to be mine. But I feel like I already took Dad from Keri, I can't take Sutton. Her eagle." She funneled her powers into her hands, pouring out her feelings to Pam as she worked the lotion into her belly and ribs. She was trying to keep Pam's spirit connected to her body, and as badly as Carla hungered, if she could force Pam's physical body to feel it enough to reach her spirit...it might help. Silently, she reached for Pam's spirit, trying to strengthen the threads that bound her to her body.

"Oh, sweetheart. You didn't." They worked together to turn Pam over.

Carla looked down, thinking she had a pretty back. No scar. *You have to come back, Pam. This wasn't your fault.* She reached up to rub her temple, smelling the soft jasmine scent of the lotion. To her mom, she said, "Every time I bring Sutton to the astral plane, we're both naked." She looked over to see her mom's reaction.

"Sounds nice. You can feel him there? Touch him like you have corporeal bodies?"

"Yes. I don't understand it. I've even tried to summon clothes but I can't."

Chandra lifted her gaze. "Honey, *that* sounds like your sister's interference."

"She wanted to see Sutton naked?"

"Who wouldn't?"

"Mom!" Carla laughed.

"Oh, stop it. I've taught you better than that. Sex feeds our powers, sex with the right person under the right conditions. Do not make it something less than respectful, Carla. I won't tolerate that. I don't care how much of a scientist you are, your soul is all witch. And you need touch as much as our girl Pam here." She put down the lotion, drew the cover up over Pam, then took hold of Carla's hands. "He's touched your soul. I can see it in your shimmer. It's blooming your power, and bringing out your beauty. You have nothing to be ashamed of."

She thought of the way Sutton had understood when her chakras flung open, her powers swelling inside her...she'd thought she had to control it. In her dad's lab, she'd always had to control her power. Control her mind. Everything was done by protocol.

But with Sutton, she was all witch, and he'd encouraged her to be as free as her witch's soul needed to be. She took a breath. "Thanks, Mom." She hugged the woman who knew her so well. Letting her go, she said, "I want to see if I can reach Pam on the astral plane."

Chandra frowned.

"I'll be careful. I'm just thinking that since I feel more power, maybe I can quickly find her and coax her back before anything else shows up." It had been four days, and she didn't think Pam had too many days left before her spirit let go of her body. "I'll just try once, then I need to go to the clinic."

"To see Max?"

"To check on the girls, and see Max," she corrected. "We're friends. I want to continue the work I do there, so we need to fix this between us." She was being honest, so she said, "I kept hoping that I'd feel something for him. I wanted to feel something for him. He seemed like the right man for me, and I told myself that I just needed time to grieve for Keri and then I'd start getting interested in him."

Her mom shook her head. "How is it that you can be so smart about other people's minds and so dense about your own?"

Gently she asked, "Speaking from experience, Mom?"

"You mean your dad?"

"You two fell in love for the wrong reasons."

Chandra squeezed her hand and shook her head. "You're wrong, sweetheart. We did love each other. I loved his brilliance, the way he believed I was special.

Losing my familiar from the curse tore something inside of me. I don't know how to explain it because you've never had a familiar. It's a bond. We do the spell by moonlight, impressing the image of our familiar on something silver and always wearing it close to our bodies. They are, well, deeper than a friend. Then the curse came and my familiar was gone. Wrenched from me. I was so worried about him. Was he okay? Was he dead? Did he think I had abandoned him?"

"And you lost your high magic."

"Right. I couldn't open my third eye and find him, I couldn't do anything. And then the murders started. It was terrifying, we had no protection. We'd always relied on witch hunters to protect us and now they were killing us. The curse was destroying us all. I started selling cookies out of my kitchen, both as a way to survive and to keep busy so I didn't lose my mind."

Carla sat on the edge of the bed with her mom, still holding her hand. "Then you met Dad."

"I got a guest appearance on a morning show. It was kind of exciting, and I decided to call myself the Cookie Witch. And there I met this brash young scientist that most people, mortals, thought was crazy." She looked out the window, her eyes losing focus.

"Do you know how amazing it was that your father, a mortal, believed? Most men are afraid of us on some level, even if they don't realize we are witches. They subconsciously recognize our power and it makes them uneasy. But not your father, he was intrigued. We starting dating, and he told me about his research. I told him about the curse, and what it was like trying to live without my familiar and high magic. Jerome didn't just listen, *he heard me.*"

Carla knew what that was like. Sutton had heard her about problems like her father and being forced to choose.

"Your dad was fascinated, asking questions, trying to understand what the curse had done. How the link between the witches and familiars had broken. He believed that science could fix that."

"It was magic, Mom."

She shook her head. "I know that, Carla. It was a demonic curse. Now we understand that our souls halved and familiars couldn't bond with us any longer. But then...we didn't know. Witches were trying everything to reconnect with our familiars. Nothing worked, no spells, no ceremonies, no amount of meditation. So why not science? Your father believed the curse created a genetic flaw that could be repaired once he identified the witch gene. Like cloning or something...I don't know. I just believed. I clung to that hope and to him. But he also believed in me as a woman. He taught me the things I needed to know to live without high magic and he encouraged me to open a real bakery. He believed in me, the whole me."

Carla was taken by surprise. "Mom, that's lovely."

She smiled that secret smile of love. "There was real love there."

"And you had Keri and me."

"When I got pregnant, your father was thrilled, but he was even more ecstatic when he found out you were girls. Twin girls. He knew you'd be witches, and he thought, believed, hoped that he could learn the genetic code of witches and reverse the curse."

Softly, she said, "We are his daughters, Mom, not lab rats."

She lifted her gaze to Carla. "Oh, honey, don't you see? He was racing against time to find the cure so you and Keri would be safe. Your father knew about rogues, and he was scared that he couldn't protect you. All he had was science. He wasn't physically strong enough to fight off a huge, blood-crazed rogue. He was terrified for his daughters. Before you were born, he'd lay with his head against my stomach, and we'd talk about the future for hours. But then you girls were born and time went on with no answers."

She paused and Carla sat quietly, letting Chandra take her time.

"Witches were being slaughtered. Your father got more and more obsessed, and the fear between us got bigger every day until we couldn't even look at each other without seeing the fear. It became bigger than our love."

"Mom," she breathed, feeling the woman, not her mother, but the woman through their joined hands. "The love is still there."

Chandra looked her directly in the eye. "Yes. All our fear didn't do a damned thing to save Keri. All it did was wrench us apart when we needed each other the most."

Regret snaked up her throat. She thought of her dad telling her that all he had was science. And then this morning, when she turned to Sutton, he'd said she obviously didn't need him. Maybe they all had some blame in this. After all this time, Carla finally understood. "Dad blames himself for not finding the answer to prevent Keri's murder."

"He loved her, Carla. She scared him because she was led by her heart." She reached up and stroked Carla's hair like she used to do when Carla was small. "Let's see if you can reach Pam."

"Okay, but Dad..."

"I didn't tell you this to make you feel guilty. Jerome's obsession was an ugly thing, and it hurt you girls. But there were real reasons for it. Being a part of freeing Keri from the knife will help him. Right now, you need to focus on Pam."

Her mom was right. Carla let go of her hand, and turned to rest her fingers on Pam's shoulder. Her first four chakras had been bubbling with excess power all day, now they burst out like an explosion from a soda bottle.

The lightbulb in the bedside lamp shattered.

The candles blew out.

The stereo playing sounds of the rain forest turned to loud static.

"Carla, pull in, focus."

She was trying. Keeping her hand on Pam's shoulder, she struggled to bring all her elemental power of fire, earth, water, and air into a singular line to flow up to her fifth chakra. The static in the air around them settled and her throat tightened, a signal that she'd gotten her energy under control enough to push the chakra.

She'd never had this much power at one time.

There you are, a male voice said in her head. With brutal suddenness, her mind was yanked from her body and slammed into a small steel space. Cold, metal darkness clamped down around her, getting smaller and smaller, pressing in on her mind with increasing pressure from every side. The ice-cold agony sliced deep into her brain and shut down her powers.

Her mind screamed out the only word she could remember, "Sutton!"

Sutton stood in the living room of the Branch Bed and Breakfast with his arms crossed, keeping an eye on Drake. Phoenix and Key had left with the two women to find Acacia Branch. Everything was contained, but he was still uneasy.

When he heard a car pull up out front, he walked to the window to see if it was Key and Phoenix returning with Mrs. Branch. Two feet from the window, he felt the room begin to spin. "Shit, not now!" He grabbed his head, struggling to stay in his body.

The eagle went apeshit on his back, and the pain seemed to help. The room was spinning like he was in the center of a tornado. His sense of balance vanished and he dropped to his knees. Blue-and-white fog was filling his vision. "No! Carla, not now!" He squeezed his head between his hands, fighting to...

Carla's scream of agony exploded in his head and he was ripped out of his body and into a vortex of spinning fog. He forgot about his body, and let the vortex sweep him where he needed to be.

With Carla.

Her scream kept ricocheting around him as if the sound came from each molecule of the fog. He had no body, no form, just his mind hurtling in this tornado until he crashed into something hard and unyielding.

His doppelganger body slid down to the hard ground. It felt like cement. "Carla?" He sat up and looked around. He appeared to be in some kind of dark room. Not bedroom-dark, but total-absence-of-light dark. Getting to his feet, he bumped his left shoulder into something hard. He carefully ran his hand over it. Cold, smooth metal.

Raising his right hand, he felt brick.

His eagle started to fight, trying to force wings out of Sutton's back. "No," he told the bird. If the creature somehow got free of his back in this tight space, he'd break his wings in panic. "Easy," he soothed. "We'll find her."

The eagle settled down, but both of them were tense.

Carefully, Sutton walked forward, using his hands to guide him. In a few seconds, he figured out that they were in a small, round room with walls made of brick. The walls went higher than he could reach, or even jump. In the center was some kind of steel structure that was about the size and shape of a refrigerator.

"Carla?" He called again. This was the room she'd described Styx trapping her mind in. He hadn't felt a door along the walls.

There was no response from Carla.

Don't panic, he told himself and the bird. He felt around the steel box and after what seemed like miles of nothing but cold metal, he found a lever. He pushed it down and the door swung open. "Carla?" His voice echoed.

"Sutton?"

"Where are you?" Her voice had sounded faint and muffled. He reached out and touched another steel box. "Jesus," he whispered.

"He's got me trapped. I don't have my powers."

He ran his hands over the front of the box to find the lever while wondering: How could Styx take her powers from her? He didn't understand all the rules of magic or psychics. He knew from previous experience that he was in his doppelganger body. Because his mind was out of his body on the physical plane, he had no idea what was happening to it, only what he was experiencing in his doppelganger form. But Carla always had her powers in either body, so why not now?

His hand hit the raised metal bar and he exhaled in relief at finding the lever. This was some strange shit. He pushed down the lever and opened the box.

He wished he could see. In normal darkness there was enough ambient light for his eagle vision to see pretty well, but this was dark as a grave. And why was Carla inside these steel boxes?

What kind of game was Styx playing?

He swung the door open as far as he could. "Carla, talk to me."

"I'm trying to connect to Keri to get you out."

Her voice trembled, he couldn't tell if it was fear, fatigue, or intense concentration. He reached out and... "Son of a bitch," he snarled low in his throat. The eagle screeched frustration in his head. Another, smaller steel box. "Honey, I'm not leaving you." He quickly found the lever, pushed it down, and opened the door.

"Leave. Keri, help me get him out!"

Her voice hit the same pitch as his eagle's screech. She was terrified. He could smell it now. He wrenched open the door, reached in and found air. Okay. She had to be here, maybe on the floor. No more games. His entire body coated in sweat as he dropped to his knees to feel around the inside of the box. His hand landed on the sharp corner of something.

A bad feeling snaked down his spine. "Carla?" He felt around the sharp corner. It was another box, about the size of a box of computer paper. She couldn't fit in there. "Carly, are you in here?"

"He's caged my spirit and soul in steel. No body, no chakras." The box shivered in his hands. "I can't reach Keri. Can't help you."

The desolation in her voice was breaking his heart. His eagle started pulling at his skin, trying to break free. Sutton didn't know if he'd ever get real wings like Axel, but he knew it couldn't happen in this confined space. He lifted the box, then sat on the stone floor and leaned his back against the brick to keep the eagle contained. The bird didn't give a shit about the rules of the soul mirror. He wanted out, and if he got through Sutton's skin, he'd destroy his beak and claws trying to free Carla. Keeping the bird pinned, he ran his hands over the box. "I'll get you out, Carly."

"I heard you. Heard you tell me not to bring you here. I tried..." her voice broke.

Jesus.

The box was closing in, tighter and tighter.

The eagle threw itself against his skin, the force of it bouncing his entire body off the wall. He felt around the steel container, believing there had to be a latch.

Nothing. Smooth as glass.

He began to pray silently to the Wing Slayer. *I'll do anything, just don't let that bastard Styx destroy Carla.* Not her, not his beautiful golden witch. Every instinct told him to keep searching. Some kind of psychic shit was keeping him from finding the latch. *There has to be a latch.* Styx was purposely delaying him from releasing Carla. Why? What was the bastard doing?

First things first, he had to free Carla. He could do this, he knew he was connected to her deeper than any of Styx's psychic shit. He slowed down, took a breath and concentrated. He stopped searching the way he would on the physical plane. They were somewhere else, on some alternate plane of existence. His connection to Carla had brought him to her, and it would find her. He used his fingers to feel for her soul, the other half of his soul.

A warm circle appeared beneath his right index finger on the side of the box. He stroked that area gently, and a small button rose under his fingers.

Sutton said a quiet, "Thank you," and pressed the button, then carefully lifted the lid. It was absolutely dark where they were, like being wrapped in black velvet. But as he lifted the lid, sparkles of silver light began to float from the box.

His eagle tat sighed.

Sutton stared in awe. He was seeing Carla's spirit, and it was more beautiful that anything he'd ever witnessed in his life. The lights flowed toward him, turning to a shimmering gold as they wrapped around him. Then he slipped from one dimension to another with barely a bump.

SOUL MAGIC

Carla's first indication that she'd successfully returned to her body on the physical plane was the agony in her head. It felt like several long prongs had rooted deeply into her brain. She had to close her eyes and center herself with her chakras to contain the pain.

"Carla, sweetheart, you're scaring me," her mother said.

She opened her eyes and stood up. "I'm okay, Mom. It was Styx, and he's getting stronger. I have to call Sutton. Now." Containing her building panic, she quickly checked Pam.

No change. She hadn't even had a chance to attempt to find her. She hurried out of the bedroom and across the family room to her small office.

Her dad looked up. His face was even more haggard, the skin around his eyes and jowls appearing papery and loose. "What?"

"Styx did it again. He grabbed me and shoved me into a steel box. It's like he was forcing me to call Sutton. And I did it, I called him." She reached for the phone on her desk, sickened by her weakness. She had heard Sutton tell her *not now*. How she'd heard him, she didn't know. Maybe Keri had conducted his voice?

The prongs in her head flared red-hot. Her hand shook and pissed her off. Jabbing the buttons, she dialed Sutton's cell number, and while waiting for the call to connect, she worked to control her powers. She needed to isolate the pain and send healing energy to those locations. Her powers flow toward her brain.

Then the energy suddenly bounced back and pinged around inside her. Weird. At the same time, Sutton's voice mail picked up. Why wasn't he answering? She hung up and dialed Darcy.

She answered on the first ring. "Carla, something wrong?"

"Yes." She didn't question how Darcy knew. She

wasn't psychic, but she was a very powerful witch. Her knowledge chakra must have shown her something. Quickly, Carla explained what had happened. "Sutton didn't pick up his phone. He'd know it was me. I'm worried. Why did Styx do it? Fun and games, or is he up to something? Or what if Sutton had been flying the airplane and..." She couldn't say *crashed*. "Please tell Axel. Tell him to find Sutton."

"Hang on," Darcy said.

Carla looked at her dad. "I need shields, Dad. What do you know about shields against psychics?" She was a witch, not some helpless mortal. She would not be this bastard's pawn one second longer.

Jerome rubbed the back of his neck and frowned. "You can use mental shields, like visualizing a wet blanket over the intruder or imagining silver lights protecting you. Too vague." He dropped his hand and said, "What do you feel now? Exactly?"

"Pissed."

"I mean in your mind. You've been having headaches, right?"

"Right. Only now it's more specific. Like prongs have been driven into my brain."

"How many?"

She heard Darcy talking to Axel in the background, but she let that slip to white noise and concentrated on the pain in her head. "Four. I can feel four prongs." She had to think in spite of the pain. "Why four?"

Her dad's eyebrows rose and his eyes grew keen. "How many times has Styx attacked you psychically?"

She counted, while realizing that Darcy was now silent on the phone, obviously listening to her. "The first time when he showed up was when he showed Sutton and me the missing witch hunter Brigg. The second time while I was talking to you, Dad. The third time when I was healing Sutton on the astral plane and the last time was just now. Four. He's been marking my brain! Using Keri's connection to me to establish pathways." She shook with anger, frustration, and pain. "I tried to send healing energy to the areas that hurt and the energy bounced back."

Her dad's face hardened. "You have to mentally pull the prongs out."

"But what about Keri?" Her mom asked as she came into the room. "What will that do to her?"

"Carla, can you feel Keri at all?" Jerome asked.

"I'll try." She closed her eyes and tried to feel her sister. The scar on her back warmed and tingled, but more important, she felt Keri in her blood moving through her chakras. A spike in power confirmed it. "Yes. I feel her." She opened her eyes. "Keri's connected to me, in my blood and chakras."

Chandra breathed a sigh of relief.

"Carla," Darcy interrupted, "Axel's working on contacting Sutton, Phoenix and Key. The three of them flew to Colorado."

Her stomach tightened. "Sutton isn't answering for Axel?"

"Not at the moment, but Axel's trying the other two. They might be out of cell range—it is in the mountains."

"True. Okay, you'll let me know?" She had to be satisfied with that.

"Yes. Do you want me to come over? I might be able to help with the prongs."

"No, stay there until we know what's happening with Sutton, Key and Phoenix." If they needed healing, Axel could get Darcy to them faster if she stayed where Axel was. "Call me as soon as you know anything about Sutton."

"You got it, and you call if you need my magic to help with the prongs." Darcy hung up.

Carla turned to her mom as she set the phone back in the cradle. "I need your help. We need to funnel as much pressure as possible against Styx's shields to get those prongs out."

Chandra answered, "It's going to hurt, Carla. We need the Circle Witches. They can funnel some of their energy to us, and maybe help with the pain."

She opened her mouth to argue, then snapped it closed. "We can use their help. How long will it take to get it?"

"Few minutes." Chandra walked over to the desk, leaned over Jerome and said, "I'm going to open the Circle Witch loops over your files."

Carla watched her dad inhale slowly, like he was drawing Chandra into his body. He tilted his head with her hair laid against his cheek. It was a sensual, intimate act filled with longing and regret. Jerome still had feelings, very deep feelings, for Chandra. How had Carla not seen that before?

Instead of typing, her mom magically connected to the Circle Witches through the computer and spoke, "We need all witches to send their energy to Carla Fisk. She's suffered four separate psychic attacks, and we need to break the connection." She went on to explain.

Carla walked around to the other side of her dad and stood there, waiting for responses to come in. She looked down at the gray T-shirt her dad wore, seeing the tension in his thin shoulders and neck. Swamped by a need to connect with her dad, she laid her hand on his shoulder.

His muscles froze for a second, then he put his hand over hers.

For the first time in two years, she felt something big and painful ease between them. All three of them wanted one thing—to help Keri.

Carla could almost feel Keri's sigh flutter through her blood.

A magically sent voice said, "Has Carla retrieved the mortal yet from the astral plane? We can't risk her breaking her connection to the mortal. We must not harm mortals."

Silver, she thought, and the prongs dug deeper, but Carla managed to keep her voice civil. "Pam is fine. I can't get to her on the astral plane because the psychic interferes. I need to break this connection he has with me in order to help Pam."

"Silver," Chandra added, "if you don't want to help Carla, that's your choice. But you do not have the right to try to stop other witches from helping her. We choose our own paths."

A new voice said, "I want to help."

A second voice added, "I will join the circle to send power as well."

"Me, too."

More witches joined in, all offering to circle their powers around Carla and help. Gratefully, she said, "Thank you. Thank each of you for your gift." Circling powers was a form of meditation. It worked better if they could open up to their sixth chakra, but even with only the first four chakras, it helped. Witchcraft always responded to positive energy.

"And what if this psychic, who Carla and Chandra claim is so dangerous, attacks the Circle Witches? What if Carla gives him access to us?" Silver demanded.

Oh dear, she hadn't thought of that. Carla looked at Jerome. "Is it possible?"

"He'd have to grab on to a power trail. It's unlikely, but he did track you through Keri, or something..." he trailed off, unhappy that he didn't have the answer.

"Each of you should make your own decisions," Silver continued.

Carla knew the Circle Witch couldn't hear her father as he didn't have the magic to communicate in the Circle.

Silver added, "But I have to remind you that we have worked very hard to keep our Circle safe."

The first witch that offered to help said, "I suppose I'll have to withdraw then."

"I'm sorry, Carla," another witch added.

Carla didn't blame them. She should have considered this before she let her mom approach them. "No need to apologize. We must protect the Circle at all costs."

"My daughter is a witch in need and you all turn your backs?" Chandra's voice rose.

"Mom, they have a point."

"I'm not turning my back," Darcy broke in, her voice rich and firm. "I'll open my third eye and help you, Carla."

"Show-off," Silver muttered. Then she said more clearly. "I am *advising* the witches with the best interest of the Circle as a whole, not any one witch."

Carla looked over her dad's head to her mom, and, dropping the magic that pushed her voice through the Circle, she said, "She's going to try for the position of Moon Witch Advisor. But she doesn't have high magic, she can't open her sixth or seventh chakra. I'm not sure about her fifth chakra."

"In these desperate and dangerous times," Silver went on, "it's becoming apparent that we may have to consider electing an advisor among ourselves."

Chandra looked back at the monitor. "The Ancestors choose the Moon Witch Advisor. We don't elect them."

"That was before the curse. I am seeking to protect the Circle so that we can do as much good for mortals as possible while dealing with the loss of our powers."

Carla stood up and rubbed her temples. "Darcy has tremendous power. She has shown us all that there is hope. Yet you want to turn our backs on our beloved Ancestors?" She was furious, sickened by the idea. The drilling in her head didn't help. "The Ancestors chose to not reincarnate but stay in Summerland as our spirit guides. Each of our lifetimes is a journey of learning and growing, each of us on our own separate path. What binds us is our reverence for the Ancestors and seeking the very knowledge and lightness of soul that they have attained. We do not elect a leader, but we listen to the advisor our Ancestors give us. We still make our own decisions." Few people understood that witches were fiercely independent.

Silver said, "The Ancestors are not providing us with a leader—"

"Advisor!" Chandra snapped.

"—and so we must take matters into our own hands. For instance, many of you would have jumped to Carla's aid, out of a sincere desire to help anyone in pain or distress, but you didn't think of the dangers. I did."

"Actually," Darcy said, "I had considered the danger and considered Carla's life and value to be worth more than the very minimal risk. This psychic has worked hard to get to Carla, and he has used her dead twin sister trapped in a knife to do it. I don't see how he could reproduce those efforts that quickly."

"Says the witch who has a witch hunter to protect her. The rest of us do not. We have no protection." Silver's voice hardened on the last words. "And yet, you didn't think of warning us."

"Enough," Chandra said. "Silver, if you continue down this path, you will cause a split among us. In the meantime, I am going to follow my path and help my daughter." She raised her hand to break the magical connection.

Darcy's voice caught her. "I'll open my third eye when you need me. Just let me know."

Chandra said, "Thank you, Darcy. You're a credit to all witches." Then she broke the connection with the Circle Witches.

≋ 15 ≋

THE SMELL WRENCHED SUTTON BACK to consciousness. His skin was on fire and there was a *rage* in his head. He smelled witch blood. The dark, spicy scent filled his head with a clawing craving. He began to struggle, then realized he was chained and lying on the dark wood floor. He saw the stones of the massive fireplace from his right peripheral vision. It all came swimming back to him—he was in the living room of the Branch Bed and Breakfast. Carla had pulled him from his body.

Shit! Now he was chained up. Rearing his head up off the floor, he looked down his body. He'd been stripped to his boxers and chains wrapped around him, anchoring his arms to his sides, his legs together. There were massive padlocks holding the chains.

A muffled scream shattered his confusion.

He smelled copper. Even better; he smelled the rich spice of warm, living, witch blood. His veins lit on fire, the craving taking hold. His nose tracked the scent and he found it to his left. Brigg Cusack and another rogue stood holding a witch. She was a big woman, close to six feet, with spiked salt-and-pepper hair; dressed all in black with a thick silver dog collar

224

around her neck, matching bracelets around her wrists. Her eyes were wide with helpless terror over the thick duct tape wrapped around her head to keep her cries muffled. She had two slices, one through her pants on her thigh, a second one on her bare arm.

Her tiny top and low-rider pants left five or six inches of bare skin. Sutton knew what was coming next. He wanted it, and hated himself for it.

Brigg moved quickly, flashing his knife at whip-speed and cutting the witch on her side. Sutton couldn't stop looking at the thin river of blood welling up from that slice, then dripping down in streams of pure bliss.

Brigg turned his head from the witch and said, "Welcome to your Ceremony of Induction. Oh, wait, first there's a test, isn't that right?"

The bastard was toying with him, mocking the induction ceremony he would have had into the Wing Slayers—had he not gone rogue. He narrowed his eyes. "You failed your test. You've lost your soul, asshole." How long had he been gone from his body? How long before Phoenix and Key got back? Where was Drake? He was trying to focus and think, but the words, *witch blood,* kept pulsing in his brain. *Want it, need it, mine.* He struggled against the chains, but he was fighting a bigger battle in his head—against the curse taking root deep in his brain.

Brigg regarded him with the baby-blue eyes in his smooth face. "The outline of the tattoo on my back is gone. It vanished. Witch blood makes us fucking powerful, dickhead."

"Wing Slayer erased the tattoo when he took your soul. And how powerful do you need to be to cut up a helpless witch?" He tensed all his muscles trying to break the chains. "You're afraid of me, so you're not that strong."

"Not afraid. Just making this interesting. Witches

cursed us and stripped Wing Slayer of his god powers. He's nothing to us. We're taking back our heritage by killing every witch. Then we'll have our immortality back." He pressed the flat of his silver knife into the vivid crimson tide pouring out of the witch. Then he walked to Sutton, stood over him. "Smell that?" He inhaled the scent, then looked down at him. "Think you can resist?"

He didn't answer, his body fighting a raging battle. Part of him wanted that knife on him. Oh, God, he wanted it. His veins felt as if a thousand butane torches were burning him. He wanted relief.

He wanted the power!

He'd felt it before, two months ago when he'd touched Carla's blood. He'd fought it then, but now he was losing the battle. He craved the sensation of pure power sliding over his fingers and sinking into him.

He heard his father's voice whisper in his head to fight against it. Get free, kill the rogues, and then himself.

While he still had his soul.

Brigg dropped down to his haunches, waving the knife up to his face.

Droplets of the witch's blood splattered on his chest.

His body arched into the cool pleasure followed by a kick of power that raced through him, more potent than an orgasm, it made his heart thud and his cock fill with blood.

Sutton wished to God his father was here now to shoot him in his heart. "Kill me. Go ahead, do it. Or don't you have the balls? Maybe you're afraid you'll miss my heart, and I'll break out of these chains. You know I'd kill you and turn you shade." He was goading Brigg, the rage in his brain turning into a vicious bloodlust. He fought not to look at the witch. Not to breathe. Not to...

Brigg slapped the knife onto his chest, wiping every drop of the blood onto his searing skin.

His body convulsed, he heard moans come from his mouth and he bit down hard on his lip. Tasted his own blood. But he didn't care about his blood.

He wanted witch blood. The power fed through his skin, blasted into his veins and sang. His whole body began to rock and hum to the tune. It raced around inside him and made him feel all powerful, all-fucking-powerful!

He shook his head, trying to clear the vibrating hum kissing and licking his nerves.

He heard the witch cry out and break into sobs behind the tape. He began to fight, to thrash against the chains holding him. He had to fight this!

Her sobs increased.

He forced himself to look, and his stomach seized up while his nerves screamed for more blood. They had cut her so many times he couldn't count the cuts, and they were covering their hands in her blood. He fought harder, he had to stop them from hurting her any more. Had to stop them from turning him rogue. They were keeping this witch alive for him to kill. One witch kill and his soul would be gone. He fought the restraints, fought with everything he had.

"Now!" Brigg said.

The two men fell on him, smearing her blood on as much exposed skin as they could find. His stomach, his chest, his thighs. He managed to use his body like a whip and smash the legs out from under Brigg...then the power-kick took hold and his mind exploded with fireworks. The last thing he heard was the front door burst open and Phoenix snarl, "They've blooded him!"

Carla sat with her mom on the small patch of grass

surrounded by the flower beds in the backyard. They needed the feel of the elements—the late-afternoon sun, the cooling air, the damp earth beneath them. Even though this was not spell magic, they still needed the earth, air, fire and water to feed their chakras.

Between Carla and her mom was a ceramic bowl filled with water. For fire, they had candles placed to the north, south, east and west. They had chosen a white candle for purification, a blue candle for psychic and spiritual awareness, a purple candle for speeding healing, and a gold candle for protection.

As added security, her dad and Joe stood back and watched. Joe had more men out front, but he was giving them as much privacy as possible.

Carla took a deep breath, soaking in the elements to saturate her first four chakras. She was concentrating with everything she had to do three things: keep out Styx, not call Sutton, and control her powers, all in an effort to mentally pull out the probes.

"I'm here." Darcy's voice materialized in her head.

Carla opened her eyes and looked across the water bowl. Darcy's image shimmered there. If she reached out, she would be able to pass her hand through it. "Silver's right, you're a show-off."

Darcy grinned. "I'm projecting my image into what I can see with my third eye. That way we have a circle."

"Join hands," Chandra said.

Carla took her mother's hand, letting Chandra take the lead. Darcy might be the most powerful, but Chandra had lived before the curse and had real experience. Carla watched as her mother laid her hand across the image of Darcy's hands. Carla did the same. Magic was symbolic in many ways. Just the symbol of holding hands would create the circle.

Chandra looked at her. "Once you open your communication chakra, you must work fast, Carla.

Darcy and I are going to circle your mind with our powers, but you have to pull the prongs out. Fast. No matter how much it hurts. Because Styx is inside you, our protection will only hold him down for a few minutes."

Carla took a breath. This was her weakness and she knew it. Facing pain made her want to analyze, not act. But she would do it. She steeled herself, using all the energy of the earth to shore up her bravery. "I will, Mom."

Chandra turned to the shimmering image. "Darcy, ready?"

"Yes," her likeness answered.

Carla closed her eyes and concentrated. She felt the energy of herself, Darcy and her mom beginning to mingle, moving in a slow trail around the circle. She and her dad had discussed the need to be absolutely precise, like doing surgery. She'd done her best to isolate each prong. It was time. Using her chakras, she funneled the energy up to her fifth one. A quick tightening of her throat, and the chakra opened.

She didn't let surprise at the ease of that throw her off. Immediately, she began directing the energy to her brain. Once she established the flow, she started pulling chunks of power from the swirl of her mom's and Darcy's magic around her, like braiding hair, she kept adding pieces of power.

The first streams bounced back.

Carla worked with single-minded determination, pulling the returning power back into the "braid" of combined power and funneling it up.

The prongs in her head grew hotter and more painful, as if they sensed that something was trying to seize them. Her mom's hand tightened on hers to keep her focused and not let herself doubt or think negative thoughts. She took in a breath, relieved to find that the stream of energy attacking the shield was doing it with

JENNIFER LYON

less effort on her part. She'd established the pattern and now the energy followed it.

She felt the first crack in the shield. She sent her healing energy to the fracture. Seconds later she felt thick ropes of furious energy snaking down from the crack. Styx! He was trying to choke off her magic.

"I got it," Darcy said.

Carla left Darcy to deal with the psychic. She pushed the power harder against the shield and, like safety glass, it formed spider cracks, then disintegrated.

She was in!

"Now," Chandra said.

Carla couldn't see her brain, but her powers would go where she directed them. She concentrated hard on the first prong. Her powers grabbed it and pulled it free. She actually heard a wet pop.

Then she felt a blast of fierce pain that made sweat break out on her body and her stomach heave. In response, her powers retracted and her chakras quivered in shock.

No, she told herself. She had to accept the pain.

The three remaining prongs began *moving.* Pounding up and down like a jackhammer in her brain. It was excruciating, jarring out all thought. Her body started to tremble. She had to let the pain wash over her. If she fought it, her chakras would close up. She summoned up Keri in her mind, remembering the time Keri had fallen on cacti on one of her searches for her precious eagles. Carla and their mom tried to dull the pain as they pulled out the cactus needles, but Keri grew impatient, and in one magical shove, she drove all the needles out at once.

Carla tried to emulate Keri. Without hesitation, she reached for the next prong and yanked it out.

The pain slammed her as if she'd ripped out a bone without anesthetic.

You were always so much braver than you knew.
Carla felt her sister's words whisper to her and her
heart swelled with grateful love. She found the third
prong and tried to magically latch on to it. A red mist
of sheer agony exploded behind her eyes.

"No!" Styx screamed, ramping up his psychic
battering. "I'll lock you in a box forever, you fucking
bitch!"

The memory of the box chilled her, while the pain
made her hot. She lost her grip on the third prong.
"Keri, help me get ahold of it," she said, furious at her
own weakness.

Then she felt her mom's and Darcy's comingled
powers shoving against his assault, pushing him back
when Darcy's stream of power suddenly thinned.

Styx rammed against them harder.

Carla's powers shriveled and tried to run back to
the shelter of her chakras. She struggled to stay calm
and keep the powers flowing to give Darcy a chance to
regroup. Her brain almost sizzled with the fiery pain.

Carla, hurry, rip off the damned Band-Aid.

Keri's words brought her powers out of hiding, and
together, she and her twin reached for the third prong.

"Carla," Darcy said, her voice weak, "I have to go.
I'm sorry!"

No! Keri screamed.

Pain exploded in her head, snapping her link to her
powers. *Can't do it.* Keri's words faded as her essence
settled back into the scar at the base of Carla's spine.

She opened her eyes and saw that her mom had
tears running down her face.

"I felt her." Chandra's hand shook in Carla's. "I felt
Keri."

"I'm glad." Carla's body was unbearably weary. The
agony in her head made her queasy. But she was
happy her mom had been able to touch Keri, however
briefly.

"You're saving her, Carla. Keeping her soul alive. Once we free her and she goes on...it'll be all right."

Her throat hurt from the emotion choking her and from her failure. "I have to get those prongs out. If I don't have enough power to do even that, how am I going to find Keri?"

Chandra's green eyes darkened. "You got two out and I'm proud of you for that. We'll try again. Maybe you can only do two at a time. You're doing everything you can."

"It's not enough." She wasn't strong enough, powerful enough, or brave enough.

Her dad hunkered down between them. "Carla, you need to rest, then you can try again. You don't need Darcy."

She frowned. "Darcy wouldn't have left unless she had to. Something's wrong." A chill began at the top of her neck and traveled down her spine. Getting to her feet, she said, "The interruption in Darcy's power was odd, too. Something must have been happening while we were trying to remove the prongs."

Her mom touched her shoulder. "Maybe she just couldn't hold the magic."

Carla shook her head as fear spread through her stomach. Whatever happened, it was bad. Feeling a warning sensation at her back, she turned and saw Axel Locke striding across the yard, his feet not making a sound. He wore jeans and was shirtless, a sign that he'd most likely used his wings as transportation. His muscles bulged with tension, his square jaw was tight, and his green eyes were grim. Something was wrong, seriously wrong.

"Sutton?"

He reached her. "He's been blooded, Carla."

"Ancestors, no!" She remembered the vision she'd had where both she and Sutton had seen Brigg blooded. The horror of it choked her. "He's rogue?"

Her Sutton? The man who had held her, kissed her, brought her father to her, fought by her side to save her sister's soul...not him. He couldn't be rogue.

Axel's words corralled her scattered thoughts. "Not yet. But he will be if we let him loose. He won't be able to stop himself."

She couldn't let that happen! "What do we do? There has to be something!"

Axel looked at her, then at her parents standing behind her before answering, "Either I kill him now while he still has his soul—"

"No!" Her knees gave out.

Axel caught her elbows, holding her up, supporting her, while he looked in her eyes. "Or you can try to save him. You are his soul mirror."

Her mom's hand on her shoulder tightened. "Too dangerous! Carla, he'll kill you! And it'll destroy Keri's soul."

It was like being back in Styx's metal box with the sides pressing in on her. What did she do? How did she choose? Sutton? Or Keri? She loved them both!

"Carla, I'm sorry, but you have to decide. We can't risk Sutton getting free." His face shifted suddenly, the mask of the leader slipping away to reveal a man in pain. His cheekbones jutted out sharply, he closed his eyes, and his hands on her elbows tightened. "I have to try to save him."

Her heart wrenched. She thought of Darcy, of what it would be like to be forced to kill her best friend, but her mind couldn't comprehend it. "Take me to him."

"Carla!" her mom cried.

She turned to Chandra and hugged her, tears clogging her nose and throat. "I have to see him."

Her mom squeezed her. "What if he kills you? Like Keri was killed."

She thought of Sutton, all the times he'd been in pain around her from the curse, all the times he took care of her. What had he told her on the astral plane? *Yes, you'll let me go with a free heart. You don't have to ever choose, just let me go.* Sutton had known he was so close to going rogue, and he'd given her permission to let him go. She pulled out of Chandra's embrace and said, "I don't think so, Mom."

Axel broke in with, "I won't let him hurt her."

Jerome said, "What about Keri? If you do this thing, if you bond with Sutton, you'll lose Keri. I thought we were fighting to save her! I thought you loved your sister."

What was she supposed to do? Let Axel kill Sutton? "How am I supposed to choose?" Her heart wrenched and twisted, and in her pain, she did what she'd always done: reached for Keri.

"Keri's your sister!" Jerome yelled. "She's begging for your help!"

He was right. Oh, God, she thought in despair when she caught the scent of incense. Her scar warmed and itched.

Save the Eagle!

Chills broke out on her arms as she felt a deep tug on her chakras. "Keri?"

The four candles flamed up, then settled back to a steady flicker. She looked at the bowl of water in the center. Floating on the surface was her sister's panicked face. "Keri," she whispered and rushed to the bowl, dropping to her knees. "I can't let you go, Keri, but I can't let him lose his soul."

Save the Eagle. Then find me.

"Where are you?" She reached out to touch the edge of the crockery bowl, wishing she could touch Keri.

Don't know. Eagle can find me. I know he can.

Her throat ached with the pain. "Keri, is Sutton your soul mirror?"

Keri's image began to break up. *Save him.*

234

The scent of incense disappeared. "She's gone." Chandra wrapped her arm around Carla's shoulders. "I couldn't see her, but I could feel her."

She turned to her mom. "I have to go to him."

Her dad said, "You swore you wouldn't do this. You're going to get killed, and lose Keri."

Carla got to her feet to try to make her father understand.

He whirled around and stormed into the house.

Carla shuddered.

Axel put his huge hand on her shoulder and looked into her face. "I'm forcing you to make an impossible choice. I'm in the wrong here. I'm the leader of the Wing Slayer Hunters. It's my job to make the decisions. I was trying to push that off on you. Go inside. Darcy will call you when—"

You don't have to ever choose, just let me go. She felt his whisper in her mind and the comforting brush of his eagle's feathers. Sutton was right, she didn't have to choose. But she would because she loved him. She snapped her head up. "Hell no. Not a chance. I'm going and I'll do whatever I can to save him."

Axel looked momentarily startled, then he lifted her in his arms and his wings snapped out of his back. He looked down at her. "Whatever happens, I will never forget your courage. If I have to do the unthinkable, Carla, I will do it with an easier heart knowing we tried everything." Then he took two steps and leaped into the air.

≋ *16* ≋

SUTTON WOKE UP IN A rage. His veins felt like they were filled with Drano, his head pounded, and the light seared his eyes. He tried to move.

Cold metal bit into his wrists and ankles. Chains? His eyes were too heavy to open but he heard voices...

"We killed the rogues who were outside the bed-and-breakfast, but the two inside ran out the back before we could get them. They had sliced the witch's throat and thrown her down on Sutton to bleed out all over him."

"Sutton was out of it, all jacked up from the bloodlust. Key and I dragged him into the shower and got as much of the blood as we could off him. He started fighting us, bellowing that he wanted more blood, so we tranquilized the hell out of him and brought him back here."

The blood memory surged through him. His heart started to race, his skin tightened until he felt like it was being ripped off, one inch at a time. Spasms tore through the muscles of his arms and legs. His stomach burned.

Withdrawal.

He'd been blooded. The curse had won.

That was why they'd chained him up. Peeling his lids off his dry, oversensitive eyes, he looked around. He was in his room in his cabin. The voices were coming from the front room.

"He still has his soul," Ram said. "He has his lifelines."

Sutton twisted his head, the movement causing pain to knife through his skull. He could see his right wrist chained to the bedpost. Opening his hand, he struggled to focus.

Lines. He saw lines.

But he wanted witch blood. The craving burned through every vein. His skin pulled tighter and he could see his veins growing bigger, demanding witch blood.

Carla.

If he could get out of these chains, he would hunt her down, he had her scent. Oh, yeah, he'd find the little witch was...she couldn't hide from him. *His.* Carla was his, he'd cut her and...

Something clawed his back.

No! A sane voice in his brain screamed trying to beat back the curse taking over his mind. The eagle tat clawed at him, trying to save Carla from him. Sutton struggled, fighting the bonds and the ugly realization that if he got near Carla, he'd kill her. He needed to get away, as far away from her as he could, and do what he had to—just like his father had done.

"There's one hope. One way to save him," Ram's voice said in the other room. "Axel went to get Carla."

Carla. He could almost smell the Arabian-coffee aroma of her blood, that darkly erotic scent. Where was his knife? He thrashed against the chains. He needed a knife to cut her, to get all that powerful blood. He only wore a pair of boxers, no holster for his knife. His leather wristbands were gone, too.

The eagle clawed his back again.

Fight it! The sane voice vibrated in his head. His

mouth was dry and his tongue thick, but he croaked out, "No. Not Carla. Don't make her choose!" He didn't want her to have to choose, and he didn't want her to lose her sister. More than anything, he didn't want her to see him like this. What if he killed her? Rolling and jerking on the bed, he tried to rip apart the thick wood frame. He had to get away. He could feel the curse spreading in his brain.

"Shit, his arms are bleeding, he's tearing open his skin trying to get free." Phoenix stalked up to the side of the bed.

Sutton bared his teeth at the hunter and croaked out, "Kill me."

"Give me the tranq." Phoenix's voice was raw and furious.

Ram came into the room holding a syringe. Phoenix reach for it, and Sutton's vision narrowed in blinding rage. Then all he could see was the arm coming closer, with the needle aiming for his hip.

He tracked that hand and needle, pulling his feet up to use the few inches of slack in the chains, and coiled his muscles. Just as the hand got close enough, he snapped his hip up under Phoenix's wrist.

A loud crack echoed in the room, followed by, "Shit, he broke my wrist!"

The syringe flew out of his grip.

"Get back!" someone yelled. Voices shouted.

Sutton ignored them, wrenching his body against the chains, determined to get free and kill them all. He heard a crack by where his right hand was chained. The post of the headboard was breaking.

Oh, yeah. He slitted his eyes and looked around. Ram was bent over Phoenix's wrist. Key was on the left side of the bed filling another syringe.

Now! Just as Key started moving toward him with the loaded syringe, he focused all his strength on his right arm and yanked with everything he had.

The post snapped off.

Sutton used the momentum to swing the post at the end of the chain at Key's head.

The hunter ducked and yelled, "He's getting loose!"

Phoenix and Ram both turned and took a step.

Sutton swung the chain and post threateningly. "Give me the key to the locks!" They couldn't get near him or he'd bash their brains in.

No! That annoying voice said in his head. He hated that voice.

"Stay back." Ram snapped the order out, then pulled out a gun and pointed it at Sutton. "Don't make me kill you, Sutton."

Vicious pain in his back burned out the rage enough to think. A voice in his head ordered, *Tell him to kill you*. He looked down at the hand he'd wrapped around the chain that he'd been swinging as a club. He forced his fingers open and studied at the lifeline on his palm.

His soul-line.

His sanity came rushing back and grunted out the words, "Kill me." He knew the clarity wouldn't last long, that his brain would become soaked in the bloodlust of the curse until all that mattered was witch blood. Once he killed a witch, his soul, and lifeline, would vanish.

Ram stared at him, rock steady, not a hair or crease out of place.

"Do it," he demanded.

"Ram," Darcy's voice cut through it. "Axel said to wait."

Sutton knew why and it made him furious. "Cowards!" He yelled at them, his mind darkening with suspicion. "Or do you want it? Bring the little witch here and see her butchered, and maybe some of the blood will splash on you?" Bastards, they wanted to steal his witch. They were luring her with Sutton, telling her she could save him—

"Sutton, oh, God, what have you done to him?"

Carla. Her voice blasted through him. Sutton turned to see her in the doorway of his room with Axel looming behind her. Her hazel eyes went wide with horror, her delicate face paled and her witch-shimmer seemed to pull from her skin toward him.

His guts twisted with humiliation, and shame made him hot. "What the hell is she doing here?" He glared at Axel. "Get her away from me!" He couldn't look at her, couldn't let her see what he was...becoming. The smell her blood made his heart pound and his head cloud in a red haze of pure bloodlust.

"Sutton, you're hurt!"

"No!" He didn't want to kill her! Yet, the animal in him wanted to cut her pale skin and feel the sizzle of her power pouring over him. He surged his weight against the chains. "Axel, you made a goddamn vow!" He hated them, hated that they had done this to him. He could have borne anything but letting Carla see the animal that he really was.

"Help me hold him," Axel said to his men.

Sutton swung the bedpost club, aiming for Axel.

The club vanished by magic. *Darcy,* he thought. It threw him off-balance long enough for Axel and Key to grab his shoulders and shove him to the mattress while Ram held down his legs.

He looked up into Axel's green eyes. "Fuck you." He'd trusted Axel with his life and soul and the bastard had betrayed him.

Axel's face darkened but his gaze was steady. "I swear I won't let you hurt her."

He narrowed his eyes. "Gonna watch, Axel? Watch me fuck her? Is that your plan? Or are you going to give me your knife and watch me bleed her until her screams die off?" He bucked against the hands on him and the remaining chains, fighting against the red haze of bloodlust. He shuddered and struggled, the blood memory sluicing through his veins in a ferocious burn. Chills broke out on his skin.

Axel lowered his face. "Carla can hear you, asshole."

Sutton's eagle cut through the skin on his back in reaction to the words. The sharp pain broke through the bloodlust. More shame and humiliation poured over him. "You brought her here. You let her see this. Would you want Darcy to see you?"

Axel's green eyes shadowed with doubt. "I—"

Darcy's voice cut him off. "Ready, Axel."

"Out," Axel said to Key, Ram and Phoenix. "Back to the warehouse."

Sutton felt Key, Ram and Phoenix's relief as they hurried from the room. Then Axel let go, and he moved with Darcy to the door, where they stopped to stand guard. Would Axel's immense strength and speed, or Darcy's magic, really be enough to stop him from hurting Carla? Sutton remained frozen, trying to decide what to do.

Then Carla's magic slammed into him, and the chains broke away from his arms and legs. Her scent, the sweet lavender scent of her skin mixed with the darker spicy aroma of her witchcraft washed over him. The dual needs in him exploded, bloodlust and sexual lust. He reared up and off the bed and hit the floor, ready to spring.

His legs refused to move. Magic. He felt it, smelled it, and it didn't belong to Carla. He raised his head and looked at the doorway where Axel and Darcy stood.

Darcy's witch-shimmer sparkled as she clasped her hands tightly together, using her magic to keep his feet anchored to the ground. Her power didn't incite the bloodlust, something to do with her soul being bonded to Axel. But he could feel Carla...

Unwillingly, he tracked his gaze to her and his breath locked in his chest. Standing in front of the opened sliding glass door, the moonlight bathed her in pure whiteness, making her hair shine ethereally. She wore a white top with a tidy little row of buttons up the center and jeans. She'd taken off her shoes. While he watched, she lifted her arms, tilted her head back, closed her eyes and absorbed the light of the moon.

Her magic unfurled, rolling out and saturating the room.

Cut her. Take it. Take the power. The whispers circled in his head. He didn't have a knife, but he could break the sliding glass door and use the glass. He fought Darcy's hold on him, but couldn't escape it.

No. This is Carla, my Carla. He pounded her name into his sick brain, reminding himself how she had healed him on the astral plane, how much the sane part of him cared about her.

"We were joined, then parted," she said. "Forced to walk alone. With singular courage, the mirror of my soul came to me and I turned away. It's my shame to bear..."

Her voice choked and Sutton saw tears running down her face. She was so incredibly beautiful in that stream of moonlight, so pure in her craft, so goddamned honest in her words.

"I beg the Ancestors, bring my soul mirror to me that I can make him whole. I give myself to him, skin to skin, heart to heart, soul to soul."

Her words hung suspended as Carla arched into the light of the moon.

Then her powers ruptured the very air. The light by the bed went out. A wind rose and howled, blowing so strong that it pushed Axel and Darcy out the bedroom door and slammed it. Freed from Darcy's hold on him, Sutton stayed rooted in the whirlwind of raw energy. The eagle on his back lifted its wings, trying to catch the currents of her witchcraft. Her powers swirled and danced on the wind, caressing him, touching him, filling him with the same pure light that bathed Carla.

As she had chosen him, she now unleashed everything she had to save his soul. To save him. The bloodlust drowned out under the waves of her magic, and what rose in its place was a fierce hunger to mate with the other half of his soul.

When her magic settled, Carla stood in front of the sliding glass door with her arms raised, her head tilted back, her hair hanging down her back, and completely nude. Except for the silver band around her left biceps.

His bloodlust struggled to surface but it was the *hunger* that took hold of his muscles and walked him to his destiny. With every step, the curse pounded at him, breaking his body out in chills and sweats, ringing his head with the lancing pain of withdrawal. Shivering him with the bloody cravings. But just ahead of him was Carla...his witch. *His*. He knew what she was sacrificing for him.

With each step another wave of agony was driven into his tendons and bones.

Two steps away from her, away from the part of him that had been missing all of his life, and Sutton realized his boxers were gone, too. His cock had risen to the call of her power. Her magic had stripped them both down to their skin and laid their hearts bare. He didn't care.

One step and the curse roared with the viciousness of a blowtorch to each muscle, each vein, each cell of his body. His body locked up, his brain on fire.

And yet, there Carla stood, eyes closed, magic sparkling, her arms raised, body arched...so vulnerable. She'd even pushed out the protection of Axel and Darcy, so that nothing stood between her and him. He could do anything to her. Anything. She'd laid herself open to him to save him.

He would not hurt her. Ever. Using all his will, he took the last step, reaching out to her and laying his hands on her full, rounded hips.

His palms sizzled, the simple act of touching her roared through his blood, chasing the curse, cornering it and caging it. The curse hissed and sputtered, but it was lost beneath the feel of her skin and the knowledge that once their souls joined, the bloodlust would die forever.

"Carla." He wanted to give her words as exquisite and real as hers had been, but his brain was empty of everything but her.

She opened her eyes slowly, as if her lids were too heavy.

He sucked in a breath. Her pupils appeared swollen, and the green, brown and yellow colors swirled within, revealing the soul of his witch. His heart pounded, his blood pumped, his cock was rigid and painful. He had to get inside her, had to seal her to him.

He had to ease the power thrumming in her, making her hurt, ache and undulate.

Lifting her in his arms, he took her to his bed. He rested her on his knee while he yanked the chains off the bed, then stripped back the covers to reveal fresh sheets. He settled her on the center of his bed and looked at her.

Her silvery witch-shimmer was filling with gold until the sheer beauty made his throat hurt. Her breasts were swollen, almost distended, and her dark nipples were tight and ready for his tongue. He loved the flare of her hips with the soft belly in between. His cock leaped with excitement and brutal need at the sight of her triangle of blond hair at the juncture of her thighs.

She was his. His to love and care for. It just...shook him. A woman of his own, a witch, a soul of such significance that it took a man and a bird to be worthy of her. A ripple rolled over her, thrusting out her breasts, then her stomach, then her hips. He recognized that power surging in her, causing her pain.

She needed him to touch, stroke and fill her until the two of them were joined at their souls. He leaned down and traced her lips with his tongue.

She sucked in her breath.

Sutton gave her his tongue, sliding it in between her lips to stroke and tease and taste. He ran his hand down the side of her neck over her shoulder then circled one breast, then the other.

Her body shuddered, her magic filling her. It tangled with the scent of her musky desire and lavender skin. As much as he loved kissing her, loved plumbing the intimacy of her mouth, he needed to taste all of her. He shifted away, licking a trail down her throat.

"Please." It was almost a sob.

Sutton spread his hand over her ribs, feeling both her fragility and her power. So damned enticing. When he felt the curve of her breast beneath his lips, he lifted his head. Looked into her eyes. "Tell me."

Her eyes pleaded with him. "Too much power. It's rolling and shifting inside me."

He looked down at her breasts, trailing his finger over an ethereal blue vein until it disappeared under the dark areola. Sexy as hell. "Here?"

"Yes!" She curled her fingers at her side.

He dipped his head down, dragged his tongue over her nipple, then suckled until her body rose off the bed.

He slipped his hand from her ribs to her belly and shifted his mouth to her other breast, nipping and laving until she was squirming with sighs and moans that nearly made him come. He let her nipple fall from his mouth, and watched as he slid his hand into the triangle of hair. She was wet and swollen there, her folds parting for him. Her breath caught.

He forced his gaze to her face. "Here, baby? Does it ache here?" He slid one finger into her. Her walls were warm and slick and tugged at him.

"Yes."

"More?" He asked in a voice that was sex-rough.

"Yes." Her voice was soft and desperate.

He slid in a second finger, and good Christ, she took him. Her body sucked him in. A tremor rocketed through him. The idea of being able to thrust his entire cock into her excited the hell out of him. She was so close now.

He stopped.

She whimpered and writhed.

Sutton knelt on the bed between her thighs. "I'm going to taste you, my golden witch. I need to." He spread her thighs, looked down and forgot how to speak. With her knees spread wide, he could see that she was swollen with desire for him. She was his witch, his soul mirror. His to love.

He leaned in and dragged his tongue all the way up to her swollen clit.

She went tight, her back bowing with tension, while her scent surrounded him. He caught her clit, drawing it gently between his lips to suckle her, and filled her with his two fingers. He drew on her and thrust his fingers inside of her until she came apart, crying out, her body shuddering against him.

He couldn't stop, couldn't get enough of her. Yet his own lust had him panting against her, his hands burrowing into her soft hips. He needed...

She curled up, reaching between her legs to caress his head with her hands. "Come here, Sutton. Come inside me."

Yes. Now. He lifted his head and pushed up the

length of her, and looked into the swirling colors of her eyes. She had climaxed hard against his mouth, but she needed more. He could see it building in her again, pulsing and begging. His cock throbbed and twitched with the matching agony.

Carla reached down, and wrapped her fingers around him.

He sucked in a breath, arching into her hand.

And then she bent her legs, and pressed the head of his cock to her entrance. Her damp fragrant skin, so soft and delicate, touched the head of his cock and he surged inside her.

His heart shot up to his throat as the perfect moment stretched out, going deeper and deeper into a snug, slick bed of magic that tightened his balls and sent lightning strikes of pleasure through him.

Her hands dug into his shoulders. "I...more," she cried.

The colors in her eyes quickened, and he felt her body pull at him. Her magic was pouring around him, circling his cock and beginning to spin. Trying to draw him deeper into her body.

She needed this as badly as he did. He couldn't stop. Wouldn't. He thrust again, surging so deeply inside her, he felt something touch and fuse between them. And then, he just felt. His need, hers. He was pumping into her, harder and wilder, Carla's sweet noises pushing him on, her body bucking against him, meeting him, sucking him.

And then she touched his eagle and cried out the words that sealed them. "I choose you."

White-hot pleasure raced up his spine. He looked down at her face, seeing her head thrown back, watching as unbearable pleasure opened her mouth on sweet cries, saw the spinning colors in her eyes fragment into a stunning kaleidoscope.

Then his orgasm hit. He buried himself in her, his

body bowing with the spasms of raw, soul-shattering pleasure.

Finally he caught his breath, braced his arms around her head and kissed her. When he looked again into her eyes, he saw the brilliant, incredible colors had settled into place.

Except now, Carla had a tinge of a blue ring around her hazel eyes. The same color of blue as his eyes.

She belonged to him. His Carly.

"I feel like I'm resting on wings." Once Sutton touched her, the maelstrom of sensations and powers had picked her up and cast her off a cliff. It had been exhilarating, sexy and terrifying. Then the terrible second where her sister left, and she was alone and freefalling. Everything in her was breaking apart, re-forming...

And that was when she'd felt wings catch her, hold her. Cradle her. Then all she had felt had been Sutton surrounding her, his skin against hers, his heart against hers, and his soul uniting with hers. He'd thrust inside her, becoming a part of her and taking her to heights of pleasure and unity that still sent tingles through her.

Sutton pulled out of her, rolling to his side and propping himself up on his right hand. With his left hand, he sifted through a length of her hair repeatedly, the back of his hand brushing by her breast with each stroke. "He's holding you. You opened up, pulled us in..." He looked into her eyes. "I don't know, baby, I'm not the witch. But something happened, something so magical, I can't grasp it. I just knew you needed the eagle to catch you and hold you."

The feathers stroked her back and arms in time with him sifting her hair through his fingers. "You're doing that?" It was soothing and caring. "You have magic to be able to do that."

His face flushed. "Nah. The bird reacts to you and your magic. It's just a tattoo on me." He leaned down, brushing his mouth over hers. "It's your magic, your power."

That embarrassed him? "The eagle is part of you." She wanted him to know how amazing he was.

"He's your familiar. I don't have magic."

She tried to understand. "What do you mean?"

Sutton lifted another thick lock of her hair, watching the strands slide through his fingers. "We don't know how the soul-mirror bond works. I may never have real wings and the ability to fly. But I can help you with your powers." He let go of her hair, and the sensation of feathers disappeared. Instead, Sutton slid an arm under her shoulders and pulled her into his chest. Over her head, he said, "Carla, Christ, you saved me. I could have killed you." His arms tightened. "You heard the things I said. I don't know why you didn't just leave me then."

Horrified by the idea, she curled into him, desperate for his arms to keep her anchored to him. "I almost destroyed you. It was my fault." Psychologists don't believe in accidents. Witches didn't either. Everything happened for a reason, by design.

Had Carla designed this? Had she unconsciously set this up to be forced to choose? It made her sick to think that maybe she had. Carla knew Keri better than anyone that Keri would tell her to save Sutton. Keri believed that was what magic was for. So had Carla somehow set this up so she'd end up with Sutton, and Keri was alone and dying in a rogue's knife? She got everything and Keri got nothing.

Sutton's fingers settled under her chin, tugging her face up to look at him. "Carla, the rogues did it, not you."

She shook her head. "I let Styx use me to separate you from your body. I heard you tell me not to pull you out. I tried not to...but I obviously did."

He rubbed his thumb along her jaw. "Thank the Wing Slayer you did. He had you trapped. How is he doing that? How is he grabbing your mind and trapping it?" Her head started to ache just thinking about it, but she explained to him about the prongs, and how they had been trying to get them out.

His eyes hardened to a steel-blue anger. "That bastard marked you. Can you get the remaining two out?"

"I have to. I will. But until I do, we have to be careful. I can't keep pulling you out of your body." She wasn't sure what this weird connection was, or how it might change with the soul-mirror bond. "It was a setup. Styx trapped me and kept squeezing until I pulled you to me. We can't let that happen again."

He slid his hand around her jaw and into her hair. "You come first. Before everything else, you."

No one had ever told her that before. Her throat started to close up, her eyes burn. And guilt made her stomach churn. "I lost her. Keri's gone." Where was Keri? Without the link to Carla, how long will her soul survive? How did she find her sister in time to free her soul to go on? "If I don't find her soon, her soul will die off."

His face softened. "I know. I felt the break." He reached over her with his left hand, laying his palm on her back. Then he skimmed downward to the smooth skin. The scar was gone.

His touch seared through her heart like a hot lance. She dropped her head against his chest and sucked in a breath and forced out the words, "It's okay. I knew it would happen. I'll find her. I have to."

He rolled to his back, lifted her on top of him, her head tucked into the curve of his neck, her legs tangled with his, and his hand covering the unmarked skin where some part of Keri had burrowed for two years. "We're going to find her. She's a part of you, and we'll find her. She knows that."

"What if she doesn't?" This wasn't fair to him. Sutton had never tried to make her choose.

"Carly..."

She couldn't take it anymore. "She told me to save you." Her voice broke as tears burned her eyes, and sobs tore from her throat. She didn't know how long she cried, but finally, she was exhausted. So tired. Her head throbbed, her eyes ached and she had nothing left. Wiping her face with her hand, she said, "I need to go."

He kept his palm over the spot missing Keri, and the other hand stroked her hair. "No. I'm not finished taking care of you. I'll never be finished taking care of you. You're mine." With ridiculous ease, he rolled her to her back. Then stroked his fingers over her face. "Close your eyes."

Her powers had locked away in her chakras at her sobs. Now they flowed out in a happy little river, following his touch over her forehead, over her closed eyes and down her cheekbones, chasing out the pain and swelling from her tears. He thought the eagle responded to her? Her powers loved him.

"Turn over."

She opened her eyes and found him watching her face.

"Please," he said softly. "Let me."

She rolled to her stomach, turning her face toward him, her left cheek on the cool sheets, her gaze on his chest. Carla knew the power of sex, but this intimacy that Sutton drew from her made her tremble. She wondered what he saw when he looked at her.

"I see my golden witch."

She realized he'd heard her thought and answered

aloud. Then she forgot everything when his hands lifted her hair off her back and over her shoulder.

He kissed her shoulder blade and forged a trail to the middle of her back. His mouth was warm, his breath damp, inciting shivers. Then he drew his tongue down the length of her spine.

Carla curled her hands into the sheets, feeling exposed and yet, safe.

He reached her lower back, the place of the missing scar. He didn't stop, but he slowed down to kiss her from one side to the other, laving and licking, until the spot that had been so empty a minute ago now felt filled with the sensation of him.

Her powers followed his touch, swirling and tingling and making her feel alive.

Sutton's large hand cupped the curve of her butt, moving down to the back of her thigh, traveling across to her other leg and back up.

Her magic followed, creating a need between her legs that caught her breath and made her squirm.

He moved up beside her, then pulled her onto her side so that her back pressed into his chest. She felt his erection against her buttocks. He pillowed her head on his arm and spread his palm on her stomach. His breath stirred her hair, and she was just thinking about turning and climbing up on him when a feathery sensation brushed her nipples.

She exhaled in surprise, her body arching into it.

Sutton's body tightened behind her, clearly reacting to touching her breasts with his feathers. Even though his bird was only a tattoo still, it felt real to both of them. His hand on her stomach pressed lightly. The feathering sensation grew more vivid, circling her breasts, then drawing over the tightened nipples. Hot sensations arrowed downward. She grabbed on to his hand, needing to hold on.

"I can't get enough," he said into her hair, his voice shaking.

The feathers tickled down her stomach, over their joined hands.

He slid his hand from hers, around the back of her hip and underneath her thigh. Parting her legs, he pressed his cock deep against her folds. She arched back, wanting to ease him inside her.

He shifted his hips, found her entrance and pressed in, just an inch.

At the same time feathers slid over her clit. Back and forth, around, sliding away then back, finding that little spot that made her buck and cry out his name.

He pushed against her, sliding in another inch. Then another. "Only as much as you can take. This way is, damn." He canted his hips, driving into her. All the way, filling her up, while the feathers danced over her swollen flesh and her powers raced.

"Carly, baby, I'm all the way in." His hand supported her leg. "I didn't think I could get in this deep." He rocked his hips.

"Magic," she panted, "no one else, only you."

His arms wrapped around her, holding her as he rocked against her harder and harder, hitting her spot over and over until she was feeling only Sutton and pleasure.

"Just feel," he told her. "I've got you. I'm in you, touching your magic. That's it, oh, God, Carly...you're ready. Now."

He was saying words and rocking his cock inside her while holding her, and the pleasure just kept winding tighter and tighter. She leaned her head back into him. Gave herself to the pleasure of Sutton. Her orgasm started small, then burst into fiery, racing, heart-wrenching waves.

"You're squeezing me," he said, then buried himself

in her, and bucked with his release, over and over until he was panting behind her.

A gentle breeze blew in from the opened slider, cooling their skin, and scenting the air with the ocean and pine. She relaxed into his hold, unable to move. He still throbbed inside her while his heart pounded against her back.

His mind had touched hers. It had crowded into her head, filled the space with a blinding sense of protection, caring, and random thoughts: *mine, Carla, Carly, golden witch, protect her, find her sister, eagle quivering for her, oh, God, she's pulsing around my cock, her pleasure, how good she smells, going to come, I'm coming, hold her, hold her while I come into her...*

Other thoughts that she couldn't catch.

"Sutton?"

He shifted his hips, his cock sliding from her. "I heard your thoughts, too." He reached up and pulled the pillows beneath them. "Cold?" He shifted her deeper into his side and put his heavy thigh over her hip.

"No."

"Scared?"

She thought about it. "Maybe."

"I'd kill to keep you safe. And I will find Keri. We know Styx has her. I'll find him and get the knife your sister is in. Then you and Darcy and your mom can free her. But she was never mine, baby. It's always been you."

She desperately wanted to believe that. But men like Sutton, they'd always gone after Keri. She was the vibrant, outdoorsy, passionate one. "I'm not like you. I don't rip the Band-Aid off."

He was silent for a few seconds. "That's a metaphor?"

"For 'I'm a big coward.'"

"Yeah, I could see that tonight. Clearly. You shoved Darcy and Axel out of the room, locked them out, so that no one could help you if I'd gone after you. Coward." He snorted.

She rolled her eyes. "I knew you wouldn't hurt me."

"Did not. You gambled."

She sighed, then tensed. "They aren't still here, are they?"

His chest rumbled. "Little late to be shy now. You stripped us both right in front of them."

"They didn't see anything." She'd pushed them out. She had wanted Sutton, only Sutton. And regardless of what he thought, she knew he wouldn't hurt her.

He leaned down and kissed her head. "They left once they were sure you were safe with me. I heard them leave."

She realized that she was more or less stranded. "I don't have any way to get home."

He sighed. "Carla."

"What?" She was drowsy.

"You are home."

≈ 17 ≈

CARLA WOKE UP ALONE AND cold. She slipped out of
Sutton's huge bed, found a big blue T-shirt and pulled
it on. It smelled like him, musk, pine and all man.
Walking out of the bedroom, she crossed the hall into
the kitchen, where she smelled coffee.

Not her choice of morning beverage. She held
out her hand and summoned a mug of aromatic chai
tea.

"That's her, that's Pam."

Carla recognized Sutton's voice. She crossed the
living room and went into the opened computer room.

Sutton sat at the L-shaped console wearing only
jeans. His massive chest and arms were bare as his
fingers flew over the keyboard while he stared at the
screen. The eagle on his back watched her, his wings
fluttering as if begging her to touch him. The man and
bird were a powerfully sexy combination.

"Found her, Carla. Pamela Elaine Miller of Arizona.
That's our Pam. She worked at a hair salon in Yuma.
It's another piece to the puzzle. I called and talked to
the owner, she said Pam quit to go on a reality show."
Sutton looked over at her with fury burning in his
gaze. "That's how he's getting the women. He's luring

them with a promise of a reality show. Unfortunately, the salon owner didn't have any more details."

Carla stared at him in amazement. While she'd been sleeping, he'd been working.

He pointed over his shoulder to the monitors on the left side of his computer console. "I'm in the Rogue Cadre network. I'm just barely finding my way around, but I'm hoping to cross-match Pam and get a location. They've encrypted their physical location, but I guarantee someone has slipped up and I'll find it." He met her gaze. "We'll find Keri."

She walked to him, setting down her mug next to his empty coffee cup. "How long have you been up working?"

Sutton reached out and pulled her down onto his lap. "I like my shirt on you."

She studied his face. His eyes were bright with the thrill of the hunt. "How long?"

"Few hours."

Her heart swelled. "You're looking for Keri."

"I told you we'll find her. I won't let you lose her, Carly." He stroked his large hand down her hair. "I don't sleep a lot anyway. The last couple months have been even worse. I had nightmares of cutting you. I'd wake up and come in here to work, to try to get that image out of my head."

Her feelings for Sutton were growing so fast, they seemed to stop up her throat, and make her ache to have him inside her. Her chakras opened with soft pops, and her powers poured out in pulsing streams to pull him in. "You're free of the curse."

His hand froze where he was stroking her hair. "Good Christ, baby, your magic is lighting me up like a firecracker. The eagle can smell you and he's quivering all over my back." His voice dropped to a growl, "Lose the shirt for us. Please."

With the computers humming behind her, Carla

shifted on his lap to grab the shirt and pull it off. Her hair slid around her bare skin, making her shiver. Her nipples swelled and the peaks hardened.

Sutton's gaze burned flame-bright. "So beautiful." He ran his hand down the outside of her right thigh. "I want to see all of you, Carly." He put his hands on her waist and lifted her.

She swung her right leg over so that she was straddling him. Then he sat her down with her butt resting on his jean-clad thighs. Sutton made her feel beautiful and free to be who she was—an earth witch who craved this kind of sexual intimacy that fed her powers and her soul.

He cupped her shoulders, leaned forward and kissed her. When he raised his head, he said, "Lean back on the console. Good," he added when she rested on her elbows.

Sutton rubbed his hands up over her shoulders and down to her breasts. Using his thumbs, he teased her nipples.

She writhed on his lap, dropping her head back and arching as his thumbs stroked back and forth.

"Oh yeah." He dragged his hands down her belly, and wasted no time parting her soft curls. "You're already excited. Your little clit is swollen and exposed." He stroked her with his thumb and Carla's thighs tightened, her body jerking at the shock of pleasure.

She opened her eyes to see his blue eyes were burning with heat, the crests of his cheekbones were deep with color. "You're wide open for me." He slid his finger down to push deep inside her.

Her body clenched hard.

Sutton used his free hand to grasp her nipple and pinch just enough, wrenching a moan from her.

"Carly, your hot little body is sucking me in." He thrust a second finger into her. Dropping his hand from her nipple, he slid his thumb along her clit, rubbing and petting. "I'm going to watch you come. Then you'll be so hot and slick, my cock will slide right in and hit your sweet spot. And I'm going to ride you until you come apart again, crying out your pleasure."

She grabbed on to his arms, feeling the ripe muscles move as he thrust his fingers into her while stroking her clit. "Sutton!"

He lifted his eyes to her face and said encouragingly, "Go, baby."

She splintered into an orgasm while he kept saying soft words to her, telling her how gorgeous she was when she let go for him.

Carla was still panting when she realized she was in Sutton's arms. He'd pulled her forward, pressed her body to his chest and rubbed her back as she trembled. She felt his warm hands and the soft feathers of his eagle as they both stroked her. There was no feeling like this. Giving him control over her body.

Unless it was taking control of his. Carla felt his throbbing erection locked in his pants beneath her. Her powers bubbled and stirred against her spine. She used them to make his jeans vanish, and to lower the chair.

"Someone's a greedy little witch," Sutton nearly growled.

She put her feet flush on the ground and lifted her head, then raised her hips and took him into her body while looking into his eyes. "This time, I get to watch you while you come."

"What's wrong?" Carla noticed that Sutton's fingers were white on the steering wheel of his truck. They were driving to her house after showering. Carla was sure she could bring Pam back today, then they could concentrate on finding Keri. But Sutton's tension was distracting her from her thoughts. "Why are you so tense now?"

He frowned, his eyebrows drawing together as he glanced at her. "Nothing's wrong."

She could feel his anxiety, and reached over to lay her hand on his arm above his wristbands. His muscles bulged with stress. "Something's wrong." Maybe he was worried about her expecting them to move in together and set up housekeeping. "Sutton, you have your own life, I know that. I'm not expecting anything."

His jaw tightened. "You are my life."

Nice, but he didn't look happy about it, so he was confusing her. "What's making you tense?"

He turned suddenly to look at her. "Do you want a ring? We could go get a ring."

"No. What would I want that for?" Now he was really losing her.

"Hell if I know. Women like rings, they're a sign of commitment, right? Are jewelry stores open now?" Her hand slid off of his arm when he reached for his phone. "I'll see—"

She grabbed his arm, stopping him. "Sutton, I don't want a ring."

He pulled his mouth tight and frowned like he was concentrating on a massive problem. "What would you like?"

His hard, dangerous face was rigid, while his steely-blue eyes were desperate. "All I want is to understand what is bothering you," she said softly.

He turned back to the road. "I don't know how to do this."

He'd known exactly how to be with her last night and this morning, so Carla began to grasp that this wasn't exactly about her. Sutton was confident and capable, what could he possibly not know how to do? And why was he suddenly in a panic about rings and commitment? "Do what exactly?"

He scissored his jaw.

"Tell me," she said gently.

"It's your mother."

It was so unexpected that she almost laughed, except that he looked miserable. "What about her?"

"I don't know anything about mothers. What do they expect? I mean, look at you." He turned his gaze on her. "Smart, elegant, and so pretty it takes my breath away. Then me." He swung his stare back out the window with his fingers fisted around the steering wheel. "I'm not educated, I was born rough and lived rougher. Maybe she'd accept me easier if I got you a ring or something." He lifted his phone again, accessing the Internet while driving.

Carla felt like she took a direct hit to her heart. Oh, God, Sutton's mom left him when he was three. He'd grown up motherless. He thought her mom wouldn't like him.

He was scared.

Of her mother.

Big bad Sutton West was scared.

Her heart melted for him. "Sutton." She reached out and took his phone out of his hand. "You don't need to buy me a ring."

He lifted his eyes, the pupils large with panic. "I can afford a ring. I can afford anything you want. Just name it."

She would be offended if she didn't know him so well. He wasn't trying to buy her, he was trying to give her mom a gesture that would make her believe Sutton was good enough for Carla. "I don't need a ring. All I need is you."

"But your mother...she doesn't like me. She threw stuff at me." He wiped the back of his hand over his forehead. "She has reason to hate me now." He wrapped his fingers back around the steering wheel.

"Keri. You think she'll blame you. She won't."

"It's my fault. I never wanted you to make a choice between me and your sister. Now you've lost her." He closed his eyes, his face heating.

Carla reached over and took his hand. "I know that." He'd spent half the night on his computer looking for ways to find her.

He pulled into the driveway, shut off the truck and looked over at her. "Carla, I don't want to make this harder than it already is for you. Tell me what to do. How to make your mother like me. Is it the cookie thing? Do I buy all her cookies? I can do that."

She unlatched her seat belt and climbed into his arms.

He hugged her to him, lowering his face to rub his cheek over her hair.

She put her hand on the back of his smooth head and said, "You don't have to come in, you know."

He frowned at her.

She smiled, knowing that Sutton would never take the easy way out. "You don't have to do anything but be yourself."

He sighed, opened the door, lifted her and stepped out of the truck. He put her down, then said, "Fine, but stay behind me when we go inside. I don't want you to get hit by flying mixing bowls." He put his arm around her shoulders and walked with her to the door.

Carla had never had anyone try so hard for her. Sutton fighting rogues for her, looking for Styx, saving her from locked metal boxes, that stuff he did without any fear. He was huge and brave and fearless. But this truly scared him on a level that would send most people into hiding. Not Sutton.

They walked into the house. The smells were delicious: coffee, orange peel and cinnamon-sugar cookies. They went into the family room and toward the kitchen. Her mom and dad both sat at the table, talking.

The coffee pot was drifting a lazy path from the counter to the table.

Sutton whipped his arm off her shoulder and shoved her behind him, his body tense and ready.

Carla stared at his huge back covered in a dark blue T-shirt and tried not to laugh.

"Sutton, why are you hiding my daughter?" Chandra asked.

He shifted from one hiking boot to the other. "Just being safe, ma'am."

"Safe," her mom said.

Carla slipped to the side.

Sutton stepped in front of her.

"Mom, put the coffee pot down. He thinks you're going to throw it at him."

"Oh, I see, and Sutton, you supposed that I am such a poor aim that I'd hit Carla?"

"Your aim seemed very good to me, ma'am," he said stiffly.

"And yet you're still shielding my daughter."

He shrugged. "I don't take chances with Carly," he said softly.

"Carly?"

Carla looked up to see the back of his neck and head flush a dull red. "Carla."

She leaned her head against his back and struggled to keep from bursting into giggles.

"Chandra," Jerome said, "may I have my coffee?"

"Of course."

Sutton flinched, and Carla was fairly sure that her mom had waved her hand to send the coffee pot to her dad.

"How long do you plan to stand there shielding my daughter from me?"

He sucked in a deep breath. "Until I'm sure she won't get accidentally splashed with hot coffee or hit with a stray spoon or bowl." He sighed and added, "And when she's done laughing into the back of my shirt."

Her whole body was shaking with laughter now. She couldn't help it. He was embarrassed as hell, unsure of himself, and the sweetest man she'd ever known. She put her arms around him and hugged him. "I'm not laughing, I swear."

"You are laughing, witch doctor. I can feel you laughing your little ass off." He practically growled at her, but put his huge hand on her arm and squeezed gently.

"Hey," her dad said. "Watch how you talk to my daughter."

Sutton ignored him, clearly focused on her mother. "Sorry, ma'am. I meant she's laughing herself sick at my expense."

"You seem to care a great deal for her."

Sutton took hold of both her arms around his waist and locked her there, with her face buried in his massive back. "Yes, ma'am. I care for her in a way that seems to be making me look like a total fool, but I can't help myself."

Carla felt her eyes fill with tears. It stopped being funny. She thought her chest would burst with love for him. "Sutton," she said softly.

He rubbed his thumbs over the skin of her arms.

"Then my girl's a very lucky witch. I'm not going to throw anything at you or her."

"Yes, ma'am." Sutton let go of her arms and stepped to the side.

Carla walked into the kitchen and went to fix herself some tea. "Want coffee?" she asked Sutton and reached up to get two cups.

"What about Keri?" Jerome demanded.

The cups slid from her hand and hit the tiled counter.

Sutton scooped her up and spun, shielding her from the flying ceramic. He set her on her feet, keeping his body around her.

"Jerome," Chandra said softly. "She's been through enough."

He got up. "There's no reason for me to be here any longer. Is there, Carla?" He walked out.

"Stay here with your mom," Sutton said.

Carla straightened up, reached for him and missed. "Sutton."

He stopped at the edge of the bar and looked back.

"You stay here. This is something I have to do."

Carla found Jerome in her small office, using the phone to call a taxi. She lifted her hand and magically cut the call.

Jerome turned, fury pouring out of him like alcohol fumes. His straggly hair was combed back, and she noticed he had shaved. But his face was still red. "Fine, I'll walk."

Carla stepped in front of her dad. "If you run out on Keri now, I'll never forgive you."

"You're the one who threw her away, Carla. You chose a man over your sister. You always made the wrong choice. And Keri keeps paying for it."

Her chakras closed up. But her heart took the hit. She'd always known he blamed her. "Why couldn't you just love her as she was?"

Furiously he said, "I knew her, Carla. Better than you think. Keri was a rare mix of witch and psychic empath. She felt people's pain vividly. It hurt her, and drove her to use magic to help people. I wanted to isolate her to keep her from feeling that pain, and keep her from being among too many people where she'd run into a rogue." He rubbed his hand over the slack skin on his face.

"She needed people to keep her magic alive enough to filter the pain."

"She wouldn't let me help her! I tried to devise other ways, and keep her alive. She was too damned vulnerable! The last fight before she left to open the Holistic Healing Clinic, she yelled at me that she'd rather die doing magic than live trapped in science."

His pain was coming off him in waves. "Dad, God, no, she loved you. She was just like you! Stubborn and passionate. She believed in what she was doing. And when she died...when those bastards were killing her...when I opened that door and heard her scream, she was screaming for you! Not me or mom with all our magic, she was screaming"—Carla's throat seized up on the word—"Daddy."

The blood drained from her dad's face and his body crumpled so that he sort of folded into a sitting position on the desk. "Oh, God."

She went to him and hugged him.

"She called for me?"

"She loved you, Dad."

Jerome wrapped his arms around her and cried.

"Sit down, Sutton."

He would rather be out hunting down rogues or getting blown up. But Carla's mom told him to sit, so he sat. The chair was small, and he was pretty sure he looked like a giant bruiser, not the kind of man she'd wanted for her daughter.

Chandra waved her hand over the mess of broken pottery. The pieces shivered, then lifted off the ground and counter, and reassembled themselves into two mugs. "Coffee?"

"Uh, okay." Sutton watched as she held up one cup and the coffee pot lifted off the table, floated to her and filled the cup. Sutton felt the magic, much like the beat of far-off music, but it didn't light up his insides like Carly's did.

Carla. Everyone called her Carla.

"My magic doesn't bother you?"

"No." The bloodlust was gone. He watched the cup float over and gracefully land on the table between his hands.

Chandra sat down next to him.

She had long hair, a darker blond than Carla's, and the top layer was caught up in a clip. Her eyes were pure green and amused. "She lets you call her Carly."

He felt like an idiot. "I didn't ask her. She's just...Carly. To me. I mean..." He rubbed his forehead.

"Maybe you mean she's soft and vulnerable enough with you to be Carly. She trusts you like she's never trusted anyone else."

He dropped his hand in surprise.

Chandra smiled at him. "I know you wanted to go after her father and tell him off."

He didn't deny it.

"Yet you let her go."

He raised an eyebrow at that. "Let? No, ma'am. He's her father, she makes the call."

"She made the call last night, didn't she?"

"What?"

"About saving you. About bonding your souls. You didn't send Axel here to get her."

He sighed and leaned forward on his elbows. "No. I never wanted her to choose between me and her sister. I'm sorry as hell that she was forced to do it." He thought of her crying last night, her body shaking with grief on top of his. The only thing worse than that had been her trying to bear her grief alone, that she thought he would let her. "The scar on her back is gone."

Chandra closed her eyes, her witch-shimmer dulling. "So she did lose her."

"The break was terrible for her. But Carla's powers will be stronger now, and together, we're going to find the knife Keri's trapped in and I'm going to get it. Then you all can set her free to go to Summerland."

She opened her eyes. "Thank you."

He shook his head. "I don't want or need thanks, ma'am. I'm going to get Keri for you and Carla. Then I'm going to kill Styx for hurting them. All the thanks I need will be turning that bastard into a shade for eternity."

Chandra sat back in her chair.

He'd scared her. Damn it. But he wasn't going to apologize, not for that. Not for making sure Carla and her family were safe. Instead, he sat back and stared at the coffee. His eagle tattoo started to fret and fuss at him.

Carla. She was upset. He could feel her churning emotions. His exceptional hearing easily picked up the conversation between her and Jerome, making him clench his jaw. This was something she needed to do, and Sutton understood that, but the eagle didn't like it. He wanted to touch her, stroke her and comfort her. To show his displeasure, the bird was pecking at the inside of his back. He shifted in the chair and tried to think of something to fill the silence with Carla's mom, but nothing came to mind.

"Sutton, I think you're bleeding."

He shrugged.

"On your back."

He hunched forward. "I won't get blood on the chair."

She put her hand on his arm. "I don't care about the chair. Why are you bleeding?"

Stunned, he looked down at her hand. She was touching him. Like she, like...he didn't know exactly.

"The eagle. It's pissed off, uh, mad, because I won't go to Carla. It'll stop soon."

"It's hurting you not to go to her?"

He shrugged again. "He's just looking out for her. He's not doing anything wrong. I don't mind."

"He's slicing up your back!"

"It heals real quick once the bird is sure she's okay."

She shook her head. "You tell the eagle to stop it right now. I won't have him hurting you when Carla is fine. I don't think Carla will like it either. Does the eagle want her to be mad at him?"

The creature froze on his back like he'd been slapped. Sutton stared at her. "I think you scared him." The eagle sure as hell wasn't scared of Sutton. But then, he wouldn't yell at him for taking care of Carla either. Her mother was kind of mean. "He just wants to take care of her."

"That's fine if Carla's in real danger, Sutton. But he's just being cranky because he can't touch her, is that right?"

"Maybe."

"He's going to stop that. Are we clear?"

"Yes, ma'am." The eagle was cowering in the tattoo, the big baby. While Sutton was sitting there getting scolded. Stupid bird.

She patted his arm. "Call me Chandra." Then she reached out and picked up a plate in the middle of the table. "Have a cookie."

His hand was nearly as big as the plate. Feeling clumsy, he picked up a golden cookie shaped like a heart. He wasn't really big on sweets and didn't get the hunters falling all over themselves over her cookies. But he took a bite, intending to love the damned thing. His mouth flooded with the flavors of butter and cinnamon. "It's actually good. Really good." He shoved the rest of the cookie into his mouth.

Chandra set the whole plate of cookies in front of him and smiled. "Of course they're good. I'm the Cookie Witch."

The astral plane was a sea of endless blue. Carla had opened her chakras, even the fifth one at her throat, with little effort. "Pam?" she called softly.

The scene appeared in front of her. Not the club that Carla had seen her in before, but a couch in an apartment. Pam was just sitting there in her green dress, looking at nothing. She lifted her eyes. "Dr. Fisk?"

Her doppelganger image looked faded and tired. "Yes, I've come to take you back to the physical plane and your body."

"That light is gone."

Carla felt a wave of grief. "I know."

"I thought maybe the light was supposed to take me somewhere. You know, how everyone says to go into the light."

Carla walked over and sat down next to Pam. "It's time to go back to your body."

She frowned. "Am I in jail? I think I should be in jail." Carla placed a hand on Pam's forearm. The skin felt waxy and cool. Her spirit was losing its tether to her body. "No. You don't deserve to be in jail, Pam. You were brainwashed into shooting Sutton. But he's fine, and I'm going to help you."

"I trust you," Pam said, her words slow and thick. Carla looked at the woman's eyes, latched onto her spirit with her communication chakra, and slipped from the astral plane. She had to hold tight to Pam. While Carla's spirit aimed for her body with unerring accuracy, Pam's spirit was disoriented from five long days on the astral plane.

Carla felt the weight of the physical plane settle over them and she directed Pam to her body. Just as she did that, she felt a "bounce" like a ripple of energy, and then she was hurtling through a tunnel.

Pam was still in her grasp.

Everything stopped. The quiet was ominous.

"What is it? What's happening?" Pam cried. "Oh, God, is that you on the floor? That's you, Dr. Fisk!"

"No." It wasn't her, it was Keri. They were in the clinic. The other two witches and Carla's patient were in the back rooms, but Keri was in the reception area. The pale green walls were stained with her blood. The bamboo floors...more blood. Even the bamboo reception desk, the one Keri had special-ordered, was splattered in her blood.

The chairs were overturned, magazines scattered. Keri had fought them and now she lay dead in a heap. Her green eyes were vacant, her skin hanging from the endless cuts with no blood left. Then she saw Keri's mouth move. "Why? Sutton was mine. Why?"

Horror slithered up her throat, and her heart cried out in agony. "I'm sorry! I..."

Sutton's voice broke in, "Carla, take my hand."

She turned, and saw him standing in front of the desk, dwarfing it. He wore black pants over hiking boots, and a dark T-shirt. His close-shaved head with the gold earring in the left ear, massive shoulders, and rippling arms looked out of place.

The Holistic Healing Clinic was a place of peace and healing.

Sutton looked like some kind of warrior.

And she was beyond relieved to see him. She reached out her arm and he closed his massive hand around hers, feeling warm and real.

Keri moved on the floor. "My eagle."

Carla said, "I'm his soul mirror." She knew she was

arguing with a vision, with something that wasn't real, but...

"Twin bond. You knew that, Carla. You're the smart one."

She wanted to believe Sutton when he said he recognized her as his soul mirror, but he could just as easily be feeling Keri. Oh, Ancestors, what had she done?

Next to her, Pam trembled. Sutton wrapped his arm around Carla's shoulders. "It's not Keri. It's Styx screwing with you. There's nothing here for us. Let's take Pam back now."

She kept her hand on Pam's arm and nodded. Taking a breath, she concentrated.

"Don't leave me!" Keri screamed.

Sutton shifted, moving around the front of Carla so that all she could see was him, see the huge chest where he'd held her while she cried. He kept his hand on her shoulder, and took hold of Pam's fingers with his other hand.

"I shot you," Pam said, her voice thin and confused.

Carla turned to Pam's fading image and blocked out the scene of her sister's murder. "He's fine, you can see that, Pam. And he's not angry at you." It was time to fight back against Styx. "I need you to look at me, focus on me."

Sutton kept his hand on her, but now he was quiet.

Styx was in her head, and possibly in Pam's. She concentrated hard on the room where Pam lay in the physical plane, built the path in her mind, then raised a mental wall around the path.

"I'll get through, you bitch," Styx screamed at her, but his energy bounced off the walls.

Her head screamed in pain. The prongs were red-hot, like two long skewers heated over a flame and driven into her skull.

The physical plane appeared. This time, Carla funneled her magic in a strong stream to place Pam in her body. Then she let go of the woman, and her spirit fell into her body, the pain of the prongs shutting down her chakra.

≋ 18 ≋

CARLA SAT ON THE SIDE of the bed, her hand still on Pam. The horror of Keri's accusation sloshed in her stomach.

But Keri had told her to go to him!

The headache had been a low throb this morning, but now it was a brutal, jackhammering assault. She closed her eyes and drew in a breath. She needed to get those damned prongs out of her head.

Both of Sutton's hands settled on her shoulders. "It wasn't Keri."

His voice was tight with rage, but his hands were strong and warm on her shoulders. The pain began to ease. With him standing right behind her, touching her, it was easier to focus. She needed to take care of Pam.

Go ahead. I'm right here.

It dawned on her that they weren't talking aloud. He was talking in her head. She turned to look at him.

Sutton smiled at her. *Can't get rid of me now, little witch.*

His grin turned his stern and hard face wickedly sexy, while the words in her head were heavy with pride. It made her want to climb up his body and kiss him stupid while holding him tight. She could handle this, handle anything, while Sutton was with her. They'd beat Styx and free Keri. It was an effort to pull her gaze away and turn back to Pam.

He used his thumbs to knead the knot between her shoulder blades. The headache had dimmed to a steady thump, and her horror had turned to fury at Styx.

Turning her gaze back to the woman in the bed, she said, "Pam?"

She opened her eyes slowly, squinting against the light.

Carla forced a smile, trying to ignore the headache. "Hello. How do you feel?"

"Dr. Fisk?"

"Yes." Pam's pupils contracted as her eyes adjusted to the light. A faint color was warming her skin tone. All good signs.

Pam blinked. "I know you, but...everything else is confusing. Why am I here?"

The brain damage Styx had inflicted on Pam with his memory-shifting was fairly extensive, and Carla wasn't surprised that Pam was confused. With Sutton touching her, it was easy to open her chakras and funnel calming energy to the woman. "You've been in a coma, Pam. Before that, you suffered some brainwashing. But you're safe now and we're going to take care of you. I'm going to make arrangements to have you moved to where I work. It's called the Transitional Clinic. There I will have a medical doctor take a look at you, and you can rest while we work together."

Pam plucked at the top of the blanket. "But why can't I remember anything? Did I have an accident, or..." Her gaze moved to Sutton. She paled and sank back into the covers in fear. "Do I know you?"

Carla summoned more calming energy and poured it into Pam. "He's here to protect you, Pam."

"He looks scary," Pam said.

Carla squeezed her arm gently. "You are safe, Pam, and we're going to help you get well. The confusion will go away, I promise. You just need to rest and trust me."

"Okay, I'll try," she answered, her face relaxing.

There was a knock on the bedroom door, then it opened, and her mom walked in carrying a tray. It smelled like soup and cookies.

"Pam, this is my mother, Chandra."

"Is she a doctor, too?"

"No. But she's been helping me take care of you."

Chandra set the tray down on the nightstand. She smiled down at Pam. "It's good to see you awake, Pam. You were starting to worry us."

Pam sat up a little. "I recognize your voice."

Carla reassured her, "That's because Mom spent a lot of time in here with you."

"Oh."

Pam was overwhelmed. Having three people staring at her didn't help.

"Carla, go make your arrangements," her mom said. "Pam and I will be fine."

She smiled across the bed at her mom. "All right. Pam, I'll be back in a little bit. If you need anything, just let Chandra know." She took her hand from Pam's arm and stood up. Sutton shifted with her, keeping one hand wrapped around her neck as they walked out into the hallway and closed the door.

Carla took a deep breath and said, "My head doesn't hurt as much when you touch me."

Sutton towered over her. "That right?"

She led him into her room next door. Once inside, she looked up at him. "You know it is. How are you doing it?"

He shrugged and reached back with his free hand to shut the door. "Don't know. Probably your magic is sending the pain to me."

She was hurting him. Again. She turned to move away from the hand curved around her neck. "Let go. Don't—"

He took his hand off her.

Carla sucked in a gulp of air as the pain drove into her brain. Her knees trembled, and she began to sweat. It was too much, too fast. She forced her eyes to stay open, focusing on the window across the room.

"Come here," Sutton said softly from behind her.

"No. It's okay. Just sudden."

"Don't do this, Carla. Don't make me watch you suffer." His voice was low and furious.

She could do this. Get the pain under control, then find a way to get the prongs out. "I'm not going to hurt you. I'll adjust in a second."

"Did I look like I was hurting to you?"

He hadn't. But she couldn't think...

"It doesn't hurt me like it does you. Carla, I'm not going to watch this. I won't."

She turned slowly, looked up. The veins in Sutton's arms were pulsing against his skin, the muscles were popping and twitching, his jaw was set and his hands curled into fists at his sides. He was holding back from touching her. Now he looked like he was in pain, whereas before... "I don't understand."

He opened his arms for her. "Just come here, damn it."

She took a step and he folded his arms around her, pressed her head against his chest.

And then he relaxed.

It only took a minute for the burning lances in her head to fade to a mild ache. But Sutton didn't even twitch, his arms stayed firm around her, his heart beat strong and steady against her cheek. She asked, "You don't feel it?" Maybe she was mistaking what was happening. Maybe he eased her pain but wasn't actually feeling it himself.

"Yes. Stabbing in my head." He pressed his cheek against the top of her head. "Wing Slayer Hunters were built to handle pain. It's not a big deal. But for witches, you feel it immensely. And yet, you take pain and heal others."

His arms felt so good. Warm, strong and safe. "Usually it only lasts a few minutes. Normally our chakras break the pain down and get rid of it."

"You don't have to go to the astral plane to get the prongs out, do you?"

"No. When I did it with my mom and Darcy, we went outside so I'd be closer to the elements. But I thought maybe with you and the eagle, I could do it in here. That's what I came in here for."

"You should have tried this before getting Pam."

"I needed to get her back to the physical plane first. She didn't have much time left."

He was silent, but his hand circled her back.

"And I thought maybe the break with Keri... I thought maybe he wouldn't be able to reach me anymore."

Sutton raised his head.

She looked up at him.

"You're my soul mirror. Not Keri. That wasn't Keri talking." He used both hands to brush back her hair.

She believed that, at least on an intellectual level. Keri had told her to save the eagle, she wouldn't blame her now. It was Styx's mind tricks, but the sheer horror stayed with her on an emotional level. She shifted the subject a little with, "We are obviously connected, since I pulled you in again. This is dangerous. I have to get the prongs out."

"Tell me what to do."

"I just need to open my chakras and concentrate. It was so much easier to open my chakras with Pam, so I must be getting stronger. I felt the eagle, too. He was helping me."

Sutton looked down at her with his intense eyes. "He loves the feel of your power flowing through us. You are getting stronger. Sometimes the flow starts to bulge in spots, like it's going to burst out of control, like a bulge in a hose. But the eagle smooths it out and keeps it going."

"It must be weird for you."

He leaned down and skimmed his mouth over hers, back and forth.

Carla dug her hands into his waist. The feel of his lips against hers ignited her nerve endings, and made her stomach clench with need. She felt his erection stand up against her belly.

He lifted his mouth. "Weird? I feel your power, that deepest part of you, streaming through me. It makes me want to taste all your skin, then taste your core until you are covered in the scent of your power. Then I'd spread your thighs as far as I could, slide inside you, and ride the feel of your power around my cock. I'd want to come right then, but I wouldn't, not until I drove you to release, the release that sets you free to fly just like my eagle. And then I'd come, pumping in you while flying with you. So *weird* doesn't even begin to cover what it feels like."

Her thighs clenched while her core pulsed and swelled. The raw essence of his words, along with the intimacy of being so closely connected to him, made her almost hurt to feel him inside her.

Her chakras snapped open like rapid gunfire, adding to the waterfall of sensations. It was too much, too fast. Winds swirled around them, lifting her hair and billowing her shirt. Electricity crackled. The TV on the wall flipped channels. Her powers were bouncing all over, searching for a connection to Sutton and his eagle.

Sutton held on to her and grinned. "Having a little trouble, witch doctor?"

"It's not funny." She tried to glare at him but the

wind whipped her hair into her face. She twisted her head to look at the TV.

It went off.

The snaps of electricity calmed, but the wind kept blowing.

Sutton left one arm around her back, and used the other hand to pull her hair from her face.

She went stiff, trying to stop the yawning ache opening inside her. "My powers are searching for you."

His amusement vanished. "I'm right here," he said softly.

All her life, she had carefully shown people the part of her they wanted to see. Witch, or scientist, or lab rat. She had dated smart men, and they'd wanted the smart woman, not an emotional witch. She'd always had to divide herself, hold back. But this bond forming between them, it meant she had to pull him into her, melding them so deeply, he saw, felt and experienced all of her.

Deep enough to eventually know if she really was the other half of his soul. She knew that kind of thinking was exactly what Styx wanted. He was trying to weaken their bond and control her. Then destroy her and Sutton.

She had to get the prongs out, not just for her, but for Sutton. She was going to get him killed if she pulled him out of his body at the wrong time. Firming up her resolve, she said, "Okay. The quickest way is probably sex."

The winds settled down. Sutton dropped her hair and rubbed her face with his thumb. Gentle strokes from the corner of her mouth to her ear while staring into her eyes. "Yeah? You think sex is quick?"

Her powers responded to that, bubbling and popping. She tried to think of something clever to say, but sighed instead.

Sutton moved fast, dropping his hands and pulling off her small T-shirt.

She was left in her pale-green bra and jeans. "That was quick."

He grinned again and gazed at her breasts. "Pretty." He cupped both breasts with his hands and stroked her nipples through the material.

She put her hands on his chest and his shirt disappeared. Sutton reached for the button of her jeans and slipped it free. He grasped the zipper, tugged it down and parted the denim. "Very pretty. Green panties." He slid his finger over the material. "Silky."

Heat blasted through her, making her muscles soften and her skin tingle. Her five chakras were open, her powers chasing his touch.

He eased her pants down her legs, pulled off her sandals, then her pants.

Leaving her in just bra and panties. And him kneeling on the floor, his massive shoulders bunching and relaxing. She could see his big eagle tattoo spread out on his back. Carla reached down and stroked the bird.

He lifted his feathers beneath her fingers. It was incredibly sensual to feel the feathers slipping between her fingers and over her palms.

Sutton stood up.

She eyed his pants, staring at the huge bulge where his erection strained against the material. She wanted him naked.

"Uh-uh. Not while I'm working."

She frowned, looking up. "What?"

"Working, baby. Helping you. If you're a good witch, and we get those prongs out, then you can have your way with me."

She tilted her face up. "Is that a bribe? Are you bribing a witch? Do you know the penalty for bribing a witch?"

He grinned at her. "What's the penalty?"

She had never felt this way with a man before, free and wild. She glanced down at his pants again. "Tasting you. As long as I want to."

His cock leaped in his pants, straining harder. He slid a long finger into the cup of her bra and lazily played with her nipple. His voice throttled down to a sex growl. "Then I confess, I'm bribing you. Most definitely bribing you. Do you want that in writing?"

Witchcraft pulsed behind the nipple he touched, making her push against him and moan a little. "Your confession is noted. No mercy will be given." To make her point, she pressed her palm against him.

Sutton made a noise in his throat and his eyes flared. "No mercy, then." He moved so fast she was staring at the empty space in front of her before her mind registered that he was behind her. She felt his hands undo her bra, then he slid the straps down her arms and let it fall to the floor.

His mouth brushed over the curve of her neck.

Her nipples tightened into pebbles and she leaned back against him, arching into his stroking fingers.

Sutton whispered against her skin, "This is working sex, remember?"

"Yes." Had to get the prongs out. Right. "I need to focus and channel my powers."

He lifted his mouth from her. She shivered, not quite knowing what he was going to do. He traced the top of her panties across her back. Then he hooked his fingers in them and drew them down her legs.

Her heart hammered.

He rose, put his hands on her hips and pulled her down on the corner of the bed between his spread thighs. She could feel the material of his pants against the outside of her legs. He smoothed her long hair down her back, then put his hands on her shoulders and pulled her back against him. He cupped her breasts, teased her nipples, squeezed gently, then stroked them in layers of sensations. "Carly."

She closed her eyes, letting her magic rise and reach for him. Opening herself. "Hmm."

"I feel your magic, baby."

"It's working. Your eagle, he's touching me." She trailed off, feeling his wings slip around her, holding her. Keeping her safe.

"He's going to hold you." Sutton leaned down and drew his tongue over the sensitive spot on her shoulder.

She tried to concentrate, drawing her powers into a stream she could funnel up to her head. To the spot where Styx had marked her.

"Easy, you're thinking too much." He dropped his hands from her breasts to her thighs, and lifted her legs, hooking her knees over his hard thighs. That left her spread open. He kissed along her shoulder, moved up to her ear, sucked the lobe.

Carla leaned into his mouth, let her legs relax.

He moved to the shell of her ear. "You're going to let me in, right Carly?" He parted her with his fingers, then stroked her, tracing her seam, up and down, his fingers soft and teasing.

Her powers went wild, suddenly blooming in hot waves, spreading out and out.

Sutton growled low, his chest vibrating with it.

Her desire became desperate. She pressed against his hand, looking for relief. Witchcraft raced and pinged and popped inside her. Her skin was so sensitized that any touch drove her wild. The feel of his naked chest against her back, his mouth tracing her ear, his fingers stroking between her legs.

"Let me help you. Pull me in." He rubbed his fingers up and down along her exposed flesh, teasing her clit, then sliding down to circle the entrance to her body, and back again, until she couldn't bear it any longer.

Carla grabbed his thick wrist, shifting her hips until one finger slid inside of her. Almost filling her.

"Yes. Hell yes. Take another finger."

She wasn't doing it anymore. All she did was hold on to his wrist while he slid in a second finger and pumped. "Push, Carly. Push your power."

All the popping, sparking, racing powers suddenly found their mark. They gushed toward her spine and starting flowing up in a stream.

"Good, good, I feel it."

She shuddered, his fingers buried in her, propelling her higher. She had to concentrate when all she wanted to do was feel.

"Hold on, not yet." He drew back a little. "Can you find the prongs?"

Tears of frustration burned her eyes but she focused hard and pushed her powers toward the pain-memory that had formed in her brain.

They hit a shield and bounced back.

No! She pushed harder, pulling the returning powers back into the stream and packing them tighter. Eagle was with her, sweeping his big wings, catching the magic and funneling it into a stronger and stronger stream of pressure. Together, they were more powerful than ever.

A backwash of magic spread in her, making her swell and hurt. It went beyond desire, beyond lust, to a cellular level.

Sutton eased his fingers out of her and lifted his other hand to cup her forehead, pressing her head against the curve of his pectoral muscle.

Her magic ramped up, fighting the shields, battering them in an almost animalistic attempt to get to his hand. Then, in a move of sheer cunning, her powers found a way around the barrier, around the prongs, and piled up at her forehead.

A throb began right between her eyes. Not the

prongs, but something else. All her skin hurt and her organs felt like overfilled water balloons. The throb built, and her powers kept feeding it. She couldn't stay still, the pressure was so intense, she arched and hissed.

"Enough, damn it." Sutton pulled his hand off her forehead.

"Wait," she cried, not knowing what was happening, but it was important. All her instincts told her to let the power keeping building.

"No." He lifted her in his arms, turned and laid her on the bed. Carla forced her eyes open, but they wouldn't focus. Everything was blurry. The white ceiling looked like fog. Where was Sutton?

Then she felt him, his hands lifting her legs, sliding his hands beneath her thighs to her butt, and cupping her. Then she felt his head press between her thighs. *Oh!* He was...his tongue touched her. She couldn't see, but she could feel. The wet slide of his tongue set her on fire. She bunched the comforter in her hands, squirming against him.

The pressure in her head built with each stroke of his tongue. But the pleasure...she was splitting in two.

He penetrated her, licking deeply. While he used his thumb to stroke and tease her clit.

"Sutton!"

He growled against her and her world splintered. Spasms of pure ecstasy gripped her, wrenching cries from her. She surrendered all control, holding nothing back. At the same time her magic crested and exploded. A kaleidoscope of colors burst between her eyes.

Sutton was there gently lapping at her, stroking her, keeping her on the waves of pleasure.

The colors kept spinning until her sixth chakra shot open. Her regular vision went completely blind as her third eye opened. The spinning colors slowed and crystallized.

She saw a bird's-eye view of a group of buildings. There was a ranch house, a barn, a row of bunkhouses, and some structure with a brick chimney jutting out of it. The sun was just setting, trees and thick brush surrounded much of the flat stretch of land. Vehicles were parked around the edge in neat lines. There was a two-lane dirt road leading up to the area.

What was she seeing?

The scene moved closer, the buildings becoming clearer. She could see that the shelter around the chimney was just a roof and four legs, which was odd.

Getting closer and closer, she saw beneath the roof.

More brick. Boxy, maybe an outdoor barbecue sheltered from the rain?

The scene blinked, and suddenly she was inside the barn. It smelled strongly of copper and blood. She recognized the cement floor that slanted to a drain. It was the same room as the visions she'd been pulled into by Styx.

Fear kicked her hard, making her skin itch with sweat and she felt herself panting, wanting to pull away. Her third eye blurred.

Then she felt the heat of a large hand sliding beneath her hair and kneading her neck.

Sutton.

Just the feel of him sharpened her third eye. She looked left to the stables.

Styx.

He stood in the middle of a raised walkway stretching past what looked like six stalls. For a witch hunter, he wasn't very big, maybe six feet and one-eighty. She barely took in his dishwater-colored, tousled hair, his lean face and thick chest, and jeans. What she zeroed in on was the knife in his hand.

Her third eye showed her the image of her sister in

the shiny silver. Keri was in that knife! *We're coming, Keri.*

Her sister's hazel eyes locked onto her from the knife.

Carla couldn't feel her, not like she had before she'd bonded with Sutton, but she thought Keri heard her. Thought that would give her the strength to hold on. Hope and excitement surged in her heart.

Keri's likeness in the knife lifted one hand and pointed to the stalls where Styx was staring. Like she had something important Carla needed to know.

Then Keri started to fade and her image melted away, as if whatever magic Keri had used to show herself to Carla had drained her.

No, Keri come back! We're close, we'll find you! Fear skittered through her. Keri was leaving, her soul dying. She'd used a burst of residual magic to show herself to Carla. No, she'd wanted to show Carla something.

She realized she was hearing whimpers. Not her sister, she hadn't been able to hear Keri. The sounds were coming from the stalls that Keri had pointed to; Carla peered in and saw five witches held captive. Ancestors help them, she could see the electric wiring threaded around the stalls and into the floors. They had five witches, all of them standing, trying not to touch anything. Two of them stood on one foot at a time, another one kept jumping up and down.

Styx watched them all, his thin mouth curving into a nightmarish parody of a smile.

A hiss sounded and there was shuffling, then screams...

Oh God, the screams.

Styx laughed, throwing back his head and roaring with amusement.

Fury slammed into Carla. She didn't need magic to know what the sadistic bastard was doing—regularly shocking the witches to keep their powers disconnected.

Fast as a snake, Styx jerked his head around. "Where are you? You can't hide from me!"

The lances in her head burned. He was trying to grab her mind again. Not this time! She concentrated on building walls sizzling with electricity around her mind.

"What the fuck!" Styx stumbled back against the wall of the barn—as if he'd been shocked. He glared around the barn. "You're going to pay for that." He shot up to his full height and curled his mouth into that creepy smile. "Oh, yeah, you're going to pay, right about now."

The eagle screeched in her head, followed by Sutton's voice in her mind saying, "Shit, the rogues found us!"

≈ 19 ≈

ONCE SUTTON HAD FELT CARLA'S magic bloom bright and vivid in his guts, he'd risen from between her legs, and lifted her into his arms. The intensity of her power told him that she'd opened another chakra, and that she was doing something important. His own arousal kept ramping up as her magic streamed through him.

He didn't mind. Sharing in Carly's magic was intimate and so damned sexy. He kept her calm, rubbing her neck, stroking her hair, letting her know she was safe. He would keep her safe while she did what she—

His cell phone beeped an alarm. Shifting Carla in his arms, he grabbed his phone and checked the screen. The sensors around the property had been breached. He switched to the camera views. He couldn't see what was tripping the alarm with the regular camera and he hadn't installed infrared at this house. The fact that his cameras couldn't see the intruders meant one thing. *Shit, the rogues found us.* They were approaching with their invisibility shields. He sent a 911 to the Wing Slayer Hunters.

"What?" Carla's voice was full of worry.

"Get dressed. Rogues."

Her face was flushed, her pupils were large and dilated from so much magic. But she stood, lifted her hands, and was instantly dressed. Then she turned to him and said, "What do I do?"

His phone beeped a response from Axel that they were on their way. "Get in the room with your mom and Pam. Both of you seal the door and window with your magic." It would slow the rogues down, but it wouldn't stop them. He shoved his phone in his pants and pulled out his knife. With his other hand, he was already walking Carla to the door.

"My dad—"

"No time. I'll try to get to him." He looked down into her eyes, saw the hazel colors filled with yellow worry. "I just have to hold them off until the other Wing Slayer Hunters get here. We'll be okay."

Carla's face was pale and tight. "Right."

Sutton watched her fight down her fear and deal. And she thought herself a coward? He moved in front of her, opened the door, and checked the hallway. He could hear faint movement outside the house and coming closer. Pulling Carla out, he hurried to the next room, opened the door and pushed her inside. He took in her mom and Pam's surprised expressions but there was no time for explanations.

"My dad," Carla said softly.

"I'll get him." Sutton pulled the door closed. He drew up his pant leg and grabbed his gun so that he was armed with his knife in his right hand and his gun in his left. Then he hurried out of the hallway to cross the family room to the small office.

A series of explosions rocked the house. He heard glass breaking, caught the acrid scent of gasoline and then the whoosh of flames.

Fire. They were shooting in gasoline-soaked rags to force them out of the house to pick them off.

The family room couch exploded in flames.

Jerome raced out of the office. "Fire!"

Carla ran out of the hallway and said, "Dad, I got this. Go in the room where Pam is. Protect Mom." She turned and aimed her magic to the couch, putting the fire out. Then she leaned into the office to douse the flames that had taken hold of the drapes in there.

Sutton was torn between wanting her safe and the hard reality that they needed the fires extinguished or they'd be forced from the house and killed.

"They're out," she said.

A warning crawled up the back of his neck. "Hurry, get back in—" Too late. He shoved Carla into the office behind him as at least a dozen rogues poured in through the sliding glass door and other windows. Sutton aimed his gun and fired, dropping four in rapid succession.

Another one got a shot off.

He heard Carla's gasp.

His eagle screeched. Rage burst in his head, and instinct took over. Nothing mattered but his mate. He stabbed the rogue sidling up on his left, he emptied his gun into a few others, then tossed it and snapped his wrist so a blade slid down from his leather band into his hand. He threw it dead center into another rogue's heart. He was moving so fast, it was hard for the rogues to get close enough to get a bead on him. But he never left an opening for the rogues to get through the door to Carla.

He heard more rogues pouring in, then the sound of fighting in the backyard that told him Axel had arrived.

All that mattered was keeping Carla alive.

Sutton threw another blade and kept fighting, ignoring the injuries piling up on him.

Then Brigg shoved aside a rogue, and aimed a .45 at Sutton's chest.

He threw his knife.

Brigg danced aside and with cold hatred in his blue eyes, sighted the gun on Sutton and began to squeeze the trigger.

Sutton couldn't move, if he did, the bullet would go through the doorway and could hit Carla. Axel had fought his way inside but he was too far away. Sutton had to believe that Axel would protect Carla if he died. His thoughts were lightning-quick as he calculated how best to keep her alive...

There was a movement in the hallway behind Brigg. Linc burst in, leaped over dead bodies, and slammed into Brigg's back.

The gun went off before the two landed on the ground.

The bullet tore into Sutton's side. Damn, that burned. He held his position as Linc and Brigg rolled on the ground. Snapping his wrist, he dropped a blade into his hand, ready to kill.

"No," Axel said.

Sutton eased back in response to the command and surveyed the area. He didn't see any other living rogues, so he watched.

Linc threw an elbow into Brigg's throat, and Brigg doubled up, choking and gagging. Using the distraction, Linc rolled on top of him, sat up, and shoved his knife into Brigg's heart. He rose, his blade dripping, and growled, "I wanted to see your traitorous face when you died and went shade. You could have used that knife to kill yourself, you didn't have to kill the witch. You didn't have to go rogue."

Everyone was silent out of respect for the hard choice that Linc had made.

Then Carla broke the silence. "You're bleeding," she said as she slipped up beside Sutton, her hand reaching for the wound in his side.

Sutton turned out of her reach and looked her over. "Were you hit?"

She shook her head, her hazel eyes wide. "Is it over? Let me see to your wounds."

"Later, we have to get out of here."

Ram walked in. "Clear outside."

Axel inclined his head in acknowledgment and said, "Let's go to the warehouse."

"We can't," Carla said. "My mom will incite the bloodlust in the hunters, and I don't know, maybe I still will, too."

Ram shook his head. "Nope. Not sure if you recognize me, I'm Ram. And all I'm getting from you is the scent of a witch, but no spike in the bloodlust. Your mom, though, I can smell her and you're right."

"My cabin. We'll go there and videoconference."

"Sutton"—Axel crossed his arms, his eyes glittering with determination—"you have responsibilities. Linc made his test and we'll do the Induction Ceremony tonight. You will be there."

Blood was running down his side, seeping into the waistband of his pants and irritating the crap out of him. He had a couple gashes on his forearms, but the rogues who had done that were now shade, so he was good. "Carla and her family come first."

"Sutton!" Carla said.

He turned to see her pale face. "I'm not leaving you vulnerable to satisfy Wing Slayer's ego. Not a chance. He and that demon Asmodeus are battling for power and we're paying the price. I am sick of this shit." He could have lost her. He didn't ever talk about it, but yeah, he remembered his mom walking out that door and leaving him. Because his god hadn't had enough power to prevent a demon from throwing a curse that had the ability to turn him into a soulless monster.

And Wing Slayer hadn't done a goddamned thing. Nor had the god lifted a finger when his uncle lost the battle with the curse and his father had to kill him. Or when his dad was so close to turning, he'd flown his airplane into the side of a mountain.

Sutton would fight the rogues and do the shit he could to win against the demon, but if it came to a choice, protecting Carly or serving Wing Slayer? No contest.

"He's not going to take her away from you," Axel said.

Sutton eyed his friend and leader. "Damn right." He took Carla's arm. "Let's get your folks and Pam. My house is isolated enough, the rogues won't get the drop on us."

Axel got in his face. "Don't insult us. You got a problem with Wing Slayer, you'd better work it out. But don't you dare insinuate that we would allow harm to come to Carla."

That brought him up short. He was jacked up from fear for Carla, the fear that he might not have the ability to fully protect her, and acting like an ass. He looked into Axel's furious eyes and calmed the hell down. "I crossed the line there."

Axel stepped back. "I'll meet you at your cabin, we'll videoconference with the others from there."

Sutton felt a twist of shame. Axel was going to his cabin as added protection. "Thanks."

Axel reached out and clapped his shoulder in acknowledgment, then turned to deal with the mess.

"Sutton, you're bleeding too much. Let me heal you."

He wasn't going to let her take any pain, but now wasn't the time to argue. "Later. We have to get your mom, dad and Pam, and get to safety."

Sutton should have known she'd be difficult.

Carla put her hands on her hips, her long hair

swaying around her blood-stained shirt. She wasn't hurt, she'd been trying to heal him, and he kept taking hold of her wrists, gently, and moving her away. His blood had gotten on her hands and now on her shirt.

Exasperated, she said, "If you don't cooperate, I'll pull you onto the astral plane and put you to sleep. Then I'll heal you."

He was standing at the sink in the bathroom connected to his bedroom, wiping up the blood and trying to fashion oversize butterfly bandages to close the eight-inch gash in his side from the bullet. His side burned every time he moved, so his temper was getting short. He didn't need Carla badgering him. "Don't be stupid. You'll leave both our bodies unguarded."

Axel snorted as he walked into the master bedroom with Carla's suitcase. He tossed it on the bed and said, "Unguarded? What am I, a helpless mortal? I can kick your ass while drinking a beer."

Sutton had put Pam and Chandra in the second bedroom next to the master, and Jerome could sleep on the couch in the living room. Carla would sleep with him. "Damn it," he muttered as another gush of blood made him lose his hold on the torn skin.

"Stupid." Carla glared at him. "I should just leave you like this!" She started to turn around.

"Carla, what are you yelling about?" Her mom walked into the bathroom.

So much for his privacy. Sutton looked up at Chandra and said, "She wants to heal me. I told her no and she's being stubborn."

"Me?" Carla practically screeched. "You're the one bleeding all over the place!"

"Enough, both of you," Chandra said, her voice stern.

Sutton jerked his gaze up, and the eagle in his back

burrowed deeper into the tattoo. The little coward was hiding.

Chandra said, "Why won't you let Carla heal you?"

He realized he could get her on his side. "It'll hurt her too much. She healed me when I was burned, and the pain tore holes in her witch-shimmer." He shuddered at the memory.

"I see. Well then, Carla and I will do it together. We can siphon off the pain quicker that way, and we'll hardly feel it."

He stared at Carla's mom. Why would she do that? "Ma'am, I heal fast. The wound won't slow me down if we're attacked again."

"Ah," Chandra said. "So it's okay for you to get shot protecting me."

He didn't know where she was going with this, or why Carla was standing next to him looking smug. He knew it was a trap but he couldn't see how. "Yes. Carly loves you, you're her mother." He knew mothers were important. He wasn't that much of a hick.

"And you're her mate. Isn't that correct, Sutton?"

Trap, trap, trap! But he still didn't understand it. "Yes."

"Then that makes you important to us. Like a son." She smiled at him. "I never had a son. But I can assure you that if I did, he wouldn't argue with me. Now stand still."

He stood frozen to the floor. Both women closed in on him. Carla laid her hand on one side of his wound, Chandra on the other.

Carla's power unfurled inside him, and heat centered on the big ugly gash. Looking down, he saw both their small hands emitting a pale light. The ragged edges of the cut began coming together and mending.

He gathered Carla's hair up in one of his hands and pulled it back to see her face. Her silver witch-shimmer dulled a little bit, so marginally that he had to look hard to see it. She was breathing fine, and seemed okay.

He looked at her mother. She had her head down, obviously concentrating. Her hair wasn't straight like Carla's, but it had a soft wave to it. Did he dare touch her? Just so he could see her face and make sure she was okay? But he had to know if she was hurting, Carla wouldn't like her mother being in too much pain. He reached out and pushed her hair back.

She had a witch-shimmer of soft peach. He had no idea why, but the color looked okay. Her face didn't look overly stressed.

And his pain was easing.

"Carla, stop, so I can see," Chandra said.

Carla shifted her hand around his back and stroked his bird.

The eagle evidently decided it was safe and lifted his feathers at her touch. The dumb animal preened happily.

Chandra studied the wound.

"It's closed," Sutton said, feeling unsure of what to do. "Uh, thank you."

Chandra looked up. "You're welcome." Then she stretched up on her toes and kissed his cheek.

The small peck on his face went straight to the part of his heart he'd thought long dead—the part his mother had trampled on her way out of their lives. He had the urge to hug Chandra...like he might hug his own mother. But he kept his hands at his sides.

She stepped back and said, "I'm glad you're okay. Now be good and let my girl take care of you." She turned and walked out.

But he was supposed to take care of her. That was his job, his reason for living. Taking care of Carla and those she loved. She'd saved his soul. Made a choice that no one should ever have to make. These witches were confusing as hell.

Carla lifted her free hand and used her powers to close the bathroom door. Then she lifted his left arm and laid her fingers lightly across the knife wound there.

He shifted his gaze to her and felt his heart swell and ripple. He loved her. He wanted to take care of her. Make her happy. Her magic was a gentle spray working through him, but the arousal exploded, his dick going hard and ready in mere seconds. His gut cramped with the need to be inside her, to feel her magic and strengthen the bond between them.

"Carly." He cupped the back of her head, feeling her silky hair, and begged for mercy. "Please, baby. Please stop." He could barely speak, the drive to mate with her was coursing through him. Her scent was burgeoning, getting richer with desire. He had to get himself under control.

She lifted her eyes.

He forgot to breathe. The blue ring, the one that he wasn't sure anyone else could see, was smoky.

"Water," she said.

A second later, the water in his shower burst on and steam started filling the bathroom. Their clothes magically disappeared. Something deep and unspoken was happening between them.

People were in his house.

He didn't care.

He lifted her in his arms, and strode to his oversize shower. The fear he'd been barely controlling since he'd first heard the warning beep on his phone grabbed him now.

He could have lost her. She could have been hurt or slaughtered. He didn't have wings, and therefore hadn't had the ability to get her out of there when they were attacked. Pulling her closer, feeling her skin against his, he stepped into the walk-in shower done in earth-colored tiles and spraying warm, pulsing water from multiple jets.

"Sutton, put me down. I want—"

The image flashed in his mind. Carla on her knees, her soft hair sliding over his hips and thighs as she sucked him. Oh yeah, he wanted that, but not now. "I need to—"

Her beautiful, amazing eyes cut him off. "I see it," she said, her unfocused gaze shifting color hypnotically. "You want to come inside me." She laid her hand on his biceps. "Hurry."

Her breathless voice urged him on. He could feel her need rising to meet his. The water pulsed on their heads and backs while steaming the shower into a world when there was only the two of them. He moved his hand under her sweet butt and grasped the back of her left thigh "Hold on," he grunted, praying he could go easy, not hurt her.

She clamped her hands on his shoulders.

He shifted her, getting a grip on her right thigh. The steam swirled thickly around them, but he could see her, see her face flushed and her bright eyes. "Your shimmer is filling with gold."

She smiled.

He pulled her thighs apart, going slowly, his cock leaping and jerking with excitement. Then he lowered her until the head touched her folds.

Jesus. It was too much, he wanted her so badly. *Slow, easy*. He pressed against her slit.

She tightened her thighs around him. *Don't hold back.*

He heard her clearly, and leaned down, taking her mouth. *I'll never hurt you.* He eased the head of his cock into her and shuddered.

She filled his mouth with her tongue and rocked her hips, trying to take more of him. *Won't hurt. My magic can take all of you.* Then she circled him with her magic, stroking the sensitive tip of his dick with her powers, while kissing him deeper.

His control shattered and he thrust into her, all the way up her channel until he was buried ball-deep. He tried to give her a second, but she rocked her hips again, driving him insane. He lifted her and thrust.

Then again.

Thrusting and filling her, touching her very center.

"Carly." He breathed her name against her mouth, tasting her while he bucked into her, again and again. "My golden witch."

She cried out, her body spasming. He lifted his head to piston his hips and spurted hard jets of raw pleasure into her. While he watched her eyes lose focus, her head tilt back, her wet hair clinging to her.

Another lightning strike of pleasure shot through him.

His. She was his.

Carla laid her head into the curve of his neck. Yes.

But he felt that kernel of worry, that tiny knot of doubt. How could she doubt this? She was his mate.

⇒ *20* ⇐

CARLA SAT ON ONE SIDE of Sutton, Axel on the other, in the computer room. The four other witch hunters looked out from separate squares on the largest monitor. Key was the cute, hip one with the spiky hair, gray eyes and killer smile. Phoenix had dark hair, dark eyes, wore black leather and oozed sarcasm with a backhanded charm. Ram had a discipline he wore like armor, but there was fire in his incredible blue eyes. And the new guy, Linc. He was all about expensive clothes and hair unless pissed off. Then he shed the superficial to reveal the man she'd seen today when he'd saved Sutton's life by killing Brigg.

They listened as she explained that she'd opened her third eye to see Styx, her sister, and those five caged witches. She finished with, "Keri used her last burst of magic to show me the witches. She's dying, just fading away to nothing."

"We'll find her," Sutton said. "In time."

The silence hung for a long second, then Linc said from the screen, "I was in the area when the rogues attacked because I was tracking Brigg. I didn't want to believe he was rogue, but after he blooded you, Sutton, I had to deal with the truth."

Axel interjected, "Linc alerted me that an attack was being launched right about the same time you sent the 911."

Sutton shrugged. "I'm not questioning Linc's actions or why he showed up when he did. Linc is one of us now, that's good enough for me."

Carla could see the very subtle reaction in Linc. His chest and shoulders expanded a fraction, and the guarded look in his eyes thawed slightly. He'd had to kill a man he'd considered a friend, and he was marked by that, but the acceptance by the Wing Slayer Hunters helped him cope.

Linc said, "I heard some talk while I was tracking them. Styx is their leader, as we suspected. He's convinced Quinn Young that he can track witches and Wing Slayer Hunters with his psychic powers."

"I'm his test case," Carla said, and she wished she was back in the shower with Sutton, surrounded by him, filled by him, until it felt like they were the only two people in the world. Where the ugliness couldn't intrude.

Axel turned to look at her. "Did you see where he is?"

She wished she could answer more clearly. "I saw the place, a ranch or something like that, but I didn't recognize it so I don't have any way to know where it's located." The throbbing in her head started dialing up to painful.

Sutton reached out and took hold of her right hand.

He had felt her pain and eased it. That made it easier for Carla to lift her other hand to one of the blank computer monitors mounted on the wall and concentrate. It took longer than she expected to open her communication chakra, which seemed odd. It had opened so easily earlier. Maybe the constant headache was wearing her down. She focused her powers to

302

imprint the image she'd seen with her third eye onto the screen. "There, that's the wide view I saw."

Axel studied it. "Can you four see it?" He asked the men on the big screen.

"Yeah, but it's not familiar," Key said.

Ram frowned. "The isolation and forest terrain will make it hard to find, and difficult to attack. We can start mapping out probable areas."

Axel added, "I'll fly over, looking for the landmarks you saw. It's almost dark now, but I can start first thing in the morning."

It wasn't soon enough. She thought of those five witches and her chest hurt. "I can try again, maybe get a fix on the location."

Sutton squeezed her right hand. "What?"

She realized he was feeling her uneasiness. "Styx felt me there, knew I was seeing him with my third eye."

His fingers tensed around her hand.

"He tried to get into my mind, but I borrowed his idea of the electrified fences he used on the witches, and I magically built them around myself. When I did that, I saw him physically rear back as if he'd been shocked, then he said, 'You're going to pay for that, right about now.'"

"That's how he found us," Sutton said. "Through his connection to you."

She tried not to flinch. It was the truth, and it made her a danger to all of them. "Yes. And it's not going to stop as long as I have these prongs. He's got them shielded and I can't get to them to remove them."

Axel considered that. "Maybe Darcy can help?"

Frustration made her tense. "We could try, but I had Sutton helping me. We pushed my powers hard to break the shield, and we couldn't get through it. Instead my powers forged a path around the shield and opened my third eye."

"So basically you're a psychic homing device for this dude?" Phoenix asked.

She looked to the screen and into the hunter's dark eyes. "I'm learning to block him, but it's not fail-proof. His connection to me is strong."

Sutton pulled their joined hands over to rest on his thigh, his eyes on her face. "We're going to find him, and we'll get your sister for you. While Axel does his flyovers, I'm going to hack into the Rogue Cadre network. It's how I found out who Styx is in the first place. I'll find more on his location. We're close, baby."

"Okay," was all she could say. They might be close, but were they close enough to find Keri before her soul died off?

Axel rubbed the bridge of his nose. "We need to talk about the Induction Ceremony."

Sutton looked over her head. "I'm not leaving her. You heard Carla, that bastard is tracking her with the prongs in her head."

She had to help convince Sutton so she said to Axel, "Tonight is important, isn't it?"

"Very." Lowering his gaze to her, he said, "Wing Slayer's god powers strengthen from being acknowledged. Losing Brigg was a blow, and inducting Linc with a ceremony will help. And it's important for all of us to show our allegiance. To make a stand. We can never, ever deny Wing Slayer again."

Carla felt the truth of that. "Like Quinn Young did."

"Exactly," Axel said. "He renounced Wing Slayer, creating the loophole Asmodeus needed for his demon witches to throw the curse."

"All right, I get it." Sutton's hands wrapped around her arms and tugged her back to his chest, his chin resting on her shoulder. "I'll go as long as I can be sure of Carla's safety."

"That's why I propose we do the ceremony close by here. We put the witch hunters not yet inducted in the cliffs on the other side of the access road. They can watch out for Carla and her mom from there, and still keep an eye out for any rogues trying to sneak up. That should be far enough away from the cabin that Chandra won't incite the blood curse in the unbonded hunters."

"But close enough to see the cabin. And hear any trouble." Sutton thought that was doable. "I'm on board with that."

Sutton was uneasy. "You don't look good. Your witch-shimmer is kind of dull."

Carla moved around his kitchen, making tea. "It's just the headache from Styx. And I'm tired."

She did look tired, making the eagle beat his wings beneath Sutton's skin in concern, but he didn't cut the skin. He hadn't done that since Carla's mom had yelled at him. Sutton caught Carla by the waist, turned her and cradled her face in his hands. Previously, the pain had flowed into him like a spigot he'd turned on full blast. Now it just trickled sluggishly. "Why don't you go to bed? Try to sleep, and I'll be back soon." The idea of her already in his bed when he came back pleased him. To be able to slide in and pull her warm body into his arms was pretty damned cool. The eagle liked it, too, sighing and fluttering his wings.

She touched his hand on her face. "Sutton, stop worrying. You can't hold off my pain twenty-four hours a day."

He couldn't help worrying. Carla was his life. "We're going to find a way to get those prongs out. Until then, I don't mind holding off your pain. I'll only be gone an hour or two. I should hear you if there's trouble, but we all have our cells linked up to the alarms on the house, too. You'll be safe."

She slid her hand over his wrist to his forearm. "I know." Her eyes softened. "You're hoping Wing Slayer acknowledges you tonight with wings."

"It doesn't matter." It didn't. He had Carly. As long as he had her, it didn't matter if Wing Slayer didn't give him wings. It was just that wings would give him the ability to fly, and that would make him better at protecting Carla. Then he could fly over the terrain where they thought Styx was, find and kill the bastard to free his mate of this pain. He'd get the knife, too, so Carla could free her sister. She wasn't going to be truly happy, or truly believe that she was his mate until Keri was free to go to Summerland. Then she'd be his with nothing standing between them.

She stroked his arm with her fingers. "Of course it matters, but it's nothing you've done if you don't get real wings."

This was exactly the shit that stood between them and threatened their bond. "Baby, you are my soul mirror. Styx was screwing with you in the vision. You know that. Keri loved you."

The yellow in her eyes spread. "I know that wasn't Keri talking. I know she told me to save you. But that doesn't mean you are mine. It means that she cared enough for you to save you from going rogue no matter what the cost to her. And we wouldn't know because of the twin bond. It could confuse you and your eagle. And that could be why your wings haven't come out."

His eagle shoved hard against his back, trying to break free and get to her. They both loved her, and it made him furious that she couldn't accept that. And that was another reason he wanted his damned wings, so she'd believe they were soul mirrors. "I don't believe that." He wasn't good at all this romance shit, and he couldn't be something he wasn't so he just told her. "I love you. *You.* Not your powers and not your sister."

Her eyes widened, then filled with green. Her witch-shimmer brightened. "I love you."

He believed her. Felt the truth. And yet, her fear still stood between them. It was frustrating as hell. "Is it that my love isn't enough?" It hadn't been enough for his mother to stay. Or even his father.

"Oh, Sutton. Yes, your love is enough, it's everything. I swear by the Ancestors! I just have an uneasy feeling, like I'm missing something, or..." She shrugged, her hand tightening on his arm. "It's like I can't hold on to you no matter how hard I try."

He pulled her into his arms, stroking her hair. "Carly." She was in pain, he couldn't bear it. "Sweetheart, do you think some of this might be from the break with your sister? And then today, you saw her fade in that knife. Could your uneasiness be from grief?" Since she'd come back from that vision, she'd felt different. He wasn't sure how to explain it, like her powers weren't as vivid. He hadn't even realized it until now, but surely grief could affect her like this.

She rested her palms on his chest. "Maybe. It could be."

She had paid a steep price to bond with him. "I'll get her for you. I swear it." He would do anything for her, with or without wings.

She slipped one arm around his back to pet his eagle. "Whether we get her or not, I wouldn't change my choice. I love you."

Sutton had never felt this way. Sure, her touch and words made his cock ache, but he ignored that. It was the bond that meant he wasn't alone anymore. He had Carly to care for, to love, to comfort, and to seek comfort from. He had her to gang up on him with her mother so she could heal him. Carly made him feel like he mattered, like he was worth fighting for. God, he loved her. He didn't have any more words, he only wanted to stand in his kitchen and hold her.

Carla leaned back and smiled at him. "You need to go. This ceremony is important."

He shifted his hands back to holding her face. He knew he had to let her go, let her deal with the pain of the prongs while he was gone, but he played for time. "Only if you promise to drink your tea and go to bed." He rubbed his thumbs over her cheeks. "Promise me."

"All right."

He leaned down, pressing his mouth to hers. She felt a little warm, but she'd promised him she'd go to bed and he'd be back soon. He lifted his mouth, slowly took his hands away, and watched her as the pain went back to her. It happened quickly, like a rubber band snapping. That didn't seem right to him. Frowning, he asked, "Okay?"

"Yes. It's just a headache." She pushed her hands against his bare chest. "I'm going to drink my tea and go to bed."

Her shimmer looked a little brighter than when he'd first come into the kitchen. "Naked?"

She smiled. "You'll have to hurry back to find out."

Sutton left feeling better. The witch was turning him into a worrier. He kind of liked it.

The air was damp and rich with the scents of dirt, pine and chaparral. They gathered in the clearing between the cliffs and the woods. Trees along the edge of the open space swayed in the moonlight, making shadows sway and dance over the twig-covered ground. It was eleven o'clock, and the deep cool night prickled the bare skin of his chest. They were all shirtless to honor Wing Slayer with their tattoos, the first symbols of their loyalty.

Axel took it to the next level, his real hawk wings spanning at least six feet.

The air was heavy with reverence as they each took their places. Axel faced them with his back to the cliffs. Sutton stood at his left with Ram by him. Key and Phoenix were opposite. They were in wing formation.

Axel nodded, and Linc broke from the other witch hunters standing by the cliffs. He walked to the center and handed his silver knife to Axel.

"Your test."

Linc answered, "Follow the law of justice by killing a friend who went rogue."

"Even though he was blooded by the enemy?" Axel asked.

Linc's shoulders rose, so that the light of the moon reflected on the outline of the unfinished falcon on his back. "He still had a choice. They gave him a knife to kill off the witch. He could have turned the knife on himself, saving his soul."

Sutton felt pride in Linc. His test had been brutal. But he had passed it, and would be a stronger, more just fighter for it.

"Accepted," Axel said. "Your vow."

"I vow my allegiance to Wing Slayer, god of the witch hunters. I take the ancient oath of protection for the innocent and justice for the damned. And I swear to fight the curse to my death."

"And your sacrifice." He handed the knife to Linc.

Without hesitation, Linc took the knife and sliced the inside of his arm. "My life's blood for protection and justice in the name of Wing Slayer."

The blood dripped silently onto the dirt.

Sutton felt his shoulders and neck tense with thick anticipation. This was the moment that Axel believed Wing Slayer would show his acceptance of Linc.

The moment Sutton hoped for a sign of his own. He didn't need a big public splash of his wings breaking out; just a quiet acknowledgment, like the mark of wings on his knife or whatever Wing Slayer wanted.

Then he'd know that his wings would come out when he needed them.

Nothing seemed to happen. Just the roar of the ocean, the rustle of the tree branches in the breeze, and the shifting of the men as they waited. No dramatic cloud cover, no sudden explosion of lightning and crash of thunder, no earthquake.

Then a shift, a sudden tension in the air. The breeze turned into a fierce wind, blowing the trees, making the shadows shift and weave eerily, dust and twigs blowing around their legs. A tangy yet sweet scent surrounded them as a large, winged shadow fell over Linc. Was this it?

Then the shadow vanished, gone as quickly as it came. The wind faded back to a breeze, the trees grew calm, the twigs and dirt settled. The scent weakened until it was only a memory.

Axel said, "Lincoln Dillinger, take your place in our wing formation. You are marked a Wing Slayer Hunter."

Sutton blinked, surprised. He'd felt a presence, something, but then it was gone. He reached behind him and slid his fingers over the hilt of his knife sticking out of the holster.

It was still smooth. His eagle tried to reach Carla, suddenly feeling desperate to touch her. Sutton felt the same disappointment as the bird, but he had to stay focused on the ceremony. They both had to be patient.

As Linc started to turn, his face as baffled as everyone else's, the moonlight narrowed into a beam of light directly onto the man's back.

The tattoo was finished. It showed a falcon in incredible detail. The bird's abdomen had gray bars across the white background, and the chest had teardrop markings in the same color. His long, pointed wings were spread, revealing a glimpse of the intricate gray barring on the underside, and the darker solid feathers on the outside. The bird had a distinctive yellow eye ring, along with a mostly yellow beak and yellow feet.

After a second of sheer silence and awe, the beam of light faded to normal. The men all broke formation, going to slap Linc on the back. Sutton reached him first, and said, "That's a hell of a mark."

Key added, "Would have taken me days to get all that detail."

Linc grinned. "Looks good, huh?"

The eagle went from disappointment to panic and started clawing his back. Ripping his skin, screeching and desperately trying to get out. Blood welled and slid down his back in warm rivers. For a second, Sutton thought maybe this was a temper tantrum over not getting wings. But no, he could feel the eagle's genuine need to get to Carla. She was in trouble! But why didn't he feel it from her? His heart rate shot up, and before he took his next breath, his knife was in his hand.

"What?" Axel appeared at his side with his wings folded up into his tattoo.

Ram had his cell phone out as he ran up. "No warning from your alarms, and the cell's working."

"Jesus, Sutton," Phoenix said. "Your eagle's shredding your back."

He didn't care. Sutton went invisible and launched into hyperspeed. All that mattered was getting to Carla. He raced to his cabin, covering the distance in seconds. Now that the eagle had him moving, he didn't bother clawing his back, but he was pitching himself against his skin, still trying to break free.

He knew the other Wing Slayer Hunters were behind him. He vaulted up the steps, stopped at the door, and inhaled.

No copper scent.

He listened, and heard Carla's soft cries. Shoving

open the door, his eyes adjusted to the darkness, and he saw Jerome asleep on the sleeper sofa. He ignored him and hurried to the bedroom.

She was in one of his T-shirts and curled on her side, her arms over her head. "Carly?" he called softly. Materializing, he walked to the side of the bed and sat down. Her hair was sticking to her head and arms and he could smell sweat.

Fear rocketed through him.

He put his hand on her shoulder. The shirt she wore was damp with her sweat and, even worse, he felt almost no pain from her. Shit. He should feel her pain!

"Sutton." Her voice was thready.

He lifted her and turned, setting her in his lap. "Carly, you have to open your chakras." He was pretty sure he could siphon off her pain then.

"Can't. Tried. Won't open."

He felt Axel walk into the room and absently smoothed the shirt down over her thighs to cover her. "It's the prongs in her head. They are causing her severe headaches." He felt so fucking helpless.

"You can't take her pain?" Axel's voice was soft.

"I have been, but something's going wrong. Her chakras are closed and she says she can't open them."

"What's going on?" Chandra's voice came from behind Axel.

Axel turned out of the way.

Chandra wore green pajamas, and her hair was pulled back in a loose ponytail. Worry lines appeared on her forehead when she saw Carla.

Sutton couldn't get on top of the panic. His eagle was fretting and softly keening. "She's sicker. In pain. I can't get her pain to come to me. Tell me what to do."

Chandra came to the bed, knelt down and put her hand on Carla's head.

"Mom?" Carla said.

"Yes, honey. I want you to just rest." She looked at

312

Sutton. "Her chakras are closed, and she's running a fever."

"Can you heal her?" She was a witch, she had to be able to heal her.

Chandra closed her eyes, and her peachy shimmer brightened with her effort. Then she opened her eyes and looked into Sutton's eyes. She shook her head. "We need to try something else."

"What?"

She stood up. "Axel, can you get Darcy?"

"Darcy's already yelling at me to get her. I'm on my way." He turned and strode out.

Chandra said, "I'm going to go out and talk to Jerome. I want you to try to force her chakras open."

"How?" He wasn't magical like them.

She put her hand on his shoulder. "Just touch her, try and draw her magic out. That might open her chakras. Try, okay?" Her voice ended on a plea.

Sutton reached up and put his hand over hers. "Anything. I'll do anything."

"I know you will." She looked slightly relieved and a whole lot scared. He squeezed her hand. Chandra left, closing the door.

"Carly," he coaxed her, "sweetheart, we're going to do this together." He laid her on the bed, then hurried, gathering up one of his clean shirts and a pair of her panties and dropped them on the end of the bed. Then he raced into the bathroom, grabbed a washcloth and ran it under cool water. Returning, he sat down again.

"You didn't get wings." She closed her eyes, took a breath, and forced them open again. "I'm sorry."

She was in agony and she was sorry for him? It choked him. He gently stripped the shirt and panties off her. Then he ran the cool cloth over her face and neck. "Just get better. I don't give a shit about the wings. Please, you have to get better."

She closed her eyes.

He knew she was conscious, it was the pain pulling her away from him. He felt what he could only describe as an echo of her pain. He moved the washcloth down, over her breasts, ribs and stomach.

He made a round trip to the bathroom to wet the cloth again.

Then he turned her over, scooped up her damp hair, and ran the cool cloth over her neck and back. Dropping the cloth on the floor, he climbed over her, not caring that he had his boots on, and pulled her back to his chest. He slipped his arm under her head. "I'm going to touch you and bring your powers out. Then I can take your pain."

She stiffened. "Too much pain for you."

He kissed the top of her head. "We'll share the pain, baby. The two of us and it won't be too much." *Liar.* He was going to pull all the pain from her. Every last drop. He slid his right hand down her belly and spread it over her triangle of hair between her thighs. Then he moved his hand up over the skin of her belly, between her ribs and breasts to her neck.

Then down again.

And back up. Gentle touches.

She sighed.

"How do your chakras feel?"

"They're trembling but can't open."

"They feel me?"

"Yes."

Hope flared into him. He slid his hand into the tangle of hair, scooted back enough to settle Carla on her back and nudged her legs apart. He would get closer to her first chakra this way. "Just you and me, Carly. I want you to open for me, let me share your pain." He stroked her folds, then separated her.

She relaxed deeper, letting her thighs fall open, allowing him to touch her.

Her trust humbled him right to his soul. She knew

he'd care for her, including listening to make sure no one came in. This wasn't sex—she was too sick and weak for sex—this was intimacy. He was easy with her, working in one finger, then leaned over her and brushed his mouth over her forehead. Her chakras went from her pelvis to the top of her head. He figured if he touched her from both ends, he could force something open.

He felt her responding clench around his fingers.

A small spasm of power breaking free.

Then her pain started filling his head. Thank the Wing Slayer. He took his hand from between her legs. Keeping one hand on her to continue siphoning off her pain, he slipped on her clean panties, then pulled his shirt off over her head. Sutton lay back down and pillowed her heat on his arm. He fitted his chest up against her back, and put his hand on her bare arm. Skin-to-skin contact was important.

She said softly, "Only two chakras opened."

"It's enough for right now." He didn't dare push her any further, not until her mom and Darcy checked on her. He lifted his hand from her long enough to grab the comforter and pull it up over her.

≈ *21* ≈

CARLA LAY IN THE COCOON of Sutton, his chest against her back, his biceps under her head, his arm curled around her. The pain had notched down to a bad headache. Her legs and arms were heavy.

There was a soft tap on the door.

"Come in," Sutton said.

Her mom came through the door, her face lined with worry or fear. She knelt on the floor, her cool hand brushing back Carla's hair. "It worked?"

Carla was so tired. "Two chakras. I'm losing my power, Mom."

Chandra's eyes welled up. She squeezed Carla's hand. "I thought the soul-mirror bond was supposed to make you stronger."

She tried to force a smile, but it was too much for her.

"You're my soul mirror." Sutton pulled her tighter against him.

She couldn't say anything.

Two more people walked into the room, Jerome, looking like a mad scientist with his blond hair sticking up all over, and Darcy, her hair pulled into a tight ponytail, and wearing jeans and a T-shirt.

Darcy went to the bed and sat down. Her eyes were dark and worried. She laid her hand over Carla's and said, "I'm going to see what I can get from my third eye." She closed her eyes.

Axel moved silently into the room and stood next to Darcy. She leaned against his leg.

Carla felt Darcy's magic rise and swirl around her, then sink deeper and deeper into her. She tried to keep the two chakras open, giving Darcy access. But even with Sutton touching her, it caused sweat to break out on her body and her hands to shake.

Darcy pulled back and opened her eyes.

Carla looked into the brown depths. "Tell me. I know you don't want to."

Tears welled up in her friend's gaze. "The prongs, they are...you're dying."

"No!" Sutton yelled behind her. "She's not dying! I'm her soul mirror, I can make her stronger! Get out, I'll—"

Carla felt his rage and pain. She didn't know how to help him.

"Out! I'll save her!" Sutton yelled. He let go of Carla and jumped to his feet. "I won't let her die!"

Axel moved to face him. "We'll figure this out. Maybe ask Wing Slayer—"

"Wing Slayer!" Sutton roared. "He doesn't care! He hasn't claimed me or Carla. You told me he wouldn't take her from me. But look at her! Wing Slayer can go to—"

"Sutton, no!" The pain exploded in her head and her vision blurred. Ignoring them all, she crawled across the bed, trying to get to him. She reached out a hand, finding his hip. She latched on to it. "Don't."

He swept her up into his arms, pulling her close to him. "Carly, I can't lose you."

She sighed against his chest. Her two chakras stayed open and the pain trickled out of her and into him.

Sutton carried her to the corner and sat in the chair between the sliding glass door and the fireplace. "What do we do? Someone tell me what to do because I am not letting Carla die. I don't give a shit if she's my soul mirror or not, she's mine."

He finally believed her. Tears burned her eyes and fell on his chest.

"Don't cry. Please Carly, I'll find a way. I swear."

"That's not why."

He leaned down, kissing away her tears. "Why?"

She forced her eyes open. "Because you love me. Just me.

He stared into her eyes. "I love you, just you. Powers or not, soul mirror or not."

"That's enough for me. Whatever happens, that's enough."

His jaw went stubborn. "I won't lose you."

"I have to talk to my dad."

"Okay." He helped her sit up. "Lean against me."

She let him situate her against his chest. Her mom covered her with a blanket, then Sutton folded his arms over her. Once they were done fussing, she looked up at her dad, noticing her vision was blurry. "You know what's happening, don't you?"

Her dad pulled in a dining room chair and sat on it with his arms braced on his thighs. His face dropped into craggy lines of despair. "All the times I was so desperate to be right, to prove to everyone I was right. And the one time I'm right, I'm desperate to be wrong."

Because he loved her. And Keri. "But you're not, are you?"

He shook his head. "I've studied this from every angle I can think of. We know Keri was linked to you to keep her soul alive. The twin bond made that possible. Both of you pulled Sutton in and formed a power matrix. Then Styx got ahold of the knife Keri was in."

Carla said, "Asmodeus found it from the magical trail she used to get to me."

Axel said, "And I'm betting he sent Quinn Young to retrieve it. Young then gave it to Styx to torture Carla."

Jerome looked around at everyone in the room. "Makes sense. Styx knew Keri was in the knife, and Keri enhanced his psychic powers. I'm guessing he cut himself with the knife and established a bond. Then he used Keri's twin bond with Carla to reach her psychically. Each time he was embedding the prongs in Carla. Those prongs gave him easier access to her."

Darcy said, "We were able to get two prongs out. But Carla couldn't get the remaining two even with Sutton's help."

Carla knew the answer now. It was what had been eluding her all along. "Because I broke the twin bond."

Her dad looked at her with heartbreaking sadness. "The prongs were in both you and Keri. You were bonded. When you broke the bond, you sealed in the prongs."

She closed her eyes. "And the prongs link me right back to Keri. When I broke the bond and separated us, we both started to die."

"No," Sutton said, his chest rumbling at her back. "Carla's powers spiked when we bonded."

"Because Keri had enough of me, and me enough of her to last for a day or so. Then once Keri started weakening in the knife, my chakras and life force started shutting down." She closed her eyes and remembered Keri's fading image in the knife. "She used the last of her residual power to show me the witches, to save them." *Oh, Keri,* she thought, her chest tightening in grief.

Sutton leaned his face against her head. "But we bonded like soul mirrors. You saved me from the

319

curse. I should be able to help you." He paused, then added, "That part just doesn't make sense."

She opened her eyes and said, "Twin bond and power matrix. We formed a power matrix, you, me and Keri. You touched my blood when Keri was in me, I touched yours, and we both bonded to you in a weird way. It was enough to bring our souls together and rid you of the curse but not enough to hold them." She looked intently at her dad. "Right? Keri's his soul mirror, not me."

"That's my best hypothesis," he said gravely.

"Just tell me what to do. How to save Carly."

Jerome said, "Get the knife. Re-form the twin bond, then you can get the prongs out and Carla can free Keri."

Carla struggled against the weighty fatigue. "He'll know Sutton's coming, won't he? Styx is counting on his psychic powers to stay one step ahead."

Sutton's muscles went rigid. "Nothing he does will stop me."

Jerome said, "Carla's right. He's staying one step ahead, layered in protection. He wants you to come to him. He's sure he has learned your weaknesses and can use them to kill you."

She knew that was true, and she pressed her hand over Sutton's bulging forearm to get him to listen. "The mortal women he's brainwashed. Sutton will hesitate to kill them. Styx will know that." Sutton was hardwired to protect the innocent and Carla knew that no matter what Styx brainwashed the women to do, it'd be hard for Sutton to kill them. He hadn't killed Pam when she shot him, and that was all Styx needed to know. "How do we beat him, Dad?"

"We let him draw Sutton to him, then we beat him at his own game. I've been thinking about this. I've seen witches project their voices and images through computers, right?"

Carla didn't have the energy to answer. Her mom did it for her. "Yes, like you saw Carla and me talking to the Circle Witches."

"Carla, honey, are you listening?" her dad asked.

"Yes." She forced herself to open her eyes and focus on the increasingly blurry figure of her dad.

"Can witches work together to project a barrage of thoughts through an electronic device? All at once? If Sutton turns on the Bluetooth on his cell and aims it at Styx, a barrage of thoughts will bombard his brain waves and short-circuit his psychic ability."

In spite of her fatigue and weakness, her heart rate picked up speed. "You think the mortals he's brainwashed have mental prongs or links to him, like me." It made sense, they thought Styx had leeched power from both witch blood and Keri to get stronger, and then he could have marked the brainwashed women to keep control of them. "Disrupting the brain waves like that should work. It'll take a massive and collective effort, though."

"The Circle Witches," Darcy said. "They'll do it. Your mom and I will convince them."

Her hope dimmed. "How?"

Darcy touched her shoulder. "Let me worry about that. I'll convince them."

Sutton kissed her head. "We'll get the knife, Carly. You just rest."

Sutton dug deeper and deeper into the Rogue Cadre network until he finally hit pay dirt...a cell phone number for Styx. They'd all been working fast and furious trying to get some place to start the search for Styx, and this was it!

He was working from his bedroom with his laptop on one thigh. Carly lay with her head pillowed on his other thigh. Darcy and Chandra had combined their powers to settle her into sleep while Sutton kept siphoning off her pain.

Even though it was dark, Axel was flying over the possible sites where Styx and the knife were. Working furiously, he hacked into the cell phone company's network, activated the GPS and now he had a cell tower location. *Yes!* "Axel," he said into the headset hooked on his ear. "I'm in." He shifted to Google satellite maps and started looking for the areas closest to the cell tower. He looked up to the big-screen TV where he'd put Carla's map. "Try these coordinates." He sent Axel to the closest rugged area.

"On it," was his Hawk's reply.

He dropped his hand onto Carly's head, loving the feel of her hair. He couldn't lose her. He didn't care if Keri was his true soul mirror, Carla was the love of his heart and soul. He wished Keri well, and he wanted her soul freed for Carla's happiness.

Chandra walked softly into the room.

Sutton looked up at the woman. He was watching her age over the night hours. He saw more lines appear around her eyes and mouth each time she came in.

She said, "It took some doing, but the Circle Witches have agreed. We're nearly positive this won't invoke witch karma since we're simply disrupting the path Styx uses to brainwash victims. This isn't causing direct harm."

"I'm grateful to the witches." But now he had to find where Styx was.

"Do you mind if I sit with her? I'll just pull the chair over and sit by the bed."

He looked up from his laptop. "Chandra, you need to rest. You've done all you can until we have a location. Lie down next to Carla and close your eyes. You'll rest better if you know you can hear her." He stroked Carla's hair. "She'll rest better too, if she feels you nearby." He reached over and pulled back the covers so Chandra could slide in next to her daughter.

Her eyes were filled with worry, but there was relief when she lifted her gaze to him. "Thank you." She slid into the bed, resting her hand on Carla's back.

"Carly needs you. You're her mother." He went back to studying a Google map then frowned and looked over at Chandra. "Pull the covers up so you don't get cold."

She smiled and reached down to grab the covers. "Do you boss Carla around like this?"

He couldn't help but grin as he studied the map. "Not so much. She's a little stubborn." He glanced over. "No offense."

"How can the truth offend me?"

He shrugged, moving the map to study the next section. "I don't know. The guys, they tease me because I don't know much about mothers. I don't know the rules."

He was startled when Chandra touched his arm. "There are no rules. You can't offend me, Sutton. The way you love my daughter would make any mother love you."

His hand froze on the touch pad. He suddenly felt big and clumsy. "My mother didn't." Damn it, why'd he say that? It was the fear, rage and terror. All centered on the woman lying half next to him, and half on top of him. *Carly.* He was terrified of losing her. It was making him too vulnerable.

"Your mother was a fool."

He stared hard at the screen. Was he supposed to say something?

Carla moaned and shivered. He slid his hand to the bare skin of her neck beneath her hair and felt the thick, sluggish pain barely seeping into him. It was getting harder and harder to siphon off her pain.

"She's cold?"

Sutton looked at Chandra, seeing the same helplessness in her eyes that he felt. Maybe he didn't know shit about mothers, but he could read in Chandra the desperate need to hold her sick child. "Maybe you should move closer. I mean, if you don't mind getting close to me. She'll be warmer between us."

Tears filled Chandra's eyes but she didn't speak, she just snuggled up to Carla's back, curving her arm around Carla's waist.

A second later, more of her pain bled into him, as if the spigot had opened a little bit wider. Relieved, he said, "Must be your magic, Chandra. I can feel more of her pain coming to me."

She lifted her head, her eyes so tired. "I'm sending healing energy, but the backwash pain should flow to me, not you."

He didn't like that. "No, it's better this way. You and Darcy need to be rested to funnel all the witchcraft into my cell phone when I confront Styx. And you'll be taking care of Carla, too."

"What can I do for you? The pain must be awful."

"Nah, it's just a headache for me. But for her, it's like someone is pounding stakes into her head. Now try to sleep. You'll hear me talking." He tapped the hands-free device in his ear. "Axel and I are searching for that knife. But if Carly needs you, I'll wake you."

She turned to the big screen on the wall where Sutton had the map Carla had magically created from what her third eye had shown her. "That's what you're looking for?"

He studied the structures. "Yeah, we know the general area, but I'm trying to narrow the search. I've looked for old ranches and private schools in the general vicinity, anything that might give us a clue. No luck so far. See that chimney sticking out of the lean-to type of structure?"

"Yes."

"That's unusual and a good landmark for us to spot either on the maps or for Axel to see flying overhead."

"It looks like an outdoor kiln."

"What?"

"For making pottery. Maybe it was a commune at one time, and they made and sold pottery. Commune members liked isolation to live as they chose, and that looks isolated, yet close enough to take their pottery to the beach areas and sell it."

Commune. Kiln. Weren't kilns used for cremation ovens, too? If they were big enough and burned hot enough, it would fit the rogues' needs. He kept that dark thought to himself. "You might be on to something, Chandra. I'll check it out."

She smiled at him and said, "I'll go to sleep and leave you to work if you promise you'll wake me if you need anything, too. I don't care if it's just a glass of water. Promise me."

"I promise." He didn't want to bother her for dumb stuff, but it seemed important to her. Hell, she made him feel like he was almost as important as Carla.

Ten minutes later, her breathing settled into a regular pattern. He was searching fast and furious, looking for intel on all known communes that might have once been in the area, and updating Axel. He narrowed the search to one that had achieved some notice for its pottery. He plugged in the address to the satellite map and when it came up, he stared at it. He could clearly see the chimney. "Axel, I think I've got it." He flicked his glance up to the big screen to double-check. It was a match.

"Where?" Axel said.

He gave him the coordinates and looked at the time. Three-thirty A.M. "I'm sure this is it."

"I'll check it out."

He waited, desperate to do something, anything. Looking down at his witch, he noted her face was pale, her shimmer dim and grayish. How could this happen? How could he have found someone to love, to have for his own, and lose her? He'd done everything he was supposed to, he'd never given in to the curse, he'd killed rogues, he'd helped Darcy and other witches.

Yet Wing Slayer had turned his back on him. No wings, no acknowledgment, and now the cruelest thing of all, taking Carly from him.

He wouldn't allow it. Whatever the cost. He didn't care. If the god wanted his soul in payment, he could have it. If he spent his eternity as a shade, fine. But Carly wasn't going to die like this, the life sucked out of her by a sadistic psychic.

And where the hell were her Ancestors? Why weren't they helping? Were they punishing her for saving his soul? Pissed because she mated with her sister's soul mirror? When all she'd done was keep him from going rogue? He brushed her hair back from her face. "You don't deserve this, baby." He'd been so incredibly proud that she'd chosen him, mated with him, and that he would be her familiar. So fucking proud. He loved channeling her powers, loved supporting and helping her. Carla did so much good helping brainwashed and brain-damaged victims.

And it turned out he was killing her.

His mom had been right to leave him.

Axel, Darcy and Chandra hadn't grasped it yet. They didn't quite understand what Sutton was going to have to do.

But Jerome did. Yeah, he'd looked into the man's eyes, seen the regret. He knew.

Carla was strong, though. She'd...

Hell, he couldn't stand it. He moved the laptop to

the floor. Then he gently moved Chandra's arm off Carla. The exhausted woman was in a deep sleep.

Sutton lifted Carla onto his lap and put her head on his chest.

"Sutton?"

"It's okay. Go back to sleep." He pressed her face against his skin, needing to feel her. Then he wrapped his arms around her.

"Thank you."

He closed his eyes, wondering what the hell she was thanking him for. He had insisted over and over that he was her soul mirror. Why hadn't he listened to her? Why hadn't he just left her the hell alone?

"I love you," she said thickly and drifted off to sleep again.

Oh, God. He couldn't bear it. "I love you, too. More than you can know, Carly. Too much to bear." He rubbed her back, feeling her drift back to sleep. He hoped she knew that, he hoped she'd remember that. Always.

Because to save her, he was going to have to break his bond with her. It was the only way she'd be able to reconnect with Keri. It tore him up to realize the truth.

Carla was lost to him. Forever. All he could do now was make sure she lived and got her sister back to free her.

He could feel her warm breath against his chest. She'd fallen back into a deep sleep. He kept rubbing her back in gentle strokes, but the urgency beat at him. Keri and Carla were inching closer to death with each minute that ticked by. He said to Axel in his earpiece, "What's your status? Anything?"

"I'm closing in on the location."

"Hurry." Sutton wrapped both arms around Carly and waited.

Would this be the last time he ever held her?

Axel said, "This is the place. The kiln is on. Maybe I'd better try to get the knife."

Carla started to writhe in his arms, crying in her sleep. "Hold on," Sutton told Axel while he rubbed her back and tried to calm her.

Carla dreamed that she was on the astral plane, searching for Keri, but everywhere she turned, there were bodies of dead witches. She kept running to the witches and begging them, "Have you seen Keri?"

"I saw her in the knife that killed me," a dead witch said.

She had to find that knife! "Keri!" she yelled, but all she could hear were screams. She broke out in a clammy sweat. "Where are you? Keri!"

A man materialized in the endless sea of blue. Next to him, a huge oven with a big chimney roared, spewing out flames and thick smoke. "I have Keri right here." He held up the silver knife.

Carla froze. The pain in her head exploded and she realized she'd been yanked from a dream into Styx's psychic vision. She struggled to build a wall, but her powers felt like they were smothered under layers of wet, heavy blankets.

Styx smiled. "Yeah, sucks, huh? I'm much more powerful than you or your sister."

Violent hatred raced through her blood like a deadly poison. She shook with the fury of her revulsion.

"Carly?" Sutton's voice reached her from a distance. She felt his hand on her back, but he wasn't here with her.

Styx narrowed his eyes. "Tell Sutton that I will throw Keri in the kiln if anyone but him shows up to try to take this knife from me."

"I won't! You'll kill him!" The twin spikes in her head burned.

Keri appeared between them, lying on the ground, cut so many times that her skin hung in clumps of sagging gray flesh. "Eagle! My eagle!" she cried, reaching out a bloody hand.

"Stop it!" Carla screamed, the spikes in her head getting hotter and pistoning brutally.

"Carly! Wake up!" Sutton's voice was loud and demanding.

She forced her eyes open, and her blurry gaze filled with Sutton's face. He'd sat up, shifting her so she lay back in one of his arms, his other hand stroking her face. "You were screaming."

Her mom was kneeling on the bed next to them, her hand on Carla's shoulder. "You're shaking and clammy."

Sutton's gaze darkened. "It's Styx, isn't it? He got to you."

The dry terror made it hard to form the words, but she told them what Styx said about throwing Keri in the kiln if he saw anyone but Sutton.

"He can't!" her mom said, reaching for her. "You'll die with Keri!"

"The hell she will," Sutton snarled, his body jerking and shuddering with some internal force. He switched his phone to speaker and said, "Axel, stand down. Styx told Carla that if he sees any other Wing Slayer Hunter, he'll throw Keri in the kiln."

Axel said, "Problem here. There're screams coming from the barn, and a couple hunters have dragged out a witch. Get here, Sutton. I can't just let them slaughter witches." His voice was furious. "I'm sending Linc to watch the outside of your cabin."

"Axel, I'm on my way."

Carla stared at his hard, determined face. "How can

329

you get there in time? Styx is playing with us, isn't he? He's going to win."

"No, I'll get there. He won't win, Carly." His entire body jerked and shuddered again.

"What is that? Your eagle?"

He looked down into her eyes. "Yes. He's trying to get out. For you. He's tried before, but this time, he's coming out and we're going to get Keri and save both of you."

The surge of fearful adrenaline was draining, making her more tired than she'd ever been. The feel of Sutton's arms comforted her, but she yearned—"I wish I could feel the eagle again, but that magic is gone..." She trailed off, the pain growing bright and vicious in her head. She closed her eyes, took a breath, then forced her lids open. She wanted him to know this. "I love him, too. You and the eagle both. Whatever happens, it was enough, Sutton."

He stood with her in his arms, then turned and laid her in his bed. With one hand on her face, he leaned down and kissed her. "I love you. Together, the eagle and I are going to get the knife because we both love you." Then he looked at her mom. "Can you help her with the pain?"

"Yes. Hurry, Sutton." Chandra put her hand on Carla's head.

Sutton turned away.

Carla and her mom both gasped. His powerful back was bulging and undulating with the force of the eagle trying to break free.

≫ 22 ≪

SUTTON WAS STILL BARE-CHESTED, WEARING only his pants and hiking boots as he hurried out of the cabin and down the steps into the dirt. Breaking into a run, he went to the edge of the cliff overlooking the ocean. It was early morning, the night was deep and black but he could make out the waves. He knew the coordinates of the old commune, he could get there.

If he had wings.

The eagle shoved hard enough so that the skin on his back stretched and nearly tore. It burned. But it wasn't enough, damn it.

How did he help the bird? Slice the skin on his back? He didn't know. The bird never listened to him, not the way he listened to Chandra the day she yelled at him. She had scared him. How had she done that? Because she was a mother? Or was it because she had told the eagle that Carla would be mad at him? That gave him an idea. "Did you hear Carla? She loves you."

The eagle lifted his wings against his skin.

He had the creature's attention. "You and me, we don't care what Wing Slayer, Ancestors, or a curse say, Carla belongs to us."

He flapped harder, the fine bones of the wings pricking his skin.

Sutton knew this wasn't going to be the flawless magic that Axel had. Axel's wings popped out of the tattoo with no blood, no apparent pain, then folded back up into the tattoo. But Sutton didn't have that magic. He only had sheer love and determination. "She'll die if we don't get that knife. We're out of time. I don't care how much damage you have to do to free your wings. Do it." Then he added the one thing he thought might work. "Carla will be proud of you."

His back erupted in a blinding flash of agony and a whoosh. The sudden weight on his shoulder blades almost knocked him on his ass. Adjusting swiftly, he shifted his balance and turned his head.

He could see the wing spanning several feet to his right. Brown and black feathers, some sprinkled with dark spots of blood. Ignoring the warm flow of blood down his back, he quickly looked to see a matching wing on his left. The wings fluttered. Quickly, he experimented with his muscles, learning how to move the wings.

There wasn't time! He had to get in the air. "Let's do this. Let's get that knife and save Carly." Sutton took a breath and leaped off the cliff.

For an instant, he was falling straight down. He sent frantic commands to his muscles but they jerked and fumbled while the rocky ground blasted up to meet him. At the last second, his wings caught a current and started pumping, stopping him from hitting the ground.

Then he was in the air, rising higher. He only fumbled when he thought too hard. Flying, apparently, was instinctive.

Like the instinct to save the woman he loved.

He let the eagle take care of flying, while he concentrated on the direction they needed to go and on shielding himself so he wouldn't be seen. It was both weird and exhilarating to be soaring across the sky, but the fear for Carla was too big to allow him to enjoy it. His focus was entirely on the mission of getting the knife and saving her.

Soon, he spotted the smoke trail from the kiln and he followed it to the commune. The layout was a simple U shape carved out of a section of forest. Cars stood lined up, pointing toward the road. On the left side of the U was the barn. A large house was straight ahead. On the right side was a long row of bunkhouses.

The kiln chimney was set back in a clearing between the house and bunkhouses.

Sutton flew over and saw an amazing sight; Axel had his wings out and was dive-bombing the rogues in the center of the commune. They had a witch and were trying to cut her on the dirt and fight off Axel at the same time. Sutton knew Styx was at the kiln as that was what Carla saw in her vision. As long as Axel didn't approach the kiln, he wouldn't throw Keri in.

He caught sight of a rogue lifting an uzi and taking aim just as Axel pulled out of another dive-bomb. That's when he realized Axel was leaving a trail of blood; he'd been injured, maybe shot. Being immortal made him really hard to kill, but if they got him on the ground and cut off his head, that would do it. So would Quinn Young's Immortal Death Dagger, if Darcy wasn't close enough to use her blood as an antidote. Sutton had to get to the kiln and get the knife, but he couldn't let Axel get caught either.

He copied Axel and dive-bombed them, dropping his shield just as he was ten feet away. He didn't have Axel's skill or finesse, instead, he slammed into one man, and both of them flew into the group of rogues. Tucking his body, he did a front roll. His wings curled around him, and he was able to spring up to his feet.

He snapped his arms down, dropping two blades from his wristbands into his hands by the time he whirled around. Two were on their feet bringing up their weapons.

He hit them both dead center in the heart. He grabbed one of their guns, flipped it over, and fired into the rogues running toward him until the weapon jammed. He tossed it to the ground.

Axel swooped in, landed on his feet, scooped up the bleeding witch, and leaped back into the air.

Sutton fought through more rogues as he headed toward the kiln.

A hellish scream came from the bunkhouses.

It was a game, a way to divert his attention and kill him. He had to kill Styx first, then Axel or the other Wing Slayer Hunters could help the screaming woman. Axel would have sent out a 911. Ram, Phoenix and Key were coming, so he forced himself to ignore the sobs coming from the row of bunkhouses.

He stalked to the kiln, pulling out his phone, and dialed Darcy to open the line. "I'm almost to the kiln."

"Say 'now' when you're ready for interference," Darcy said.

A bullet tore into his calf. He whipped around, snapped down a blade and threw it straight into the heart of the tall, thick rogue who shot him. The man dropped his gun and slumped to the ground.

Still holding the phone, he turned back. "Got it," he said as he passed between the house and bunkhouses to the kiln. The chimney stuck out of a roof supported by four posts. He was sure that the rogues had been using the kiln to get rid of bodies, both witches and rogues. Focus, he told himself, and he went silent and invisible. He moved past the massive oven, the loud roar of the heating elements sickening him. He saw the man standing in front of the oven door, surrounded by six armed female guards. They stood shoulder to shoulder in a tight circle, but the man was a full head taller than the women.

It had to be Styx and his brainwashed mortals. From what he could see, Styx was just over six feet, with dirty blond hair, brown eyes, a soft face and hairless arms. He was holding a knife and running his fingers over it. He recognized the knife from the vision.

It was Keri.

And that bastard was touching her.

"I know you're there. I'm psychic, possessing powers you can't even imagine."

Sutton dropped his shield. "More like you can see the blood from my leg in the dirt." He was aware of movement behind him. Probably rogues or maybe other mortal women. It was a trap, of course. Luring him there with the hope of saving Carla then killing him, too.

Styx's gaze traveled over him, wings and all, then he shrugged. "You can't doubt me. Look what I've done to Carla. Even now, she's dying. And when I throw this knife in the kiln?" He grinned. "Toast."

Hatred exploded in Sutton's mind. He'd never been an emotional fighter, and he determinedly ignored the pulsing rage. Too much was at stake for him to get stupid by trash talk. He had to be cold, analytical and fast.

With his knife in one hand, and the opened phone in the other, he took a step that brought him just below the roof of the shelter.

Styx said, "So here's the question. If I throw the knife in the oven, will you dive in after it—to a fiery death—to save your witch's life?"

Sutton wanted to get the best advantage before scrambling Styx's psychic waves. As casually as possible, he looked around, noting the dozen or so rogues behind him.

Psychic or not, Styx didn't get how the Wing Slayer

Hunters worked. They had each other's backs. It was just a matter of how long it would take the men to arrive. Once they got there, Sutton wasn't worried about all the rogues behind him.

His concern was the brainwashed women. He hoped their plan worked and the witches could confuse Styx's psychic powers enough to cut his link to the women. Then he could get the knife without killing them. Were the others here yet? The roar of the kiln would mask the sounds. He decided to draw this out a few more minutes. "If you throw that knife in, what's to stop me from killing you?"

Styx laughed. "You can't kill me. Oh, you can try, and these women will kill you. Or the men behind you will kill you. Or maybe I'll kill you."

His arrogance and confidence were unchecked. This man had been getting away with everything from rape to murder by using his psychic gift. He'd manipulated his own father. And he'd enhanced his skills, both by witch blood and by using Keri in that knife. He was scum.

Styx grinned. "Do you want me to tell you how I train my girls?"

Sutton tightened his grip on the phone. "You mean brainwash."

"First I destroy their memories that define them. Then we break them. The boys all like that part. Rape, pain, humiliation, beatings. And once they are broken, I decide who they are. Watch this. Megan and Paula, throw Kelly in the kiln."

Two of the women reached for the girl between them. She looked to be no more than nineteen. They grabbed her arms and—

He couldn't let this happen. "Now," Sutton said and held up the phone. The cell grew hot and started to vibrate in his hand. In seconds, a low drone like a swarm of bees began to fill the air.

"What the hell!" Styx yelled.

Megan and Paula let go of Kelly, who fell to her knees, holding her head. Several of them dropped the guns, or seemed startled to have them. They began to talk at once.

"What's happening?"

"I don't know."

"My head hurts."

"I can't think!"

Styx was standing still, a thin line of blood running from his nose. The interference the witches caused was working! Strong enough to burst a blood vessel in his nose. Taking advantage of his confusion, Sutton rushed the rogue psychic, keeping the phone opened. His used his right wing to shove the women back, away from the kiln.

Styx snapped out of his fugue, drew his hand back and threw the knife toward the fiery oven.

"No!" Sutton dived for the knife and stretched out his hand. He was too far away! If that blade went into the kiln, Keri and Carla would die.

Styx shouted, "Kill him!" to the rogues.

Rage slammed down on Sutton and his eagle screeched. Both man and bird reacted, snapping out their left wing and blocking the path to the oven.

A blast of vicious heat scorched the feathers, and the knife slapped against the inside then fell to the ground.

All hell broke loose. Wing Slayer Hunters rushed the rogues swarming into the shelter.

Styx grabbed the woman closest to him.

Sutton kept the phone up and moved closer. "It's over, leech. Let her go."

"I'll kill her!" He shoved a knife up to the woman's throat. "Whatever you're doing, stop it!" A thin necklace of blood bubbled up on the terrified woman's throat.

He wasn't going to let him kill the woman, or hurt anyone else. Styx and his mind games ended now. Lifting the phone higher, he said, "Phone for you. It's the witches. They're destroying your power."

Enraged, he screamed, "No! They can't! I can destroy their minds!" His nosebleed began to gush.

Sutton dropped the phone, snapped his wrist and caught the thin blade. He hurled it past the woman's head and into Styx's right eye.

"Kill him!" Styx screamed, dropping his hold on the woman to yank the blade from his eye. He tried to grab another confused woman, and Sutton leaped, using his right wing to knock the woman free and slam Styx into the ground.

Styx smashed the heel of his boot into the gunshot wound on Sutton's calf.

Sutton jammed the heel of his palm into the bastard's bloody eye, shoved his elbow into his throat, and while Styx writhed and grunted beneath him, he grabbed Styx's knife and stabbed it into his chest.

Styx's good eye shot open in shock.

Sutton shoved off him. "Don't need to be psychic to know you'll spend eternity as a shade."

The life drained out of that eye, and he was dead.

Sutton hurried to the kiln and found the silver knife on the dirt just two feet from the yawning mouth of fire that would have destroyed Keri's soul and killed Carla. He leaned down and gently picked up the knife. It was hot, too hot from being so close to the opened oven. Blisters formed on his hand, but he ignored that, unwilling to let the knife go now that he had it. "I've got you, Keri, and I'm taking you back to your sister and mother." He picked up his own knife that he had dropped in the leap to save Keri and put it in his holster. The heat of the oven made his left wing hurt worse, and his right calf screamed with each step.

Leaving the shelter, he saw that dead rogues

littered the compound. A group of women was gathered in front of the bunkhouses and Key was talking to them, calming them down.

All the hunters were torn and bleeding, but they were alive.

Axel limped up. "That wing looks like shit. Can you fly?"

He dropped his gaze to the knife that held Keri's soul, then back up to Axel. "Yes." He hoped like hell that was true. *Come on, eagle, we have to reunite the sisters. One more time, for Carla.* He took four steps and leaped into the air like he'd seen Axel do.

The eagle spread his wings and took them home.

Carla was dying. She had made the wrong choice, the selfish choice, and she was dying for it. For loving Sutton. For choosing him over Keri.

For taking Keri's soul mirror, her eagle.

The drilling in her head made her nauseous and her vision was dimming. She was cold and shivering. But she could see Darcy, standing in front of the sliding glass door framed in the glow of the breaking dawn, her hands stretched out to the side, palms up, as she was channeling power from the Circle Witches through the cell phone attached to her ear.

She didn't need clear vision to know that Darcy was beautiful in her power.

Carla's mom was on the bed next to her, the laptop on her thighs. She was working with the Circle Witches, sending her power along with the rest of them.

Jerome sat on a chair at the end of the bed. Worry and grief made him appear thinner and smaller. "Carla, is Styx trying to reach you?"

"No." Her mouth was dry and her lips rough from peeling.

"This will work," he insisted.

She didn't tell him that she could feel her life force leaving her. She wasn't going to survive. But it was Keri that she was worried about. Keri's very soul was dying. That wasn't fair, and it was her fault. She tried to focus her eyes. "Dad, if I don't survive, please tell Darcy to try to free Keri. Even if there's just a spark of a chance that her soul will survive and go on."

Her mom inhaled sharply.

"You're upsetting your mother," Jerome said in a choked voice.

"I'm sorry. Please, promise me, Dad." Keri can't die off forever. Her soul was too passionate and loving, too caring, too full of life. She had to go on to her next life.

Her father dropped his head. "I'll tell her."

"Thank you."

"Carla, don't give up hope," her mom said, breaking her concentration. She put her arm around Carla's shoulders. "Sutton will get the knife and get back here."

Sutton. Her throat tightened, her eyes burned and her heart ached. She loved him and she had felt their souls touch each other. How had it all gone so wrong? Because he wasn't hers.

"Okay," was all she managed before hundreds of voices filled her head. They were singing, but it was a horrible jumble, different words, different tunes, even different languages. They kept getting louder and louder, the volume rising steadily.

Stop! Styx screamed in her head.

Then a blast of heat swamped her and she couldn't breathe. Her chest locked up while sweat popped out on her skin. "Hot." She struggled in the bed, weakly trying to kick off the covers.

She felt her mother's hand on her head. "You're burning up!"

Jerome leaped out of the chair. "Is she breathing?"

"Yes, but she's too hot! Do something!" Chandra cried.

She tried to grab her mom's hand, but her limbs were too heavy. "Keri's hot." The prongs in her head were vibrating violently. She could feel her sister's soul struggling feebly but there was nothing to hold her. Just the hot silver of the knife suffocating her.

Was she in the kiln? Carla's eyes filled with tears, but she was too weak to do anything but feel. *I'm sorry, Keri. I'm so sorry.*

She tried to open her eyes but everything was dim and far away. And colder. A chill raced along her skin and sank into her bones. And she was so tired, her muscles too heavy to even shiver anymore.

"Carla?" Darcy said.

Carla could feel Darcy's hand on her arm, but she couldn't see her. It was too hard to talk.

"Carla," Darcy said more urgently. "Hang on! Sutton is coming! It's over, he's got Keri and he's coming."

"Try," was all she could manage.

Sutton landed outside the cabin in the front. The sun was beginning to rise, revealing the isolation he had always loved. He heard the waves crashing below, the birds singing and his heart thudding.

Linc walked up to him. "Everything's been quiet here."

"Thanks." His attention turned to the sliding glass door to his bedroom as Darcy raced out, her long ponytail flying. "Sutton! Hurry!"

He rushed toward her, ignoring his right calf screaming in pain where he'd taken the bullet. He passed Darcy and headed for the door.

The wings folded tight against his back so he could get through the opening. Distantly he wondered why the wings didn't disappear, but maybe the burned wing couldn't do it. Or maybe the wings were permanent since he and the eagle had forced them out. He didn't care. He clutched the knife in his hand and hurried to the bed.

Jerome and Chandra were standing on the other side of the bed. Darcy had come in behind him, but all he cared about was the woman under layers of blankets. She lay still and pale as death. There were obscene dark circles under her eyes. His heart jerked and pounded. The eagle let out a keening sound and his wings opened up, trying to reach her. "Carly?" His voice came out a croak.

Her eyelids fluttered.

He reached across Carla and set the knife in Chandra's trembling hand. Knowing Keri was safe with her mother, he pulled the mountain of covers off Carla and lifted her into his arms. "Baby, I have the knife. I have Keri."

She opened her eyes slowly. They were unfocused. "Cold."

His wings wrapped around her. Now Sutton knew why the wings hadn't faded into his tattoo. The eagle wanted to touch Carla, comfort her, love her. "Better? The eagle has his wings around you."

She blinked, turning her face into the feathers touching her.

He looked up, his gaze landing on Jerome. "What do we do? Styx is dead, why isn't she better?" Carla felt insubstantial in his arms, like she was slipping away from him. His heart pounded hard enough to burst.

Jerome shoved both hands through his wild hair. "She and Keri are too weak. Cut her with the knife. If Keri's soul is strong enough, they will re-bond and

Carla can pull Keri out of the knife. That should save Keri, which will in turn save Carla."

Oh, hell no. He'd known he'd have to break their bond somehow, but this? It sickened him. He couldn't hurt her, he couldn't do it. This was his nightmare, the one where he'd seen his hand holding the silver knife and cutting Carla. How many times had he woken, craving witch blood and hating himself for it? Telling himself he was one day closer to having to end his life so he didn't become the monster that cut Carla.

Chandra walked up to him, holding the knife carefully. "You have to."

Panic raced over his skin, making his head roar, and the wings tried to cover Carla, to shield her from him. He stared at Chandra, "I can't."

Jerome said, "Has to be you. You have to do it to break your bond with her or she won't be able to re-bond with Keri."

Darcy sucked in a breath.

He looked over at Carla's best friend. He wasn't sure what he'd thought he'd have to do to break the bond...but this? "True?"

Her brown eyes filled with gold agony, and her witch-shimmer was almost gray with worry. "Yes."

"She'll feel it? The blade and the break?"

He saw her struggle with what she should say, but he knew she was telling him the truth when her shoulders slumped in defeat. "Yes. She has to feel it for it to work."

He had to hurt her. Goddamn it. How could he do it? He knew he had to, and he knew that by doing it, he was irrevocably cutting her bond to him. Forever. Carla would not make the same mistake twice. She knew now that he and Keri were soul mirrors.

But he wanted Carla. Loved Carla. Lived for her. He was going to stab the woman he loved.

He was a monster. Like his mother said, like his dreams showed him. This was what he brought Carla with his blind insistence that she belonged to him.

Carla's breath labored and started to rattle. Her body shuddered from the effort to draw air. She felt so fragile in his arms.

Darcy said, "You have to do it, Sutton. Now. Both Carla and Keri are getting too weak. Time's running out."

Chandra held out the knife, her hand shaking.

He stared at that silver knife. "Where do I cut her?"

Jerome answered, "The scar. Keri will recognize it."

He took the knife and closed his eyes. "Leave, just leave us alone."

Chandra brushed Carla's hair back and kissed her forehead. "Ancestors be with you," she said and turned to leave. Jerome put his arm around Chandra.

Darcy laid her hand on Sutton's shoulder. "She chose you out of love. She won't blame you for this."

He wasn't even surprised. Darcy was that compassionate and kind, forgiving him when he would never forgive himself.

When the door closed softly and they were alone, he carried Carla to the bed, sat on the edge and laid the knife on the cool sheet next to his thigh. He could feel her struggle for each breath. Maybe Wing Slayer was punishing him for not putting the god before Carly. But why did he always have to take away the ones he loved? Sutton tried begging for her life. "Wing Slayer, please, save her. I'll give you anything." He brought her face up to his and brushed his mouth over hers. "I love you, Carly."

Her mouth curved into a tiny ghost of a smile.

That one gesture arrowed through him. She trusted him.

The eagle saw it, too, and even though his wings were out, he used his claws to tear into Sutton's back in blind, protective fury. Sutton didn't flinch, he deserved it and more.

Carla choked, her body convulsing in a desperate attempt to draw in air. Her muscles went rigid, and she made horrible wet sounds in her chest. She was suffocating in her body as Keri's soul was suffocating in the knife.

Quickly, he turned her over, laying her stomach across his thighs and putting pillows under her head. He stroked her back through his blue T-shirt she wore until her muscles relaxed and she was able to draw a shallow breath.

Do it, he told himself.

He picked up the knife from where he'd put it on the bed. It was warm to the touch. He pushed up the shirt, revealing the little white panties he'd put on her, and the curve of her lower back.

He didn't want to do this. He wanted to take care of her, make her happy. Not hurt her.

His wings came around the front of him and lay protectively over her back to stop him.

Carla struggled for another breath and he couldn't stand it. Swiftly, he shoved the wings off her and leaned his forearm across Carla's upper back to hold her.

He knew exactly where the scar had been.

His hand wanted to shake, but he wouldn't allow it. He would only allow fast precision. He'd make this as quick as he could for her. Without any more hesitation, he positioned the knife and pierced her skin with the tip. Then he sliced so fast he could barely see his own hand move.

He lifted the blade just as she cried out brokenly, her back arching against his arm where he held her down. She subsided into wheezing sobs.

The eagle went at his back in fury with both claws. He let the bird rip him apart while he watched the blood well and drip from the wound on Carla's back. He looked at the knife, seeing Carla's blood on the blade. "Please, Keri, fight for her! Carla loves you, she's tried so damned hard to help you!"

All Carla's muscles went limp. She stopped crying. The blood flowing from the fresh wound slowed to a bare trickle.

No scar formed.

Gut-seizing panic roared through him. "No!" He dropped the knife, flipped Carla in his arms, and said, "Carly! Open your eyes!"

Nothing. Her head rolled to the side.

The eagle let out a piercing cry and wrapped his wings around her.

Carla stopped breathing. He felt it the second she left him. "No!" He shot up off the bed and roared out, "You can't take her! Take me! Not her!" The thought of Carla getting to Summerland and not finding her sister made him sick. She would know Keri had died and was gone forever. The grief drove him to his knees. He couldn't bear it, couldn't...just couldn't. "Wing Slayer, I beg you! Take me, let Carla live and free Keri."

He cradled Carly to him, holding her close while the eagle stroked her and cried with him. Tears ran down his face. "She only tried to do good. The people she helped..." Everything inside him broke. The pain was worse than anything he'd ever known, worse even than when his mom walked out, worse than when his father died. "It was me that pushed her, me that made her choose."

≽ *23* ≼

"WE DON'T HAVE MUCH TIME." The voice reverberated through the room.

Sutton didn't answer, didn't care. He held Carly against his chest, covered in the eagle's wings so she wouldn't get cold. She had been so cold. Would she be cold in Summerland?

Would she ever forgive him for losing her sister?

He'd never forgive himself. Never.

A shadow fell over him.

He frowned and looked up to tell whoever it was to go away. That Carly was cold and shadows would make her colder. He knew he was in some kind of shock or denial, but he wanted to stay there. He wasn't letting her go. No one would take her from him. So he looked up to tell the shadow to move and—

His brain blanked. Hovering between him and the sliding glass door was a huge male being, over seven feet tall, with wings made of rich gold feathers woven into tight, masculine arcs that shimmered like the sun. They reached up maybe twelve feet high at the tip and when spread wide, they measured a width of at least fourteen feet. His massive arms were covered in bronze bands stamped with wings. "She's cold," he finally said while his brain stumbled around in the dark, bumping into the walls in his mind. A dim light clicked on. "Wing Slayer." His god.

"Sutton. My warrior who fought for a witch who isn't even his."

The pain lanced through him, ripping open the wounds. "Don't punish her. Take me. Let her live. She can free Keri to go on to Summerland."

"She's not yours, Sutton."

He'd rather be a shade for eternity than hear that. But he finally and irrevocably conceded, "I know." How could he have ever thought Carla belonged to him?

"You have to let her go. She'll re-bond with Keri, but you aren't letting go."

He stared at his god. "I cut her. Hurt her. That's the last thing she'll ever know from me and you don't think I broke our bond?" He cradled her body, unable to stop holding her. "I killed her."

Wing Slayer bounced on the air, his wings darkening to a burnt color. "If you don't, Carla's soul isn't going to make it and neither will Keri. Carla's soul left her body and is trying to pull Keri, but she can't form the bond with her that she needs to. She's still holding on to you. If you don't break your bond with her, Keri will die off and Carla will fade into a shade."

"No!" he bellowed, his mind twisting and bending with the sheer horror of it.

"Let her go. If you truly love her, let her go."

He closed his eyes, wondering how Carla had done it. How she had made the terrible choice to let her sister go to save him. But if he didn't do it, Keri's soul would die, and Carla would end up a shade, roaming the between worlds, no longer able to feel the sun or moon or love that witches needed. He couldn't let that happen. And finally, he was totally humbled and prostrate before his god. He kept his head bent and said, "Tell me what I have to do."

Carla looked around in surprise. She was back in her body. What was happening? The last thing she remembered was Sutton, holding her begging her to live and Keri to help her. Then a strange lightness took hold of her and she had been able to see him holding her body. She realized she must be dead and had tried to reach Keri in the knife to pull her soul out, but she hadn't been able to do it. So she'd just hovered near Sutton.

She took in her surroundings. Beautiful vines with large white and purple flowers that wove alongside a long graceful road paved with colored stones. Up ahead, the path gave way to soft grass surrounding a rock waterfall that splashed into a pool. A gentle mist lightly touched her skin. She wasn't even walking, but gliding while a soft breeze lifted her hair.

She recognized where she was, the astral plane, the place she'd pulled Sutton into that first time. She didn't understand. Was she dead? She thought she was, but she was clearly in her doppelganger body, dressed in the same T-shirt and panties she'd had on earlier. How was that possible?

And why?

She turned and saw Sutton walking beside her. Seeing him made her vividly aware of her heartbeat, and she couldn't take her eyes off him. He wore the same pants and boots he'd worn on the physical plane, only now the wings of his eagle jutted out from his back, the brown and black feathers spreading out across her back. Sutton's arms, chest and stomach were even more powerful than she remembered to support such a majestic bird.

"You have your wings. That's wonderful!" She wanted to touch him, to feel all his skin and feathers, but something felt off.

He turned to look at her, his eyes lighting up.

Then Keri appeared in the pathway in front of them. "Carla, you're here! You and Eagle!" She held out her hands.

Sutton's head whipped around. His wings lifted and fluttered in excitement. "Keri."

"Sutton?" Jealousy and fear bubbled like a rancid stew in Carla's stomach. She loved Keri, and wanted to rejoice in seeing her. Except now she understood. She'd had this dream before as a warning. The Ancestors hadn't been able to reach Carla then, so they'd blessed her with a dream of warning. But she'd ignored it. She'd known Sutton wasn't hers, and she'd taken him anyway.

Now Keri was here to claim him. How? Keri's soul was still in the knife, how could she appear here? She wore the black yoga pants and top she'd died in, only there was no blood on them now. Something was wrong. Carla put her hand on Sutton's arm. "It's a trick! Asmodeus or—"

He didn't look at her, but stared at the image of her sister. "No trick."

She dropped her hand. He didn't want her touch, he wasn't there for her. He had never been hers. Her nose clogged, her eyes burned and her stomach twisted in agony of rejection.

The eagle wing pulled away from her back. Sutton finally turned, his face remote, his eyes dull. "I'm sorry, Carla." Then he jerked away from her, as if he couldn't leave her fast enough, and strode toward Keri.

Although she was wearing a T-shirt that fell to her knees, she felt naked and exposed as she watched him leave her. The majestic wings spread out, his shoulders and back rippling with muscles to handle the wings.

Wings for Keri. Not her.

She wanted to scream at him to come back to her, she wanted to throw herself on him and beg. But she couldn't. She wouldn't. He wasn't hers.

He hadn't really loved her. He'd loved Keri. He'd felt Keri through the twin bond. Sudden and shattering pain ripped down the center of her chakras and broke the false soul-mirror bond forever.

Broke her.

"No!" Keri's voice crackled like thunder. "How can you do this?"

Confused, Carla forced herself to look at the scene in front of her. Her sister attacked Sutton, her small fists beating his arms and chest.

He stood there, taking it, not moving, not even looking at Keri, but somewhere in the distance. The wings on his back were beginning to droop, as if they were unbearably sad. She didn't understand. Why was Keri angry and Sutton unhappy?

She told herself to walk away, to just keep walking until her soul found its way to Summerland. Her doppelganger body should start fading since her physical body was dead.

But she was gliding, without a will of her own, being pulled to Keri and Sutton.

Keri stopped beating on Sutton and threw herself at Carla. "Don't let him do this."

The confusion inside her kept multiplying, but a lifetime of love opened her arms to catch her sister and hug her. Carla closed her eyes, inhaling the light incense scent that always clung to her sister. Her first thought was that Keri felt odd, almost like something was missing. Then she felt the scar on her back, the place where Sutton had cut her, heat and tingle. Keri started to feel more solid.

She leaned back and looked at Keri. "Did you feel that? What happened?"

Keri's face filled with joy. "You've pulled my soul from the knife!"

Carla felt it then, the bond that had been with her for a lifetime. She and Keri joined once more, and she felt her sister's utter relief and joy at being freed from the knife. Her smile was shaky, but heartfelt. "You can go on now. Find your way into your next life." Tears filled her eyes. "Please forgive me. You saved my life and I failed you and took your eagle." The shame and grief bubbled over inside of her, a thick bitterness that burned her throat.

"Carly, it wasn't your fault," Sutton said in a low voice.

She jerked from Keri's hold and said, "Don't call me that. My name is Carla. I'm not your Carly. I am not yours!"

He folded his huge arms over his chest as if to protect his heart. "Sorry, I won't. *Carla,* I didn't want to break our bond, but I had to. You died. I tried to save you, I swear I did. I got the knife and I tried to reunite the two of you."

She remembered that. "You cut me. But it didn't work."

The skin tightened on his face and he nodded. "You died anyway. Wing Slayer came and said you wouldn't leave, that cutting you hadn't broken the bond. I didn't believe him at first, I cut you. Hurt you. You trusted me and I cut you."

Carla's skin pebbled at the pain in his voice. "I knew why you did it." She hated that her heart bled for his pain. But now she knew that it was the Wing Slayer's god-magic that had brought them all there.

"Wing Slayer said Keri's soul was going to die and you were going to end up a shade if I didn't break our bond. He told me that you don't belong to me."

Her chest hurt like two hundred pounds of rocks were being piled on it. She had done this. She had known the truth. It was her fault. "You were reacting to the twin bond. To Keri."

He looked miserable and frustrated. "I couldn't let you go shade and suffer like that! And even if you somehow found your way to Summerland, I couldn't let you get there and find out Keri wasn't there. You can hate me, you can believe I didn't love you. But I can't let you suffer."

His words were so real, so Sutton. Just like her headache, when she had told him not to touch her, and then he'd appeared to be in pain. But when he was taking her pain, feeling her pain for her, he looked fine. All the time he'd held, kissed, or touched her. Made love to her. *Her.* Not Keri. He had fought to save her, screaming at Keri to fight for her.

He looked even worse now. His skin tight and stark over the bones in his face, his crossed arms bulged with tension, his hands curled into fists. His wings, his beautiful wings, drooped on the ground like a pile of wet feathers. And his eyes were full of misery, looking at her.

Not Keri.

Her.

Wings. "How did you get wings?"

His shoulders bunched. "Desperation. I told the eagle you'd be proud of him and he forced out wings." The wings lifted an inch or two off the ground and fluttered.

Carla's heart squeezed at the truth. They had loved her, the man and the eagle. Her eyes filled with tears, her nose burned and her throat ached. She looked away, unable to bear it. "So you'll find Keri? When she reincarnates?" Why the hell was she asking? Keri had her arm around Carla, trying to comfort her. No one did this, no one intended for this horrible nightmare to happen. It just did—Sutton and Carla were soul-crossed lovers. They weren't supposed to fall in love.

Keri and Sutton were supposed to be soul mirrors.

The pain made her head spin. "Don't answer, please don't answer." She heard her sister crying almost as hard as she was.

Then Sutton's hands were on her arms, hauling her up against him. "I had to let you go." His big hand covered the back of her head, pressing her face against him. She could smell the musk and forest-pine scent on his warm skin and her heart broke all over again. She just nodded, unable to speak as sobs racked her. How could her astral plane body feel so real? How could she be dead and hurt so much? In seconds she felt herself being pulled from his arms, separated by a force they couldn't see.

"Please, Wing Slayer, a few more minutes," his voice was thick and his arms held her tighter.

She was yanked from the astral plane and snapped back into her body.

Sutton was on his knees between the bed and the wall in his room with Carla in his arms. The grief for her choked him, made his chest hurt and tears leak from his closed eyes.

A soft sigh drifted up from Carla, and Sutton went rigid. He didn't move a muscle.

He could feel her breathing!

He snapped open his eyes. The woman in his arms lay quiet, her eyes closed, but she was breathing. Her skin was a natural tone and her witch-shimmer glowed silver. He could see her breasts rising and falling beneath the shirt. "Carla?" He didn't call her Carly. She had told him not to.

She gave a long sigh. The seconds stretched out.

Sutton heard the hushed conversation outside the door, along with Jerome's strident tones. But in this single moment of time, he didn't have room for them, not even Carla's mother. Only Carla.

Then she slowly opened her eyes. "Your wings are gone."

His wings didn't matter. "You're alive." A whisper was all he could manage. His heart went wild in his chest and the eagle bounced joyfully inside the tattoo on his back. "How can you be alive? I felt you die."

"I don't know. I don't feel sick anymore. I feel fine." Her eyebrows drew together. "Except for my back. It burns a little where you cut me."

Sutton couldn't get a grasp on reality. Seeing her on the astral plane had been hard enough, and then she'd been ripped from his arms and he'd been flung back to his physical body, believing she'd gone on to Summerland with Keri. How could she be alive? And what did the burning in the cut mean? "Is it Keri?"

She tried to move her hand to her back, but Sutton held her too tight.

"Hold on." While still on his knees, he shifted her to her feet so that her back was to him, and slid his hands to her waist to steady her. "Let me see."

She reached back and lifted her shirt.

Dropping his hands from her, he saw the backs of her thighs, then her butt in the little panties and struggled to keep his mind on the cut. Not Carla's body, not the feel of her skin, not the lavender scent of her.

She wasn't his. Wing Slayer had told him that. He knew that was why his wings were gone. What he didn't know was why she was alive. But he was grateful to Wing Slayer and would honor his god's decree that Carla wasn't his.

The hem of the shirt lifted past her panty line and he saw it. The scar was there, just like it had been before they'd made love the first time. Seeing the jagged line tripped a swirl of emotions, it was visible proof that Carla wasn't his and it hurt. But he knew how much Keri meant to Carla, and being able to free her soul would make her happy. He wanted her happy. Fisting his hands to keep from tracing the line, or touching her in any way, he said, "The scar is there. You have Keri with you."

Carla reached her hand back, her delicate finger sliding along the scar. Then she dropped the shirt and turned to look at him. "I have her. She's free of the knife. Sutton, we did it."

He rose to his feet, noticing that there was no pain in his calf. The gunshot wound was healed. Wing Slayer, he guessed. "Can you release her with a spell or something?"

She frowned. "It's a spell. I thought..." Her witch-shimmer dimmed and she looked lost in his huge T-shirt. She said, "Why are your wings gone? Turn around, let me see!" Her voice rose.

He shook his head. "Carla, don't do this to yourself. Don't." He couldn't bear it if she got upset.

She stared at him, the yellow in her eyes edging out the green and brown. "Try to make them come out again." Tears welled up in her eyes. "Please."

He hated seeing her hurt like this. His arms ached to hold her but he couldn't. He forced the words past his tight throat. "You know I love you. You know it, Carla. But I can't have you, and there's no reason for the eagle to exist. The wings are for our soul mirrors, and you're not my soul mirror. The eagle and I forced them out in desperation to save you, but now they're gone."

She shook her head, like she was in denial. "Turn around."

He had no idea what his back looked like. But what did it matter now? He sighed and turned.

She gasped. "Sutton!"

He flinched when she slid her fingers along his skin. Her touch made him burn to strip his shirt off of her and make love to her until no one, and no god, could ever separate them again.

Except that she wasn't his.

It ripped through his heart.

Her fingers kept tracing. "You're scarred. Two huge scars where the wings came out. But your eagle is still here." Her fingers brushed his feathers. "He's watching me. Your wings must still be there."

He didn't know what to tell her. "If they are, I don't know how to make them come out, at least not without a huge mess." He didn't care about the wings.

She stroked his eagle. "I can't believe the two of you did this for me. It had to be agonizing."

Sutton's world was crumbling with each of her soft caresses. He moved away from her, two long steps, and turned. "It was nothing compared to losing you. When you died...my world went dark and cold. I begged Wing Slayer for help and he gave it to me. He saved you somehow. And for that, I will give him my loyalty until I die."

She dropped her hand and looked down at the floor. He hated her misery.

"Carla, you'll find your real soul mirror." The thought of that wrenched a hole in his chest and made the eagle tattoo burn with jealousy and sadness. But her happiness mattered. "You'll forget—"

She snapped her head up, the green in her eyes blazing. "Like Keri is your real soul mirror?"

He reacted before thinking. "I love you. There's no one else for me. Not ever." He clenched his fists in an effort to keep from hauling her up to him. If he touched her...he wouldn't stop.

She closed her eyes, taking a deep breath. "I made the wrong choice."

The words echoed in the hollowness of his chest. But she was accepting the truth. Both of them had to accept it.

She opened her eyes and stared at him, her shimmer taking on a steely-blue determination. "I'd do it again exactly the same way."

He jerked back, surprised. He couldn't have heard her right. "What?"

She stepped to him, put her hand on his chest, and said, "I love you, and I'm going to fight for you right until my last breath and beyond." She took her hand away, turned, and walked around the bed. Her clothes changed midstep. The huge T-shirt was replaced by jeans and a mint-green sleeveless shirt.

He was so shocked, he hardly noticed the familiar way her power sizzled through his insides. "But Wing Slayer..." He stopped himself when it sank in. "I felt it."

With her hand on the door, she looked back. "Felt what?"

"Your power when you changed your clothes." Like a magnet, he was drawn to her, walking toward her before he could catch himself. "I felt your power!" The eagle fluttered on his back, trying to reach her.

Carla dropped her hand off the doorknob. "Your eagle! I can feel him!"

Sutton's control snapped and he rushed to her, taking Carla's hand and pulling her into his arms. He dropped his face into her hair, inhaling her. "I don't understand. You're not supposed to be mine." But she was his.

She leaned her head back and looked up at him. "Wing Slayer has his reasons, Sutton. But he's not punishing you. You've vowed your faith to him, now trust in him."

Could that be true? With Carla in his arms, anything seemed possible. And he would be damned careful. "We had to break our bond, at least you had to believe it was broken on the astral plane in order to get Keri."

"That makes sense. I'll talk to my mom and Darcy, and try a spell."

He lifted his hand to run his fingers and palm over her silky hair. "We can't break your bond with Keri until we can send her soul on to Summerland." He didn't care. He could wait. Yeah, his dick was hard and straining against his pants to mate with her, but he could wait. This time, they'd do this right, making sure Keri was safely released. "Carly." He lowered his mouth to kiss her. Taste her. She was warm and alive and his. Breaking the kiss before he completely lost his head, he said, "You were going to fight for me."

She smiled at him. "I always will."

≫ 24 ≪

"I WANT TO THANK EACH of you for your help," Carla said into the laptop. She was out on Sutton's porch, enjoying the late-morning sunshine. The Circle Witches had helped break Styx's psychic hold and allowed Sutton to get the knife from him. "You saved both me and Keri and I am forever grateful."

Silver appeared on the screen and said, "You're welcome, that's what the Circle is for."

Skitters of unease ran up Carla's back. She looked over at Darcy sitting in a matching redwood chair and staring at Silver on a second laptop.

Realizing that Darcy was refusing to look at her, Carla dropped the magic that propelled her voice through the computer and said, "What did you do?"

Darcy finally looked away from the computer. "Silver was causing some difficulties. She said she feared the magic of the Circle would be used to help Sutton murder Styx."

Oh, crap. That would be a valid argument for Silver to sway the witches, given that witches were not allowed to cause harm with their witchcraft. Darcy was her friend, and her mother, well Chandra loved Carla and would have promised anything to save her. She guessed that Darcy had to negotiate with Silver. "How bad?"

Darcy said, "Your mom and I both promised we'd support a vote for Advisor if no one was chosen by the Ancestors in a moon cycle."

Carla thought of the moment when she'd walked out of Sutton's room. Her mom saw her first, jumping up from the table and hugging her. Chandra had cried when Carla told her that she had Keri with her. Jerome had been next, hugging her tightly. Carla had told him that his science had helped save her and Keri and he'd cried, too. And then Darcy had hugged her. They were all talking at once, so happy. And they'd all had a part in saving her. Darcy and her mom with their magic and her dad with his science. Carla couldn't blame Darcy or her mom for what they'd promised Silver. If it had been one of them dying, she'd have done the same thing. It meant she had a month to convince Darcy to try the spell to become the Moon Witch Advisor.

She turned back to the screen and reengaged her magic. "Thank you, Silver." Silver had added her power and Carla was sincerely thankful for that.

Silver answered, "You're welcome. When will you do the spell to free Keri? I'm sure we'd all like to add our power to ensure a safe journey for our sister-witch's soul."

Carla didn't have to look to know Darcy was rolling her eyes. "Tonight at moonrise. We'll do the spell down on the beach so I can tap the ley lines that run there, and use the salt from the ocean. Thank you, Silver and all who wish to add their magic to the circle for Keri." She shut the laptop.

"Since when has Silver ever offered to help?" Darcy slammed her lid closed.

Carla set the machine on the ground, stood up and stretched. "Since she's so sure she'll be the Advisor.

You have no choice, Darcy. You're going to have to try the spell to see if the Ancestors will choose you as the Moon Witch."

"Maybe. But let's concentrate on the spell tonight. How many chakras can you open?"

Carla wasn't sure why Darcy was resisting the Moon Witch, but she was right about the spell. "Not sure yet. I was able to open six chakras and get to my third eye before my power started failing."

"Try now."

She closed her eyes and started opening chakras.

Sutton stood on the cliffs waiting for Axel. He and the men had saved four of the five witches at Styx's commune. Joe and Morgan had the witches in a safe house. Finally, he saw a growing shadow in the sky. Seconds later, Axel landed on the rocks about ten feet from him and folded up his wings until they disappeared into the tattoo.

Sutton asked, "Styx still dead?" He had to make sure. Yeah, he'd killed him, but he had seen Carla come back to life. He had to make damned sure Styx wasn't going to come back to life to torment her.

Axel walked over. "Very dead. We disposed of his body."

Sutton knew how—in the kiln. But at least he could be sure now that the sadistic psychic was dead.

"Carla wants to do the spell down there?" Axel indicated the beach below.

"Yes, she said she needs the ley lines and the sea salt."

"Yeah, witches are partial to the ley lines that run where the water meets the shore." He rubbed his eyes, looking tired. Dropping his hand, he said, "We can secure it."

"I'm not going to lose her now." As it was, his body was in a constant hum, a perpetual readiness. The bond between them wasn't completely broken as he'd believed, but it was disrupted and every cell in his body needed to reseal the bond.

Sex.

He was desperate to be inside Carla, his Carly. They weren't soul mirrors, but they were powerfully bonded.

Axel looked over at him. "Damn, Sutton, I can feel the tension coming off you."

He stared at the ocean and said, "I'm staying away from her until the spell. I'm not going to screw this up again. She needs to take care of her sister."

"Rough. But it gets better. As your mental bond grows, when you can reach out and feel her, the physical part is easier to control."

He shrugged. "Maybe." He didn't know exactly what was going to happen since they weren't true soul mirrors. They might not have that kind of mental bond. He'd had a taste of it though, and he already missed having Carla in his head. But he was more concerned with the unease running through him. "What am I missing? Styx is dead. Did you find any sign of Quinn Young?"

Axel shook his head, his dark hair lifting in the breeze. "No. But we're not letting our guard down. You and I will protect the women during the spell. We'll put the other hunters back into the cliffs where the magic won't incite their bloodlust, but they can get to us if something happens."

He nodded, then was caught by a sudden sizzle building inside him. The tattoo beneath his shirt woke up and started fluttering his wings. "Carla."

Axel looked over at him. "She in trouble?"

He shook his head. "She's doing magic. Trying to kill me." He could barely breathe as her power built and poured through him. "Damn." He turned and headed to the cabin.

He broke into a run, unable to keep himself from her. He found Carla standing on his porch, her back to him. She had her arms down, her palms were facing out and fingers spread. She tilted her head back so that her hair swung free, grazing her jean-clad butt.

His gut cramped, his cock jerked and throbbed, and his eagle shuddered in pleasure.

Darcy looked at him, then got up and went into the house.

Axel moved past him and disappeared into the house.

The witch on the porch had his full attention. He moved up the steps silently, going around to the front of her. "Carly, baby, you're killing me."

Her eyes were closed. "You feel it?"

"Yes." Hell, yes. Her scent was sinking into him, while her powers rushed over his skin and through him like liquid lightning. The eagle shoved against his skin, working his wings to corral her power.

Then it stopped.

Carla opened her eyes. "I almost reached my seventh chakra. I can do this tonight. I can do the spell. With you. The closer you got to me, the higher my power climbed."

He didn't understand it. "How is this happening if we're not soul mirrors?" Then he knew. "It's Keri, isn't it?"

"Yes."

His heart seized in a painful gasp. "Carly, when she's gone, it won't be the same. You won't have this much power."

She moved up to him, slipped her arms around him, and laid her head on his chest. "I won't need it then. All I'll need is you."

God, he hoped so.

Carla walked down the trail to the beach, grumbling each time she tripped on rocks and loose sand. It was hard to keep her footing on the trail while holding the flowing skirt of the delicate gold dress out of the way. She'd magically created the dress she had worn when she and Keri played Ancestor dress up. It was probably silly, but Sutton had understood that was a special memory to her. It was dark and getting cold, and she clutched Sutton's jacket tighter around her bare shoulders.

She had thought walking down the road would be easier than when she'd walked up it to find Sutton the first time.

She stumbled again on another rock and tumbled forward.

Sutton caught her around the waist, then he swept her up into his arms. "Honey, you are not an outdoors-woman."

She looked up at his face in the moonlight. The face she loved with his bald head, his eagle earring and those incredible blue eyes. "How do you see where you're going?"

"Eagle vision." He grinned at her, then his grin flattened. "You're not wearing underwear." His voice dropped huskily.

"Spell work requires freedom."

He dropped his gaze to her face. "You're torturing me, baby. I'm going to get even."

"Hiking on these trails is torture enough." She hated feeling inadequate, but how could she not? He was already three-quarters of the way down the trail to the beach and that was while carrying her. Keri would have never let him carry her. She'd have walked on bleeding blisters before she'd given in. Carla knew

Sutton loved her, and she knew her sister was okay with that, but she still...

"Carly." His voice was low and gentle. "I can't fix people's heads. You can."

Startled, she said, "You heard my thoughts."

"No, I just know you. Most of the time, you're very self-confident. But every once in a while, you forget how damned special you are. It's my job to remind you."

Carla put her head on his shoulder, feeling the man she loved. He didn't care that she wasn't an outdoors-woman. He loved her as she was. She felt the ground level out beneath his stride, felt the cool mist of the ocean. "Put me down."

He slid her down his body, his thick thigh rubbing against her. He took hold of her face. "Once we are finished here, I'm not going to be able to wait. I need you. I need to..."

Her breath caught and her body went soft and wet. "Me, too." She rose up on her toes to kiss him.

"All right, let's get to work," Darcy said with Axel by her side.

Carla broke the kiss and bent down to pull off her shoes.

Her dad came up to stand beside her.

She dropped the shoes, feeling the cool sand on her feet, and looked at his face in the light of the three-quarter moon. The shadows and dips on his clean-shaven face marked his grief. His hair was neatly combed and he looked solemn. She put her hand on his arm. "What is it?"

He said softly, "If you see her and can talk to her, tell her I love her."

Her heart twisted for him. He had loved Keri, but fear for her had gotten in the way. His grief was compounded because Keri's murder took away his hope of ever fixing his mistakes with his daughter.

"She knows, Dad, I promise you. But I will tell her."

He put his arm around her shoulders and squeezed her in a hug. Then he walked away to the rocks. He was going to stay outside the salt circle to observe.

Her mom, Darcy, Axel, Sutton and Carla would be inside the circle.

Carla turned to where the waves lapped at the shore. Ley lines were formed where two powerful forces met, like where water met the earth along the shore of an ocean. Carla was going to draw down the moon in order to create a magnetic force that would tap into the ley lines, pulling even more power up through her chakras.

She needed a familiar—Sutton's eagle—to control that extra power. The eagle would be on lookout for demons, who also had the ability to pull power from ley lines. The salt circle should protect them, but demons were exceedingly tricky.

Carla took a breath. *Ready, Keri?* She didn't expect an answer.

The scar warmed.

Carla smiled then, and her first four chakras opened with gentle pops. Keri's soul had been trapped too long. Keri, who loved the freedom of hiking, running, or biking, was long past ready to be free.

"Everyone is set," Darcy said.

"Thanks." Darcy and her mom would funnel power from the Circle Witches. Sutton would help her. Axel was there as a guard, and he always funneled Darcy's powers.

Sutton moved up behind her. "I can feel your power already."

Just his nearness caused her fifth chakra to vibrate at her throat, then open. Her awareness of Sutton intensified, until she could feel the very beat of his heart. His eagle focused in on her with a hunter's concentration. She couldn't imagine Sutton without his eagle. Would they lose him when Keri was gone?

The sensation of feathers brushed over her shoulders, followed by the warm touch of Sutton's hands. They'd be fine. His eagle might leave, her magic would dim back to previous levels, but they would have each other. She leaned back against him, her chakras yawned with the effort to draw him in.

He leaned down and said softly, "Give Keri a proud send off, baby."

She smiled, knowing how Keri would like that sentiment. Feeling strong and ready, she said, "We'll do it together."

He pressed his mouth to her ear. "Always."

Her skin was sensitive, and the feel of his breath sent shivers through her. Ready, she took a step away from Sutton and checked everyone's place. Sutton behind her, Darcy and her mom to her left, and Axel behind them. Facing the ocean, Carla raised her arms in front of her to form a circle with the tips of her fingers touching. Feeling the cool light of the moon on her skin, she began with, "Pure in its whiteness, born of the earth, consecrated by the sea, feared by the dark, embraced by the light, salt rise and circle your protection."

She visualized the circle in her mind while keeping her eyes closed. There was an eerie silence for a tick of time, as if all the waves went still. Then the roar of a tremendous wave rising and crashing, leaving the sharp scent of wet salt in its wake.

She opened her eyes to see that a perfect white circle had formed around them on the sand.

"Beautiful, Carla," her mom said softly. "The salt streamed from the ocean and drew the circle. It was better than I could do when I had my familiar."

A warm feeling spread in her, but she was careful not to lose her focus even though a part of her wanted to bask in her mother's praise. But now that she'd started, Carla had to work quickly. She was going to open ley lines, which made it easier for demons to use the lines. And she was going to expose both her and Keri's souls until Keri separated from her once more. Even with a salt circle, she didn't want to tempt demons or any other kind of trouble.

High magic was dangerous.

She raised her hands and conjured four candles, situating them inside the circle at the points of the four cardinal directions. She pointed at the red candle for earth and a flame burst to life from the wick. She felt her first chakra swell with more power. Carla didn't hesitate now, she pointed to the green candle for air, the orange candle for water, and finally the yellow candle for fire so all were blazing.

She could feel the pulse of the ley lines reaching out to her chakras in recognition. She leaned back and raised her arms in the silvery moonlight spilling on the beach. "Ancient as time, powerful as the sea, the moon is our source, let her light guide and fill me."

Her skin went tight and damp as power poured down over her, filling her with high magic. Her sixth chakra shot open and the moon created a magnetic effect, drawing up more power from the ley lines.

In seconds the powers collided and began to spin around her spine and chakras. Her skin felt hot and sensitive, her nipples swelled and began to ache, while her womb throbbed. It built until she felt as if even her eyelashes were swollen with power. She couldn't control it all. She couldn't even draw a breath and began to pant and grow dizzy. Her heart skipped and stuttered.

Then Sutton put his huge hands on her waist, steadying her. In seconds, her heartbeat slowed and regulated, following each beat of Sutton's heart. She *felt* his heart reach out to hers and synchronize the beats. She didn't know how it happened. And the eagle was there, funneling her power, helping her as magic filled every cell and pore.

The center of her forehead began to ache and throb. Her regular vision faded and her third eye opened. It was time.

Carla turned to the east, and Sutton turned with her, his hands holding her. "We are born of the east, like the light of the new day, and die of the west, slipping quietly into the ocean. But our souls live on, carrying the knowledge and lessons of each lifetime. A witch's soul must travel her journey until she has reached that of a Blessed Ancestor."

She faced west. "Our sister Keri has reached the west in this lifetime. Her soul rests with me." Her mind filled with images of Keri, of the two of them playing as children, laughing as teenagers, baking cookies with Chandra, of Jerome pushing them on swings, of dates and tears and secrets. Her entire lifetime with her sister swelled her heart and tears poured down Carla's face. She expected and embraced both her grief at Keri moving on and each treasured joy Keri would leave with her.

Carla lowered her head in reverence. "Ancestors, I bow before you and beseech you to give Keri's soul wings and safe journey to your welcoming arms."

The scar at her back burst open, causing her to gasp in shock and pain. Then she accepted it, embraced it. She was willing to endure any amount of pain for Keri. Raising her head, she lifted her eyes to the ocean. But the ocean was gone. There was only a violet-colored fog so vivid in color she was astounded.

Then Keri walked out, wearing the white dress she had worn as a child playing dress up, and a vivid smile. She lifted her hand to Carla. "Come with me."

She could not deny her sister. Carla took her hand

and was pulled into the swirling deep-purple fog. Time ceased as they floated, hand in hand, through a continuum that had no form. There was no fear, no worry, only sheer trust and the feeling of Keri's hand in hers. Then brilliant lights appeared like thousands of crystal stars in a velvet sky. Carla *knew,* and turned to look at Keri. "Summerland."

"Yes. It's exquisite and peaceful. We always said we'd make the journey to Summerland together." Keri turned to face her. "I knew you'd save me, Carla. I knew you'd find a way to free me. I love you, and I've been blessed to have you as my sister."

Tears welled up and ran down her face. "I don't want to let you go, Keri. I love you."

Her sister's face was changing, going from her natural beauty to a soft glow that radiated love. "But you have to. Sutton is waiting for you."

Carla squeezed her hand, trying to hold on to Keri for just a little longer. "I never meant to take him from you."

Keri pulled Carla into her arms. "His heart belongs to you. Live and love, Carla, with my blessing. And always carry with you my love."

She pulled back and added, "Tell Dad that I know he loves me. Tell both Mom and Dad I love them, too. And that I'm at rest now." Her image broke apart and reformed into one of the brilliant lights and so floated in a singular beauty.

"Goodbye, Keri," she said softly, grateful that if she had to let her go, as least she was given the gift of seeing her safely to Summerland. Peace settled over her bruised heart.

"We choose you."

The voices were like an echo of crystal bells, so pure it felt like twinkling whispers in her mind. "Blessed Ancestors?"

"Yes."

Humbled that they would address her, Carla expressed her gratitude. "Thank you for bringing Keri safely here."

"We are pleased she is here, Carla. We have waited a long time for Keri. And for you."

She wasn't sure she understood, but she stood quietly and waited.

"You have knowledge."

That was why she had instinctively understood what was happening. She had opened her seventh chakra, and the Ancestors were filling her with knowledge, as much knowledge as she needed right now. Too much knowledge, and she wouldn't be able to handle it. "Thank you."

"We choose you as our Moon Witch Advisor."

She could only feel Sutton's hands on her waist and nothing else but sheer light. "I'm honored." She let her thoughts gather and added, "I will serve you and our sister-witches as best I can."

"We chose you for your ability to blend magic with knowledge. Time is up."

She was spinning in a vortex of vivid violet when the eagle screeched a warning.

Carla's third eye closed and her vision returned with crystal clarity. She barely got a breath when she saw the sand on the outside of the circle start to undulate, tremble, and then glisten like thousands of worms.

Her stomach lurched. "Demon attack of some kind! From the ley lines!"

The sand fell away as the things slithered all over, many of them hitting the outside of the salt circle then disintegrating into husks. They couldn't get in the circle but they were pouring out of the sand everywhere on the outside of the circle. They scuttled across the beach with snake-like speed in colors of wet greens, blacks and browns.

Carla's dad clattered up on the rocks, stood up and swatted at his legs. "Leeches!"

The witch hunters that had been back in the cliffs began jumping off the rocks and running toward the waves. They were yanking the shiny swollen things off them and bellowing in disgust.

"Jerome!" Chandra turned, took a step, then stopped herself before she broke the circle by walking through it.

More hunters were running into the ocean, desperate to get the things off them.

Ram and Linc were trying to get to Jerome, who was climbing higher and higher to escape. Almost every inch of his arms, legs and face was covered in the shiny mass of writhing bloodsuckers.

"Carla! We have to do something!" Chandra said.

Desperately, Carla said, "It's demon magic!" What should they do?

Axel said, "Asmodeus, he's creating a diversion. Rogues must be—"

Jerome's scream cut him off.

Carla whipped her head around to see her father teeter on the edge of a rock, lose his balance and begin to fall. She reacted, raising her hands to summon and compact the air beneath her father. Halting his fall, she then used the air to shove him back up on the rock.

Ram grabbed Jerome's arm, catching him before he could fall again.

"Shit, circle's broken." Sutton grabbed her, lifting her into his arms as the slithering creatures poured in.

Too late, she realized she'd broken the salt circle by aiming her magic outside the consecrated line to her dad. The mass of leeches covering the beach caused a scream to build in her throat, but she fought it down.

Rogues poured over the cliffs and down the rocks to launch an attack. Instantly, Carla, her mom and

Darcy were shoved together and the Wing Slayer Hunters put their backs to them and fought the rogues.

Carla had fallen for the trap, breaking the circle to help the others. Fury roared through her. She was a witch, the Moon Witch whom the Ancestors believed in. She would fight back with her powers and knowledge.

Suddenly, Jerome was thrust in with the three women. Chandra raised her hands to use magic to help pull the remaining leeches off him.

Carla felt time running out, that something worse than the slimy leeches was coming. Worse than the rogues who the Wing Slayer Hunters fought while ignoring the leeches climbing all over them.

An earthquake-like rumble rocked the ground.

"Asmodeus," Darcy said, grabbing her arm. "We need another salt circle."

"We'll never get the line between the Wing Slayer Hunters and rogues!" Carla thought rapidly. "I already set a circle, using the salt from the sea. It's consecrated—it should work to destroy the leeches since they are demon magic. And..."

The ground rumbled again, and cracks appeared, then dark oily smoke and the stink of sulfur.

"Hurry!" Darcy said. "You consecrated the salt so you have to do the spell. Bring the salt over the beach." Darcy grabbed her hand and Carla grabbed her mom's hand. Jerome moved around them, pulling off leeches, kicking away the ones slithering closer. And he tried to keep the fighting hunters from slamming into the women.

As a greater rumble tilted the earth, Carla held on tight to Darcy and her mother, and gathered every ounce of power she could. The ley lines tried to writhe and snake away from her. The eagle screeched, and in her mind's eye, she could see the bird dig in his claws, fighting with the demon for control of the ley line.

The rumblings grew. Carla's body heated from the struggle, and then the lines stopped moving and allowed her access once more. She dragged in a breath and said, "From the depths of the oceans, to the sands of the beach, salt rise up and pour out your consecrated purity on the writhing mass of darkness!" The ley lines shot up through her, almost like being hit with a fire hose, causing the soles of her feet to burn. Carla held her position, letting all the power run through her.

The ground shifted and rolled, but the witches held their circle. And a second later, a massive wave rose, climbing higher and higher, curling and reaching out until it hung over the entire beach, blocking the moonlight.

Carla concentrated, squeezing her mom's and Darcy's hands. The amount of magic it took to control this massive wave, to freeze it long enough for it to separate and drop the salt, was rapidly draining her. Men were exclaiming, unable to believe what they were seeing.

Darcy and Chandra fed her more power from the Circle Witches, and finally, millions of tiny white grains began to rain down on them.

Salt!

Carla barely registered it, struggling to hold the wave while the salt flowed down. If the wave fell on them, it would crush them and pull them out to sea.

Time to push it back. The eagle funneled all the power flowing through her to force the wave back. Would it be enough?

The wall of water began reversing its enormous arc until it retracted far enough out, and then it crashed in a deafening roar.

Then there were only the sounds of the waves and the men breathing. No fighting. Carla looked around.

The salty sand was littered with dead rogues, and the rest were climbing the cliffs to run away. The leeches had disappeared entirely.

Between them and the cliffs, there was a shallow crater, with thin ribbons of putrid-smelling smoke rising between the glittering salt. Asmodeus had failed to break through. They'd pushed him back.

She looked at Sutton, saw the streaks of dirt and blood on him, but he was whole and safe. "We did it."

Sutton wrapped his hands around her waist and lifted her high off the ground. "You did it. That wave scared the hell out of the rogues."

Axel added, "It was an ambush. Look."

They all turned to the top of the cliffs the farthest from Sutton's cabin. A huge man stood up there, his long black trench coat blowing in the breeze.

Sutton set her on the ground, putting his arm around her. "I see the knife burned into his arm. Quinn Young."

"He can't approach us. Dumb bastard took the mark of a demon on his arm, so he can't touch the consecrated salt." Darcy's voice was cold with anger.

Carla reached out and took Darcy's hand. Quinn Young was her father, and he'd murdered her mother as a sacrifice to Asmodeus to get that hideous Immortal Death Dagger.

Axel put his arm around Darcy, so that the four of them all stood in a row. "He and Asmodeus thought they could kill the four of us in one battle. That Death Dagger would kill immortals like Darcy and me, and prevent you two from having the chance at immortality."

Carla felt Sutton tense next to her.

Axel went on, "Carla, Wing Slayer has asked that you and Sutton go to the astral plane."

Confused, she asked, "Why?"

Axel's green eyes were amused. "He's half demon

and half god. All this consecrated salt"—he looked around at the salty sand—"It's a problem for him. He wants to see you. Don't keep him waiting."

"Carla," Sutton said, "take us to him."

"Okay, but first—" She let go of Darcy's and Sutton's hands to turn and look at her parents. They both stood behind her. "I saw Keri. Dad, she knows you love her. And she said to you both, Mom and Dad, that she loves you and she's at rest now." Carla smiled then, a smiled filled with the memory of Summerland. "It was beautiful. Where Keri is now, she's a free soul. She just had to tell you both that she loved you, then she was free."

Chandra turned to Jerome.

He opened his arms and pulled her to him. They hugged tightly.

Carla reached for Sutton's hand and took them both to their appointment with Wing Slayer.

≈ 25 ≈

SUTTON RECOGNIZED THE FOLIAGE AND flower-lined path leading to the waterfall. He held Carla's hand and walked toward the grassy area. He had no idea what would happen.

Wing Slayer appeared.

Carla stopped, her hand tightening in his.

Sutton dropped to one knee. "Wing Slayer. You saved Carla's life. Thank you." He owed the god his life and his soul for that.

Carla settled on her knees next to him and stayed silent.

"She's a very impressive witch. The Ancestors have claimed her as their Moon Witch."

Wing Slayer's voice reverberated through him. Surprised, he lifted his head and looked at Carla. "What's that?"

She turned to him, her eyes full of rich autumn colors. "An advisor between the Ancestors and the Circle Witches."

His chest swelled with pride in her. He had seen what she could do on the beach, and he was just so damned proud. "You opened your seventh chakra. I knew it! I could feel how much power you...wait,

Carly, if they claimed you as that, you'll still have all your powers? All your chakras?" Worry began to gnaw at him and his eagle twitched restlessly. He looked at his god, huge and powerful where he hovered in front of the waterfall. His wings did not get wet, nor did his hair. Lights sparkled off the bronzed bands wrapped around his arms, revealing the wings of his hunters. "Do I have to give her up? Because she's not my true soul mirror?" Sutton couldn't take all that power from her.

Carla sucked in a breath, and her hand went damp with worry in his.

Wing Slayer's wings lightened to a gossamer gold. "But you are soul mirrors. Your love has created a soul magic that has bonded your souls as surely as Darcy and Axel are bonded."

He was stunned to silence.

"We're soul mirrors?" Carla asked. "But how? Keri—"

Wing Slayer didn't seem to mind her questions. "Sutton and Keri were soul mirrors. When Sutton touched your blood, he was touching your sister's blood, too. Then when you touched his blood, Keri touched it as well and the eagle stirred to life, sensing the soul-mirror bond."

"The twin bond," Carla said quietly.

Sutton rubbed his thumb over Carla's wrist. "You told me over and over, but I didn't believe it. I couldn't. I fell for you."

She turned to him, her eyes blooming yellow. "But if you'd seen Keri—"

He shook his head. "I did see her. Right here, when I had to break our bond. Carly, I saw her, but to me, she's just your sister. It's you I love."

"He's correct, Carla. He did fall in love with you, and so did his eagle tattoo. Enough so that the both of them forced out wings when they should not have had the magic to do so."

"I'm not doubting you, Sutton. Not ever," she said softly. "I know you love me."

He turned to Wing Slayer. "She forgave me for breaking our bond."

Wing Slayer shook his head. "Your bond didn't break. But you caused her such tremendous pain that the bond retracted. And Carla, in her pain, did what she'd done all her life, reached for her twin sister, Keri. That moment of pure desperation for Carla pulled Keri from the knife."

Sutton looked up at his god. "She told me you weren't being cruel. That you had commanded me to do it for a reason. She told me to have faith in you."

His wings lifted behind him. "Your faith invoked enough of my god powers to restore Carla's life. We can't say exactly how, but your love and the twin bond created soul magic. You and Carla are true soul mirrors."

Carla asked softly, "Will Keri find her own soul magic?"

Wing Slayer smiled at her. "She knows how much you love her, and she willingly gave you the eagle. You know that, do you not?"

Carla's witch-shimmer softened and tinged with pink. "Yes. Keri didn't love him. She instantly recognized that I did."

He gazed at her with a surprising gentleness. "She'll find her way, Carla. You and Keri are very special. That the two of you could keep her soul alive for two years while trapped in a knife is a miracle. Do not worry for Keri's happiness, it's our job to look after her now."

Grateful, Sutton bowed his head. "Both of us thank you and the Ancestors. Carly's heart will be at peace knowing her sister is okay now."

"Lift your joined hands," Wing Slayer thundered out in his gut-trembling bass.

Sutton looked up and saw a knife appear in the god's hand. He recognized it as his own. Without hesitation, he lifted their joined hands.

The god drifted forward, filling the air with the scent of metal and flowers. Then the knife flashed and a perfect ring of blood welled up around the base of both their thumbs.

Sutton stared at it. He felt the pain of the cut, but he knew Carla did not. He knew it because he felt Carla's pain, too, as he should. But what robbed him of thought was the significance of the cuts.

Immortality. Wing Slayer was granting them immortality. His god found him worthy enough of Carla and immortality. Carla would be his to love and protect for eternity.

Wing Slayer's voice rang out once more. "Carla, your Ancestors are here, do you feel them?"

She closed her eyes and Sutton felt her power swell as she opened her chakras. "Yes." She opened her eyes. "They're here."

Sutton was stunned when he saw the picture in his mind. Bundles of incredible light floated around their joined hands. Carla was showing him what the Ancestors looked like. She was in his head. The joy was unbearable.

Wing Slayer wrapped his hand around their joined ones. The touch of his god sent a bolt of electricity through him. It raced from his hand through all his cells and then back to his hand. It was so strong, he saw Carla's long hair lift in a static reaction.

Wing Slayer pronounced, "We claim you as soul mirrors. May you reflect the faith, courage, honor, strength and cunning to fight the curse and protect the innocent. We give you the gift of time to aid you."

There was a flash of light that exploded into billions of colored fragments like they'd been thrown into a kaleidoscope. When the colors faded out and the astral plane reappeared with the huge rock waterfall ahead of them, Wing Slayer was gone.

"Thank you," Sutton said, knowing now that Wing Slayer heard him.

"He left your knife," Carla said.

Keeping his fingers intertwined with hers, he used his free hand to pick his knife up off the ground and held it up for her to see. "Wings. He impressed the hilt with wings." He couldn't take in all that had happened.

Carla touched her finger to the hilt. "You're important to Wing Slayer. He has marked you to show the world."

Sutton slid his knife into its sheath and lifted both her hands in his to look at the ring around each of their thumbs. "He marked *us*. Immortal thumb rings." She was his for eternity. The eagle spread his wings in happiness inside the tattoo, while Sutton stroked the perfectly healed ring around both her thumbs. Realizing they were both still kneeling on the pavers, he stood, then tugged her to her feet. Just the feel of her hands in his slammed into his groin, filling him with the heat to have her.

"I'm not taking us back. Not yet."

Oh, yeah. "No?"

She let go of one of his hands and turned toward the waterfall.

Her magic sparked inside him, and in the next instant, they were both naked. God, he loved her magic! She tugged on his hand, heading to the soft grass at the edge of the waterfall.

He let her lead, lagging behind to see the scenery; her long straight hair sliding over the small of her back that flared into her butt. His hands itched to cup her ass, to feel her... He stopped. "Carla, your scar."

Her hair swung as she turned her head, clearly showing him the scar.

Sutton lifted his eyes. "It's a perfect crescent moon and it glows silver."

"Moon Witch," she said. "I felt the scar burst and bleed when I freed Keri, and I guess the Ancestors used the scar to mark me when I was in Summerland."

Did she have any idea how amazing she was? He pulled her to him. "You're beautiful. All of you." She was his, a witch so special it took a man and a bird to care for her. He kissed down her cheek to the corner of her mouth.

His need for her pounded, his dick ached and his balls tightened with lust. The eagle shifted restlessly, wanting to touch her, scent her, feel her.

She lifted her head, her eyes full of color. *Let him loose, Sutton. Let the eagle out.*

She was in his head and he loved it. The eagle bounced, wanting out, as desperate as he was for her. But Sutton didn't know how. "Uh, I don't know how it works. Last time, there was a lot of blood." Carly had a disturbing habit of healing him and taking his pain.

Her witch-shimmer took on more gold. "That's a problem. I'm afraid we're going to have to change our plans." She drew her small hand over his ribs, down his stomach and then, with maddening slowness, along the length of his cock.

"What?" He knew she was teasing him, but her fingers were wrapped around his dick, leaving him unable to think. Then she used the very tips of two fingers to stroke his balls. Her magic vibrated softly and he thrust against her, trying to get more.

"This will be working sex."

"Huh?" He'd do anything. She wanted him to work for it? He'd lay her down on the grass and lick all of her, taking the most time with her sensitive nipples, and the folds between her legs. He'd—

"To bring out your wings." Her breath was hot

where she touched her lips to his chest, then drew her tongue over his nipple.

He shuddered like a teenager.

"Got to bring those wings out." She slipped down to her knees. "We're going to push you until you sprout wings." She leaned forward.

Sutton sucked in a breath and watched her. So beautiful it made his chest hurt. Her white-blond hair spilling around her and sliding against the coarser hair on his thighs. Her back curved forward so he could see her narrow waist and the swell of her hips. And her face, so expressive and elegant. She parted her lips, and her tongue darted out and touched the slit at the end of his cock.

His blood raced, his heart pounded and he reached down, stroking his hands over her silky hair.

She traced the aching head with her tongue, her fingers squeezing his hips, pulling him in tighter...until she sucked him into her hot little mouth.

He saw stars, bright snaps of light. He tried not to thrust, not to give her more than she could take.

Give me your magic, Sutton, your wings.

He would give her anything. He gathered her hair in his hand, gently tugging her head back so that she released him. He loved the frown that built between her eyebrows. She liked tasting him as much as he loved lapping at her center. *I need to be inside you.* He dropped to his knees and swept her up in his arms to lay her on the soft grass. He shifted so that he knelt between her legs. He stroked the soft skin of her inner thighs, then he pressed her legs apart to look at her. Her flesh was damp and infused with gold, telling him how much she wanted him.

The eagle cried out something, he didn't know what, but it made him shudder once, as a force inside him released, and the wings exploded from his back. No pain, just a pure magic.

Carla arched into the touch, her eyes closing as she gave in to the pleasure.

Sutton could *feel* her with his wings, feel her slick folds, her tight, aching clit, her need. "Carly," he said in a hoarse voice, and he leaned over her.

The wings pulled back, quivering with the same deep desire.

She opened her eyes and wrapped her legs around his hips. *You're majestic and you're mine.*

He lost control, lost any thread of himself as separate from her, and he thrust into her, sealing them together.

She moaned, lifting her hips to take more.

Sutton felt Carly around him, her magic tingling and clutching while her folds swelled and pulsed and he thrust again and again, driving them both higher, higher than they ever dared go before.

Because now they had wings.

Carla cried out, throwing her head back, her long hair framing her as the orgasm took her and she soared.

Sutton roared with his own release, soaring high with his witch. Feeling the wings keep their pleasure going until they were wrung dry and they drifted back to the astral plane. Panting, he braced himself on his arms over her and looked down at her, his Carly, his golden witch.

His gaze drifted to her silver armband. "Carly?"

"Hmm?" She looked up at him. "Your wings are sexy."

"They aren't just my wings," he said, feeling the joy.

"What do you mean?"

"Your armband." He shifted his weight to one arm and lifted his hand to trace the silver that had re-formed from the elegant infinity loops to a pair of intricate eagle wings wrapped around her biceps and overlapping as if they hugged her tightly. "It's beautiful, like you."

She looked over at the silver wings, then back to him. Her autumn-colored eyes were tinged with the thin blue ring. "You have your own magic, Sutton. I didn't do it and the Wing Slayer didn't either."

He loved her so much. But she still didn't understand. He leaned down to kiss her, then he said, "Carly, you are my magic."

The End

Dear Readers,

Thank you for reading Soul Magic! I really hope you enjoyed Carla and Sutton's story of star-crossed lovers who find a way to defeat demons and destiny with the power of their love. But there's still more to come! The next book is Night Magic, the tale of an undying love that won't be denied.

I hope you'll continue reading the series set in a world of magic and danger where the real power is love.

Wishing you all a little magic in your lives!

~Jen

OTHER BOOKS BY JENNIFER LYON

THE WING SLAYER HUNTER SERIES

Blood Magic (Book #1)
Soul Magic (Book #2)
Night Magic (Book #3)
Sinful Magic (Book #4)
Forbidden Magic (Book #4.5 a novella)
Caged Magic (Book #5)

THE PLUS ONE CHRONICLES TRILOGY

The Proposition (Book #1)
Possession (Book #2)
Obsession (Book #3)
The Plus One Chronicles Boxed Set

ANTHOLOGY

The Beast Within Anthology
with Erin McCarthy and Bianca D'Arc

Writing as Jennifer Apodaca

Once A Marine Series

The Baby Bargain (Book #1)
Her Temporary Hero (Book #2)
Exposing The Heiress (Book #3)

The Samantha Shaw Mystery Series

Dating Can Be Murder (Book #1)
Dying To Meet You (Book #2)
Ninja Soccer Moms (Book #3)
Batteries Required (Book #4)
Thrilled To Death (Book #5)

Single Title Novels

The Sex On The Beach Book Club
Extremely Hot

Anthologies

Wicked Women Whodunit Anthology
with Mary Janice Davidson, Amy Garvey & Nancy J. Cohen
Sun, Sand, Sex Anthology
with Linda Lael Miller and Shelly Laurenstron

ABOUT THE AUTHOR

Bestselling author Jennifer Lyon lives in Southern California where she continually plots ways to convince her husband that they should get a dog. So far, she has failed in her doggy endeavor. She consoles herself by pouring her passion into writing books. To date, Jen has published more than fifteen books, including a fun and sexy mystery series and a variety of contemporary romances under the name Jennifer Apodaca, and a dark, sizzling paranormal series as Jennifer Lyon. She's won awards and had her books translated into multiple languages, but she still hasn't come up with a way to persuade her husband that they need a dog.

Jen loves connecting with fans. Visit her website at www.jenniferlyonbooks.com or follow her at https://www.facebook.com/jenniferlyonbooks.

CPSIA information can be obtained
at www.ICGtesting.com
Printed in the USA
LVOW07s2127041217
558590LV00004B/1041/P